ANIME
SUPREMACY!

MIZUKI TSUJIMURA

Translated by Deborah Boliver Boehm

Art by Hwei Lim

VERTICAL.

TABLE OF CONTENTS

ANIME SUPREMACY!

CHAPTER 1:

"THE PRINCE & THE BEAST TAMER"

"Why did you get into the anime business?" people asked her from time to time.

"That's a good question," she might say with a thoughtful tilt of her head, but now and then she replied straightforwardly: "Because I like anime."

Occasionally she responded with a bit more passion, and heat. "It's because I've always loved anime, for as long as I can remember. I adore everything about it: the characters, the voice actors, the art, the settings, the directing, the soundtrack, the theme songs, the worldview. Just—everything."

It was true: she never ceased to marvel at the way the visual images and sounds flowed across the screen in perfect harmony, as if the protagonists' facial expressions, and the costumes, and the dialogue, were all conspiring to cast an overpowering spell that simply bewitched her.

She couldn't even begin to count the number of anime that had left her dazed and wondering, *What's going on here, anyway?* That happened so many times when she was younger, but it was still difficult to explain the feelings of amazement and delight.

Her whole body had seemed to go numb, leaving her totally un-moored and befuddled, and she'd find herself making a mad dash to press the Record button for that very week's episode.

Whoa. Yikes. What's going on here?

And then, simply: *Wow—this is awesome!*

Of course, that was in her teens, when she never thought she'd end up where she was today: with a full-time job at Studio Edge, a mid-level anime production company. Her job title was produc-tion director—producer, by any other name—and now that she was working behind the scenes, her innocent adoration of anime seemed to have morphed into something more professional.

Of course, because she started out as a fan, there were still times when she got a bit carried away at work. Since she had de-veloped a more discerning eye, she was better able to appreciate the nuances of the art form, and she frequently lost her mind over some minuscule detail, screaming things like "I love this part so much I can't stand it!" More often than not, those engaging details tended to be some cerebral bit of *moe*. That word meant irresistibly captivating adorability and wasn't supposed to be in-tellectual.

As for her early "Wow!" responses, it was the sad fate of anyone who ended up working behind the scenes to have those youthful feelings of bedazzled wonderment vanish into thin air.

Or so she thought.

But then—this was when she was twenty-seven and had been in the industry for five years, ever since graduating from college—she saw *Yosuga*.

Yosuga was the popular abbreviation of the series' full, official name: *Yosuga of the Light*. It was the seminal debut work of anime director Chiharu Oji, who was frequently referred to thereafter as "the guy who made *Yosuga*." At the time he was one of the young-gun directors at Tokei Animation, a large, old, prominent company, and everybody said that with this one groundbreaking work of art he had singlehandedly propelled the Japanese anime industry ten years into the future.

Amazingly, Oji was only twenty-four years old at the time.

At a glance, his name seemed like a nom de plume, especially since Oji literally meant "prince" and Chiharu was usually feminine, but no—that was the name he was born with. (Incidentally, a reporter for a certain anime magazine who touched on that matter apparently hit a nerve and was sent packing in mid-interview—though not before the young director had remarked, "If I were Kamille, you'd have gotten slugged, bye and Zeta Gundam." That particular protagonist also hated being told that his name was less than manly.

She, Kayako Arishina, had been one of *Yosuga's* viewers.

Needless to say, it would have been unimaginable for anyone in the anime business *not* to have witnessed that spectacular debut. And as she watched, Kayako once again felt the old, familiar, full-body frisson: *Whoa. Yikes. What's going on?*

On a purely personal level, Kayako was amazed that she could still experience that kind of unfiltered thrill. She was no longer a teenager, yet here she was again, utterly spellbound by what she saw on the screen. She had never imagined that anything new could overwrite the influence of the anime she'd watched as a malleable schoolgirl.

Everything she'd viewed, and read, and listened to during her early, impressionable years when she found it difficult to put her reaction into words formed a treasure trove of accumulated experience that informed the work that she did. Yet as she became more knowledgeable about what she loved, she gradually acquired the big-brained skill of critical thinking, and the instances when she gushed unconditionally and indiscriminately about any current series—*Omigosh, how can this be so good?*—decreased accordingly.

When she was a child, the contours of the anime world had seemed all the more mysterious and attractive because she had only the barest understanding of the genre, and the process. But now that she had learned some tricks of the trade and become fluent in industry argot, those beguiling mysteries just seemed like an organic part of the job.

At that point in her career, Kayako assumed that even if she were to become the fan of a certain anime creator's oeuvre, her response would just take the form of respectful admiration toward a fellow professional in the field. Never again (she thought) would she develop a giddy schoolgirl crush on any one director's work, or moon about all day thinking of nothing else.

Yet while she was watching *Yosuga*, she was murmuring to herself, *Wow, this is great*, although she only realized that in retrospect. At the time, she couldn't really put a name to what she was feeling.

When Kayako fell back to earth, she actually had chills. She'd found something she was mad about right now, for the first time in ages, and even though she'd only just finished watching it herself, the thought that others had, too, filled her with jealousy. She wanted to own it, as her find.

Note to self: *Remember the name Chiharu Oji.*

The young genius was three years Kayako's junior. They belonged to the same generation, and Kayako was able to gather from various details that she and the creator of *Yosuga* had grown up watching—and being nourished and shaped by—all the same anime. They had read the same manga and novels, and played the same games, as well. None of it was old and would still seem fresh to the kids of today, Oji proved through his work with all his might.

He had breathed the same air as Kayako, growing up, and then he had gone on to create this astonishing story, just for her. She couldn't get past the preposterous feeling that she didn't want it to be seen, or understood, by anyone else. As an industry person she was involved with other projects in development at the time, but thanks to *Yosuga* she actively resented the other viewers, the very same anime fans who were supposed to be her customers.

I'm sorry, people, but you don't get it, not the way I do.

From that galvanizing moment on, Kayako Arishina understood deep down inside why she had chosen to work in the world of anime. No matter who asked that boilerplate question, she would never again tell the truth.

Q. *Why did you get into the anime business?*

A. *Oh, that's easy—so I could work with Chiharu Oji someday.*

If Kayako hadn't had that shiny new goal to cling to, she might not have stayed in the anime industry at all. Over and over, she kept telling herself: *I'm going to work with Chiharu Oji someday. That must be what I've wanted all along, more than I ever knew.*

◆

"So it looks like we already have a winner in the spring supremacy stakes."

Their meeting had just wrapped up, and gazing out the window at the unobstructed view, Kayako had taken a sip of the black tea dispensed by the Unimat machine. With a start, she looked around and saw Osato grinning at her.

"Way to go!" he said. "I'm really proud of you."

"Oh, thanks," Kayako blurted out reflexively, feeling a bit guilty about having been so thoroughly lost in her thoughts. As a result she missed her chance to ask exactly what he meant by that word "supremacy." Was he talking about artistic merit at all in addition to sales prospects? While she pondered, Osato leafed through the materials.

"Are you guys going to stick with the working title '*Fateful Fight: Ryder Light*'?" he asked.

The question caught Kayako by surprise, halting her hand mid-drink. However, nothing about her colleague's tone or body language suggested a hidden agenda. Not even bothering to glance at her, he was studying the initial character sketches in the PowerPoint printout.

"Oh, right, and the wardrobe for the Jyuri character looks really good," he continued after the briefest of pauses. "I love the challenge that her hairstyle poses."

"Um, yes," Kayako said noncommittally, lowering her cup.

After every appearance of the current project's title—*Fateful*

Fight: Ryder Light—on the pages Osato was holding was the bracketed notation "[TEMP]." The character he'd mentioned, Jyuri Towada, was the anime's protagonist.

Summoning a smile, Kayako answered Osato's question. "Actually, that title is pretty much settled, but someone must have forgotten to remove the 'TEMPs' from the printouts. It shouldn't be too long before we're ready to announce it officially."

"Oh, I see. Actually, the other day Mr. Kakiuchi over at Animarket mentioned the possibility of replacing that working title with something a bit more impactful. And before that our CEO was also suggesting that it might be better to give the show a title that could be abbreviated down to the name and still mean something, like *Yosuga*."

The overtones in that instance: remembrance, memento.

Osato was the director of planning for Blue Open Toy (Bluto for short), a studio that took pride in being the leading creator of anime-character figures, and he loved them so much he worked on the prototypes himself. Like the anime and game industries, the figurine business had enjoyed breakout success in recent years, and it appeared (both visually and in actuarial terms) to be populated primarily by young people. At the tender age of twenty-nine, Osato was already a department head. His retro-trendy black-framed glasses and purposefully long hair—worn loose and parted on the side—seemed to evoke an English rock star from the eighties rather than someone living and working in contemporary reality. As Kayako saw it, only a person with a high degree of self-confidence could pull off such a stylized look.

Osato was actually quite popular, and his admirers included a number of Kayako's coworkers. When those female colleagues returned to the office from a meeting at Bluto they often had an appreciative twinkle in their eyes, as if to say, *Mmm—a guy who looks handsome wearing glasses.*

Osato was personable, he was great at his job, and he loved figures so much that he actually helped make them. "Compared to our most popular in-house designers, I'm just an amateur," he had said once, but despite dismissing himself as a hobbyist, people in the know spoke very highly of his creations.

He also excelled in diplomatic relations, and when it came time to liaise with other development shops, including Studio Edge, he was unusually deft at broaching difficult topics. "Well, now," he would say smoothly, putting everyone at ease, "shall we take the plunge and talk about the bottom line?"

Whether it was anime or figures, men or women, people who worked in and around this industry were, as a rule, vulnerable to "love." They were easily impressed and even moved when someone's behavior proclaimed, "I take pride in what I do" and "I really adore my work!"

Even after financial problems that couldn't be resolved by good feelings alone arose in projects launched amidst such excitement, even as everyone started feeling overwhelmed by the hellishly hard work and the endless complications, the memory of that initial surge of love comforted them and helped them make it through the rough patches. Inevitably, there were regrets and disappointments along the way, but they became bearable.

"In any case, I'll be back," Kayako said. "I need to pay a visit to your president to talk about the title, among other things. Oji should be with me then, as well."

"Thanks, that sounds like a plan," Osato replied. "I'll be looking forward to it. Can you give me a rough idea of the projected completion date for the first episode?"

"That hasn't been decided yet. We're working on the third episode now, so I think the first three should be ready to show you before too long."

"Okay—sounds good."

Osato was a sharp guy, but for now, at least, he didn't appear to suspect that anything might be amiss.

I mean, it's not as if I'm telling any outright lies, Kayako assured herself, mentally crossing her fingers behind her back. The tea she'd been sporadically sipping had grown tepid and tasteless.

Bluto, as an increasingly active player in the industry, had for the past several years been joining in more anime-production joint ventures than they had in the past. In the case of *Fateful Fight: Ryder Light* [TEMP], for which Kayako was the main producer, Bluto had been on board since the earliest planning stage. In other words, they had paid in.

"The announcement is scheduled for the end of next week, right?" Osato said. "It's bound to get a lot of attention. After all, this'll be Oji's first new project in ten years."

"Nine years," Kayako corrected. She took a shallow breath and smiled. "If we aren't precise about details like that, Oji might get mad at us. You know how he is."

"Oh, my bad. But anyway, that included, he never breaks character, does he? Not just his work, but he himself, as a person, is endlessly interesting. I mean, for starters, he has that name, and of course you know about his looks."

"I do, yes," Kayako nodded while thinking, *You're no slouch in the looks department yourself.* To cover her discomfiture at being forced to discuss Oji, she tilted her teacup and peered inside, but it was now completely empty.

At one point, the media had dubbed Oji "the little prince of the anime world." That adjective probably wasn't intended as a serious allusion to St. Exupéry, nor to any aspect of Oji's own work, and was no more than a teasing aside. He'd also been labeled "the dishy director" and "the pretty-boy genius."

In fact, the first time Kayako saw Oji's photograph in a magazine, she was surprised. A "dishy so-and-so" was usually only that in the context of his field, but in Oji's case, it was no exaggeration. Even when you saw him alongside the most glamorous actors, whether on television or in the pages of magazines, his level of attractiveness didn't pale in comparison.

While *Yosuga* was at the height of its popularity, the director's face had often adorned the covers of magazines devoted to anime or "subculture" in general, and it didn't look at all out of place on the racks in bookstores.

—I like *Yosuga*, but does the director have to be that good-looking?

—All the exposure he's getting is annoying so I'm passing

on *Yosuga*.

It got to the point where such green-eyed remarks came to be heard from anime fans.

Even Kayako, who had fallen madly in love with the director's work on *Yosuga*, found herself in reluctant agreement and thought the backlash was a terrible waste. People were turning against an unquestionable masterpiece because of something as trivial as the director's appearance. While good looks could win die-hard followers, it wasn't worth it when you considered the risk of alienating other fans. The free advertising in the form of celebrity-type media coverage was too valuable to pass up for the production side, but average looks might have served him better at this rate.

Those were Kayako's thoughts, from the viewpoint of a producer in the same business. On a personal level, all things considered, she was surprised by her own fairly rational and stoic mindset. The "dishy director" attracted legions of female fans with his charisma, but the thing that made Kayako's heart beat faster was his work, and his work alone. Perhaps, as attractive as he was, he simply wasn't her type appearance-wise.

She remembered feeling even a little shocked when she had a chance to see Chiharu Oji in person back then. Kayako was just a shade under five and a half feet tall, and Oji was at somewhere around five foot two. She had always thought that he looked like a boy with his tidy facial features and loose, floppy hair—but he actually came across to her, without exaggeration, as a cheeky brat.

Nine years had passed since *Yosuga*.

Oji had left Tokei Animation afterwards and moved from studio to studio before going freelance. Along the way, he had worked on various projects as an associate director or episode director, and while some of those individual works had been quite well received, he'd gone nearly a decade without headlining a project.

Chiharu Oji's specialty was the so-called "magic girl" genre, a category that *Yosuga* fell under as well.

The primary plot invariably features a teenage girl who acquires magical powers, transforms into a supernatural version of herself, and dashes around doing battle with an assortment of foes. Magic-girl stories have been popular for ages, and because the basic plot points are both perennially appealing and easy to configure, there haven't been many flops. The tie-in merchandising, too, always has an excellent chance of succeeding. Young fans continually clamor for character figures and whimsical "sticks" (generally resembling magic wands), while the same figures, as well as other collectibles, find plenty of adult buyers as well.

One notable characteristic of Oji's work was that his magic-girl narrative was more suitable for adult viewers than for children—by a long shot. That is to say, the façade of his magic-girl anime may seem to suggest "children's programming," but the actual content could be quite violent and mature. Segments involving cruelty or so-called bed scenes were present, though in a veiled, ambiguous way designed to go over the heads of younger viewers. Oji's anime had been widely lauded for showing the often-painful coming-of-age process for teenage girls vividly, and honestly.

Unprecedentedly for a magic-girl anime, with its usual focus on *moe* and the cuteness quotient, the majority of the show's fans and supporters were adult women, rather than children or males of any age. More than anything, *Yosuga of the Light* had attracted attention because a show that was groundbreaking in that regard had been created by a man.

Fateful Fight: Ryder Light [TEMP] was going to be that acclaimed auteur's long-awaited new project, after nine years of relative obscurity. And the genre was his trademark magic-girl saga.

In the story, the heroine, Jyuri, was able to harness her own spiritual power to transform her motorbike into various other shapes, and that's how she charged into combat. The focal point of each episode was going to be a climactic battle in the form of a race. The mechanics of the magical motorbike were being outsourced to a designer at HITANO, an actual manufacturer of motorcycles.

"Ryder Light" was the general term for the type of motorbikes ridden by the young girls.

This anime was the biggest project Studio Edge had undertaken in many years, and the details had been carefully kept under wraps. At the end of the following week, though, they were planning a press conference featuring Chiharu Oji, in a live broadcast via Niconico, Japan's version of YouTube, during which the title would be revealed.

"But what happened today? Why did you favor us with your presence, Ms. Arishina?" Osato's tone was playful, but Kayako's spine stiffened in alarm. "What?" she said, wheeling around, but Osato added with a laugh, "Oh, no, it's just that Mr. Omiya is the go-between for most of our dealings with Studio Edge." His expression clouded over with concern. "Is Oji worried about something having to do with the figures?" he asked. "Is that why you came?"

"No, nothing like that," Kayako assured him. "I just happened to be nearby on other business."

An anime production usually had multiple producers assigned to it.

The production company where Kayako worked only made anime and didn't release them, and in that sense resembled an artist signed by a recording company. A packaging company handled broadcasting and sales for the works that the artist produced, and in Edge's case, that was major industry player Animarket.

It took a massive amount of funds and manpower to create an anime series. In this instance, there were a total of four producers, starting with Kayako from Studio Edge and including ones from Animarket and the TV station. On top of that, assistant producers and production planners from each firm were attached to the project. They had various roles ranging from keeping an eye on the budget, following up with the original author and clients, or, like Kayako, attending to the director and other staff who actually created the work.

From Bluto's perspective, Kayako was fully on the creative

side—they saw her as being in charge of the director, Oji. She couldn't have felt more dispirited as she eked out an excuse.

"Also, Oji loves the work you've been doing at Bluto, so I stopped by today to say hello and see how things were going to provide him with some additional motivation. When he heard that a master figure-maker like Ms. Marino agreed to be involved, he was really happy."

"Yes, the last I heard, Marino was all fired up about this project," remarked Osato. "I mean, with Oji as the director, and Mr. Gin doing the character design, she was saying she'd have to be out of her mind to pass on it."

Kaede Marino was an in-demand master designer of anime figures, and her schedule (Kayako had heard) was packed to the gills for years to come with commissions from players in the anime world who wanted to be sure their figurines were as good as they could possibly be. Yet Marino had somehow managed to find time to squeeze in this extra work, saying, in effect, "Anything for Oji."

Production teams started talking to a figure-maker as soon as an anime project booted up, and actual work usually began six months or so before the anime hit the airwaves. For *Ryder*, they must have been right in the middle of the process.

"I'll be sure to share that with Oji," Kayako said with a smile. Bowing her head, she added, "Thank you very much for everything today—I know you're super busy."

She left the conference room, and on her way to the main exit she stopped to survey Blue Open Toy's busy workspace. The company was headquartered in a multipurpose building in the Ikebukuro district of Tokyo that was also a prime destination for sightseers. Bluto occupied the thirty-seventh and -eighth floors. The exterior walls were mostly glass, providing sweeping views of the cityscape below and beyond. Inside the company's workspace, Kayako never tired of the magnificent spectacle of anime figures adorning dozens of cubicles.

Without exception, every single desk displayed a row of expertly made three-dimensional renderings of characters from anime and games, in various poses. Just one quick glance around the room delivered a clear sense of what was generating the most excitement in the anime world at any given time. Each individual team member had personal favorites among shows and characters, but the turnover rate was high, and it was the inevitable fate of older figurines to be pushed out by new arrivals made with more advanced techniques and to lose their places atop a desk.

Kayako's own desk at Studio Edge was decorated with a few figures from shows she'd worked on so far as a producer, but there wasn't a single item of *Yosuga* memorabilia.

She turned away from the work area and pasted on the forced smile she'd developed for public consumption. She was about to head for the lobby when Osato called out from behind her, "Ms. Arishina, could you wait a minute, please?"

Kayako stopped, and her neck immediately tensed up. Holding her breath in apprehension, she looked around. Osato vanished into a nearby room and returned after a moment holding a box, which he placed in Kayako's hands. When she peeked inside, her mood brightened immeasurably even at a stressful time like this.

It was a figure of a character from a series Kayako had been in charge of. In this specialty version, the creature was portrayed with a gigantic head perched on a disproportionately small body.

"It's Miele!" she gushed.

"You were saying the other day that you liked Miele, and I just happened to come across this," Osato said. "It isn't anything major, but I thought it might amuse you. Or—you don't already have one, by any chance?"

"No, I don't. Thank you very much. I never dreamed one of these little cuties might still be kicking around in the stockroom."

"Actually, there aren't any here at the main office, but if I go to the warehouse they'll usually have whatever I'm looking for. If there's anything else you want, please let me know. I'd be glad to try to find it for you."

Kayako glanced briefly into Osato's eyes. They seemed to be brimming with sincerity, and she was so moved that she found herself unable to speak. After taking a short breath she finally said, "You're a very kind person."

"Right back at you!" Osato smiled broadly. "You know, I've thought about this a lot while I'm working, but there really don't seem to be any bad people in my corner of the business. I think the same is true of the anime world in general, too."

"No bad people?" echoed Kayako.

"Oh, I'm not saying that in a hypocritical, holier-than-thou way, but rather as a kind of natural inevitability. It's a small community, so rumors spread quickly, right? If somebody does some slipshod work, or bags on a project, the news will be all over town in the blink of an eye, and things can get difficult for that person, going forward."

"I get it."

Kayako understood what he was talking about only too well. Anime staffs were made up, to a large degree, of freelancers who pinballed around among various studios, and once a negative rumor began to circulate about someone, that person's work opportunities could simply evaporate. It wasn't just a matter of skillset or job performance, either. If there was talk about questionable behavior—for example, if a male director got into a relationship with a female subordinate—that type of gossip would spread like wildfire, too.

"So does this figure come with some kind of hidden agenda?" she asked. "Does Bluto want to ask us for a special favor, or something?"

"No, absolutely not! Nothing of the sort," Osato said, shaking his head gently. "It's not as if this is a major gift or anything. It's just a small way of saying 'thank you.' Well, then, I'll be off."

As they exchanged yet another farewell, Osato gave a little wave, then bowed his head. It pained Kayako to think that he'd be holding that pose until the automatic door shut. She exited in a hurry, and checking that the door had closed behind her, she slowly raised her face and felt a surge of relief at finally being alone. The moment she leaned against the wall in the empty hallway, all her tension seemed to melt away like chocolate left out in the midsummer sun, and she slid down to the floor.

After a moment, she looked up at the ceiling and took a deep breath.

The thoughtful gift she was holding in her hand—the cute little figurine—was outlandishly heavy. She bit her lip to fight the mass of emotions that assailed her. She was filled with remorse. *Today, too, I couldn't fess up that Oji disappeared.*

Kayako had a throbbing headache. Pulling out her mobile phone, she checked her inboxes, but there were no emails, texts, or voice messages, or even a missed call: no signs of communication whatsoever. It was a week already since he had abandoned an anime series in the midst of production. This was an unmitigated disaster.

Kayako stood up and faced forward. Stashing the gift in her briefcase, she made a decision: before getting back to her office, she'd duck into a restroom somewhere along the way and cry her eyes out for exactly two minutes.

◆

"You're no small woman, are you, Ms. Arishina?"

That's what Chiharu Oji said, out of the blue, during the tête-à-tête where Kayako pitched him about joining her new project as director.

She had been so startled that she barely managed to stammer out an incredulous "Huh?"

They exchanged glances, then Oji said in a jocular tone, "You probably thought I'm pretty short," making her feel doubly disconcerted. "You look like a model," he went on.

"Oh, no," Kayako denied modestly. "Not at all."

"No, really, you do. Yup. You look like a plastic model that somebody built from a kit. You'd better be careful to stay out of the sun, so you don't melt."

"Wait, what?" Kayako's eyes opened even wider with surprise, and it was a few minutes before she realized he was teasing her.

The fact was that she had been getting the "You look like a model" line, in its usual sense, quite frequently at the time. At her workplace (which was usually a cross between a war zone and the aftermath of a hurricane), she was once told in a snide, mean-spirited tone, "Gosh, it must be nice—you're tall, and with your long hair, you're always so beautifully put together."

Makeup? Her facial features were so clearly defined that they didn't really need embellishment, so even if she went completely barefaced it wasn't really noticeable. When it came to fashion, it was certainly true that she bought—and wore—whatever she pleased, but there were frequent stretches when, too busy to go home, she ended up walking around in the same hideously wrinkled skirt for several days in a row. In fact, nights when she only managed to grab a couple of hours of sleep at the office were actually the rule rather than the exception. And as for her height, you'd think people would know that there were a lot of women in the world who felt awkward about being taller than average.

At that meeting, a feeling of exasperation welled up inside her. Her conversation with the potential director seemed to have lurched off the rails and crossed the line into absurdity. *Why are you ragging me about my appearance?* she thought indignantly. *Isn't it natural that I'd make an effort to look presentable today? After all, it's a meeting with you, Chiharu Oji: my anime idol, and the person I admire most.*

"So how old are you?" her idol asked.

Kayako found the question offensive and irrelevant, but she replied politely, "I'm thirty-five."

"Oh, that makes you three years older than me. So when I was in sixth grade, you were already in your second year of junior high? Or maybe third year? You really are a full-fledged grownup, aren't you?"

Kayako had no way of knowing how much (if any) sincerity lay behind this interrogation, and she was at her wits' end. They'd been talking about *Yosuga of the Light*—what she liked about that anime in particular, and which parts struck her as particularly effective.

Many years had passed since the *Yosuga* series first rocked her world. The realization that she was actually speaking directly to the person who created such a marvelous thing was making Kayako nervous to the point of frequently finding herself at a loss for words. Oji's side of the dialogue mostly consisted of injecting standard space-fillers like "I see," "Mm-hmm," and "That's right" from time to time, in a tone that suggested a kind of leisurely boredom.

Kayako's expectations of a lively exchange about how much she loved *Yosuga*, and why, had been crushed almost from the outset. Their conversation was like a deflated ball, and she felt as if she were being forced to undergo some ascetic trial where she had to keep on kicking it. The director seemed to have absolutely no intention of allowing her to pay him any compliments.

In the past, Kayako had used love—her passion—as a negotiating tool, or weapon, and those same techniques had been effectively used on her, in return, so not being permitted to praise Oji at all was especially hard to bear.

As long as they were making small talk the director was quite loquacious, but the moment the discussion turned to his own work, his facial expression changed, as if he were somehow testing Kayako, or taking her measure. He avoided eye contact, and his emotions seemed to switch off.

The more she tried to share her feelings and impressions, the more Oji seemed to dismiss her as just another fan, and the words she wanted to use to explain the profound impact of his work on her life seemed to slip far, far away. She liked and loved and admired that work so much, and as the time ticked away she felt increasingly frustrated at not being allowed to convey her feelings, and acutely aware of her own foolish inadequacies. Finally, when she seemed to have run through her entire stock of words of praise and persuasion, she concluded by saying simply, "I'd really like to work with you."

At that, Oji spent a long moment seemingly lost in thought, elbows languidly propped on the empty surface of the desk, not saying a word.

Kayako's heart ached. She'd intended to go on pestering him, stubbornly, for as long as it took even if he turned her down flat. The excruciating silence went on and on. One minute…two minutes…maybe longer. At last Oji opened his mouth, and that, of all things, was what flew out.

"You're no small woman, are you, Ms. Arishina?"

Kayako was bewildered by this bizarre sidestepping of the matter at hand. Her mouth dropped open for a moment, and then she swiftly came to terms with the fact that it was over. Her proposal was going to be rejected.

Oji's eyes seemed to darken, and his face was virtually expressionless.

Now that she thought about Oji's behavior, there had been telltale signs from the beginning.

Clutching her aching stomach, Kayako walked past Studio Edge's reception. Small though the company was, three years earlier it had invested in a sophisticated security system, and now Kayako swiped her ID card to enter. En route to her desk in the planning department on the second floor, she cut across the area where the animators were hard at work. There, it was almost always preternaturally quiet.

Since anime, as an art form, was created by a large group of collaborators, the finished products were essentially the accretion of steady, conscientious labor on a variety of tasks. Naturally, there were meetings and simple exchanges during the process, and even a modicum of gossip, but it was rare to hear chatty whispers on the floor while people were engrossed in work. Individual staff members mostly sat at their desks, silently absorbed in the jobs at hand. Many animators sported headphones or earphones, the better to retreat into their own little worlds.

Wandering through the first floor, a visitor would hardly hear a sound, yet there was always a clear sense that a large number of people were assembled there, hard at work. Inside the company, even at high noon, it always felt more like the middle of the night.

As Kayako passed in front of the separate rooms for *genga*, animation, finishing, and filming, the door opened and a man came charging out. (Genga, or original pictures, are the endpoints of the cuts that compose an anime.) After nearly colliding with Kayako, he said, "Oh, sorry." Kayako looked up and gave a silent, secret gasp of alarm.

It was the genga artist Sakomizu: stoop-shouldered posture, disheveled hair that didn't appear to have encountered a brush anytime lately, and the old-school type of glasses you rarely see nowadays, with clunky frames and thick, milk-bottle lenses. Kayako remembered hearing that Sakomizu had worn those same frames since junior high school, and just kept ramping up the strength of the prescription as the years went by. His skinny body was engulfed in a T-shirt bearing the likeness of one of Studio Edge's anime characters. It must have been at least a size too large because there was quite a bit of extra room in the shoulders, and the overall impression was that the T-shirt was wearing the man, rather than the other way around. More than likely, the shirt hadn't been intentionally purchased but had just been passed along by someone in the company.

Sakomizu and Kayako noticed each other at the exact same moment. The man kept his eyes conspicuously averted and didn't acknowledge her presence at all. He had evidently been on his way somewhere, but he whirled around abruptly, as if to return to his lair.

"Keep up the good work," Kayako said. Her bravado-fueled bluster, an attempt to keep up a front of civility, elicited no reply. The door slammed angrily in her face.

Kayako wasn't sure whether she felt insulted, or just empty and frustrated; those emotions were all mixed up together. And then a moment later, when it hit her that he'd gone back to wearing his old glasses, a faint sadness welled up in her, and she felt suddenly short of breath. *Wow*, she thought, *I've grown so weak.*

Needless to say, in this day and age prescription lenses have become much thinner, and frames are available in a vast variety of cool-looking styles.

Kayako was the one who had prodded Sakomizu into updating his glasses, as a way to change his image.

When he'd showed up at work wearing the new specs, his fellow animators all crowded around, saying, "Wow, you look so different!" to which Sakomizu responded, "Oh, you really think so?" with a smile.

Kayako had decided not to worry too much about the current awkward situation. When you were moving about in the world, this kind of minor problem was bound to occur. Having a colleague snub you was no big deal. It was fine. In a month, or in half a year, the whole thing would blow over.

Willing herself to put her distress behind her, Kayako started up the stairs. As soon as she reached the second floor, the tranquility of the studio below became a distant memory. The department where she worked was a perpetual whirlwind, dense with noise, movement, and activity. Someone was always talking, and she could hear voices in the midst of phone conversations—"Hello, this is Edge" and "Yes, about that matter..." Voices raised in anger were a normal part of the second-floor cacophony, as well.

Once, when she'd referred to the second floor as "the office floor," an animator had asked her with a bitter smile and bloodshot eyes, "Who's really doing the desk work here? I have to finish a whole stack by tomorrow."

"I'm back," Kayako announced quietly, draping her bag over her chair.

She was aware of a number of furtive but concerned glances aimed in her direction.

Oji had been absent and incommunicado for a week now, and his disappearance was already a topic of conversation among a number of her colleagues. The only people who knew about it, officially, were the company president and the producer and other core staff who were directly involved with *Ryder*. Because no one wanted to do anything to upset the hands-on animators, that group hadn't been told yet.

However, in a small office like this where everyone ate from the same metaphorical rice pot, word inevitably got around.

Kayako wondered how much longer the disastrous turn of events could be kept secret.

She was on the verge of sitting down when she heard a voice behind her. "Ms. Arishina, the president wanted to see you as soon as you came back." It was Kawashima, one of the production assistants on *Ryder*.

Kayako and the director were overseeing the overall process, but there were a number of staff members below them who were in charge of each thirty-minute episode.

With a troubled expression clouding his face, Kawashima said in a low voice, "Has he contacted you?"

Thinking that he shouldn't ask such an obvious question, Kayako snapped, "No, of course not." Then, immediately regretting taking it out on him, she added, "Believe me, the minute I get any news I'll be sharing it with everyone, and we can hoist a celebratory glass or two. It'll be party time, for sure."

"True."

"Listen, I'm sorry," Kayako said.

Seemingly startled by the apology, Kawashima shook his head. "It's not like it was your fault."

"Thank you for saying that."

While they talked, Kayako made her way toward the president's office. She could feel dozens of eyes boring into her back, and she couldn't help thinking, *No, when it comes down to it, I guess it really was my fault.*

"President's office" was something of a euphemism. In actuality, one corner of the room had just been partitioned off to create a private chamber, or the illusion of one. Kayako knocked twice on the door, then went inside.

"Welcome back," Mr. Eto, the company president, greeted her in a sharp voice.

She had repeatedly advised him not to eat while he was working, but the minute Kayako entered, the aroma of snacks filled her nostrils. She spied a bag of consommé-flavored potato chips on the desk.

President Eto, who would turn forty-five this year, had toiled in the anime trenches for many years and had been involved in producing a large number of projects. He followed the same career path as Kayako, rising through the ranks to become a producer, and founded Studio Edge while he was still in his thirties. In his youth he'd been the very model of a delicate, sensitive literary type, but no one would ever have guessed that from the way he looked today. As the man himself was fond of saying, "There's a ton of stress in this line of work, so what can you do," and as if to prove his point, his weight had more than doubled.

One time, when Studio Edge was being attacked online for putting out mediocre fare, someone posted a message-board thread titled "The president looks like a giant white pig." Eto had gone around the office saying huffily, "Actually, my facial features, at least, are still in pretty good shape."

When Kayako walked in, President Eto was staring blearily at his computer screen. Raising his eyes to meet her gaze, he asked, "So, were you able to tell them? How did they react?"

"No, the thing is...."

Studio Edge was planning to inform every company with a seat on the production committee that there was a possibility the *Ryder* project might have to change directors. That decision had been made in a meeting two days earlier. Kayako had been the sole voice of opposition, insisting until the end that they ought to wait for Oji to reappear.

The press conference to announce the production was still a week away. Oji was well aware of that timetable, she reasoned, and would surely return before then. In addition, assuming he did come back, a big public uproar over his disappearance in the meantime would brand him as "the director who ran away at one point." Their relationship of trust with clients and sponsors would be destroyed, and it would be impossible for work on the project to continue in a normal way.

That's the case Kayako tried to make, but she was unable to get any of her colleagues to agree.

The eminently rational conclusion that emerged from the meeting was this: if they waited until the last minute to tell the other members of the production committee about this situation, it would create serious and ineradicable trust issues going forward. Kayako understood their decision. She understood, and yet now that the chips were down, she found herself unable to get up in front of people who'd been attracted to the project by Oji's name and tell them he had run away.

It was already November. The series was slated to begin airing in spring, in less than five months. To have the designated director be absent and unaccounted for at this stage was a crisis of the direst magnitude.

Perhaps sensing some subtext in Kayako's inarticulate response, Eto blew out a huge cloud of breath with a prolonged *phew*. He plunged one hand into the bag of consommé-flavored chips, and there was a rustling sound as his fingers scrabbled around.

"Arishina, you aren't mistaking me for a nice guy or anything, are you?" he asked.

"No." Kayako's shoulders almost began to tremble, and it wasn't some figure of speech.

There was no way she would. From the day she'd joined the company, she had been well aware that in this tempestuous business, an endless roller coaster of ups and downs, a mid-sized shop like theirs had managed to survive thanks to Eto's rather fearsome personality. Being scolded by him was always a terrifying experience.

A producer and director were basically joined at the hip for the duration of a given project—united by a practical bond that was, in a sense, deeper and more intimate than the connection between entertainers and their managers.

There were many occasions when progress would come to a standstill if the director didn't show up, and that was why Kayako's management of Oji extended beyond the workplace to his private life.

She had to be on top of every detail: when he came to work, when he finished for the day, how much sleep he was getting, and when he would be ready the following morning, since she needed to be at his place to pick him up.

There had even been times when he said, "I'm in the middle of doing laundry right now, so you'll need to wait another hour," and the two of them ended up hanging out by his room listening to the humming of the washing machine. (When Kayako offered to take over the laundry duties, Oji responded in a tone of displeasure, "Thanks, but no thanks. I'm a sensitive boy and I'm at a tender age.")

If something was bothering him she had to remain at his side, day or night, and she was always standing by to pick up his late-night phone calls and stay on the line with him for four or five hours at a stretch, if necessary. True to his reputation, Oji was the genius type and was also willful and selfish—that was one nuance of the nickname "the Little Prince." He suffered excessively over the artistic aspects of a project and thought nothing of dragging other people into his fraught, frenetic orbit.

This kind of behavior wasn't unusual among superstar directors who presided over a workplace where a colossal amount of work was divided among a huge staff, but Oji took the prima donna routine to an extreme Kayako had never encountered before.

Nevertheless, she'd been enjoying herself immensely. She felt that Oji's attitude of "wanting to make something really great" was the real thing, pure and unadulterated. To that end, she was willing to humor him all the way.

A week earlier, she had gone to his apartment building in the morning as usual, to pick him up. She rang the bell for his unit, but Oji didn't appear. *That's odd*, she thought, still at the mildly annoyed stage. *What a brat—he's probably still asleep.* She called his home number, then his cell phone. When there was no answer on either line, she went to the front door and knocked repeatedly, then gave it a few swift kicks. However, there was no response whatsoever.

That's when she first started to get a bad feeling.

One after another, she phoned every place Oji might possibly have gone, and every person he could conceivably be visiting.

One of her earliest calls was to his family home. "Oh dear,

please forgive my son," his mother said in what struck Kayako as a rather laid-back voice, considering. "That boy has been like this forever—whenever things are tough, he always gets mad and runs away." Kayako pressured the mother into making a call to the building superintendent, who let her in with a master key.

There was no sign of Oji's cell phone or wallet. Work materials were still scattered around the apartment, and he hadn't left any kind of a note. Dialing his cell phone over and over yielded only a recorded message: "Your call cannot be completed at this time. This may be due to connectivity issues in certain locations, or the device may have been switched off."

Had the battery run out of juice, or had Oji deliberately switched off his phone? There was no way of knowing, but as the day wore on and there was still no word from the director, it became clear that he was off the grid.

Everyone was assuming that he had run away.

Gazing absently around Oji's vacant apartment with her mouth hanging open in disbelief, Kayako had no clue how to go about dealing with such a development.

To be sure, Oji had been plunged into a perpetual state of gloom in recent days, saying that he couldn't come up with the screenplay from the fourth episode on.

For series anime that are broadcast on television, the staff usually includes a scenario writer who serves as story editor. That person is responsible for scripting the overarching narrative, while sub-writers compose each individual episode down to the actual lines the characters will speak. An able story editor ensures that the screenplay maintains a steady flow and a solid core.

In the case of *Ryder*, however, Oji was supposed to be acting as both director and story editor. The sub-writer for each episode had to extract the narrative essence from Oji's vague outlines and hammer out the actual script in hours-long story meetings with him.

Moreover, during the production process, Oji had driven three sub-writers to quit and declared in the end, "The hell with it—I'll write the scripts myself."

Even to Kayako, this seemed like a decision born from desperation.

During the broadcast run of a series anime, working three episodes ahead was generally considered a comfortable cushion. In reality, though, a production that followed that model would soon eat up all its creative equity, so to speak, and end up in a precarious day-to-day situation that turned the workplace into a seething vortex of stress. To avoid this situation, it was essential to have a stable staff in place as soon as possible.

Series anime were usually constructed as twelve-episode programs that ran their course over a three-month period. The animators were split up into teams, with each unit taking charge of a particular episode, in rotation.

Fortunately, the scripts and the storyboards, on which the animated sequences and backgrounds would be based, had been completed through the third episode.

However, nothing was finished beyond that point. The director had failed to reach an agreement with the fired screenwriters about any of the elements they had worked on together, so the writing process was back to square one. Creative work couldn't proceed without the director's approval. This even applied to the "TEMP" designation that dogged the title and couldn't be removed without Oji's consent.

It amounted to a complete failure to direct the director. And that was Kayako's job and responsibility.

When, her face pale and drawn, she had first gone to explain the current situation to President Eto, her boss hadn't gotten angry. He had simply assessed the situation with cool aplomb. Kayako almost wished he would blow his top and yell at her, but he didn't blame her and just said in a severe voice, "We'll wait five days."

She knew what a tremendous favor the president was doing for Oji by suspending work on an anime-in-progress for five precious days.

But at a subsequent meeting, two days before, Eto had announced that the five-day grace period had expired, and the time had come to change directors. Chiharu Oji's name would be removed from the project, as well.

"The thing is," President Eto was saying now, "you promised to go over to Bluto today and explain the current situation. I could have gone myself or sent someone else."

"Yes, I know."

Every time the president looked her full in the face, she wished that she could crawl into a hole, or simply evaporate.

Since keeping Oji under control was her job, she believed that if someone had to make the rounds, offering apologetic explanations, she should be the one to do it. If she were going to foist that on anybody else, she'd much rather go tell the director that they were done with him.

Not only was Oji's disappearance Kayako's problem, she was the one who had gotten her company into the project in the first place. Going in, she didn't even care on what; she just wanted to work on something—anything—with Chiharu Oji. Since he'd left his company and been freelancing, she was sure he would bite. She had a long-cherished ambition to collaborate with him, no matter what others might say.

If things really did reach the point of changing directors, snagging another superstar who had directed a hit series or two would be impossible, both circumstantially and in terms of time. The most practical approach would probably be to promote someone from among the current sub-directors and have that person step into Oji's shoes.

The impact of the following week's official announcement, which was to have been built around the dramatic "Oji's first major new work in nine years!" angle, would be considerably diluted. On top of that, the reporters would probably feel like victims of an outrageous bait-and-switch scam if, after going to the trouble of showing up at a specially called press conference, they didn't get the big news they'd been promised.

After the meeting two days ago, Kayako had been on the verge of phoning not only Bluto but all the other partners as well, but every time—and there were many, many times—she would chicken out, excusing her cowardice by telling her colleagues that she ought to deliver the news in person. And then, today, she had gone to Bluto with every intention of telling them about the disastrous turn of events, and had chickened out yet again.

President Eto took another breath, then quietly let it out. Kayako wondered whether there was some hidden significance in the fact that the expulsion of air was so much longer this time.

"I'm not saying this because I dislike Oji or anything. To be honest, that isn't even a factor," he remarked. "Changing the director is nothing personal—it's just to protect the project. You understand that, don't you?"

"Yes."

"People like Oji think nothing of holding an entire project hostage," Eto went on. "At this stage, everything will grind to a halt without the director, and yet if they don't get their way about every little thing, they blithely threaten to abandon the project in midstream. Now that Oji has gone and disappeared, for reasons known only to himself, I'm very sorry but I'm going to have to ask him to relinquish the project. Otherwise the quality is going to go irretrievably downhill."

Hearing those words forced Kayako to concede.

Things could get worse than they were now. If it became widely known around the workplace that the director had pulled a vanishing act, morale would plummet. And of course, it wouldn't be possible to keep his disappearance a secret for very much longer.

"Do you really think he'll come back by next week?" asked Eto.

"I do think so. I really do."

I believe in him. He's going to come back. The more Kayako uttered those wishful mantras, over and over, the less certain she felt, deep down. What made her repeat them was her conviction that she, of all people, needed to believe in him.

Eto shook his head. "This is just a temporary reprieve," he warned. "Even if he comes back now, we're going to be in a serious pickle from here on out. Don't forget that Chiyoda, the most recent in the string of scriptwriters, was handpicked by Oji himself. As you'll recall, he claimed the first two we hired were no good and insisted on dragging in a third one, willy-nilly, saying 'If we use this guy, it'll be fine.' Except it wasn't fine, at all."

"I know." Being reminded of that debacle made Kayako squirm.

"And that's not all," the president continued. "Oji objected to having any agency tie-in for the theme song, and he wanted to change the voice actors. What with all his selfishness and obsessive behavior, the workplace has really turned into a chaotic mess, don't you agree? He's finally gone too far with this latest antic—this disappearance. It really is the last straw. I know you've probably been doing everything you can to make things work, but the bottom line seems to be that all the negative rumors about Chiharu Oji were correct."

"About Bluto. I'll go over there again, and this time I really will tell them," Kayako promised. "However, about changing directors, could you please wait a bit longer? I'm going to try to find Oji."

With that she bowed, excused herself, and turned to leave.

"Wait as long as you like, but keep up with your other work," her boss's voice boomed out behind her. "In any case, I'm going to replace the director."

Kayako couldn't respond. She just slipped silently through the door, unconsciously gnawing on her bottom lip.

The person Oji had handpicked to be his scriptwriter was named Koki Chiyoda. He was an author of so-called light novels, or YA fiction, and Oji claimed to be one of his biggest fans, from way back.

When Kayako heard Oji say, "I respect Chiyoda, so I promise I won't complain about his input," she immediately phoned the novelist and begged him to join the project. Chiyoda protested that he'd never even tried his hand at writing a screenplay, but they finally compromised by hiring him to write the third episode, on a trial basis.

Fortunately, Chiyoda had seen Oji's *Yosuga* in its entirety and announced that he was a mega-fan. On top of that, the writer said that he'd seen every single anime Oji had worked on in the intervening years. You would have thought it was a match made in heaven, except—

Even now, just hearing the name of Chiyoda's publisher, Daidaisha, filled Kayako with remorse. And every time she remembered the heavy sarcasm that Chiyoda's editor Kuroki regaled her with during the exit negotiations, she broke out in a cold sweat.

Koki Chiyoda's third-episode script was wonderful. Everyone agreed that the work not only met Oji's stringent requirements but surpassed them. The lines had a great beat and tempo to them, and the writing was so vivid that it conveyed a sense of the anime's world even with no images attached. You could feel the atmosphere and see the scenes unfolding before you, and the exchanges between Jyuri and her rival, Kiyora, were particularly masterful.

This is it, at last, Kayako thought at the time. Without a doubt, *Ryder* was going to be a success. Not only was the work going to be powerful, but having both Oji's and Chiyoda's names attached was a huge plus in terms of glamor and prestige. There was no reason to think the series wouldn't be the talk of the town.

However, it didn't take Oji long to throw cold water on the optimistic mood. "Uh, no," he said. "This isn't right. Yeah, it doesn't look like Chiyoda's gonna be the answer, either. His writerly sensibilities are just too overpowering, and I really can't handle it."

Inside Kayako, something seemed to shatter.

Do you wanna die? she asked her director. Quietly the first time, and yelling the second time: *Do you wanna just crawl off somewhere and die?!*

"Mmm." Oji shook his head. "I mean, this is just impossible," he dared to say. "Chiyoda is definitely an incredible writer, no question about it. But his words are so powerful that they don't seem to need any images. No, even more than that, it's almost as if pictures would get in the way. Okay, then, I've made up my mind.

There simply aren't any other options at this point. Since Chiyoda turned out to be another bust, it's obvious that no one else can do this job. I'm going to have to write the scripts myself."

Chiyoda wasn't present for this announcement, but Kuroki was at the table, and Kayako couldn't bring herself to look him squarely in the eye.

After a long pause Kuroki finally said, "So after all that work, it turns out you've just been wasting our precious cash-cow novelist's time?" His voice chilled Kayako to the bone.

We are so, so sorry about this, she and all the staff members in the room abjectly apologized. Then Kayako turned her attention to trying to talk Oji out of his radical decision. Why not use Chiyoda's script and just do their best to vie with those writerly sensibilities?

Oji's only reaction was a brusque reply: "No way."

Nevertheless, Kayako and the others went on desperately trying to persuade the director to change his mind. Since Chiyoda's script was fantastic as a screenplay, couldn't they at least use it for the third episode? After all, they'd managed to persuade a popular writer to come and write for them.

Even Oji nodded his assent to this, but Kayako now regretted that to Chiyoda's camp, the request must have seemed brazen, shameless, and supremely selfish.

"Isn't this all just a bit too convenient for you people?" snapped Kuroki, and then and there, he went on to disallow any use of the script. Behind his spectacles, the editor's eyes were hard as flint, and the mood in the room was excruciatingly awkward. Kayako felt as if she were sitting on a chair upholstered with thorns.

When Chiyoda joined the project, his publishing house had been open to discussion about producing "mooks"—magazine-format books—as well as a novelization based on the series, and things had been proceeding apace. Now, of course, those negotiations were frozen in place, at best.

After the shakeup, true to his declaration, Oji took over Chiyoda's job and began work on his own version of a script for episode three, but it didn't take long for that undertaking to run aground. Progress, if any, was extremely slow, and since there was no script, there was nothing to add to the storyboard.

A storyboard was, in effect, the blueprint for an anime. It incorporated characters' movements, backgrounds, and dialogue, among other elements, and served as the basis for the animators' work.

On top of everything else, Oji didn't happen to be one of those anime directors who is also skilled at drawing. His storyboards consisted mostly of scribbled instructions and stick-figure characters whose faces were little more than circles punctuated with random dots and squiggles. Some members of the staff who did know how to draw got together and painstakingly fleshed out the director's rudimentary sketches, but this approach proved very time-consuming.

Right around the time when the entire staff was starting to think the entire project might be headed for disaster, they heard from Kuroki, the editor.

If the Studio Edge team still wanted to, they could use the script for the third episode, but in that case, Chiyoda's name must not be attached to it or to the project in any form.

Kuroki's voice sounded bitter on the other end. He, himself, probably wanted to refuse, but apparently, upon checking with Chiyoda, the author had said, "I'd be happy if they put it to use," a generous offer that was nearly enough to bring tears of gratitude to the eyes of the staff at Studio Edge.

"If that's Koki's view, there's nothing I can do, though this won't ever happen again. And listen up. The Chiyoda brand, the sum of his accomplishments, will not get mentioned in connection with this anime. We won't be lending you his name." And at the end Kuroki spat, "Give my very best regards to the Little Prince," before hanging up.

So that was where things stood with the script.

◆

Tokyo Telemo Center, located in the Yotsuya district, was the largest recording facility in metropolitan Tokyo.

It hosted a total of seven booths, large and small, and as a rule there was always a vacant one that production companies could use. If you made a last-minute reservation there for a job that needed to be tackled on short notice, you were more likely than not to bump into colleagues from other companies who also had their backs to the wall. The anime business was an insular world in any case, so Kayako almost always saw someone she knew.

Glancing at the whiteboard next to the entrance, she noticed that it bore the names of three other anime companies in addition to Edge. When she saw "Tokei Animation" written next to the slot for Studio A—a much larger space than the one Edge had reserved—she groaned inwardly. She didn't know which Tokei title they were recording but felt a slight but unmistakable sense of foreboding. The faces of two or three acquaintances she'd rather not encounter floated across her mind.

Praying that she'd steer clear of them, she skulked toward the studio, hiding her face as best she could.

Today was the third session of voice recording for *Ryder*. Carrying a gift—a *baumkuchen* cake, pre-divided into small pieces—Kayako entered the studio and said, "Good morning."

"Morning."

The sound director, Gojo, had already arrived and was drinking a cup of coffee. Smoothing down his dry, salt-and-pepper hair as was his habit, he squinted his already narrow eyes at Kayako. Some other staff members were there, as well, but there was no sign of any of the voice actors in the interior recording booth. Confirming that fact, Kayako breathed a sigh of relief. "Thanks in advance for today," she said, bowing her head.

Gojo was probably still in his early forties, but his demeanor was so gentle that Kayako sometimes felt as though she was conversing with her grandfather in the country. His aura of serene equanimity lent him the affect of a much older man, which wasn't a bad thing, at all.

Gojo smiled and asked, "Is the director off today, too?"

"Yes. I'm sorry for the trouble, but I appreciate your kindness."

One of the things Kayako had learned while working in this business was the importance of the sound director. That person's job was to direct every sound-related aspect of an anime, including voices and music. It probably varied according to the workplace and the director's personality, but when Kayako sat in on the voice actors' dubbing sessions as a producer for the first time, she'd been surprised by the extent to which the sound director called the shots on essential performance-related aspects and went over the head of the director to give instructions and order retakes. The director would be present in the studio for such sessions but mostly just sat and watched over the proceedings, leaving almost everything to the sound director.

Sound and voice were important elements for animated titles in particular.

Gojo was a veteran sound director who had formerly been employed in the recording department of a major studio, Tokei Animation, before going solo and becoming an independent contractor. Recording mainly involved the overall editing of voices and sound effects, and he had worked closely with Oji during the making of *Yosuga*. "He taught me everything when I couldn't even tell which way was up or down," Oji lauded the older man as a primary mentor.

During the planning phase, Kayako and her crew had proposed a number of sound directors, but at Oji's suggestion they ended up offering the job to Gojo.

Oji was willful in all sorts of ways. He had strong opinions starting with the auditions for the voice actors, and even during the actual recording sessions, he was the type to offer his own instructions rather than deferring to the sound director's judgment and expertise.

Gojo evidently understood and accepted Oji's hands-on style, and that appeared to be an important feature of their working relationship. Despite his long, successful career Gojo didn't seem to have an arrogant bone in his body, and he was a master of unflustered flexibility. Clearly, Oji had chosen a sound director who was accustomed to his peccadilloes and wouldn't raise any objections to his desire to be involved at every turn.

Needless to say, every facet of this project, *Ryder*, reflected Oji's original directorial vision. From the launch until today, the staff that Kayako and her colleagues had recommended, sound directors and scriptwriters included, had almost all been "re-painted in Ojicolor," that is to say, unilaterally replaced by the director's own choices.

And now, Gojo had ended up directing the voice recordings that Oji had been so gung-ho about actively supervising himself. The irony was that even though Gojo had willingly taken a back seat while Oji was around—serving as more of a coordinator— the older man was a highly capable sound director with years of experience under his belt. The other day, the first recording session since Oji's disappearance had gone off without a hitch, and Kayako had been immensely relieved to hear Gojo's precise instructions and insightful performance tips.

Naturally, Gojo was aware of Oji's unexplained absence. He had known the director since Oji was in his early twenties and laughed uproariously when he was told the news. Then, after a single droll comment ("Oji sure is a funky guy, isn't he?"), he immediately reverted to pragmatic mode. "What effect will that have on our daily routine?" he asked, and Kayako gratefully latched onto that down-to-earth attitude as if it were a life preserver.

The production had already contracted with popular voice actors to play the protagonist and the main cast. In any case, at this late date, there was very little room for changes in the daily production schedule.

Peering through the glass, Kayako could see everything that went on in the recording booth.

Up in the front, projected on a monitor, characters rendered in the "three dots in a circle" drawing technique appeared in sketches taken directly from the storyboards. The drawings were so primitive that it was just barely possible to recognize the protagonist, Jyuri, and her close friend, Maari.

Whether it is a live-action or animated work, the voicing can be tweaked in post-production or come after filming. However, in the case of anime, the ongoing creation of visual images tends to be perpetually behind schedule, and more often than not the voice actors need to follow storyboard frames and to perform without the final art. With a TV series, this timetable was very nearly the rule, and exceptions were rare.

So while the current situation was nothing tremendously unusual, as Kayako gazed at the unpolished sketches on the monitor, she couldn't help but realize that the visual aspect of the project was in a very precarious state.

Gojo's eyes surveyed the interior of the studio. "He's definitely going to come back," he told Kayako. "I don't know whether he'll turn up in time for the official announcement of the project, but surely this can't go on much longer. He'll be back soon—I'm sure of it."

"You sound awfully calm and carefree, but we can't be so laid-back."

"The director truly loves and cares about this project. That's a fact. It's probably because he cares so deeply that he blew out his tires, so to speak, but I honestly don't believe that he's the unreasonable, selfish *enfant terrible* everybody makes him out to be." Gojo's kindly face creased in a brief, wry smile. "I do understand what he's saying, and he isn't mistaken. That theme song they tried to bring in for purely commercial reasons totally ignored the worldview of the anime. As for the voice acting, considering what a terrific job Kagihara is doing—you know, the actress Oji chose for the part—well, I'm glad he stood his ground. And you did good, too, standing up for him."

"No, please," Kayako demurred. "It was just that I couldn't be more forceful with Mr. Oji than I was."

Producing an anime required vast sums of money.

For a typical 12-episode series, production costs usually ran between 120 million and 150 million yen, while the budget for a 24-episode series was close to 200 million yen. On average, a single episode came out to anywhere from 10 to 20 million yen. In addition, broadcasting on TV incurred sponsoring fees paid directly to the station: in other words, for that common voiceover announcement, "This program is brought to you by..." For a late-night time slot, the bill was normally 10 million yen for the entire three-month run.

There was a time when a single major company might produce an entire anime in-house, but in recent years, the staggering budget meant that a production committee had to be formed for the vast majority of projects.

At an anime workplace, where the interests of a number of companies elaborately intertwined, occasionally a certain sponsor could make a sudden, unanticipated demand. That's what happened with the theme song. The directive was to use a recently released single by an all-girl idol group as the main theme, and moreover, one of the group's members as the voice actor for the protagonist.

The person who first brought that concept over to the creative side was Animarket producer Kakiuchi, but it fell to Kayako to broach the subject with the staff. Pitching difficult or unpalatable proposals to the director was part of her job.

The proposed theme song couldn't be described as good, by any means. Nonetheless, Kakiuchi tried to make the case that using a song by the group—which had recently become immensely popular—for a late-night anime, in tandem with stunt-casting one of the singers as the lead voice actress, was bound to generate lots of publicity.

With a heavy heart, Kayako took the proposal to a sleep-deprived Oji, who'd been working madly for days on end. She herself felt insulted by the casually condescending logic that because their project was a magic-girl anime, injecting a group of teenage-girl idols into the series made sense.

She would never forget the incredulous, affronted look in Oji's eyes when she started to explain the plan.

"Are you serious?" he asked. "Is my producer really telling me this?"

The moment she saw the hurt in Oji's eyes, Kayako made up her mind to turn down the proposal. "I'm sorry," she said. "Please forget I ever mentioned it."

When she shared her decision with Kakiuchi, he flew into a rage, accusing her of coddling the director. In the end she persuaded Kakiuchi to accompany her to a meeting with President Eto, who managed to work things out. It was ultimately decided that the theme song would be a track by an indie band, Oji's wish from the outset. As for the lead voice actress, they conducted the customary audition process and settled on Yuka Kagihara, an industry veteran.

Gojo chuckled. "Well, he ran away anyway." There was an impish look on the sound director's smiling face, and he spoke so mildly that Kayako's downcast mood brightened a bit. "I'm sure wherever he is, he's aware of your phenomenal efforts on his behalf, and I don't think he'll leave things as they are for very much longer."

"I hope you're right."

During the time she'd spent with Oji over the past year, since the project launched, there had been innumerable moments when Kayako felt twinges of doubt about what she was doing. Oji didn't seem to give the slightest consideration to the possibility that he might be causing someone to run around in a panic or duck into random restrooms to weep, but she had learned to accept that aspect of his personality. *I'm quite bonkers, too*, she thought. And she always returned to this: *If only I had handled things just a little bit better.*

"Oh, I'm definitely right," Gojo replied in a tone of absolute certainty. "I mean, it was the same when he was choosing voice actors. One of his pals showed up to audition, but in the end his decisions about the lineup were based entirely on ability. It made me think he's committed a hundred percent to *Ryder*."

"I believe that, too."

"When he does come back, let's go out drinking, just the three of us, if only to lecture him about what a bad boy he's been. I'm planning to complain bitterly about how much extra work he caused for me, compared to what I signed up for, so please arrange to have Studio Edge pick up the bill."

Gojo chuckled, then glanced at his wristwatch and said, "It's time to get this show on the road." With perfect synchronicity, Yuka Kagihara's cheerful greeting—"Good morning!"—rang out inside the studio. Catching sight of Kayako and Gojo, the voice actress doffed her hat, bent from the waist in a deep bow, and thanked them in advance.

◆

Faced with popular voice actors, Kayako was always reminded of the old proverb, "The nobler the person, the humbler the behavior." The more popular the voice talent, the more modest and meticulously considerate of others they tended to be. It was the production side that needed to be thanking them, but they invariably bowed to say, "Thank you for kindly giving me this job."

On the other hand, Kayako had been shocked by some of the things she'd seen at recent auditions for female voice actors. Perhaps they were trying to appeal to the sensibilities of male directors and producers, but the actresses' costumes ran the gamut from startlingly short miniskirts that showcased their shapely legs, to outfits resembling school uniforms, to designer frocks jauntily accessorized with cat-ear headbands.

The term "idol voice actor" had been around for some time, and it was no different for *Fateful Fight: Ryder Light* [TEMP]. Kayako wanted to cock her head in bewilderment and secretly cringed at the sight of some of the more outlandish attires: *What is this anyway, some kind of cosplay event?* She was even more surprised to see that the male staffers didn't seem to think those over-the-top costumes were that inappropriate. After a while, she figured it out. *Of course,* she thought. *The actresses dress that way because it gets results.* And after that she felt a wee bit disappointed in her male colleagues.

Oji was a bachelor, and not only did he create magic girls, he himself was such a fantastical figure that he'd earned the nickname "the Little Prince." Because he didn't seem completely real, Kayako hadn't gotten so much as a glimpse of his personal penchants, interests, or inclinations. He didn't seem to act high-spirited or show much excitement in public, but didn't he, in his heart of hearts, enjoy that spectacle, too?

When Gojo referred to a voice-actress "pal" of Oji's, Kayako knew immediately whom he was talking about.

Aoi Mureno.

The popular voice actress had starred in last year's *Mermaid Nurses.*

She and Oji apparently went way back, and after the auditions were over, Kayako saw them together in the corridor, deep in conversation. As expected, there was something different about a popular performer. Kayako noticed at a glance that the actress had a distinctive aura, and she thought, *Oh, that must be Aoi Mureno.* Kayako was getting ready to greet the pair when she heard the actress say coquettishly, "Oh, Mr. Oji, you're too much. You really *are* a little prince!" Not wanting to interrupt their intimate banter, Kayako stopped in her tracks. As she'd heard, Aoi Mureno was a conspicuously cute girl.

After a moment Aoi noticed Kayako's presence and called out, "Oh, hello!" in a friendly enough voice, but her eyes were coolly appraising and tinged with suspicion. Aoi's legs were long, slender, and straight, and as soon as Kayako became aware of this, she couldn't help but brace her own feet. She was close enough to hear Aoi whisper to Oji, "So, your producer's a woman."

Perhaps Kayako was jumping to conclusions based on a very small amount of evidence, but even so, at that moment, she suddenly thought: *This girl has a thing for Oji.*

Aoi's performance at the audition wasn't bad. She might not have been suitable for the part of the heroine, but she'd be cast in some role or other, for old acquaintance's sake. In that case, Kayako was resigned to seeing Aoi again at the workplace, but contrary to expectations, Oji didn't offer her a role. *That's odd,*

Kayako thought, but she was more than a bit relieved. Having to watch that lovely, showily dressed woman hovering around the director would have been hard to bear.

A short while later someone came up to Oji and began asking him about his pal, suggestively—"Have you known that girl for long? She's super cute."

"Oh, you mean Aoi?" he responded indifferently. The familiar way he spoke her name courted vulgar curiosity in its own right, but he added, "Sure, she's cute, but real-world cuteness will never be a match for 2D." It was a brusque reply. "So whoever it is, it's all the same to me. In terms of looks and appearance."

During a break in the dubbing session, Kayako ventured out by herself to buy something to drink. Just as she reached the cluster of vending machines on the second floor, she caught sight of someone she really didn't want to talk to loitering in the designated smoking area at the rear. At that same moment, the smoker noticed her as well.

"Oh!" he said, looking her way. Kayako longed to turn around and run back the way she'd come, but it was too late.

"Long time no see," the other person said.

It was Osamu Yukishiro, a producer at Tokei Animation. The sense of foreboding Kayako felt when she saw that company's name on the whiteboard at the entrance hadn't been a false alarm, after all.

"Oh, hello," Kayako responded with a small nod. She felt her lips twitching, but the mental equilibrium required to conjure up a big, bright, phony smile had long since deserted her.

The designated smoking area was partitioned off with clear plastic, and she could see Yukishiro stubbing out, in one of the ashtrays, the cigarette he'd been smoking. *That's all right, no need to put it out. Seriously, you don't have to come talk to me,* Kayako thought, but her telepathic pleas were in vain. Yukishiro was walking toward her, all smiles.

"How's it going?" he asked, then went on, "Studio Edge is recording here today too, I see. I heard that there's going to be a press conference on Niconico to announce your new production? A guy I know is a reporter at *Animaison*, and he was griping that it was unheard-of to keep the production details a secret from the press until the official announcement. Well, oftentimes, even when you try to keep the specifics under wraps, something will usually end up getting leaked to certain people."

Yukishiro was wearing jeans and a polo shirt, which wasn't unusual garb for someone in the industry, but in his case every component of his outfit was from a recognizable fashion line. Rather than high-end brands with logos plastered all over them, though, his tastes ran more toward limited-edition shirts and "double-name" coats owing to collaborations between such and such. He didn't have it with him today, but the last time they'd met Yukishiro had been carrying a black embossed-leather briefcase that looked like something a doctor in a movie might tote around. When Kayako heard that it was an antique the producer had bought during a trip to France, all she could say was, "Wow..."

Nothing about Yukishiro seemed to be trying too hard, or going too far: not his neatly groomed brown-tinted hair, or his elegant smile. His eyes were a trifle droopy, which came across as being equal parts amiable, flippant, and sarcastic. Even so, his suave demeanor helped him worm his way into people's good graces, and there was something uncanny about his talent for winning hearts and minds—a talent he only exercised, however, when he saw some practical value in doing so.

Yukishiro was one of Tokei Animation's most competent producers, and he was widely known as a hitmaker. His name popped up in various interview articles, and not just in magazines aimed at the anime trade. He frequently used phrases such as "fast-lane success" and "feeding the Zeitgeist." The word on the street was that a great many directors were standing in line to work with him.

He was also around Kayako's age, as far as she knew. Yukishiro looked at her through inscrutable coffee-colored eyes. "How's Mr. Oji these days?" he asked.

Kayako inhaled deeply. *The anime industry's a very small*

world, she reassured herself. *It's only natural news would have gotten out that Oji's doing our next title. It's fine. There's no way anyone could have heard about his disappearance.*

"Please just let me say that I have no clue what you're talking about. At least, not for today." Kayako put it at that.

"It must be rough working with him," Yukishiro noted in an easygoing tone. Nodding to himself, he went on, "He did get his start at our company, and I feel somehow responsible that he's been causing trouble wherever he goes since he struck out on his own as a freelancer. I teamed up with him on several projects, but what can I say? He isn't what you'd call easy to work with, and I really feel for you. I'm sure the stress is never-ending."

"...Are you here to do some recording today? I gather your new title is going to run during the same season, and you'll be announcing the particulars next week?"

"Purely by coincidence." Yukishiro smiled. "I mean, like, complete happenstance, right?"

Hearing him repeat himself that way, Kayako could only reply, "Sure." She swallowed the words that rose in her throat: *You guys basically just stole our method.*

While the dates were different, she'd heard that the press conference for Tokei Animation's new show would also be streamed via Niconico.

She'd gathered that it belonged to the "schoolkids plus robots" genre.

She didn't know who would be directing but had assumed that Yukishiro would be attached as the producer. She seemed to have guessed right.

That was when the door of one of the nearby studios opened and a woman poked out her head. "Hey, Mr. Yukishiro," she yelled, "how long are you planning to stay on break, anyway? We got back to work a long time ago."

Seeing the look of displeasure on the woman's face, Kayako couldn't help but gulp.

Yukishiro noticed Kayako's reaction but didn't seem particularly flustered. He just said, "Well, then, I'll be going," with the same elegant smile. Then he added, with overly impeccable politeness, "That was Director Hitomi Saito. She did the in-game anime for *Pink Search*, year before last."

Kayako already knew that.

The action game of one of Tokei Animation's marquee titles, *Sun Angel Pink Search*, had anime portions, including the opening sequence, that were so surprisingly polished and brisk that they'd garnered more (and longer-lasting) attention than the game itself. The tie-in merchandise, a wand, had also sold remarkably well, Kayako recalled.

She'd seen that in-game anime. Tokei Animation's Hitomi Saito was one of the directors that Kayako hoped to work with one day.

Leaning farther out of the studio door, Saito noticed Kayako. Perhaps minding how she'd yelled at Yukishiro, she gingerly turned to face Kayako and bobbed her petite head.

Kayako hurriedly responded in kind.

She knew Hitomi Saito by sight, but this was the first time they'd met. The diminutive director wore glasses and was dressed in loose pants and a T-shirt. Her long hair was pulled back into a crude ponytail from which a number of strands were hanging untidily down. She looked scruffy and exhausted. Kayako was no stranger to super-hectic periods at work, and her chest tightened as she gazed at Hitomi.

Awesome. Hard at work, Kayako thought. There was something really lovable and beautiful about that. It was the look of a person who was totally serious about what she was doing.

Year before last, when Hitomi Saito helmed the in-game anime that created such a sensation, she'd only been twenty-four—the same age as Oji when he made *Yosuga*.

The director, no doubt unnerved by Kayako's scrutiny, quickly averted her eyes and urged Yukishiro, "Hurry up, please." Without further ado she closed the studio door and was gone.

"She's kinda scary, our boss," Yukishiro said amusedly. "One of these days, when the chance arises, I'll make a proper introduction. She's super interesting, that kid."

"By all means," Kayako responded. "I'd like that very much."

In recent years, the number of female directors had grown. Kayako's experience with people in that role had led her to conclude they were all sadists. Male or female—it made no difference. Oji and Saito weren't exceptions to the rule. Furthermore, in the case of sadistic women directors, there was usually a male producer who stood beside her and silently catered to her every whim with a patience and perseverance that could only be described as samurai-like. A loquacious man like Yukishiro didn't quite fit that mold, but even so, it was clear that when his director said "Jump!" he was more than happy to ask "How high?"

But what about me? Kayako wondered. *How do Oji and I appear to others? Am I managing to make Oji run himself beautifully ragged like that, and to remain steadfastly by his side all the while?*

"I hope you find him." The seemingly casual words jolted Kayako back to reality, and she saw a calm smile on Yukishiro's face. Before her eyes could even open wide, he went on, "I'm talking about Oji. I hope he returns."

"...What are you talking about?"

"I'm looking forward to the press conference next week. You'll be live streaming, and it's open to the public, right? Director Saito and I will be in the audience, with your kind permission. Oh, and that'll be a good time for the two of you to get to know each other and have a nice chat. She's a fan of Oji's, too, as I recall."

Bye then. Don't work too hard. With that, still wearing a silky smile, Yukishiro headed down the hall toward the studio where his director was waiting.

Left alone, Kayako waited until he had vanished from sight, then punched the vending machine.

Ka-blang. The sound echoed around the break area, and the floor actually seemed to vibrate underfoot. Riding the wave of adrenaline, she gave the wall a swift kick. It only caused an unpleasant tingling sensation in her foot and did nothing to improve her mood. Yukishiro's caustic smirk kept dancing around on the inside of her eyelids.

That pseudo-handsome bastard! Of course, Kayako didn't say those words aloud, but that's what she was thinking. *Drop dead! Him and Oji, and me too.*

◆

The dubbing session lasted well into the evening. After it was over, Gojo and the rest of the sound team invited Kayako to join them for dinner, but she made her excuses and dragged her weary self back to the office.

At Studio Edge, there was no such thing as day or night. The doors stayed open 24 hours a day and someone was always there, immersed in work. Even this late at night, all the rooms in the studio on the first floor were ablaze with light. Wondering whether her colleagues on the second floor had gone home, Kayako peered up the darkened staircase but couldn't bring herself to return to her desk right away. Even though she had refused the invitation to socialize with the recording staff, she simply didn't feel strong enough to be alone at a time like this.

There seemed to be signs of life in the genga workroom, so she quietly opened the door. Only one person was inside.

Oh, why does it have to be him, of all people, and why now, of all times, Kayako thought, as Sakomizu—who had cut her dead in the hallway the day before—glanced around at the sound of the door. He must have gone home since their last encounter because he had changed his clothes, trading the oversized T-shirt for a collared flannel shirt. It was tucked neatly into his trousers, which in turn were fastened with a belt.

Their eyes met.

"Ah… Still hard at work," Kayako said.

"Hi."

Even that minimal greeting, delivered in a muted voice, felt like a small token of redemption to Kayako. However, Sakomizu immediately faced forward and resumed drawing.

His glasses had switched back to the ones with thinner lenses.

Good, Kayako thought, relieved. Maybe he had just been wearing the milk-bottle lenses yesterday by chance, and not as a rebuke to her.

It was very quiet.

Shk shk. The only noise on the entire floor was the sound of the artist drawing lines on his board. Dithering over whether to leave the room, Kayako decided to stay for a while even if it would be awkward. As she had done many times in the past, she pulled up a stool behind Sakomizu, who was intensely absorbed in his task, and sat down and watched the illustrations coming to life beneath his fingers.

Sakomizu was a freelance animator.

At Studio Edge, there were hardly any in-house animators. Most of them were freelancers who brought their gear into Edge's office and used the tables and chairs provided upon receiving an order. In addition to the ones who set up at the studio, other freelancers worked at their own homes; the employment situation of animators ran the gamut.

The best were in great demand, with every company in town vying for their services, and freelancers who were juggling multiple assignments would even use Edge's facilities to do work for another firm. Managers tended to tolerate the practice, and it didn't raise Kayako or her colleagues' eyebrows.

The number-one goal at the workplace was to try to maintain quality while being as quantitatively productive as possible, so stoical silence was the default. However, when Kayako was waiting around for genga, she often initiated conversations with the animators. On that point, female producers were said to be more sensitive and sympathetic than their male counterparts. *Are you getting enough sleep? Aw, did you catch a little cold? Please don't push yourself too hard!*

With a tight production schedule where every minute counted, where people were goaded to finish up, Kayako never took these artists for granted. Once, when she casually let slip that she hadn't been home in three days, and the usually reticent animators responded with a "Huh…" and cranked out the work she needed, she was so moved that she couldn't find the words to express her gratitude.

She had known Sakomizu for a long time, and he was one of the animators she respected most. Not so much as squirming even when she waited right behind him and literally breathed down his neck, he unflappably completed his projects by the due date. More than once, Kayako had involuntarily yelped in delight when she saw the finished artwork.

Indeed, Sakomizu's drawings were, quite simply, bundles of charm. The beauty of his lines and delicate details exceeded expectations and gave everyone chills, and directors and staff alike tirelessly praised his work to the skies, saying, "Sakomizu, you're a genius!" Kayako had wanted to have him on the team for her current project, no matter what.

They'd reached a point where they could just chat, and she'd felt comfortable enough to broach the topic of replacing his glasses. One day, just as *Ryder* was getting into full-on production mode, he asked Kayako out to dinner. They'd never shared a meal together, just the two of them, but had gone drinking any number of times in a group with other animators, so she set out in a relaxed mood.

"I want to date you," Sakomizu propositioned her at the restaurant.

Kayako could sense the serious-minded man's nervousness from across the table. The open-heart necklace that emerged from the emerald-green wrapping paper that he held out seemed to tell the whole story—his sincerity, his kindness, his clumsiness—and her heart ached.

"I'm so sorry," she apologized. She had never once seen Sakomizu as anything more than a work colleague.

She felt profoundly terrible about the whole situation: the reservation at a French restaurant, the suit jacket that he looked so unused to wearing, and her choice of casual slacks, so inappropriate for the occasion.

Sakomizu, dumbfounded, stared at Kayako. "Then don't say stuff like that." The low mutter that he let out after a moment scared her a little.

"'Bundles of charm'?" he continued. "Don't say anything like that to me again. And don't be blithely calling me a genius, either. Don't worry about my health. Cut it out with the 'Shall I fix you something to eat?' And don't give out fancy chocolates on Valentine's Day. If you're gonna say it was just for work, then do it in a more businesslike way. Instead of handing them out selectively and individually, distribute them openly to everyone so we'll all know you're just expressing your gratitude for our work, and nothing more."

It was the first time Kayako had ever heard him utter such a large number of words all at once. "Stop messing around with me," he spat, and what pained her most wasn't his criticism but rather the look on his face, which seemed to be on the brink of crumpling into sobs. "Of course I'd fall for you, stop messing around with me."

"I am so, so sorry. I never meant for this to happen," Kayako repeated the same words over and over, bowing as if she were rubbing her forehead against the tabletop. *I'll never be able to come back to this restaurant, that's for sure.* After the man left, Kayako finally raised her own slightly tearful face and saw 20,000 yen lying there, enough to cover her share.

The next day, Sakomizu appeared at the studio as usual. He sat uncannily still with his eyes glued to the computer screen, his entire attention focused on drawing. Like always, he worked calmly and matter-of-factly, to meet his deadlines.

The only noticeable difference was that when Kayako addressed him, he didn't turn around. When she tried, with feigned nonchalance, to repay him for the 20,000 yen he'd spent at the French restaurant, he stubbornly refused to accept the proffered cash.

Once a genga drawing was finished, the director and the head of animation compared it in sequence and sometimes suggested certain modifications. It was Kayako's job to convey the tweaks to Sakomizu, note in hand—maybe the position of a chin or the feeling evoked by a character's eyes and facial expressions needed to be adjusted.

One day, in the middle of that process, Sakomizu looked her straight in the eye for the first time in a while and declared, "From now on, I'll only listen to the director. If Mr. Oji has any complaints about my finished work, please tell him to give me a direct explanation. Not you, nor the animation director. I will only listen to what he has to say."

And from that moment on, he blatantly ignored Kayako. A month had passed since then.

As for Oji, he had now been missing for a week. The following day, Kayako was to go back to Bluto's offices to meet with Osato again. This time, she absolutely had to tell him about the impending change of directors. No further reprieves would be forthcoming from President Eto, and she understood that they were fast approaching the point of no return.

Even at a time like this, Sakomizu's drawing, which she gazed at absently, was superb. Since he had ordered her not to praise him, she wasn't going to. But she was moved. He was incredibly good.

She'd thought he might tell her to go away, but he didn't say a word. Indeed, he seemed quite oblivious to her presence behind him and just kept adding to his drawing, in silence.

He must totally hate me now, Kayako thought. This was probably the last time he would ever agree to work on a project she was producing. However, even though Sakomizu undoubtedly felt as awkward as she did, for this project, at least, he was continuing to work as diligently as ever and showed no signs of throwing in the towel. For the sake of Oji's title, he was evidently determined to stick it out to the end.

"Mr. Sakomizu, are you by any chance doing any work on Tokei Animation's new title?" Kayako asked gently. She just wanted to talk to Sakomizu, and any topic would do.

She fully expected him to ignore her question. After a brief silence, however, he responded—without turning to look at her. "You mean Director Saito's *Sabaku*?"

"That's what it's called? I didn't know that, but it's going to butt heads with our anime this spring season. It's Producer Yukishiro's project."

"I am working on it," Sakomizu freely acknowledged.

Tokei Animation mostly used in-house animators with exclusive contracts, but any way you looked at it, Sakomizu was exceptional. It was no surprise that Tokei had sought him out.

He was a pro, so it was probably second nature for him, but once again, Kayako was impressed. She hadn't seen or heard any details about the competing project, but it was safe to assume that Tokei's *Sabaku* and Edge's *Ryder* were quite different in terms of aesthetic vision and general flavor. Somehow, Sakomizu was managing to work on both projects at the same time.

Which one do you like better? When that question nearly popped out of her mouth, Kayako realized how battered she was feeling.

As yet, Sakomizu didn't know that Oji had disappeared. She needed to keep the animator on board by any means possible, but with Oji out of the picture, there was no one at Studio Edge whose notes the illustrator was willing to look at.

"I see," Kayako said, nodding and standing up. She really wanted to say, "Don't push yourself too hard, and please make sure to get some rest," but not wanting to risk Sakomizu's wrath, she kept those expressions of concern to herself. She was about to slink quietly out of the room when, to her surprise, Sakomizu called after her.

"Ms. Arishina, it looks as if you'll be competing against *Sabaku* for anime supremacy this spring."

"Supremacy?"

"As in conquering or reaching the top."

Supremacy, Kayako echoed under her breath.

Sakomizu still hadn't glanced in her direction, while his fingers continued to move. "You hear that word a lot these days. It's because late-night anime is so competitive—like the Warring

States era," he went on. "I don't know what's going on elsewhere, Ms. Arishina, but at least, you should be able to beat Producer Yukishiro."

"Why is that?"

"Because that person doesn't remember people's faces. He's a real go-getter, but that's his one big fault."

In the quiet office, the only sound was the *scritch-scratch* of lines flowing from Sakomizu's hand. Outside the window of the studio, which was high above the street, the starless night sky spread out over the city.

"Before, when I was drawing cels, I did a ton of work for him— this was before he got to be such a big deal—and he spoke to me directly, I don't know how many times. But he apparently thought that since there were so many people on the staff, he didn't need to remember everyone's faces. Then, around the time I started to get a pretty good reputation and clients began asking for me by name, Yukishiro came by my desk, all deferential and ingratiating, saying, 'Nice to meet you' as if he'd never laid eyes on me before. He put on a polite front, but having become so successful, it was obvious from his attitude that he thought I was happy to have the chance to work with him."

Sakomizu didn't speak those words like someone who had taken umbrage; he just seemed to be candidly stating the facts.

"My case is just one example, of course. But it bothered me, so I talked to some of my coworkers and found out there are loads of people who've had the same kind of experience with Yukishiro. Not only animators, either. Voice actors and editors of the original, too. I just can't help thinking that treating people differently depending on your status is fatal for someone in his line of work."

Sakomizu's hand stopped moving, and the scratching sound ceased as well.

Kayako's heart seemed to lurch at the thought that he might finally turn around and look at her, but Sakomizu's eyes remained fixed on the computer screen. Holding that pose, he spoke again.

"You're the exact opposite, Ms. Arishina. You remembered

me—after we met a long, long time ago. I'd actually forgotten, myself, so I was surprised when you bowed to me and said, 'Thank you again for everything, that time.' And I know it's not as if you remembered me, in particular. You're like that with everyone. You praise people, you give them credit."

"It's not as if I go around lavishing praise on everyone indiscriminately. It's only for people who do uniquely wonderful work."

"I know, I know," Sakomizu brushed off her flattery, annoyed. "But that kind of attitude does make an impression, especially in this line of work."

The sketching sound resumed.

"You can definitely win," he said. "If it's against Mr. Yukishiro, you and Edge can reign supreme without breaking a sweat."

When Kayako went back to her desk and checked her email for the first time all day, she found a message from Daidaisha.

Kuroki's face immediately sprang to mind. Remembering their exchange about Chiyoda and the script, Kayako thought, *Uh-oh, this can't be good.* But it wasn't what she was expecting, at all.

The sender's address was Daidaisha, but the message was from someone called Yamao, not Kuroki. It began, "Kuroki gave me your contact info. I'd like to meet with you regarding a possible mook and novelization of *Ryder.*" The signature space named the anime business department as opposed to the literary department where Kuroki worked.

The message ended politely with "Thank you in advance for taking the time to consider this matter. Let's make some good books." A split second after she read those words, Kayako was dialing Kuroki's number on her desk phone.

It was already after two in the morning, but the editor was still in his office. Although they were talking on the phone, Kayako bowed deeply as she said, "Thank you very much." Or rather, she meant to say those words, but they came out as a breathless, husky croak. She tried again. "Thank you very much."

"For what?"

Kuroki was as cool as ever. Feeling intimidated by the man's self-possessed tone, Kayako went on, "For what you did about *Ryder.*" She had no idea how to begin to express her gratitude or to apologize for the earlier debacle. "Even after we treated Mr. Chiyoda so abominably, you went to the trouble of putting us in touch with your anime business department about a possible mook—"

"Oh, that," Kuroki interrupted, as if he'd only now made the connection. His tone was so neutral and uninflected that it almost seemed anticlimactic. "Work is work. As for what happened with Koki, it's part of my job to protect our authors. If the things I said in the heat of the moment came across as harsh, I apologize."

"But our Oji really did do something terribly rude."

"Doesn't matter, I promise you I'm not losing any sleep over it. But personally, I don't want to get entangled with you people, ever again, so please go on working with our people in the anime business department. Well, then."

"Really, I can't thank you enou—"

Before Kayako was able to finish her sentence, the call was cut off on the other end. She didn't think Kuroki was still angry. That was probably always his personality. Holding the dead handset with both hands, Kayako felt all the strength draining out of her from the shoulders down.

She felt a surge of gratitude.

Toward Kuroki, but also toward Sakomizu and their conversation a moment ago.

To the words: *You can reign supreme.*

Replacing the phone in its cradle, Kayako stared up at the ceiling. The white light from the fluorescent tubes flooded her eyes, even as Kuroki's words, which she'd just heard, sank into her heart by slow degrees. Gradually, belatedly, it began to dawn on her.

"To protect our authors," Kuroki had said.

Sometimes editors effectively became personal managers for

their writers and supervised and protected them. And that dynamic was exactly the same as the one between a producer and a director.

I want to protect my director.

Kayako had been visited by that thought many times during the course of her career. Her job was to protect the director—Oji. She'd come this far with that mantra and battle cry.

Oji was the heart and soul of the project.

There were money matters, people matters, grown-up matters. That kind of noise was always present, and an anime workplace needed a burning core that was wholly obsessed with preserving the quality and integrity of the work despite all that, almost to the point of naïveté.

That was why, presented with a theme song and voice actor that didn't jibe with his sensibilities, Oji had asked, "Are you serious? Is my producer really telling me this?" At that moment, behind the insolent words, there had been a weak gleam in Oji's eyes, Kayako was sure of it. Clearly, he'd felt hurt.

That was why she thought, *I need to protect him.*

She resolved that she, alone, would absolutely stand by his side until the bitter end.

She envied Kuroki for protecting Chiyoda, and Yukishiro for attending to Director Saito.

"Let me protect you," Kayako blurted out in a thin voice that made her chest ache to hear. She was close to tears.

She'd fight beside him, whatever it took. If they were going to fail, then they could fail together.

So let me protect you. Let me fight, she pleaded with all her heart. *That's my one and only desire.*

◆

Along one exterior wall on the 37th floor of the building where Blue Open Toy had its offices, there was an observation deck.

Nowadays it was no longer unusual for a skyscraper to be a sight-seeing spot, but there were a few tourists sprinkled around even at lunchtime on a weekday: mostly couples who appeared to be college students, and parents with their children in tow. Kayako was passing by on her way to Bluto's offices, but overhearing some random exclamations ("Eek! I'm getting weak in the knees!" and "Wow, we're up so hiiiigh!"), she made an impulsive detour into the observation area. Perhaps she'd been overly hyped up for her meeting with Osato, but she was a good twenty minutes early.

It was a flawlessly gorgeous day.

The clouds were like bits of raw-spun cotton scattered across the heavens, and a backdrop of vast blue sky stretched in the spaces between those bits of fluff. Down below, a Yamanote Line train looked like a stick as it glided slowly through the landscape. When Kayako peered directly down at the microscopic people on the sidewalks, her knees turned to jelly and she had to quickly avert her eyes.

Feeling a bit vertiginous, she backed away from the window, and that was when it happened.

"Are you thinking that the people look like specks of dirt? Goodbye, Muska."

Like an arrow, that familiar voice shot right through her chest and lodged in the center of her heart. Flustered, Kayako looked toward the source.

"If you keep being mesmerized by the pull of Earth's gravity, Char Aznable will come and purge you."

Chiharu Oji was standing there.

He headed toward Kayako, ambling along the long window that framed the sunny sky with its sprinkling of clouds.

Kayako was literally speechless. Awash in a sense of unreality, she stood in silence, barely supported by legs that felt even more rubbery than when she'd been gazing down at the distant pavement.

Oji was wearing the same clothes as the last time she'd seen him, shortly before his disappearance, and that costuming continuity almost made it seem as if nothing had gone awry during the intervening days. The figure on the observation deck could almost have been an apparition, a visual manifestation of Kayako's deepest desire.

But no: he was the real thing.

Oji smiled. "Ms. Arishina," he said. "I'm back."

Somehow, his face looked a bit thinner.

◆

Yosuga of the Light, the legendary anime that marked Chiharu Oji's directorial debut, consisted of twenty-four episodes in all.

This was a rarity for a director's initial work, but it ran during two seasons—"cours," in industry jargon. When *Yosuga* was broadcast nine years earlier, the predominant time slot for anime series, unlike now, wasn't late at night. Rather, it was six p.m., just before the "golden" prime-time block.

Even now, Kayako had a clear memory of the chilly December when those almost unbearably exciting final episodes aired. A single breath would seem to fill her lungs with icy vapor, and watching *Yosuga* was the only thing she looked forward to as she made her way home along the wintry streets.

Anime that targeted the so-called child demographic were nearly always scheduled to run during December to ensure robust sales of related toys during the Christmas-shopping frenzy. Nowadays, anime aimed at children were generally broadcast on weekend mornings, and *Yosuga* was one of the last series that brought kids sitting in front of TV sets in the evening waiting for the program to begin. There, "magic girls" still belonged to both children and grown-ups.

The main characters were four schoolgirls, with a supporting cast made up of their families and friends. Each of the heroines had her own reason to fight, her own need to gain power.

In the majority of magic-girl stories, every primary character has the ability to transform, and the girls all band together and use their various powers to defeat a common enemy. *Yosuga* significantly departed from the formula due to a certain premise: only one among the four girls would walk away with magical powers in the end.

Hence, the depicted process was what might be called magic-girl tryouts. The heroines combated evil entities bent on inflicting harm upon the human race. The ability to transform rotated among the girls, with only one possessing that attribute in a given episode. The remaining three girls, devoid of supernatural powers, would watch quietly from the sidelines while that episode's designated magic girl fought the enemy. In theory, the four were supposed to be allies, but because every character wanted to be the one to emerge victorious from the zero-sum game, they secretly wished that the current magic girl would fail or even be killed, while outwardly supporting their frenemies.

There were times when viewers, watching in anguish as the drama unfolded, felt that it might have been better for all four to have simply remained as ordinary girls. But no matter how many of those painful moments occurred, the girls themselves were continuously driven by one common goal: *I want to be special.* That was the road they had chosen, and the war they'd decided to wage, and they never took their eyes off the prize. Even if they met up with boys they liked, even when their families attempted to stop them in their quest, the magic girls were always insatiable and relentless in pursuit of their goal: to end up as the Special One. They did so with a zeal that was almost unrealistic according to some fans.

In an interview conducted back then, Oji offered an explanation. "It's because I hate the cheap, convenient, noncommittal conclusion that 'Ordinary, everyday life is the most precious thing of all' that I'm making a magic-girl anime in the first place. Unrealistic? Are you sure about that? How can you be content with being the same as everyone else and not trying to be special? Do you feel so unmotivated in taking on life?"

It was a time when there were a great many anime with open endings—that is, narratives that provided philosophical concepts and overwhelmingly powerful imagery, then left it to the viewers to interpret the story as they wished and draw their own conclusions. People assumed that *Yosuga*, too, would end in a cloud of ambiguity without giving clear answers, but Oji brought the story to a definitive close.

The ongoing battle with the enemy forces that wanted to annihilate mankind had already been resolved in the penultimate episode. With the epic foe out of the way, people expected the show to end in one of two ways: either all four main characters would cease to be magic girls, or a new adversary would appear, and the entire quartet would become full-fledged magic girls in recognition of their dedication and meritorious service to date. But true to the original setup, Oji chose just one of the four to become an eternal magic girl.

In a world where the enemy had been vanquished, one girl, and one alone, was anointed with the "special" title, while the other three set out on the same quotidian roads as everybody else.

When a writer for an anime magazine remarked that having each girl follow her own particular path was a marvelous ending, too, Oji responded, "Actually, I wanted to kill them off."

That comment didn't make it into print.

"It wasn't a marvelous ending, at all," he'd gone on. "If they weren't chosen to be special, it would have been fine to have them lose. I wanted to kill off all three of the girls who weren't selected to put a proper end to the story, but the powers that be wouldn't let me. Of course, that was to be expected. With an anime that's broadcast over network television at six in the evening—as opposed to theatrical features or OVA—there are ethical considerations, the primary one being that kids would have been traumatized. Each character had her own set of fans, and if everyone hated my ending so much that they turned their backs on the anime, it would have had a hugely negative effect on merchandising, and we wouldn't have been able to recoup the production costs."

Therefore, claiming that Yosuga had been an artistic failure, Oji left Tokei Animation.

"They wouldn't let me kill them off"—those were the Little

Prince's parting words.

◆

"Ms. Arishina. I'm back."

The instant she heard that voice, Kayako took off running. Throwing caution to the wind, she bore down on her target. When she was close enough for an embrace, she stopped, panting for breath—and then, just like that, hit Chiharu Oji in the face.

Her hand balled into a fist.

In the split second before Kayako's fist made contact with his cheek, she saw Oji's eyes widen in surprise. He was just starting to shape the word "Huh?" when she felt the thin flesh, and the bone beneath, against her fingers.

Crack! The onomatopoeic sound effect exploded inside her head.

As if he'd been blown away, Oji's waifish body lurched in an exaggerated manner and toppled over backward. His head struck a metal guardrail, filling the air with a reverberant clang. Breathing hard, Kayako stared down at her fallen director.

Following her spontaneous deed, she was suffused, belatedly, with a feeling of relief so deep it almost made her tremble. Then, at last, she was able to speak.

"You jerk."

She couldn't stop.

"You jerk. You've gotta be kidding me, you jerk. Seriously, damn you, jerk."

"Owww!"

Clutching his head, Oji looked up.

"Ouch, Ms. Arishina. What if I'd landed wrong?"

Sighing, he got up and stood in front of Kayako again.

"I can't believe you actually hit me," the director muttered. Then he swiftly turned his face toward her. "So anyway, where do you need me to go first?"

Kayako studied him. His tone was casual, but he was wearing a serious expression.

"I've already been to Edge," Oji went on. "The president told me you'd just left to pay a visit to Bluto on account of me, so that's why I'm here. I asked if I couldn't just give you a call, but everyone insisted that I needed to go find you in person. I went to the trouble of tracking you down all the way over here, and this is the thanks I get?"

"Went to the trouble"? What kind of nonsense is that? retorted Kayako, inwardly, her incredulity having rendered her speechless. At the same time, though, her heart was full. Not only had her prodigal director returned, but it sounded as though President Eto had decided to forgive him, too.

"So where should I go first?" Oji repeated his earlier question. "I mean, there must be some places I need to drop by to offer my apologies."

"You don't think your first apology should be to me?"

"What? You really want one?" His eyes seemed to be saying, *I came back, didn't I? Isn't that enough?*

Even as Kayako marveled at what a selfish, childish piece of work he was, she answered reflexively, "No need, I guess." *Good grief*, she thought, *I'm like the complete stereotype of a masochistic producer. There's no hope for me now.*

"Let's start with Bluto," she added. "We'll apologize for the lack of progress, and since their president is apparently going to be at the meeting today, you should update them on the title. Is *'Ryder Light'* still tentative?"

"No, it's official. We're going with it," Oji replied. The look in his eyes seemed to take on a sharper edge. *"Fateful Fight: Ryder Light.* Yup, that's gonna be the title."

"Understood," Kayako said.

"Oh, and also, here." With a quick movement, Oji handed her a red plastic bag.

"What's this?" asked Kayako, taking the bag and stealing a peek inside.

"It's a present from my trip," Oji revealed on cue. "Please share it with everybody at work. I only bought three boxes, so I hope that'll be enough."

Kayako took another look inside and was shocked to see boxes of chocolate candy. *Hawaiian*, it said. *Macadamia Nuts*, it said.

She had received these standard-issue souvenir sweets on several occasions from friends who'd gone to the islands on vacation or for their honeymoons. On the side of the red bag were the familiar letters: "DUTY FREE."

In disbelief, telling herself this couldn't be happening, Kayako finally asked the question she'd been dying to have answered since what felt like forever.

"So where did you go, anyway?"

"Hawaii—well, the island of Kauai, to be precise."

What "island of Kauai"? she almost said, but didn't. *Look, whatever, I have no clue, because I've never been to Hawaii in my life.* It wasn't self-control that kept her from uttering those words; rather, she was so flummoxed that she simply couldn't speak. She hadn't asked for any further explanation, but Oji continued nonetheless.

"Yeah, it was just that work here seemed to have stalled out, big-time, and I was like, hey, I could really use a change of scenery right about now. We'd just been talking about how to handle the bike-race scene set in a ravine, so I decided to go on a little field trip and check out some canyons. I really wanted to visit the Grand Canyon but that would have been a super-long trip, so I ended up going to Hawaii instead."

"So, you were hanging out in Hawaii for a week."

"Well, there's travel time and various other things, so those ate up a couple of days. I was really only on the ground for five days. I didn't get a chance to relax at all."

Like you deserved to relax? How dare you! raged Kayako, though only in her mind. She could hear the blood throbbing at her temples, and she felt as if she might faint dead away. "But why did you run off without telling anyone?" she demanded. "Everyone was worried sick about you, and the whole project screeched to a halt."

"Why? From what I heard, nothing screeched to a halt. The dubbing is finished through the second ep, and I got the impression the animation's been sailing along, too, up to the point where the script ends."

"But would it have killed you to get in touch with us, just once?"

"Yeah, about that. I was watching a bunch of anime in the airport lounge, and my smartphone battery died on me," Oji said with a showy shrug of his shoulders. "That seemed like a problem at first, but then I started thinking maybe it was for the best. I mean, I was able to combine a brief vacation off the grid with gathering material for the show. It was fun."

Oji's chatter about his refreshing, restorative trip made Kayako's head swim. The airport lounge—did that mean business class...or even first class? As if she were suffering a bout of anemia, she felt her brain fogging over. Just when she balled up her fist and considered punching the director again, Oji pulled out another paper bag.

"Anyhow, here's this, too." He extracted a bulky stack of paper and held it out in front of Kayako. When she saw the heading on the top page, she stopped breathing.

Fateful Fight: Ryder Light. Episode #4.

The thick bundle was divided into sets of a couple dozen pages each that were held together by double clips. As Kayako raised her head to look at him, Oji nodded.

"Yup, it's all there," he said. "Up to the end. Twelve eps total, in storyboard form." It was the scenario for *Fateful Fight: Ryder Light.*

Kayako received the stack with both hands and began to riffle through the pages without saying a word. Each sheet was divided into six frames, and every frame contained meticulous notes about all the necessary elements: shot composition, dialogue, character movement, even instructions for sound effects. *If we have this, we can create a shooting script*, Kayako realized. Just as Oji said, it was all there.

Oji had never been a "drawing director." His customary style was to sketch a rough outline of what should be happening on the screen—*I'm thinking we ought to do it this way*—and then the animators would take over and flesh things out. However, even with that approach, if Oji didn't provide them with a nucleus, the first step, the rest of the team was stuck. Now that they had this scenario, work on the series could proceed.

They could help Oji.

She and the rest of the staff were involved in this project because they wanted to actualize what he envisioned in his head.

"Is it okay if I read it?" she asked in a slightly tremulous voice.

At this stage, Oji should have been busy writing a basic script, but he had far surpassed that goal, producing an illustrated scenario that was very close to a full-fledged storyboard. For the first time during their reunion, Kayako felt as if she might burst into tears.

"You can read it later," Oji said curtly. "We need to run over and meet with Bluto now, right? It won't do to be late. Also…" Gazing at Kayako with upturned eyes, he added, "I really went through a lot to write this, so I want you to read it slowly, when you have more time."

"Okay. That makes sense."

"Well then, shall we hit it?" he urged with a cool, unruffled expression. After they'd gone a few steps, he turned to look back at Kayako, who was carrying the stack of storyboards. "Let's make something great, Ms. Arishina," he said.

In that instant, a world that had so recently been melancholy and dull seemed to be restored to brilliant, glorious color. Kayako's feet—which had been stumbling blindly along, in constant danger of losing their way—now stepped firmly on the ground.

"Yes," Kayako replied and followed in the director's wake. "I just have one favor to ask."

"What?" responded Oji in a grudging tone, without glancing back.

"Please don't show those souvenir chocolates to anyone else. I don't think it would be great for morale on the shop floor."

"Wait, what? I bothered to buy them, and besides, the sugar

rush will stimulate everyone's brains. They must be tired from working too hard."

"No, I'm serious. And don't tell anyone that you went to Hawaii."

Kayako noticed that the jacket he'd thrown on had some kinks around the hem, and she got a sudden lump in her throat. It looked as though he'd left in a rush. He must have chosen a collared jacket—not his usual style—because he knew they'd be doing an apology tour today.

Welcome home, she whispered in her heart.

The prince was back.

◆

"You wanted to kill them off—do you still feel that way?"

At the first pitch meeting where he'd deflected her with the "no small woman" remark, Kayako asked Oji that question.

She herself felt that the only possible conclusion for *Yosuga* had been the remaining trio going their own ways—in other words, the actual ending that the director wasn't satisfied with. Yet she couldn't help but reflect upon it. She'd have loved to witness his alternative ending, if such a wish could be granted.

As he wore a look of surprise and silently raised his head to gaze at her, she pressed her advantage and inquired, "Would you care to kill them with me?"

Kayako assured, "No matter how many fans the popular heroines attract, you could go ahead and massacre them. You'd be able to do as you see fit, director."

"You think we could get away with that kind of traumatic ending? I mean, we're living in a world where sales of DVDs and figures are impacted by the way the final episode is received by viewers. Without those secondary revenue streams, most series would end up in the red."

Typically, reservations for the first volume of a series' DVD started being taken as soon as the initial episode aired. Those numbers were an important barometer indicating which anime were garnering the spotlight during a given season and served as publicity in their own right. In the case of collectible figures, it was rare for sales to start during the early part of the cycle, and they normally didn't go on the market—even for preorders—until a series was in its final month.

Thus if the final episode was judged to be less than excellent, the repercussions could be huge. As preorder cancellations poured in, the alarming news would spawn all sorts of rumors, followed by negative online campaigns orchestrated by disgruntled fans.

"Don't worry, it'll be fine," Kayako said. *Please let my voice come across as light and easy*, she prayed, but her heart was pounding wildly. "If the series fails, that would be well within the realm of probability in any case. And you wouldn't let it be simply traumatic, would you, director? With an Oji work, it's safe to assume that an underlying reasoning for killing them off would be in place. I'm sure you thought of a way to make those deaths convincing for everyone. So let's do it," Kayako urged. "I'll set everything up: the funding, the workspace, the broadcast slot. This would be a bona fide project dedicated to finding a way to kill off popular heroines in a convincing way."

Creating an anime that would surpass *Yosuga of the Light*.

It was with hopes of doing so that Oji incorporated "light" into the name of the beloved motorbikes that the heroines would speed around on. *Fateful Fight: Ryder Light*.

He was also the one who didn't want the title to be reducible to a single meaningful term.

Kizashi, Akashi, Ikari, Hizumi. *Omens. Evidence. Fury. Distortion.* Various such suggestions were put forth at that first meeting, but Oji made himself clear: "I don't want to do the same old thing."

Instead, he explained, he was aiming to take a meaningless term and to assign it such absolute significance that anyone hearing it would recall the series. No one had any particular reaction to "Ryder Light" now, but eventually it would conjure up his latest anime project in everyone's mind.

"I would not mind doing it," Oji said. For some reason, his speech became noticeably more polite at that point. "Please don't misunderstand me," he added. "When I said you're no small woman, I meant it as a compliment. I'm looking forward to working with you, Ms. Arishina."

◆

Starting the very day of Oji's return, everyone at Studio Edge scrambled to make up for lost time on the *Ryder* project, and work resumed in a flurry of tumultuous meetings and outside appointments.

Kayako ran around all over town offering sincere apologies. To shield Oji from outside noise as much as possible, she turned down his offer to come along.

Of course, there were producers at Animarket and the TV station who didn't pretend to be thrilled about the prodigal director's return: *How do we know this was a one-time aberration? If a problem like this can arise before the show even goes on air, we shudder to think what might happen down the road...*

What gave Kayako the confidence to face those voices was already having the storyboards for all twelve episodes in hand.

At one of her stops, a sour-faced Kakiuchi, from Animarket, said in a voice dripping with sarcasm, "Well, now that we have these storyboards, we could muddle along somehow even if Oji went AWOL again, huh?" He gave his approval to keeping Oji on the team, but added, "Given who's directing, I imagine he'll continue to ask for lots of impossible changes along the way."

"Hey, if they end up raising the quality of the production, we'll all be more than happy to go along," Kayako responded with a smile.

The production-launch press conference was going to feature

some short videos—an animated opening, followed by a three-minute highlight reel from the first episode.

Now that Oji was back, the normal workflow had resumed. The animation director had already gone through the current inventory and suggested corrections, and Oji added his own notes on top of those. After that, the drawings were returned to the animators. With only five days remaining until the press conference, some staff members grumbled about the feverish pace and the constant demand for revisions, so Kayako stayed overnight at the office to keep an eye on things. *Oh, shucks*, she sighed, remembering the vow she'd made to do her best not to pull any more all-nighters.

When Kayako first started working at Edge, she had rented an apartment close to the office. Being able to pop back home at any hour put her at ease and often ended up making her stay over at the office until dawn. She'd spend days at a time having lost sight of the boundary between job and home life, so just as the *Ryder* project was getting off the ground, she boldly packed up and moved to a place several train stops away. In the anime industry, it was easy to lose all sense of time without cutoff points like the first train in the morning and the last train at night.

Initial impressions were crucial, so naturally Edge wanted an exceptionally talented artist to create the genga for the clips to be shown at the press conference, the project's public debut.

As a matter of course, it was at Sakomizu's workstation that Kayako loitered around while he finished. She didn't have any particular need to visit. An assistant director was assigned to each individual episode, and waiting for drawings was normally that person's responsibility, but since the project was in the very early stages, Kayako still had some time to spare.

As far as she knew, Sakomizu had never spent a single night at the office, no matter how demanding the schedule, and it was a rare occurrence to see him wearing the same clothes two days in a row. He wasn't a style maven, to put it mildly, but he was almost always clean-shaven and reasonably tidy.

"So, Oji came back," Sakomizu said.

For a second or two, Kayako thought her ears might be playing tricks on her, and she could barely muster a lame-sounding "Huh?" Turning around without cracking a smile, Sakomizu sighed and plopped a pile of drawings into Kayako's hands.

"Revisions," he said. "That batch is done."

"Th-Thanks a lot." Kayako took a quick peek at the drawings in her hand and gasped in amazement.

Bundle of charm: the phrase she'd used so often to describe Sakomizu's work sprang to mind, but she stifled the urge to say it out loud. Even though the image was two-dimensional, the characters' well-defined and lively movements seemed to leap off the page. The beauty of the artwork dazzled her.

"Wow." The word slipped out unbidden as she raised her head.

With a fed-up look, Sakomizu muttered, "I know you've been waiting for these. Going without sleep night after night, constantly lurking behind me."

"You're right."

Maybe Sakomizu was being sarcastic, but there was no hesitation in Kayako's reply. He could say whatever he wanted, and there was nothing she could do about it. Her endless need and desire for the animators' drawings was an indisputable fact of life.

For the most part, animators didn't tend to show their emotions openly, and that was certainly true of Sakomizu. Yet the more they fit that mold, the more likely they were to produce art of such an astonishingly high quality that Kayako and her colleagues would crave it badly enough to wait for as long as it took, going without sleep night after night and hovering behind the animators' chairs. It was a close match every time as both sides contended with the pressure.

"Thank you so much. Now we'll be able to showcase your amazing work in the opening video at the press conference." Wary of being overheard, Kayako asked in a whisper, "So you knew what was going on with the director?"

"Of course—who wouldn't? There's a huge difference in the number of revisions depending on whether or not Oji is here.

Sometimes he even asks for retakes on things he's already okayed."

Gimme a break, he complained without looking all that annoyed. "Really, though," he went on, "I'm just happy to be a part of Oji's project."

A slight smile played around the corners of his mouth, and the expression in his eyes grew softer. Kayako's heart felt suddenly full.

It's commonly said that the more stellar the animator, the harder it is for them to make a living. Payment for one drawing ranged from several thousand yen to the low five figures, at best, but the basic per-page price was usually set in advance, and it tended to be quite difficult to negotiate an increase. On top of that, the better animators were more likely to be deluged with orders for extremely intricate drawings, and as a result they often ended up with more work than they could handle. In the anime world of today, technological innovations were developing at a rapid rate, but drawings with elaborate specifications were also becoming the norm. *Ryder* was one such project.

"Thank you," Kayako repeated one more time, lowering her head in a deep bow.

On the evening of the day that Oji returned, Kayako sat in Studio Edge's conference room, all by herself, and read the entire twelve-episode storyboard for *Fateful Fight: Ryder Light.*

She could sense the animators working away on the floor below as she paged through the thick pile of paper, barely able to contain her excitement. Hoping to summon the picture in Oji's mind as it would appear in an actual anime, she focused on following the words and images.

By the time she finished reading through to the end, night had fallen outside the blinded windows.

Kayako felt thirsty. She had brewed a cup of coffee earlier, planning to drink it while she was reading, but it was still sitting in front of her, untouched.

Suddenly realizing that the overhead lights were on, which was odd since she didn't remember hitting the switch, she looked up.

Oji was in a seat in the corner close to the door, and he looked like he was trying to bury his face in the desk. She'd been so immersed in her reading that she hadn't even noticed his arrival. Kayako thought he might be asleep, but he evidently sensed her motions because he raised his head and looked in her direction.

"How was it?" he asked.

Kayako was choked up with emotion. She'd been weeping, which he could probably guess from her facial expression and red eyes. She would have preferred to talk to him later after she'd had a chance to get her feelings in order and wipe away her tears. Oji's tension, however, filled the conference room, which wasn't too large, to the brim, and Kayako sensed it.

Someone having a first look at what you've written was intimidating even for a genius. Oji had produced something he felt confident enough to share, and he'd chosen to show it to Kayako before anyone else.

"I won't listen to feedback from anyone else," he announced, "but you, alone, have the right to criticize my script."

"You're sure about what you've done here?"

"Yup," Oji replied without a moment's hesitation. "I might change a few details, but that's basically what I want to go with."

"It's wonderful."

Oji finally took his eyes off Kayako and turned away, so he was in profile, but she could see him taking a quick breath. She drew in a breath of her own— a long one—as she prepared to speak. Her nasal cavities felt prickly and sore, and tears were starting to well up again.

"Good job. It was a wonderful read."

"I'm glad," Oji let out and plunked his head down on the desk again.

As a result, Kayako couldn't read his expression, but she was fine with it because she didn't want him to see that she'd started crying again, either. Taking advantage of the moment, she surreptitiously brushed away the tears from under her eyes.

From here on, the marks on these sheets of paper would be translated into polished pictures, and those illustrations would, in turn, morph into moving images. It was almost unbelievable how happy and full of anticipation she felt at the prospect. Together with Oji, she'd be putting the vision into action.

Tidying the sheets of the finished storyboard she'd just received, Kayako put both hands on top of the pile and bowed her head in gratitude.

◆

The press conference was just a day away, and today's schedule included a meeting of the entire production committee that would double as a rehearsal for the big event.

It was the same with any title, but from the moment a new project launched, Kayako began to await each broadcast as if she were facing the guillotine. Even at the best of times there was a subdued sense of pressure, so when she received a phone call from Oji saying "I'll be late," she had a terrible feeling about it.

"Only by an hour or so," Oji went on. "Sorry, my bicycle had a flat tire."

"Why don't you just grab a taxi?"

"No way. If I leave my bike here somebody might steal it. I'll take it back home, and then get a cab from there."

"I'll come and pick you up."

"No need. I'll be fine. I can get there by myself."

After hanging up, Kayako buried her head in her hands. He probably wasn't going to be fine, at all.

For starters, why was he using a bicycle to get around? He'd shown up to meetings on his bike from time to time, mumbling something about needing to make up for his lack of exercise. The bicycle itself was a limited-edition release from a foreign car company, and Oji clearly considered it an important possession, but what if he got into an accident? The idea made Kayako decidedly uneasy.

Another time, his bicycle tire had gotten stuck in a ditch and he'd tumbled off. After receiving a distress call, Kayako had rushed to join him in searching for a metal pin that had fallen out, and they'd both ended up being late to a meeting. Crawling around on the asphalt, she'd wondered why she was going to such lengths, but she'd just shrugged it off that time, too.

I'm in the middle of doing laundry, or *My bike has a flat tire*: whatever reason Oji gave, it was always Kayako's job to explain why to the people who were kept waiting. Ultimately, the quickest route to persuasion meant spending time with the director and helping him navigate the shoals of daily life.

"I'm going to pop out and pick up our director. I'll return as soon as possible, but in the meantime, could you please begin the meeting by discussing any matters that don't require Mr. Oji's presence?"

Kayako bowed to the assembled group, then left the conference room without waiting for an answer. Sure enough, a ripple of snarky voices—"Ha, wanna bet he's skipped out again?"—followed in her wake. Exiting the building as if she were shaking free of them, she climbed into the company car and headed for Oji's home.

Once there, she walked up to the door and rang the bell, but there was no answer. Thinking they might have just missed each other, she opened the meter boxes for electricity and gas. It was a sneaky confirmation method she often used when an animator who was working at home didn't come to the door. When someone was pretending to be out, the numbers on the power meters still turning over gave away the ruse. Some artists even designated meter boxes and external washing machines as drops for drawings to be picked up.

Oji's electricity meter was spinning away. The director was almost certainly inside.

Kayako rang the bell again and banged on the door. She was dealing with a man who'd already pulled a disappearing act once, so she felt no hesitation about bending the rules a bit or using a little force. When she put her hand on the knob, however, she was surprised to find the door unlocked. It opened easily, and she stepped inside.

"Mr. Oji?" she called out from the entryway. Unlike a couple weeks ago, when the deserted apartment plunged her into despair, today the place seemed inhabited. Kayako heard the sound of water like the shower was running, and, feeling flustered, she hastily backed away. She couldn't think of a more awkward scenario than bumping into her director as he stepped out of the bathroom, but she felt a flash of annoyance, as well. What on earth was he thinking, taking a shower at a crucial time like this?

She was about to go back outside, pulling the door closed behind her, when something caught her eye: a stack of mail piled on top of the shoe cabinet.

Considering that Oji was a bachelor living alone, the heap of letters and circulars looked surprisingly orderly. Mixed in among the junk mail spread out on a monochromatic piece of designer cloth, she spotted an envelope labeled "Invoice Enclosed." The return address included the word "Travel," which suggested that it was from some travel agency.

Kayako glanced at it casually, thinking it must be a bill for some charges incurred during his runaway trip to Hawaii. The envelope had already been opened, and its content, which had been taken out, caught her eye.

"E-Z Souvenir Delivery Service," the invoice read. "Three boxes of Hawaiian chocolate-covered macadamia nuts @ ¥1,200."

"Souvenir delivery?" Kayako whispered to herself.

She'd heard about this kind of service. When people went on overseas trips, instead of spending a lot of vacation time shopping for gifts and souvenirs, they could simply order their destination's local products from a travel agency, which would then deliver those items to a home address in Japan. However, there was one detail that didn't fit. Oji had supposedly gone to Hawaii on the spur of the moment, with no advance planning, so it seemed unlikely that he would have set up a souvenir-delivery service.

And that wasn't the only strange thing.

There was the matter of the red duty-free bag that Kayako had found so intensely irritating the other day. Didn't it prove that he'd bought the chocolates either at the airport or at a duty-free shop? Pondering this, she took another look at the invoice, and her eyes widened in surprise. The date of the order, at the top of the bill, fell within the week of Oji's disappearance—the exact same period when, according to his story, he was in Hawaii.

Clutching the travel agency's envelope and invoice with the sound of the still-running shower behind her, Kayako quietly went into the hallway. Perhaps she'd seen something she shouldn't have, and her heart was pounding wildly.

So Oji hadn't gone to Hawaii, after all?

Apart from the invoice for the home-delivery souvenirs, there was nothing else in the travel agency's envelope. Kayako took an extra-deep breath as a new question formed in her mind: *If not Hawaii, then where? After he vanished, where did Oji go?*

There was no way she'd be able to keep herself from asking him once he finished showering and got dressed.

Oji probably didn't expect his producer to be waiting outside, and when he opened the bathroom door his face froze in surprise. Kayako demanded head-on, "Where were you, anyway?"

Oji caught sight of the envelope in her hand, and all the color drained from his face.

"Seriously, where were you?" Kayako repeated, and just then the air rang out with a near-shriek—*Aaaaah!*

In that instant, Kayako honestly didn't know whose voice it was, or even where the sound had come from. A split second later, Oji lunged forward with tremendous force and snatched the invoice from Kayako's hand. Then, amid a loud volley of inarticulate screams—"Aaah!" "Unbelievable!"—he proceeded to rip the document to shreds with both hands.

Kayako was so shocked by this turn of events that she stood dumbfounded for a while, unable to move a muscle.

"Unbelievable," Oji repeated, shaking his head. Finally looking at her with a deeply flushed face, he spluttered, "Really, it's unbelievable. I said you didn't need to come pick me up, so why are you even here? You're such a pain in the neck—and this is terrible! It's a huge violation of privacy. Seriously, why don't you just go to hell. I can't go on living. No, that's it—I'm done. I can't work with Studio Edge anymore."

"So really… You weren't in Hawaii?"

Oji was acting like some pubescent boy, or girl, whose mother had taken a peek at the super-secret diary—but taken aback though she was, Kayako managed to pose that question. She hadn't expected such an extreme reaction and had only suspected the possibility. Didn't the director realize that he was digging his own grave and admitting to it?

"Just shut up already! You're right," Oji blurted out like he couldn't care less anymore and was ready to level with her. "I didn't go, okay? Now are you satisfied? You really are the worst, bursting in here and trampling all over my heart. Yeah, I couldn't get my hands on any Arizona souvenirs to back up the Grand Canyon story, so I switched to Hawaii. Hey, if the scene plays dynamically enough that you'd think I actually went to see some ravines, that's what matters, right?"

"That duty-free bag…"

"Aaaargh!!" Oji clapped his hands over his ears in a histrionic gesture. He went on emitting angry, incoherent noises, pausing occasionally to mutter, "You're terrible, terrible." Astonishingly, he appeared to be on the verge of tears. "You must be thinking it was uncool to recycle a bag someone gave me. You already figured that out, so why make *me* say it? You're shaming me, that's what this is. Do you get a kick out of spotting where people are vulnerable and making them admit it? You're like a wicked demon. No, not 'like'—you're an evil demon from hell."

"Where were you actually?" persisted Kayako. Even as she recoiled from the continuing litany of insults, she thought, *This guy. I can't even.* Except she still wanted to know. How had that storyboard come into existence? Where was he when he created it?

"I was at home," Oji said, answering the question at last. Wearing the same sulky expression, he abruptly turned and looked the other way.

Kayako caught her breath.

"I was right here," Oji repeated. "I didn't go anywhere."

"But, but…" Kayako was remembering the day she'd stood in this same apartment, which appeared to have been abandoned. Hadn't he flown the coop without even bothering to take the materials for *Ryder* with him?

"I stayed away for the first couple of days, but after that I was hunkered down here the entire time, working on the storyboard."

"But why?"

"Listen, do you understand the incredible pressure of having to start from zero and create something from scratch, coaxing it into existence and giving it shape, even after it already exists in my mind? This is a situation where if I don't do it, nothing can go forward. I might make it look easy, but knowing that it probably looks that way to you just adds to the stress. I never really know for sure whether I'll be able pull it off or not. Having done it in the past is no guarantee that I won't trip and fall flat on my face this time."

Oji had tossed off this rant in a rush, furrowing his brow the entire time. Even though he seemed to be blaming Kayako—preposterously—for his own failings and insecurities, she couldn't help noticing that his face looked beautiful and oddly picturesque even when it was twisted into an angry mask. Seemingly fueled by his own outrage, he launched into another diatribe.

"I mean, it's not like I'm in any mood to go gallivanting off on a field trip. This isn't the kind of job I can perform on the side in Hawaii. You often hear directors and writers claiming that changes of scene and 'me time' are a necessary part of the creative process, and how they get ideas while they're out taking a stroll or whatever, but I think that's all a barefaced lie—unless they're geniuses, of course."

Not giving Kayako a chance to get a word in edgewise, Oji spewed out the words. Then his expression seemed to shift abruptly from irate to serious, though it was still on the far side of grouchy as he turned to look directly at Kayako.

"Scripts and storyboards only come into being through long

hours at a desk," he continued in an earnest tone. "No matter how bored or fed up, even if there isn't the tiniest shred of glamor, you just have to sit there and keep plugging away, getting things down on paper or on the computer. Anytime I get up, there's a chance something important might get lost, so I basically have to glue myself to my chair and focus single-mindedly on doing whatever it takes. Even if it kills me, I can't afford to wander off in search of a change of scenery."

An image flashed across Kayako's mind—a view of Oji's boy-ish-looking back, bent over a desk—as if she'd actually seen it. Now that they had his storyboard to use as a foundation, she and the animators would be able to help Oji at every turn, but when it came to the very first steps in the process, he was absolutely right: he had to go it alone, with nobody to lend him a hand and no one to rely on except himself.

Ahhh… Kayako felt a galvanic sensation in the very marrow of her being. *That's right,* she thought. *When he came back from his "trip," his face looked thinner and his clothes were definitely rumpled.*

"If you'd only said the word, just one word," she appealed to him, "I would have been glad to set you up someplace where you could concentrate to your heart's content, all by yourself."

"No, but that's what I'm trying to say. As it turned out, I was able to crank out the script and the storyboard, but when I be-gan, I honestly didn't know whether I could actually do it. If I hadn't had the Plan-B alternative of really running away if things went south, I could never have begun at all. That's why the whole 'locked in a hotel suite' approach was never an option."

"But your approach made everyone worry."

"Nah, that isn't true. You guys weren't worried." Oji puffed up his cheeks. "I actually thought you might worry about me a bit more—maybe stop to wonder whether something might have happened to me, and call the police or something, but instead everyone automatically assumed that I had run away. I felt really hurt by that. Shouldn't you people at least have thought about the possibility that I might have been in a car accident, or kidnapped, or fallen victim to foul play? I mean, I'm your director, and I feel like you ought to treat me better...don't you?"

"You really did run away. Could you stop painting things in such a self-serving way?"

"Yeah, but after I came back to the apartment and was working away, no one ever bothered stopping by to check whether I might be here."

That was true, and Kayako regretted it. Even though her sleuthing skills had been honed by dealing with animators who tried to deploy the "sorry, nobody home" trick—to the point where her first move in such cases was always to check the meter boxes for telltale activity—the possibility that Oji might be pulling a similar stunt had never even crossed her mind. She was too busy thinking about what people around her would say, and trying to figure out how she ought to behave.

"Yes," she said, "but couldn't you have given a little more thought to everyone who was waiting around for you, completely in the dark? Just speaking for myself, I was more dead than alive the entire time you were gone."

"I do think about them, all the time—probably more than anyone else does. Not just about the work itself, but the staff, as well. And of course about you, too, Ms. Arishina." Something about the way he said her name left Kayako at a loss for words.

Fixing her with a candid, unwavering gaze, Oji shook his head. "When a new project gets going, the people who come aboard are basically giving me a sizable slice of their time. I'm being entrusted with a big chunk of everybody's lives, for the sole purpose of giving shape to something I want to create. I think about that every single day. It's built into the fundamental nature of the director's work: if I don't ask other people to help me, the project won't move ahead. I can't do anything by myself."

Kayako stared at Oji without blinking. Even though his voice was raised in anger and he seemed to be pelting her with words, she was somehow touched by what he said.

In the case of television anime, producing just one thirty-minute episode required a sizable staff working behind the scenes.

For an entire series, the staff ultimately numbered in the hundreds.

Standing before this person—this mercurial man-child who thought pretending he'd been on a tropical island and making it look easy was mature—Kayako thought, for the first time since they'd met, *He's actually pretty cool.*

Making an anime required an enormous amount of time and overtime, and Kayako and her colleagues at Studio Edge had the same feelings about the director: they, too, were being entrusted with a sizable slice of Oji's time, and a big chunk of his life. It was, she thought, an honor to be able to run alongside him while they were all investing most of their waking hours in this project.

And now, she and the rest of the team could take the "1" that Oji had struggled mightily to wrest from zero—and turn it into a hundred or even a thousand. They could bring characters to life and watch them move.

"I just really, really hate it," Oji burst out. "Why did you have to come here, without being asked? And why the hell did you have to poke around? I seriously can't believe you read my mail." He was now reverting to his earlier tone. "You stuck your nose into the exact things I didn't want anyone to see, and now it's impossible—I just can't do this anymore," he blithely asserted the opposite of all that he'd just said.

He appeared to be on the verge of retreating into the apartment, but Kayako took hold of his arm and told him, "It's okay. We're good. But it's time to go now. Everybody's waiting for you, and the press conference is tomorrow."

"Wait a minute. I have one condition."

"What's that?"

"Don't tell anyone about Hawaii."

Kayako let out a sigh that shook her entire body. She remembered having made a very similar request just a few days ago. "Got it," she murmured, tugging Oji toward the waiting car.

She was afraid that if she allowed her mind to wander, her face would break out in a smile. As she walked along with the director in tow, she consciously crafted a stern, severe expression. Inside, though, she was thinking, *I'm so happy we're going to be able to go forward with this project, after all.*

Getting the director to the workplace safely, and on time: that was Kayako's job.

Kayako had never breathed a word to anyone about Oji's "disappearance" charade. So some time later, when she was seated at the table for a meeting with various other producers and the companies' CEOs, she was shocked when Studio Edge's president, Eto, suddenly asked, "By the way, where *did* Mr. Oji spend that time, anyway?"

She turned to face her boss, but she was so dumbstruck that her lips might as well have been stitched shut. "So what's the scoop, Arishina?" pressed Eto. "Surely you didn't think Oji had actually gone to Hawaii?"

"No way he did," Kakiuchi joined in, making her even more tongue-tied. "It was our guy Nojima who went to look around the apartment early on and discovered that Oji had left his passport and bankbook, so we at least knew he hadn't left the country."

"Right," Eto agreed absentmindedly. "Well, wherever he was, it's still a cute story. He must have wanted to make himself look good, like he'd written at his leisure while he was on vacation. Way to put on a front for Arishina, who idolizes him."

"Well, you couldn't churn out that many pages in your spare time. Not that we'd want him to take it easy," quipped Kakiuchi, who always came across as a bit of a martinet. Turning to address the still silent Kayako, he said, "Anyway, all's well that ends well. I don't know the particulars, but at least the storyboards got done. Please just go on pretending that he fooled you, Ms. Arishina, and not delve too deeply into the truth."

"Y-Yes," Kayako stammered.

"By the way," someone said, "I've been crunching some numbers..."

As Kayako sat watching the men swiftly move on to other matters, it struck her that she'd been pretty green. Oji, too. They'd never noticed that while they were having fun doing what they wanted, the adults were watching over to make sure no major disasters occurred.

Making anime is a team sport, Kayako reminded herself, and more than ever, she found that fact very heartening.

◆

The weather on the day of the press conference was as fine as fine could be.

For the most part, staffers from the Animarket and the TV station side who were accustomed to such events handled the preparations. Kayako and Oji were told that they only needed to show up on time.

However, Kayako hadn't managed to dispel the lingering cloud of anxiety that had carried over from the meeting the day before.

For one thing, the event was going to be broadcast live. What's more, the interview with Oji prior to the press conference was going to be hosted by a female announcer from the TV station, in a talk-show format.

"Wouldn't it be better to use someone a little closer to the anime industry, like maybe a voice actor?" Kayako had suggested, to no avail.

She'd never even heard of the woman who was supposedly one of the station's most popular young female announcers. Maybe people who followed that world knew of her, but the selection didn't appear to cater to the needs or desires of anime fans. Kayako was worried that they might feel alienated.

"Who's supposed to benefit from this casting, anyway?" she asked as she studied the announcer's official headshot, which showed a small face surrounded by a cascade of softly waved hair, in keeping with the current fad. But the station's producer, Tanuma, shrugged off Kayako's question as if it were absurd.

"You mean you've never seen this kid going on and on about

how much she likes anime?" he asked incredulously. "Don't worry, she'll be fine. Lately she's been doing a lot of interviews with trending actresses and dishy celebs, and so on. She's a real pro."

Kayako wondered about his examples—actresses, followed by dishy celebs. Was he saying that the announcer would, therefore, be good at interviewing Oji? Until several years earlier, Tanuma had worked in a division of the broadcasting company that had nothing to do with anime, and even now he wasn't really up to speed on the medium. It was hard to say that he understood the feelings or the collective consciousness of anime fans.

Although Kayako was dogged by a sense of unease, Oji himself, unfazed, replied, "Doesn't matter to me."

The organizers had decided that it would be a waste to limit the press coverage to the narrow realm of anime, so they had invited a large number of reporters from a variety of publications in addition to the usual suspects from specialty magazines. This, too, bothered Kayako. She knew she might be fretting unnecessarily, but she couldn't anticipate the sort of questions that might be posed by journalists from weekly magazines and sports papers whose knowledge of anime in general, and Oji's work in particular, had to be limited.

The site for the press conference was one of the large banquet halls in a high-class hotel in the ritzy Ginza district. The Halloween celebrations were barely past, and already, as if overnight, the town was starting to be decked out with Christmas decorations and colorful lights. Even though it was still November, beyond the hotel's heavy door—which was opened by a liveried, low-bowing doorman—Kayako could see a sumptuously decorated Christmas tree.

At the entrance to the lobby, she paused and took a deep breath. Stretching out ahead of her was a plush carpet, gold embroidery on a red ground, so sumptuous that she felt the need to walk on it gingerly, with an extra-light step. Tanuma had been in charge of organizing the venue for the press conference, but she had never dreamed that it would turn out to be someplace this luxurious.

However, there was no trace of hesitation in Oji's gait. He wore his light jacket with ease and didn't appear to be intimidated in the least by the posh surroundings. On the contrary, he seemed to feel right at home.

"Let's do this," he said to Kayako, as though to get them both fired up.

"Okay," she replied.

When they arrived at the second floor, there were already some reporters milling around in front of the designated banquet room. Kayako recognized the representatives of industry magazines—*Animaison* and *Cinémage*, among others—but the majority of faces were new to her. She'd heard that the crowd was expected to number around fifty, including reporters and those involved with the project.

The area in front of the banquet room had the feel of a small, impromptu cocktail party, and a number of people took notice of Oji and Kayako as they passed. One or two let out an inadvertent "Oh," which caused a great many eyes to swivel simultaneously toward the new arrivals. Kayako was flustered and didn't know where to look, but Oji marched confidently on. It wasn't that he was deliberately ignoring the crowd; he just faced forward and headed to the waiting room next door.

The meeting immediately before the live broadcast was a simple affair.

The rising-star announcer Tanuma had brought along began with the customary pleasantries: "We're very grateful for your time today," and so on. Then, with a beaming face that looked exactly like her official headshot, she added, "I've really been looking forward to this, Mr. Oji. I've been a fan of yours ever since *Yosuga*."

"Ah, thank you very much," Oji responded in a tone of languid indifference. Just as in his first conversation with Kayako, he wasn't about to give this fan an opening to gush about how much she loved his work.

The interview questions provided in advance were fairly bland and inoffensive. *This will be your first new series in ten years—how do you feel about that? Can you share some of the highlights so far, and talk a little about your vision and your goals for the* Ryder Light *project?* Etcetera, etcetera.

They took a moment to review the step-by-step plan. First, she would take the stage and announce the title. Then an opening video, which came in at just under five minutes, would be screened, followed by the trailer for the first episode. Finally the announcer would reveal the name of the director, whereupon Oji would appear in front of everyone for the first time.

During *Yosuga's* run, Oji had become famous as the "dishy director" and, whether he liked it or not, had received a tremendous amount of personality-focused exposure in magazines and elsewhere. He had to be pretty confident about not choking. And on this day Oji, a person who hated to give anyone a chance to praise him, would probably turn to face the cameras, flip an invisible switch, and do his best imitation of someone who didn't mind the attention.

When the meeting was over, Kayako wandered off and peeked into the big ballroom. Her eyes lit on a row of seats toward the back, near the exit, and she let out an inadvertent "Ah!"

Tokei Animation's Yukishiro and Director Saito were sitting there. By chance, just at that moment, Yukishiro turned and looked in Kayako's direction.

Their eyes met, and he silently acknowledged her with his patented elegant smile. His lips moved, forming what appeared to be the word "Hello."

Come to think of it, the day they'd met at the recording center, he had mentioned something about planning to attend this press conference. So he'd been serious, after all. *He has a lot of nerve, showing up here*, Kayako thought. Then she remembered the way he'd insinuated that he knew about Oji's disappearance, and a brief, chilly wave of anger revived in her. Quietly, she filled her lungs with air.

Hitomi Saito, who was sitting next to Yukishiro, didn't seem to have noticed her producer's remote interaction with Kayako. Today the young director was wearing a pretty dress printed with tiny flowers rather than the casual pants-and-T-shirt outfit from the other day. She appeared a bit dazzled by the camera spotlights as she looked toward the stage.

If what Yukishiro had said was true, Saito, too, was a fan of Oji's. She had probably been looking forward to this event.

Relax. There's nothing to be upset about, Kayako told herself.

Returning Yukishiro's gaze, she mouthed, "Hi there." Leaving the waiting room behind, she faced forward. A secret, greedy desire suddenly surged up from the depths of her being.

May they all watch—not just Yukishiro, but everyone, she murmured under her breath. That archaic phrasing had never once crossed her lips in daily life. *May they all watch* Ryder, *and may they all go home completely and utterly blown away.*

We are not going to lose.

◆

Sometimes a film sequence that only lasts a few minutes can completely change a person's life. That's what had happened to Kayako, with *Yosuga.*

Many of the people who worked in anime, and the film industry in general, had their own private *Yosuga.* Hopefully the five minutes of *Ryder* that had been edited together and were about to be shown on screen would have that effect on someone in the hall today.

Kayako might as well have been praying as she kept her gaze trained ahead with bated breath. Standing at the very back of that room, she felt as though she were offering herself up as the images unfolded onscreen.

Through a dark night, Jyuri rode her motorbike at top speed for two full minutes, during which they never saw the face of a single character. The only things visible were the front wheel tire and the headlight slicing through the blackness. The course gradually grew rougher, seemingly matching the tempo of the opening song as it swelled and gathered momentum. Here and there float-ed the shadowy rear silhouette of a person or the hint of a land-scape, but those glimpses were so faint to be questionable and far away. Just as the viewer's impatience came to a head, the darkness broke.

It was only in the final second that they saw Jyuri's face as she nimbly hopped off her bike.

"FATEFUL FIGHT: RYDER LIGHT."

When those words appeared, someone in the audience let out an "Ooh!" For Kayako, that single syllable was like a gift.

It wasn't just the one voice, either, and she was almost certain that the reactions weren't emanating from hired applauders. At least, she hadn't heard any discussion about resorting to that sort of paid puffery. Those exclamations were probably coming from genuine anime fans. Kayako found herself hoping that people sit-ting in front of their computers and watching the live stream all over the country were having the same kind of vocal reaction. *I hope they're seeing what I'm seeing*, she thought.

As the trailer began, there was a stir among the audience. "That's Yuka Kagihara," someone said in a low voice, naming the voice actress. Another voice, barely audible, asked, "Wait, is that bike a HITANO design?"

Jyuri's signature phrase, invented by Oji, echoed through the room.

—Live. *The only person in the world who can make you despair is you.*

Hearing those words clearly affected the crowd, and the at-mosphere changed instantaneously, and unmistakably. The am-bient murmurs of a few seconds ago died down, and a deafening silence enveloped the room. The screen went black, and across it the title—"FATEFUL FIGHT: RYDER LIGHT"—flashed once again, like a shooting star, and was gone.

The video portion of the program was over.

There was a single percussive *clap*, followed by ripples of applause. Gradually, the clapping grew louder, and spread.

Listening to the sound, Kayako exhaled slowly through her nose. It was only then she realized that she'd been holding her breath.

The lights came up and the screen shut.

The female announcer took the stage and introduced Oji in a voice that carried throughout the hall. "And now, let's meet the director of this work, Mr. Chiharu Oji!"

Bathed in the brilliant light, Oji's face was stunningly beautiful. Every camera in the place was pointed in his direction, and the air erupted with far more flashbulbs than were usually seen at an anime-production launch. With his fluffy hair and pale, unblemished cheeks, he didn't look at all like someone who had turned thirty several dozen moons ago. This was probably the first time in quite a while that he had appeared before such a crowd.

Go get 'em, Kayako sent her director some silent encouragement. *You can do it, because you're you.*

Oji took a seat on a billowy-cushioned chair across from the interviewer and looked for all the world like a reigning monarch on his throne. He seemed prepared to hear himself called a dishy director again, after all these years. With a gaze that was simultaneously haughty and glum, Oji greeted the interviewer with a cursory "Hello."

She continued with her smiling effusions. "I'm sure a lot of people here know this already, but Chiharu Oji is the director who made the legendary anime, *Yosuga of the Light*, ten years ago. I myself have been a huge fan of him ever since. Thank you for coming today, Mr. Oji!"

Maybe a bit over the top? Kayako felt mildly concerned about the interviewer's tone.

While it was probably true that the young announcer liked anime, people outside the industry who were hearing about Oji for the first time today wouldn't be likely to recognize *Yosuga*. This was nine (not ten) years later, and "ever since" or not, Oji hadn't headlined any other projects in the intervening years.

Kayako was starting to wish she had paid more attention to such details during the planning meeting.

Because of the intensity of their devotion to the medium, hard-core anime fans despised bandwagon fans. Liking anime and selling yourself as an otaku could turn out to be a double-edged sword if you were exposed as a pretender who hadn't paid the dues.

"Thanks for doing this," Oji said, inclining his head in the most minimal of bows. Outwardly, at least, he appeared completely cool and copacetic.

The announcer smiled. "You're picking up the director's megaphone again for the first time in ten years, which seems likely to cause a big splash in the industry. I'm wondering what everyone here thought about the videos we just saw—the opening segment and the first episode preview. Personally, I was so impressed that I was speechless. The show really looks amazing."

"Thank you very much," Oji replied. "I won't be using a megaphone, though. Anime directors don't." He more or less muttered those words, and Kayako was afraid that he might be starting to lose his temper, which had been one of her main concerns going in. There was nothing that creators disliked more than people who couldn't be bothered to grasp the nuances of the process. Oji probably wasn't happy to be flattered in such careless terms.

Though punctuated by a number of moments that were sweat-inducing for Kayako, the talk show proceeded fairly smoothly.

"Back in the day, *Yosuga* was a hot topic, and the fact that the director happened to look like a movie star got loads of attention, but how do you feel about that, Mr. Oji?" the interviewer asked. "I still remember seeing magazines all over the place with your face on the cover. Not too many people have managed to obliterate anime's nerdy stereotype the way you did."

Oji nipped such sensationalistic gambits in the bud by answering the interviewer's leading questions with a simple "Sure" and firmly steering the conversation back to his new work—"For this time's *Ryder*…"

There was nothing Kayako could do but watch and hope for the best.

This was Oji's battle, and he was the only one who could dispel his current image as someone who was unable to handle *Yosuga*'s overwhelming success and acclaim, and who now had, in effect, a nine-year gap on his résumé.

Still, wasn't allowing a fledgling announcer to conduct the interview a mistake? While the questions had been submitted ahead of time, too much extraneous info was tumbling out of her mouth on her way to them. If she wasn't actually knowledgeable about the industry, then sticking to the script and just asking those harmless questions would have been much easier on Oji.

Kayako was in the middle of that train of thought when the announcer brought up that phrase.

"By the way, these days the anime world resembles the Warring States period, and it's gotten to the point where people actually speak of 'anime supremacy.' This *Ryder* has supremacy written all over it, but how confident are you feeling right now?"

That question had never come up during the planning meeting.

"Supremacy?" echoed Oji, furrowing his brow and looking the interviewer full in the face for the first time.

"That's right," she nodded. "You don't know that term? You hear it a lot among anime fans these days, but apparently it was coined by an employee at one of the packagers, who said something like, 'Supremacy is ours this quarter.' It's gradually coming to be a sort of unofficial title to designate the most successful anime among the many created in a given season."

"Hmm. So in other words, 'supremacy' means something like bragging rights?" Oji gave his head a quizzical tilt, then added, "I get it. You just took me by surprise there." He sighed. "I thought you were pulling my leg for a minute since that word doesn't have an exactly pleasant connotation."

"What?"

"I'm just saying, I don't really care for that phrase."

Kayako felt her heart constricting.

Anime supremacy—the phrase and the goal of triumphing over the competition had given her hope and strength during her tough stretch. But now Oji was emphatically shaking his head on stage.

"I mean, who decides that?" he demanded. "By 'successful,' don't they just mean which anime made the most money? If the term originated with packaging company personnel, then that must be it. But what's the point? Does an anime need to win? If it doesn't stand alone at the summit, is it a loser?"

Turning to face the stunned announcer, who'd fallen silent, Oji continued. "Of course, it's always better to make money, and I know these projects have to turn a profit. Really, I get it. But even so, I don't have any desire to try to reign supreme over all the other anime that are running at the same time as mine, or to be the one and only winner."

His crisply dismissive tone suggested that the matter was closed. Kayako was moved. Oji's face seemed to shine even brighter under the klieg lights overhead.

My, oh, my, she thought. *This guy.*

Oji might not be thrilled by the idea of a seasonal anime champion, but Kayako was firmly convinced that their series was going to capture the next supremacy. He could proclaim his aversion to the term and the underlying concept until he was blue in the face, but Kayako wouldn't ever stop thinking so.

Unlike ten years ago, when anime still didn't air primarily late at night, these days, only the top three or so among the nearly fifty series produced each season generated enough income to end up in the black. Oji had to know from experience what it meant to toil on anime that didn't fare particularly well in the marketplace. And, needless to say, even if you won the top spot once, there was no guarantee your next project would be equally successful.

Yet that wasn't it. "Anime supremacy" no longer just meant plain profitability. That may have been its sole connotation at the start, but the term had evolved beyond its triumphalist, production-side origins and been adopted by the fans.

Which anime will touch people's hearts the most this season?

Which will leave its stamp on viewers' memories and on the times? That was what the term meant now, and sales figures were considered secondary.

The announcer mustered an awkward smile. "But anyway, the anime phenomenon is really amazing, isn't it? In the early days, it seemed as though the audience was mainly made up of otaku and a limited fanbase, but these days we speak of everyone being otaku, of a nation of otaku. Anime is also one of Japan's proudest worldwide exports, and lately even established magazines aimed at stylish women have been putting together special issues about anime, and the genre has become popularized to the point where people in general, even so-called normal people, like it. Could you speak to that, in terms of *Ryder*? As a director, what kind of role do you think you'll be able to play in the world of anime as it is today?"

This last question, a transparent attempt to change the subject, seemed to ramble, and it was hard to tell what the interviewer was getting at. *Uh-oh, Oji might get mad*, Kayako thought, but a moment later he began to answer in a self-controlled manner.

"Here's the thing," he drawled. "There are no 'normal people' in the world. When you say 'established' women's mags, I assume you're talking about *an • an* and others? Yes, I suppose anime does get its own special issues, as you say. That's simply because the publishers perceive a trend and want to capitalize on it. But I don't know how you get from that to the idea of an entire nation of otaku. As long as there are people who seek my work, I don't mind if my anime is just for otaku or a limited fanbase. Once a series is broadcast, it's no longer mine. From that point on, it belongs to whoever watches it."

Oji turned away from the announcer and scanned the audience. His gaze found Kayako, who was standing by the wall at the farthest end of the hall, and in that instant, she saw a glimmer of quiet determination in his eyes.

Oji looked into the camera once again. "Hmm. What role can I play in the world of anime? First off, has it ever occurred to you that constantly being called 'dishy' or 'pretty boy' might feel insulting and even abusive? And can you imagine what it's like for your solitary amusements, like anime and manga, not to be understood, and to spend your teenage years being thought of as gloomy or as a nerd?"

The man with the muted gray look in his eyes whom Kayako pitched in their first meeting was gone. She had no idea where this was headed and just kept gulping and staring at her director.

"As human beings go, I'm kind of a throwback," he said. "I guess I'm just not grown-up enough to wear the term 'otaku' like some fashion item. For my generation, 'otaku' was a word that people used to point fingers at you behind your back."

"Oh!" The announcer's eyes went round with surprise. "Does that mean you were called an otaku and bullied? It's really hard to picture you that way."

"See? There you go again with the superficial stereotypes." Oji exhaled a long, audible whoosh of air. "I don't know why you have to jump to conclusions and slap a familiar label on everything. That seems a bit easy, and simplistic. Being bullied may be the extreme, but there are plenty of subtler manifestations of alienation and discomfort in the world. And when people start to feel like they're about to drown in that kind of cruel reality, I believe anime can come to the rescue and save the day, most definitely."

"So are you saying that watching anime is a form of escapism?"

"No, not at all." Oji shook his head. "My viewers don't need to be gloomy, or depressed, or looking for an escape from reality. If there are people who choose to watch my anime to find the strength to survive the day-to-day vicissitudes of reality, then they're as dear to me as if they were my real brothers and sisters. If I can continue doing my work for them, rather than for so-called normal people who've turned into a nation of otaku, I'll be happy."

Dear to me. That phrase, so gentle and affectionate that it almost seemed incongruous in this setting, wafted out over the room. Oji had performed his monologue on a single breath, and now he stopped to inhale before going on.

"The catchphrase 'Live' in *Ryder Light*, in the imperative form, may sound cheesy, but I mean it sincerely. In the final analysis, we need to stay strong and take good care of our own hearts to survive in this world. There's a popular phrase, 'satisfied with reality,' to poke fun at people whose actual lives and romances are fulfilling, but a lot of people with real lives that aren't so fulfilling aren't wallowing in misery. Even if you don't have a romantic partner, even if the world doesn't treat you kindly, as long as there's something that matters to you and nourishes your soul—whether it's anime or music idols, or whatever—as long as you have something to hold on to when you feel like you might be starting to drown, you can be happy. Reigning supreme isn't the only way to succeed."

"So, Mr. Oji, if I'm understanding correctly, your upcoming anime series, *Ryder*, is a work that's aimed not so much at the general public as at otaku who might be having a hard time in their daily lives. Am I right?"

The rejoinder that the announcer inserted in her confusion made Kayako feel faint. She also felt like murdering Tanuma for his choice of interviewer.

"Mr. Oji, you seem to have a very original and unique way of thinking about otaku," the announcer added along with an expression that said, *I have no clue what this person is talking about.* Allowing her face to betray that sentiment marked the nadir of her performance.

For an instant, Oji's own face became an expressionless mask. Then, in the next second, he smiled brightly and said, "Yes." Kayako gulped.

"While the 'realies' were busy dating or having sex, I was lying awake worrying that I might be a virgin my entire life and spending the better part of my adolescence masturbating to a whole legion of anime characters. But I refuse to listen to anyone who tries to tell me that my life is pitiful for having gotten to know Belldandy and Motoko Kusanagi."

Eek, a cross between a gasp and a scream rose from Kayako's throat, and she nearly took a step forward. Someone needed to put a stop to this. No one had cornered him enough to say such a thing. Up on stage, the young announcer's face was frozen, and she clearly couldn't distance herself from Oji soon enough.

"Hey, I kind of like having my current self interviewed by a girl," he said insouciantly. "To the extent that I am what I've watched, I won't let anyone talk trash anymore about the things I've enjoyed. And if you want to say that anime is culture and a world-class industry, that's probably true. However," the director qualified, "an anime belongs to whoever watches it, so it ends up transcending those of us who were involved in its making. I may be the creator of *Ryder*, but some fans will love it even more than I do, and it's fine with me if other people end up knowing my anime better than I do. It belongs to whoever devotes the most affection to it. As for the characters and so on, people who watch the anime can make up their own scenarios about what happens after the series ends."

"What makes you look at it that way?" interposed the announcer, at her wits' end. She seemed to be asking not out of genuine interest but simply to hold up her end of the conversation.

Oji, however, treated the question seriously. "It's because I've done that exact thing with a huge number of anime and manga myself—watched and read them as though they belonged to me. I feel grateful to the creators who've gone before me for allowing the freedom to do that."

Oji turned to face the audience once again and narrowed his eyes against the intensity of the lights. His gaze came to rest on Kayako's face.

"In every era, there will always be a certain number of individuals who denigrate any pastime that can be enjoyed alone. No matter how big the anime industry becomes, that will probably never change. But if my position as a director has given me the right to express myself, I'd like to take this opportunity to say something to everyone who'll love *Ryder*. No matter who makes fun of you, however often, I won't. Sure, I'm the creator, and maybe it's not entirely convincing to hear this from an industry insider, but getting to tell you that your pleasure is something to be esteemed, and that it's fine to look down on people who don't get it, maybe makes being made to sit here today worth my while."

Finishing with his eyes still on Kayako's face, Oji cracked a smile as if to ease his own tension and requested, "Can we wrap this up now?"

◆

After the wild tornado of a talk show and the ensuing press conference had ended, Oji left the stage. The reporters and guests got to their feet and began filtering out. Kayako had started to make her way toward the anteroom where Oji was when a voice behind her said, "That was really something."

Turning around, she saw that the voice belonged to Yukishiro. Director Saito was standing next to him, and she said, "You're Ms. Arishina from Edge, aren't you? We didn't get to meet the other day at Telemo, and the fault is mine."

"Hello," Kayako greeted her hastily and pulled out her business cards.

As she handed one to the director, Saito accepted it and said in a flurry of embarrassment, "I'm sorry, I don't have any cards with me." She glanced nervously at Yukishiro, and Kayako wondered whether the director might have been told not to hand out her contact info to any outsider so Tokei Animation could monopolize her.

Still, this was unexpected. Yukishiro had promised to introduce the two women, but Kayako had never believed for a minute that he'd actually let her talk to his star director.

"Sorry to ambush you like this," Director Saito said, lowering her head. Away from the workplace, she just looked like a pretty, slim, well-brought-up young lady—not a strong-willed director who played an essential role on the production team.

"She says she wants to talk to you, Ms. Arishina," Yukishiro averred, not sounding particularly happy. Saito told him yes and nodded. Kayako sensed a certain amount of dignity, and presence, in the way the young woman interacted with her producer.

Turning back to Kayako, Saito said, "Everything was great. The video clips from *Ryder*, and Mr. Oji's press conference, too. I'm glad I came."

"Is that so."

Kayako nodded politely, but her true feelings were not so simple. She'd hoped for a stronger reaction to the videos than an anodyne superlative like "great"; she felt chagrined that people weren't so thunderstruck that they couldn't even find the words. As for Oji's interview, hadn't he expressed himself too edgily? Now that he'd gone beyond just being the dishy director, what would Oji's female fans think of their beloved Little Prince?

But Director Saito said, "He just made up his mind and went for it, didn't he?"

"I'm sorry, what?" Kayako responded, looking into the director's face.

Gazing up at Kayako, who was quite a bit taller, Saito continued, "It might be rude to say this to the party that organized the event, but to tell the truth, press conferences are a real drag. You know—getting hauled on stage, and all the praise and expectations and general hullabaloo."

Yukishiro grimaced. The new series he and Saito were working on had a press conference to announce the project coming up the following week. Kayako had heard that while it would be in a different place—a hotel in Roppongi—the Tokei event would be along the same lines as today's gathering. *Hmm*, she thought. *It sounds as if Yukishiro bulldozed it through but the director isn't entirely on board.*

"I got the impression that Mr. Oji willingly put himself out there as a sort of walking advertisement and decided to throw caution to the winds to become the public face of his work. I respect him for that," Saito said with no trace of a smile. "I'm jealous. The opening scene's direction was terrific. I envied him, I really did. Mr. Oji had his own views about the whole anime supremacy thing, but I'm aiming to win it next spring. I don't want to lose."

Kayako's eyes flew open in surprise. She could almost sense hot blue flames wavering up from the diminutive director's shoulders.

"I understand, because I admired and chased after Mr. Oji's *Yosuga*, too," Saito went on. "I've never seen him talk so much about his own work and—this probably isn't the best choice of words—use himself to sell his product. Just from that, I think he's really putting everything on the line for this series."

Saito's eyes had been tranquil and serene, but now they looked even reddish from excitement.

Yukishiro sighed. "I checked a while ago, and everybody online seemed to be talking about Oji and *Ryder*, and nothing else. Good for you," he lauded before continuing, "Well, I'm sure the same thing will happen next week when we announce our new title. I have to say, though, that Oji is like a runaway train during interviews as well. How much of that was scripted, anyway? I'm guessing taking care of the Little Prince isn't exactly an easy job."

Kayako was about to quip, "Actually, he's more like a drama queen than a prince," but then she remembered his touchingly tearful reaction when she found out that he'd faked his trip to Hawaii, and she merely shrugged.

"I'm used to it," she said, then added, "By the way, Mr. Yukishiro, please tell me our two shows aren't going to air in the same time slot, too, during the spring season?"

The prospect of a head-to-head battle worried Kayako, but when she voiced her concern, Yukishiro promptly shook his head and smiled as if he'd been waiting for that very question.

"Our show isn't going to be on late at night," he said. "We've got the early-evening slot on Saturdays, just like in the good old days."

Kayako felt as though she'd been hit on the head, hard, by some unseen force.

Since the vast majority of anime programs aired late at night, there was really only one time slot in which a show could be seen by both children and adults: early Saturday evening on the HBT network. Also known as Brand Time, it was reserved for various companies' titles several years in advance, Kayako knew, but now that she thought about it, oddly enough, she hadn't heard so much as a whisper about who had it next spring.

Yukishiro, seeing the surprise on Kayako's face, smiled triumphantly. *The bastard*, she muttered in her mind, glaring at him.

A moment later, though, she was engulfed by a wave of refreshingly positive—even festive—feelings. If Yukishiro was telling the truth, surely they must have wanted to keep it secret until the project was unveiled the following week. So why had he felt the need to brag about it today?

Because the quality of the *Ryder* clips had been so astoundingly good, that's why.

Just then, she saw Oji ambling toward them. "Ms. Arishina, what're you doing there?" he demanded.

Kayako stood up straighter. "Thanks for all your hard work today. Um, that announcer…"

"She went home. No worries, we'll be fine letting Tanuma follow up with her. You didn't show up, so I came to find you. We should go, too."

And then, for the first time, Oji looked at Yukishiro and Saito. Kayako had no objection to introducing the directors to each other but hadn't wanted Oji to run into Yukishiro.

She made a hasty attempt to wedge herself between the two men, but Yukishiro laughed and said, "Hey, long time no see. Thanks for the entertainment today. I enjoyed the *Ryder* clips and the interview, too. I was glad to see that you don't seem to have changed at all since you were at our company."

It was a low blow for the producer to make a tacit reference to their shared work history, given the way things had turned out. *That really doesn't matter anymore*, Kayako thought, and tried to intervene, but that was when Oji tilted his head in evident confusion and mumbled, "Erm, sorry, but who might you be?"

Yukishiro's eyes widened in astonishment as he stammered, "Wh-What?"

Kayako didn't know whether Oji was putting on an act, or

not. A faintly apologetic expression flitted across his face, and he asked, "I'm sorry, have we met before somewhere?"

"What do you mean, 'somewhere'?" echoed Yukishiro, his face twitching visibly with annoyance.

Wow, Kayako thought, with a delicious rush of malice. This was the first time she'd ever seen him lose his composure.

"You've got to be kidding me, Oji. I'm Yukishiro from Tokei Animation. You know, the place where you bugged out without finishing the production work on *Under*? And on *Autumn Lily*, too—"

"Oh, is that right? My bad. But if you're the person who did those two series you must be quite the hitmaker," Oji said with a carefree smile, still acting as though they were meeting for the first time.

Looking thoroughly disgruntled, Yukishiro dug out his business-card holder. Kayako was bemused to see that he viewed even an embarrassing situation like this as a potential avenue for networking.

As she watched the two men exchanging their cards, Kayako suddenly remembered Sakomizu's complaint—"That guy never remembers anyone's face"—and had to struggle to keep from bursting into laughter.

Somehow, it looked as though their director had found a way to troll the notorious forgetter of faces and gain a small measure of revenge.

There was another good thing that came out of the press conference.

Some reporters who were still hanging around came up to talk to Oji, but right around when they noticed that Saito was also there, Kayako seized the opportunity and left together with her director.

She was about to stop by the waiting room to gather their belongings when a rather unassuming voice called out from behind her, "Um, excuse me—"

Thinking it might be another reporter, Kayako protectively

ushered Oji toward the door before she turned around. She was unprepared for the sight that met her eyes: a man with terrible, slouchy posture, the lower half of his face hidden behind a flu mask. He had straggly hair and even though it was nearly winter, he wore no jacket over an orange T-shirt emblazoned with an anime character. It was Koki Chiyoda, and next to him stood the ever-inscrutable Kuroki.

"Mr. Chiyoda!" Kayako exclaimed involuntarily, and Oji stopped and glanced around. "Ah!" he said, and his face reflected the surprise in his voice.

Kayako registered Kuroki's familiar presence right away, but if Chiyoda had been alone, she might have mistaken the masked figure for a suspicious character.

"Oh, sorry, I don't have a cold or anything contagious, so please don't worry," the novelist rapid-fired and rushed to remove the mask. "I didn't want to cause any trouble for you guys, so I decided to come incognito."

Kayako was about to remark that removing the mask now might defeat the original purpose of the disguise when she noticed that sure enough, reporters were starting to sneak peeks in Chiyoda's direction.

Oblivious to the attention, he smiled benignly and explained, "I heard about today's event from Mr. Kuroki. I really wanted to see the preview, so I ended up crashing the party."

"We never dreamed you'd be here—I mean, you must be so busy."

"No, not at all. Well, I *am* on deadline at the moment, but I needed a break."

It was hard for Kayako to go on listening to that cheerful voice. Once again, she bowed her head. "I'm so, so sorry about what happened with the scenario you wrote," she said. Ever since that unfortunate occurrence, she'd been hoping to go see Chiyoda and offer a proper apology, and she felt ashamed that she'd been putting off even getting in touch with him.

But Chiyoda just responded, "No, it's fine," in a congenial tone. "Really, it's all good. I have a friend who's a professional scenario writer, and she really hates to lose at anything. So if I'd tried my hand at scriptwriting and it had turned out to be brilliant, she might have gotten mad and refused to talk to me anymore. Now that I think about it, I probably dodged a bullet there."

If it had turned out to be brilliant... That was an impressive level of self-confidence, Kayako thought, but she didn't say anything out loud. Just then she got the sense that Oji, who was standing next to her, had suddenly gone rigid with tension.

"Mr. Chiyoda," he ventured in an unusually husky voice. "Thank you very much for coming today. How was it?"

"Well, it totally made me want to write about bikes and magic girls again," the novelist confessed, then frowned and shook his head. "However, I don't think I'll be writing a bike scene anytime soon, because I've realized I'll never be a match for you in that genre, and it would just be too frustrating. So please do your very best and make something so unsurpassable that it becomes an impossible act to follow for anyone. I'm really looking forward to watching."

Kayako could hear Oji inhale sharply.

"We'd better get going, Koki," Kuroki said.

Oji bowed his head to the two men. "Thank you very much," he said. "I promise, I'll do my very best."

"By the way, I like the little sister better than Jyuri," Kuroki remarked, with no change in his usual deadpan expression. Kayako couldn't believe her ears. "Please find a way to give the sister more screen time," he added. "I'm looking forward to the series, too."

Then, with a "See you again," Kuroki began to walk away with Chiyoda in tow, leaving Kayako and Oji staring after them, faces wreathed in surprise.

"'Bye! I've got deadlines looming, so I'll catch you guys later," Chiyoda called back over his shoulder.

After the two men had vanished down the hall, Oji stood unmoving for a long beat, gazing after them. When Kayako said, "We need to get going," he responded with a vague, halfhearted "Yeah." Finally, as if he'd been brooding about something, he turned and looked up at her.

"Do you think Mr. Chiyoda will ever forgive me?" Oji mumbled those words almost as if he were talking to himself. "I respect him. I don't want him to hate me."

"In that case, we just need to create something interesting and fun and worthwhile," Kayako replied. "That's the only thing we can do."

She had to wonder if Oji only had communication skills inferior to a junior high schoolgirl's at his disposal even when he wanted to make an active effort to get along with someone.

"Mr. Chiyoda was saying that he came today to refresh his mind before going back to his deadline," Kayako tried ribbing the director, a little meanly, recalling that in his opinion authors who claimed to get ideas during breaks from work were basically liars.

Oji must have remembered, too, because he glared at Kayako and said, "So that probably means he's a genius. Seriously, though, he said he wouldn't be writing about motorbikes anytime soon, but he didn't swear off taking on magic girls."

Kayako tilted her head, trying to retrace Chiyoda's words now that Oji said so. The director seemed certain because he muttered, "That gets on my nerves. He must think he can write something on the level of *Ryder*, minus the bikes."

"But that'd be a treat to read, wouldn't it? Mr. Chiyoda's story, inspired by *Ryder*?"

"Yup," Oji admitted with unexpected ease. "I'm really looking forward to it."

◆

Exiting the hotel, they piled into a taxi. On this day, they had to go straight to a post-recording session in which voices, background music, and images would be edited into a clip, one element at a time.

After bundling Oji into the back seat ahead of her, Kayako

gave the driver the address of Tokyo Telemo Center. The cab took off into the gathering dusk, racing through wintry city streets illuminated by the festive sparkle of holiday lights.

Kayako was gazing dreamily out the window when Oji said, "Hey," in a tone of studied nonchalance.

"What is it?"

"Just...thank you."

Kayako hadn't been looking at Oji, and his words caught her completely off guard. She was fairly certain it was the first time he had ever thanked her, for anything. Turning toward him, she peered into his face.

"What?" snapped Oji, lapsing into the petulant expression he often wore. Right after that, though, he expelled all the air from his lungs.

And then he began to speak.

"You know what people were saying about me after *Yosuga*, right?"

Kayako couldn't bring herself to answer. Oji responded to her silence with a rueful smile.

She did know, of course. She'd heard all the gossip, and the rumors.

The genius director who helmed the legendary anime, *Yosuga of the Light*, had become a washed-up shadow of his former self. Nobody wanted to work with him anymore. He denied that he felt any pressure resulting from his first series' success, but he didn't manage to do a solid job on any of the projects that came his way after that. That was because in every single case where a title was launched with Oji attached as director, he dropped out midway through. Since he was incapable of functioning as director, his involvement henceforth took the form of an additional direction or scenario credit, and each of those series did reasonably well. On the surface he seemed to have been an active participant in those projects, but in fact he'd ended up abandoning every one of those commitments by the latter half of the series.

If it had only happened once or twice, people might have understood, but by the time three years had passed since *Yosuga*, everyone considered teaming up with him to be a risky proposition.

"I've never admitted this before," Oji said now, "but I was really a mess. After *Yosuga* turned into a sort of festival, I had no idea what I wanted to do next. Everyone was saying genius this and genius that, but I was afraid that the minute I released my second series they'd realize I was just mediocre."

"But you *are* a genius," Kayako objected. "No doubt about it: you're the kind of super-talent who only comes along once in a few decades." This was the one thing she wouldn't allow him to deny, even to himself.

Oji gave a small smile that reached all the way up to his tawny tea-colored eyes. "Thanks," he said again, and then looked straight ahead. "I really didn't think I would ever be able to work as a director again. I didn't think anyone would turn up who was curious or crazy enough to want to try teaming up with me, and even if they did, it would probably be some shady fly-by-night outfit, so the whole enterprise would be a gamble. I honestly never thought I would get another chance to work with a legitimate company like yours."

At the outset, when Kayako first floated the notion of inviting Oji to be their next director, no one at Studio Edge, including the president, had been receptive to the idea. Many people tried to talk her out of it, but she managed to win over the skeptics, one by one, and cautiously proceeded with the preliminary preparations.

That's why it was such a tremendous disappointment to everyone at work to have the director disappear after the project had taken shape. *See?* they gibed. *We knew it would turn out this way.* Those days were torture for Kayako, like being forced to lie on a bed of nails, but what she put faith in was Oji's final love.

This is the moment of truth: the now or never, the do or die, Kayako had nearly prayed waiting for him.

"You're no small woman, Ms. Arishina," Oji was saying now. "Partnering with me is no joke. When you filled in the moat as thoroughly as you did, I thought I couldn't possibly escape."

"There are no bad people in this business," Kayako quoted a

certain Blue Open Toy employee's words without attribution. "If someone does sloppy work, word will spread like wildfire and it'll be hard for them to get work in the future. That's why I was so certain you'd come back."

"Yeah, that was kind of a close call. You saved me." Oji laughed. Then he asked, abruptly and in a different tone of voice, "By the way, Ms. Arishina, do you have a boyfriend?"

The question took Kayako by surprise. *Ngh*, she grunted, then accidentally inhaled a large clump of air that made her cough. Finally, she managed to choke out, "Why do you ask?"

Oji's expression was cool and composed. "Seriously, I'm asking you to give a big chunk of your life to this series, and I can't help thinking that you're no spring chicken. You don't appear to have anyone in your life, and I'm just worried about your welfare."

"My social life is none of your business."

"Oh, really? Because if you're up for it, I can marry you."

After hearing something so surprising, Kayako could only squeak out a strangulated *Fwek*. She had no idea whether Oji was joking, or not. After a second she responded reflexively, "No thanks, I'm good," but that could have just been the voice of what little pride she had left. After a moment she asked, "What do you mean by that, anyway?"

"I meant exactly what I said. I told you before, didn't I? In the end, I don't think real, three-dimensional women can ever match 2D cuteness, so it doesn't make any difference to me whom I date. If you ever feel like you're doomed, we can discuss the possibility."

"Really, I'm fine. And for your information, I have a date tomorrow."

This time it was Oji's turn to look surprised. "You're lying. Who with?"

Hearing the playful spark in his voice, Kayako thought, *You little brat.* She was only too aware that she was no longer a spring chicken, as Oji so inelegantly put it. But she wished he would give it a rest.

In the way of an apology for the earlier episode, she'd been invited to the same French restaurant she'd given up ever setting foot in again. "It's not like that this time," a solemn Sakomizu had expressed his remorse and even baldly told her off, "To be honest, I don't have those kind of feelings for you anymore."

Hearing that declaration had made Kayako feel as though she'd missed out on something and now it was too late. Women were perverse creatures, indeed, she mused.

She remembered something she'd heard.

Among colleagues in the anime industry, it was said, love usually grows out of either admiration or respect—one or the other. In a business where it was quite common to have watched something that a given person had been involved in before meeting that someone, admiration for contributing to that cherished work often turned into feelings of romantic love. And respect, subtly different from admiration, meant falling in love not so much with the output itself but rather someone's attitude and stance toward the job. It was said that relationships based in admiration tended to cool off sooner, while those that grew out of respect lasted considerably longer.

However… Kayako paused to take a breath.

In this field, where admiration and respect were intertwined and diffused all over the place, romance wasn't the only form of love. Nourished by many forms of it, even sucking in the viewers' love from the other side of the screen, the driving force kept Kayako and her comrades running, day after day.

"What are you smiling about, you creep?" Oji wrinkled his nose and screwed up his face in a scowl like a sulky child.

"Sorry," Kayako answered absently, but she couldn't stem the flood of sentiment.

I'm truly fortunate to be doing this work, she thought from the bottom of her heart. *Because people who work in this industry are, one and all, vulnerable to "love."*

"Is this it?" the driver asked, jolting Kayako back to reality. She paid the fare and climbed out of the taxi while doing a mental review of the agenda for that day's dubbing session. They were running a bit late.

"Ms. Arishina, let's go," Oji said impatiently.

"Right," Kayako replied. She trotted close behind the slim figure of the director, who was striding with both hands jammed into the pockets of his jacket.

Gazing up at the dark but clear winter sky, she wondered what they would be up to next spring when the title was going to air. Oji would probably get mad if she told him directly, so instead she whispered to his back:

I'm going to see to it that you reign supreme.

Because, for me, you're anime itself. The whole of my admiration and respect.

CHAPTER 2:

"THE QUEEN & THE WEATHERCOCK"

From time to time someone would ask her, "Why did you get into the anime business?" Occasionally the approach might be a bit more probing: "Did it have to be anime? I mean, you graduated from X University's law department, so why anime?"

True, Hitomi Saito had believed that anime was a sort of cult pastime, only enjoyed by a small sector of the population. Yet at the same time she heard people describing anime as one of Japan's proudest, most visible exports. In her mind, anime seemed like something with an incredibly minor—but at the same time incredibly major—place in the world, and she couldn't conjure up a concrete image how those two opposing concepts might be connected.

Hitomi's father was terribly gullible and softhearted—the type of person who was easily conned into being the guarantor for a friend's business loan. Forced to shoulder and pay off debts in a way that made even his daughter think, *What? Did that actually happen? It sounds like something you'd see in a TV melodrama*, the household she grew up in was dreadfully poor.

"It's a waste of electricity" was a common refrain, so no one in the Saito family was ever allowed to turn on their little second-hand television.

It might as well have been an empty box sitting in the middle of the living room. The only time Hitomi got to watch anime was when she visited a friend's house or if the family went to stay with relatives, and she was completely indifferent to the girls in her class who ran around flaunting their "magic girl" wands.

Once a year, the cutthroat world of anime replaced magic girls with newer models. Hitomi's classmates, whose parents were always buying them the latest anime wands, would say, "Hitomi, do you want this?"—holding out the obsolete one from a title that had run its course. Hitomi would gaze vaguely at the proffered item, then shake her head: "No, I don't."

She knew there was no such thing as magic in the world.

Hitomi didn't harbor any desire to undergo a transformation, either. The children who were chosen to become magic girls always lived in gorgeous houses and wore a different modish outfit every day. They might be a bit clumsy and scatterbrained, but they always had cute faces, and Hitomi knew that only special girls like those were ever selected.

Her own lifestyle featured scary encounters with yakuza-type loan sharks who dropped by to harass her father when she was home alone, forcing her to summon up every last drop of courage and reply politely, "There are no adults here at the moment." That eventually led to her father vanishing without a word leaving only divorce papers and a note addressed to his wife and Hitomi that read: "I'm sorry." And it wasn't as if their lives suddenly became easy after he was gone; on the contrary, barely getting by was even more of a struggle than before. There was simply no opening for anyone to come along and turn Hitomi into a magic girl.

She and her mother left the house where they'd been living as a family, and moved into a tower block of flats outside the city limits. It was a much longer commute from the new place to Hitomi's school, but she enjoyed watching the way the light from the setting sun poured itself over the riverbank as she walked home.

I'm going to become the most magnificent person I possibly can. I'll be an awesome person, and I'll get a job that pays well. I'll live my life in such a way that my mother won't ever feel ashamed or embarrassed, and I'll even make it possible for my poor, gullible father to come back home again.

Hitomi didn't go to cram school, but she studied, and studied, and studied some more, as if to commit everything in her textbooks to memory. She figured a civil-service job would be the most practical career path, so she set her sights on majoring in law and decided to apply to the most prestigious place that might accept her. That turned out to be X University, an elite private institution in Tokyo where she received a full-ride scholarship.

Hitomi's single-minded plan was to pursue her goal of a government job. That is, until the day in her sophomore year when a friend lent her a video of an anime movie. It was the theatrical release of *Mister Stone Butterfly*, directed by Tsutomu Nonozaki. The film told the story of a group of young boys and their battle—with the help of "Butterfly," a robot they controlled—to protect Earth from sinister extraterrestrial invaders.

Hitomi wasn't aware of this, but the TV version had been immensely popular; children, especially, were wildly enthusiastic, and apparently declared it their number one program of the year in question. The associated merchandising of figures, toy robots, and so on, was also said to have been spectacularly successful.

The town where the young protagonists lived looked very similar to the place where Hitomi had been born and raised, and the apartment complex, too, was virtually identical to the one she and her mother moved to after her father deserted them. There was nothing extraordinary about the mien of the buildings, the little playground squeezed into a narrow space among them, or the group of boys, who hollered, "Let's do this, just for fun!" and fought bravely against the enemy day after day, with no thoughts of praise or recognition.

Hitomi was reaching adulthood and knew that such apartment blocks were, of late, falling into decline and coming under criticism from the vantage point of urban planning and design.

Even the complex where she came of age was now inhabited primarily by elderly residents living alone. However, the thing she found surprising as she watched *Butterfly* was that there was no sense of tragic heroism about either the boys portrayed in the anime, or their parents. It was as if all the characters were actually residing inside a moving picture that chronicled their lives in a more realistic way than even a live-action film.

The adults who worked on it had to have been aware of both the positives and negatives of living in a community where narrow spaces were divided into tiny cubbyhole apartments. But quite aside from such considerations, the atmosphere created by the young protagonist's evident love for his suburban-Tokyo town seemed to leap out from the screen.

In the movie, from beginning to end, the boys neither grew nor evolved. They just dealt matter-of-factly with whatever came up on any given day, trying to do the right thing according to their own individual lights. They often failed or argued among themselves (although they always made up), but after wiggling out of a variety of dire predicaments and surviving assorted risky adventures, they invariably returned to their everyday lives as though nothing had happened.

In the final scene the protagonist, shown in profile against a backdrop of the rising sun, yawned hugely and said, "Ahh, I can't go to sleep now, or I'll be late for class." As Hitomi watched, she became aware that tears were rolling down her face.

In the world of *Butterfly*, peril on a global scale somehow managed to coexist with the quotidian realities of everyday life, and there was no jarring sense of dissonance or inconsistency between the two. Hitomi, who hadn't known what she was getting into, was overwhelmed by the anime's expressive power, and she felt as though her heart had been captured by *Butterfly* and its director, Nonozaki.

For the first time in her life, it seemed permissible to acknowledge the unglamorous town and the shabby apartment complex where she spent her formative years. Now, at last, she could admit that she'd been fond of those places, regardless of what anyone else might say about them.

Having been pitied every step of the way for being poor and unfortunate, Hitomi had cleaved to her path in reaction to all the negativity, but now she began to feel the first stirrings of doubt.

And she thought: *Animation is really amazing. It's so interesting and fun.*

She was shocked to realize that such a remarkable work of art was theoretically targeted at children and that its existence hadn't been made known to a grown-up like her until now.

What if she had seen that movie when she was a child? Surely her worldview would have been broadened, if only by an inch, or maybe just a fraction of an inch, and enriched much sooner.

It had already been two years since the movie version of *Mister Stone Butterfly* was released, but after running from shop to shop in town, Hitomi finally found a copy of the pamphlet that accompanied the film's release. This was one of the few times she felt genuinely glad that she had decided to go to college in Tokyo.

The director's name, Tsutomu Nonozaki, came to mean something to her, and she read every interview she could find. That's how she came to realize that an anime wasn't created by just one person. Producers, supervisors, assistant directors, writers who handled storyboarding, voice actors, various types of artists for genga, backgrounds, and CGI: the list of participants went on and on. In interviews, they all talked seriously about their contributions to the whole, and it was clear that everyone went into it striving to make something really good.

Hitomi felt a desire to work with people like that welling up from the depths of her soul; there was no way to subdue those feelings, and before long they had engulfed her entire being.

It would have been futile to resist.

For her mother, for her father, for money, to make ends meet—Hitomi's path had been motivated by things and people other than her own self. For the first time in her life, feelings of hope and longing were springing up inside her, and she was powerless to do anything but follow where they led.

Hitomi knelt before her mother and received permission, on the condition of graduating from college first, to go work at Tokei Animation. In between attending lectures and working a part-time job, she squeezed in a special course in the basics of anime at a vocational school, where she also spent much of her limited free time binge-watching animated movies and TV series instead of catching up on her sleep.

"Why choose the anime business?" She was actually asked that question during her job interview at Tokei Animation. "Why come to us when you studied law at a prestigious school?"

"I want to make anime to surpass the ones directed by Tsutomu Nonozaki," Hitomi replied.

She somehow got the job, but now that her name was getting out as a directorial talent working at Tokei Animation, Hitomi still cringed, and her face felt as if it might go up in flames, whenever she remembered her astoundingly arrogant reply. *How could you have been such an idiot?* she asked herself over and over, but at the time she'd been completely serious and sincere. She'd truly intended to try to surpass the person she admired most in the world.

Tokei Animation was the company that had produced the *Butterfly* movie. That the studio was also called an industry behemoth and deemed a venerable institution had eluded her back then. Moreover, she had barely looked into other anime studios and not applied to any company other than Tokei. It was a marvel that they'd hired her, if she said so herself.

Then, in the spring of the year Hitomi joined, Tsutomu Nonozaki abruptly left the company. She had never even spoken to the famous director, much less gotten the chance to work with him. There were some vague rumors about convoluted corporate machinations—the type of intrigue that's part and parcel of any major company—and unfavorable conditions on the set. Apparently, from what Hitomi heard, the director and the studio who combined to produce such brilliant work had decided to go their separate ways because of a dispute over his salary and working environment.

The person she looked up to most had disappeared from sight, but clinging to the hope that her voice would reach him, even from afar, she set to work.

Tokei Animation was juggling several televised anime series at any given time, and as it happened, it was Tokei that sent a steady procession of magic-girl sagas out into the world—the very stories that Hitomi once couldn't relate to—in the service of selling toy wands.

Hitomi paid her dues as an episode supervisor in charge of thirty-minute segments, and her life was an endless succession of frantically busy days. Then, after a while, she was asked to orchestrate the anime component of a video game. The entire worldview of one of Tokei's current, well-received magic-girl TV series was being turned into an action game, and Hitomi was tapped to direct both the opening sequence and the in-game animation.

"We'll make them buy the wand," Hitomi said at the initial meeting as she looked around the table at her colleagues, all of whom were considerably older than she was. At the planning stage, she'd heard that one of the game's unique features and sales points was an original item—a wand designed for the occasion. The toy version would go to market at the same time as the game. "Let's try to make both Mika, the heroine, and the wand, as charming as possible. However, we can't overlook the fact that our target audience is children. The magic-girl genre belongs to kids."

Sales figures of the unique wand would directly reflect the number of people who appreciated the game's anime component. And that number, in turn, would become part of Hitomi's track record as a junior employee.

Her mark was, in essence, her childhood self, that little girl who said, "I don't want it," and let such a wand fall from her hands.

I'm going to deliver pictures and stories that will make even that girl start to want one. I'm going to make it work business-wise.

"Let's make something great," she exhorted her colleagues.

Unlike Chiharu Oji's *Yosuga of the Light*, which had turned the tables by being a magic-girl anime aimed at adults, "orthodox" iterations needed to deal with the standards-and-practices censors, not to mention the PTA, and faced various hurdles. Conventional wisdom held that the genre wasn't kind to brave departures, but Hitomi resolved to make something within the limits of the established template that would be enjoyable for children and adults alike.

In the end, "Sun Angel Pink Search: The Game" shaped up to become Hitomi's signature work. Sales of the wand that only appeared in the video game exceeded that of the main wand from the anime. While the title had completed its run, towards the end, the game's wand had begun to appear in the series itself.

The overall director of the TV anime had choice words for Hitomi and continued to give her the cold shoulder even now, but she didn't let it get to her. She couldn't pretend the situation was ideal, but she decided not to worry.

That was because six months later, the plans for a project Hitomi had been dying to work on—a schoolkids-plus-robots series—was approved.

The title was *Soundback: The Singing Stone*—or *Sabaku* for short, an abbreviation of the transliteration *Saundobakku*.

This was the genre Hitomi had dreamed of exploring from the start: schoolkids and robots, fighting together to save the world. In addition, the series would be something of an anomaly in the current landscape of anime broadcasting, which was heavy on late-night programming, in that it was slated to air on Saturdays at 5 p.m.

Hitomi's dream was coming true.

Children would watch the show in droves.

◆

"I just can't do it." The instant Hitomi heard those words, uttered in a tiny voice, she saw it coming.

Anju Mimatsu was standing in the dubbing booth, and after numerous spoiled takes and repeated coaching from the director, the voice actress emitted a wail, covered her face with her hands, and hung her head. The assistant audio engineer and the sound mixer, who were sitting in front of a monitor, exchanged a glance. The entire staff was in a state of agitation, and Hitomi, too, looked up at the ceiling in frustration.

So she did start crying...

"I'm sorry, I'm sorry," Anju said through a torrent of tears, and her shoulders were visibly heaving in that recording booth. Because the microphone was still turned on, the actress's voice echoed throughout the studio.

Anju wasn't alone in the dubbing booth. Aoi Mureno, a voice actress who had been in the business far longer than Anju, was there as well. Aoi ran over to the weeping Anju and placed a consoling hand on her colleague's shoulder. "Are you okay?" she asked.

Seemingly supercharged by that friendly contact, Anju's weeping grew even louder and more piercing.

Obviously flustered, the talent manager from Anju's agency jumped out of his chair and then appeared to hesitate, not sure if he was allowed to enter the booth. He glanced at Hitomi, who was sitting in front of him, and waited to see what she would do.

Ignoring the manager, Hitomi grabbed one of the microphones connected to the booth. This wasn't the first time she'd had to deal with a youthful voice actor's tearful meltdown. It wasn't anything unusual, or new. "What are you crying about?" Hitomi asked the woman.

"Oh, um..." Anju raised her head and met Hitomi's eyes through the glass, but before she had time to speak, Hitomi went on, "Could you please tell us what's wrong, so we can understand why you're crying?"

Hitomi didn't think the acting direction so far had been harsh enough to make a performer feel browbeaten or harassed. Still, she felt the actor's voice wasn't conveying the emotions that the scene required, and they had done several retakes while Hitomi tried to find the words to explain the effect she was looking for. The timbre of Anju's voice wasn't bad at all, but she was being too assertive about projecting the interpretation of the role she'd come up with on her own, and Hitomi, as the director, had told her to tone it down a bit.

Hitomi already knew from experience as she repeated her question that the reply would be a hundred-percent identical to those she'd heard on other occasions. She even said a little prayer: *Please let this answer be different for a change.*

Anju's cheeks were flushed and she appeared to be deep in thought, but she remained silent aside from an occasional hiccup. Aoi's hand still rested lightly on the younger woman's shoulder, and after a few moments, Anju—her downcast eyes still brimming with tears—spoke at last. "It's just so frustrating when I can't get something right," she said.

When Hitomi heard that, she came very close to letting out an audible sigh. In her experience, the reason voice actors gave for bursting into tears was always the same, almost as if they had gotten together beforehand and agreed on an answer.

First, they would take the blame, through a veil of noble tears. Then after receiving some words of encouragement, they would perk up again, declaring themselves ready to get back on track and make a fresh start.

It was a ritual that had probably occurred on many sets in the past, and if you had time to burn, maybe a little air-clearing wasn't necessarily a bad thing. Unfortunately, *Sabaku* was on an extremely tight schedule.

Turning the mic switch on again, Hitomi spoke.

"So you're saying this is the first time you've ever been aware of your own limitations? Today, right here, right now?"

This question, too, usually received a predictable answer. Sure enough, Anju nodded dolefully and said, "Yes. I just realized now, for the very first time."

"Well, you may be feeling nice and refreshed after your cathartic crying spell, but it hasn't really been enjoyable or productive for the rest of us. What do you think about that?"

From inside the booth, Anju was looking in Hitomi's direction, and her eyes flew open in surprise.

Leaving the mic switch on, Hitomi turned to face Anju's manager. "This is on you, too," she said. "From now on, please don't bring anyone to our studio who doesn't have a clear idea of what they can and can't do."

In the instant after Hitomi finished speaking, an even louder, more penetrating wail filled the air. Anju had buried her face in her hands and was bawling like a baby once again. A moment later, though, she stood up and came barreling out of the booth, with her short, flouncy skirt swirling around her.

"Anju!" her manager exclaimed in alarm and ran after her as she left the room.

Hitomi heard someone click his tongue right next to her. Hatefully. She turned her head and locked eyes with the producer, Yukishiro. He stood up to leave, and as he passed Hitomi's chair he snapped, "You may be feeling nice and refreshed after speaking your mind like that, but it isn't going to be very enjoyable for me to try to smooth things over."

Without waiting for Hitomi to reply, Yukishiro left the room, calling out "Ms. Mimatsu!" as he went.

The voice actors hired to work on an anime series committed to coming in at certain specified times over a period of six months or so. If any of them had unavoidable scheduling conflicts, their voices were recorded separately, in a special session. In the case of Tokei Animation, the goal was to arrange to have the next four or so episodes recorded for any given project.

This day was devoted to dubbing the third episode of *Sabaku*.

The bulk of the dialogue had already been recorded by the other cast members on a previous day (and having twelve voice actors lined up in the same studio was always lively and energizing), but two performers—Aoi and Anju—had been unable to make it on the assigned day, so their session had been pushed to today.

Recently, many companies were employing designated sound directors to take charge of the dubbing process for recorded voice or BGM (background music), but Tokei didn't subscribe to that system as a rule.

From her time as an episode supervisor, "after-recording" and dubbing had been part of Hitomi's job. Under Tokei's setup, episode supervisors who aspired to become directors someday were forced, for better or for worse, to forge a variety of skills via on-the-job training.

When Hitomi first joined the directorial staff, it had been a nonstop parade of bewilderment. "What do you want to do?" people kept rushing her. Scolded by senior sound personnel every step of the way, she learned about recording audio, music selection, sound effects, and so on, by doing.

This was the reason both Chiharu Oji and Tsutomu Nonozaki, who had left this company and gone solo, had taken with them the basic ability to perform every single task related to anime creation on their own. Headstrong geniuses who were teased about being one-man bands had been forged in the hectic crucible that was Tokei Animation.

After leaving the recording studio, Hitomi headed to the break room. Aoi Mureno, who'd been in the booth with Anju, was sitting alone on a couch and smoking a cigarette. "Thanks for all your hard work today," Hitomi said.

"Want one?" asked Aoi, holding out the pack.

When Hitomi shook her head, explaining that she didn't smoke, Aoi took a puff, exhaled a large gray cloud, and told her, "Sorry. Normally I wouldn't smoke during a break from recording, but I somehow found myself craving a cigarette. Please keep this a secret from senior voice actors."

"Oh, so I guess they'd be angry if they knew?"

"Well, my voice is my livelihood, so I should be taking doubly good care of my throat. Some of them are outraged at the mere idea that I might ever smoke a cigarette, and when I was a rookie, one of them actually got mad at me for slacking because I'd been careless enough to catch a cold! My fellow actors may be even stricter about this sort of thing than any manager. They're like old-fashioned craftsmen, if you know what I mean."

Needless to say, voice-acting work was all about the voice, so most performers took extra-good care of their throats and never went anywhere without a canteen or a bottle of water. Hitomi had come to see that type of meticulous behavior on the part of veteran actors as an essential aspect of their professional reliability.

But she wasn't about to make a fuss every time she discovered that a young voice actor was a smoker. The bottom line was that cigarette habit notwithstanding, Aoi's performances were first-rate. Unlike some one-note specialty actors, her range was so wide that she could play *moe* girls and schoolboys with equal ease.

Another thing that made Aoi such a valuable addition to anime projects was her instinctive understanding of her place in the larger picture. She was acutely aware that her job involved coming in for three hours to breathe life into what a staff of a hundred had created over several months.

"I'm sorry about the way I ran Anju off," Hitomi apologized.

"Oh, no, that's perfectly all right. No worries. I totally understand how what happened today would have been the last straw for you." Aoi's way of talking was a curious mixture of polite speech and peer-group argot. At twenty-seven she was a year older than Hitomi.

With soft-looking, loosely rolled hair, and small, neat hands and feet, Aoi struck Hitomi as someone who would indeed be in show business. In an industry with a high turnover rate, talent that managed to stay popular for any length of time tended to have something going for them.

Hitomi couldn't remember ever becoming more than moderately friendly with a voice actor on any of the projects she'd handled. This aspect of her job could get awkward if she didn't maintain a certain distance. Unless you were singularly adept at separating the professional from the private, getting your personal life tangled up with a project was unwise.

Hitomi had never once worn a skirt when she went to a set where most of the voice actors were female. It was as if she were erecting a barrier with all her might so the talent would think of her as a faceless, sexless staff member who was barely worth noticing.

Their present conversation might devolve into backstabbing gossip, and Hitomi hated getting caught up in that kind of thing. Aoi Mureno, too, seemed to have no desire to prolong the discussion, though she did get off one parting shot.

"Maybe Anju thinks she's an idol, and not an actor," Aoi sighed. With a self-mocking laugh she added, "But who am I to talk, right?"

It wasn't only Anju Mimatsu. Hitomi had been opposed to more than a few of the voice actors who'd ended up on the project. She couldn't help thinking how much better it would be if she had the authority to do all the casting herself, according to her own preferences, but Yukishiro, the producer in charge, had had his way.

"Are you even aware of how intensely sought-after idol VA are these days?" he asked. "For the main parts, we went and asked for the people you suggested, didn't we? For the roles where pretty much anyone could do an acceptable job, kids who'll work for peanuts despite their name recognition and popularity are the best bet. They broke out with *Mermaid Nurses*, and we get to use five of them as a set, okay?"

Hitomi felt like retorting, "I really don't think there's such a thing as a role that 'pretty much anyone' could play," but she managed to hold her tongue.

While she had never seen the anime in question, she was aware that the kids in it had gone on to hold live fan events whose tickets were snapped up in no time. As "idol voice actors," each had her own personal followers. However, the fact was that after *Mermaid Nurses* ended (it was the story of a group of nurses at a university hospital who led double lives as members of an idol group), the only one whose subsequent voice-acting career really took off was Aoi.

When Hitomi thought back to the press conference where the *Sabaku* project was first introduced, she still felt a vague sense of unease. At the event that Yukihiro had pushed to be "as sumptuous as possible," he, Hitomi, and the young voice actors had all been in attendance. The latters' fans somehow got wind of it and showed up in large numbers, and as they shouted encouragements ("Aoiiiii!" "Anjuuu!"), Hitomi realized that the actresses really were as popular as Yukishiro said. She couldn't help wondering whether the audience had gotten a real sense of *Sabaku*'s concept and aims, or whether the presentation had touched anyone's heart, as the press conference finally petered out like a case of indigestion.

"I'm really sorry for the inconvenience," Aoi muttered now.

Watching her stub out her cigarette, Hitomi said, "When voice actors start being perceived as idols, it's probably because that's what the fans want. It's not your fault."

"That might not be true. I mean, there are definitely some voice actors who're hoping to be showered with attention for doing this kind of work—though I'm not trying to imply that Anju is like that."

"No, of course not."

After the press conference, Anju had raised hell with the staff because she was convinced the spotlight had been trained on her exactly one time fewer than on the other girls. At that point, Hitomi thought, *Yikes, this kid*, but shortly after Anju left, two of the other castmates exchanged glances and whispered reassuringly to each other, "We got an extra turn in the spotlight because we deserve it more, right?" Overhearing that, Hitomi felt sickened, and it was only out of cowardice that she didn't point out to them that a stupid mistake on the staff's part was all it had been.

"I'm back," Yukishiro announced in a voice that seemed overloud as he abruptly opened the door and walked into the recording studio. He shot a glare in Hitomi's direction, and she returned his gaze with a feigned air of unconcern before glancing behind him.

"So you are. Alone, though?" she asked.

"Alone. Ms. Mimatsu went home."

"Could you get her to come back to work?"

"She says she'll return on one condition. The director has to apologize." His ill humor was on full display as he looked down at the seated Hitomi. "So, what are you going to do?" he said.

Uh-oh, Aoi let out.

Hitomi answered the producer's question with a question of her own. "What do you think would be best?"

"Let's go find her. If we can straighten it out now, we can still get all the recording done today."

"That works for me." Hitomi tucked her wallet into the back pocket of her slacks and left the studio with her producer.

Yukishiro strutted ahead as if he were in a huge hurry, and as Hitomi emerged from the building, she saw him already standing on the curb with one arm slicing the air, yelling "Taxi!"

◆

One of the curious features of the anime business is the bizarrely long story-planning meetings. Those sessions routinely last from midday till night, or from early evening until the wee hours, and as the intensity grows and the agenda expands to include art, music, and editing, the participants can begin to feel fatigued or even depressed.

After one of these meetings, Hitomi left the conference room and went into the hallway to buy something to drink.

It was already past 11 p.m., and through the window she could see a sharply delineated half moon floating in the night sky. Tokei Animation's offices were located in the old downtown section of Tokyo, a quiet neighborhood where most of the surrounding lights had been extinguished by this time of night, and Hitomi was able to make out a sprinkling of stars as well.

Work on the second half of the screenplay for *Sabaku* was underway, and with the first half already under everyone's belts, people had developed strong emotional attachments to the story and the discussions were more impassioned than ever. An outsider might be surprised to learn that work on the second half was only beginning now, when the first batch of episodes had already begun to air, but that kind of timetable was completely normal in the anime world.

An agreed-upon component could gradually morph into something entirely different that wasn't necessarily an improvement.

After pouring the contents of a plastic bottle of full-calorie cola down her throat, Hitomi let out a sigh. Outside the window there was a small pond with three humidor-type ashtrays placed around it at regular intervals, and Yukishiro was standing next to the one on the far right, having a smoke. He was using his other hand to manipulate the screen of his smartphone, and after a moment he called someone to embark upon a rather intense conversation.

Sabaku wasn't the only title he was responsible for at present. As far as Hitomi knew, he wasn't the showrunner for any other anime series this season, but a movie he was handling would be released next month, and he had probably already started prep work on the next season's offerings. Working in anime involved doing a lot of one-off films and videogames, and he was probably talking to some staff member about one of those. Or maybe his wife, a former flight attendant, was on the other end.

Hitomi had never met Yukishiro's wife, but from what she'd heard, he had married a remarkable beauty. Colleagues who had known the producer for many years went around saying, "Well, we wouldn't have expected any less from Yukishiro. From the time he was young, he always knew how to make the most of connections, so he probably only hooked up with the cream of the crop when he was dating and going to mixers and so on."

As he talked on the phone in the moonlight, Yukishiro stretched his arm high over his head and lightly shook his head. Evidently the person on the other end was refusing to listen to reason. Hitomi couldn't hear the conversation, but she could tell from the producer's body language—*I'm telling you...*

She was automatically reminded of how Yukishiro had admonished her at the screenplay meeting. "Don't let every little thing you're thinking show on your face," he'd said.

"What are you talking about?"

Today's meeting might have continued all night, too, if Yuuki, the story editor, hadn't announced that he had someplace else to be and gotten out of his seat. He was in charge of the screenplay for all intents and purposes. After all the other staffers had left, Yukishiro confronted Hitomi as if he'd been waiting for the two of them to be alone.

"It's written all over your face," he said. "You clearly think these meetings are a total waste of time."

"Actually, that's not what I was thinking at all." Deep down she felt more than a little surprised, and even as she delivered that calm reply she was wondering why the producer would say such a thing.

She certainly didn't make light of scenarios. It was, however, true that she'd never quite gotten used to spending vast stretches of time on meetings that didn't yield any immediate decisions, back since her days working as an episode supervisor on *Pink Search*.

Episode supervisors, animation directors, and story editors, to name a few—if you were to ask which of those people who served under the director was officially number two, there was no ready answer. The anime workplace was full of top deputies. The desire to give all their ideas fair consideration was understandable, as was each contributor's commitment to quality.

Even so, anime spent a disproportionate amount of time on developing screenplays—which was ironic considering that they were frequently criticized for being weak. Hitomi felt that endless scenario meetings where they discussed this, that, and the other thing until the cows came home made the team mistake the trees for the forest. Because the screenplay ate up so much time, the critical step of reviewing the storyboards ended up being given short shrift.

You could say that storyboards, which encompassed the movements of characters and shifts in backgrounds, as well as the dialogue and the flow of music, were an anime's blueprint. Making sure all those elements meshed smoothly was one of the director's most important tasks and should have merited the biggest investment of time.

Needless to say, anime wasn't just about spoken dialogue; it was an art form where the pictures tell a story. Yukishiro had certainly been in attendance as a producer at the planning meeting for *Pink Search* (the series, not the game) where Hitomi had remarked, "Having everybody draft a storyboard and consolidating all our best ideas from there would be quicker." The entire staff from the overall director on down had frozen at her words, and she'd been disinvited from subsequent meetings. Later, when they abruptly handed her the screenplay for an episode she was supervising and told her to put it into storyboard form, she got into a big fight with the director over its appallingly poor quality.

During the early stages of *Sabaku*, Hitomi once again proposed that they might try hashing out the scenario through storyboards.

She was told, "That's all well and good, but we'll also follow our usual style," and she'd sat in the long, long story meetings day after day thanks to that incomprehensible conclusion. She couldn't object when they'd argued, "Trying something new would make things even tougher on Mr. Yuuki."

Maybe it all came down to tradition. Perhaps the point was that people at least got to voice their view, to have taken part in a process. The long meetings were no picnic, but there were always some members who derived a kind of perverse enjoyment from the ordeal.

Moreover, *Sabaku* had been forced to accept a major change: the model for its setting had to be depicted clearly. Both the scenario and the art sides were scrambling to make the necessary adjustments. Identifying a location in an anime from the background and such and making so-called pilgrimages, which kicked off a mutually reinforcing cycle of publicity with the local polity, was by now a trend in the world of anime.   .

Trends were evanescent by nature, and Hitomi hadn't wanted

to latch onto the latest fad, but Yukishiro and the sub-producer in charge of promotion had gone ahead and secured a commitment of cooperation from a township and requested a meeting after the fact.

While anime didn't film actual places, location scouting played a role in drawing backgrounds.

Hitomi had gone on a scouting mission to Enaga City in Niigata Prefecture, a lushly verdant rice-farming area that she'd visited on a holiday trip with her parents long ago. While she had every intention of respecting the integrity of the scenery, the truth was that she saw no need to cater to local concerns.

She found it off-putting when the point person at the township's office handed her a sheaf of printed materials and urged, "Surely your work would want to feature the festival we put on every autumn?" Hitomi was ready to adopt good ideas, of course, but basically wanted her storyboards to include only what she wanted to show.

"Director Saito, some things that appear useless to a fair genius like you may be essential to the project," Yukishiro said.

"I see. I've never once thought of myself as any kind of genius, nor do I think of script meetings as a waste of time, but I understand."

She didn't want to quarrel but couldn't help sounding irritated. Yukishiro seemed to be on the verge of a retort but simply said, "I appreciate that," then got up and left.

After boarding a train at the station closest to Tokei Animation's offices, Hitomi only had to change once. Less than thirty minutes later, she was passing through the ticket wicket at her home station on the Tozai subway line.

It was almost the last train and past midnight, and the station's several kiosks and shops had lowered their shutters. For months, Hitomi had been hoping to make it home in time to grab a takeaway snack at the Mister Donut branch, but on this night, once again, that desire was thwarted. *Drat*, she thought. *I'm dying for a Pon de Ring and a French cruller.*

She rode the escalator up to ground level, and the first thing she saw when she walked out of the station was the monolith of huge apartment towers looming overhead. Here and there, tucked among the massive buildings, some cherry trees were blooming. Every year when spring rolled around Hitomi would be amazed anew by this discovery. *Ah, cherry blossoms, even in a place like this. Spring really is the prettiest time of year here.* She loved the sight.

Pedestrians were few and far between on the concrete side-walk, which was lit only by a sparse scattering of streetlamps. When Hitomi glanced back over her shoulder, she saw the same urban landscape of apartment blocks spreading out on the other side of the station as well. On the faces of the buildings, the small windows, like so many square holes, glimmered faintly with yellow light.

This town had famously been used as a location for Tsutomu Nonozaki's *Mister Stone Butterfly*.

It was a long commute to downtown Tokyo, and having to change trains was an inconvenience, but Hitomi had purposely moved out here as soon as she landed a job at Tokei. When she arrived home, exhausted from work, the theme song from *Butterfly* began to play in her head the minute she saw the familiar vista, and she'd feel energized again. She could think, *Okay, let's do this.*

On this night she was fresh from having been told not to let her feelings show on her face, but even so, compared to the time just after she moved to this neighborhood, she felt she had toughened up considerably and grown stronger.

She'd railed at a voice actress the other day, but the truth was that she was in no position to be pointing fingers at others over emotional outbursts. Once, when Hitomi first began working as a novice director, she'd started crying right in the middle of production: *Why can't anyone see what I'm trying to do here?* The producer and animation director said, "Yup, the director's crying. We'd better take a break," clapped their hands, and gave her a chance to gather herself. An assistant director came up and comforted her, asking, "Are you okay?" The animators quietly went back to work even as they exuded the unspoken thought, *Oh, not again*. In those days, as Hitomi tackled one task after another, receiving help from various people along the way, she constantly felt—more than she did now—that her entire soul was being scraped raw.

These days, she rarely cried about anything.

Regretting that she couldn't pause to savor the beauty, she strode quickly through this season of cherry blossoms in full flower, their branches forming canopies over the road.

Hitomi had known going in that the script meeting might drag on until late, so she'd made sure to set the DVR before leaving for work, but she made it home in time with a few minutes to spare. She ran inside, impatiently tossing her shoes aside, and hastily switched on the TV.

It was 12:55 a.m., past midnight on a Thursday.

This was the debut week for Chiharu Oji's new series, *Fateful Fight: Ryder Light*.

"Hi, Zakuro, I'm home!"

Hitomi's cat was sitting fluffily on the sofa. Her fur was a dark brown that fell somewhere between red and black on the color spectrum—hence Zakuro, which meant "pomegranate" in Japanese. After greeting her pet, Hitomi ran a quick check on the cat's food and water dishes and tended to the litterbox.

Meown, Zakuro crooned, quietly padding up next to her human. Two years earlier, Hitomi had seen some elementary-school students who lived in the same complex running frantically from apartment to apartment, pounding on every door and asking, "Please adopt this cat." Before Hitomi knew what was happening, she had volunteered.

After washing her hands, she glanced at the newspaper slot in the front door and found a letter from those same schoolboys. Inside the envelope was a scrap of loose-leaf paper bearing a message—"We'd like to see Zakuro again, so when will you be at home?"—embellished with a cartoonish drawing of a cat.

Hitomi thought for a moment, then wrote, "Dear Taiyo, I'll be here around noon on Sunday," and returned the memo into the newspaper slot so that it stuck outside.

While she was puttering around, doing this and that, the voices in the commercial that had filled the room fell silent and, after a second or two, were replaced by the *vroom-vroom* sound of a motorbike engine.

Hitomi plopped down in front of the television.

Her impression from the day of the press conference for the show, that it broke new ground, held fast.

FATEFUL FIGHT: RYDER LIGHT. The moment the title appeared on the screen, she broke out in goosebumps.

Director Oji's first chance in nearly a decade to display his real abilities, *Ryder* hadn't been generating buzz solely because of the cutting-edge visuals. There had been a lot of positive chatter about the screenplay, as well. The main point of interest was the fact that the protagonist was what people called an evolving heroine.

In the first episode, Jyuri was six years old. The competitive bike races took place once a year, and in the course of every episode, the heroine and the people around her—friends, family, magic-girl foes—all aged a full year. By the time the twelfth and final episode aired, the protagonist would have turned eighteen.

Thus, there would be twelve of the annual motorbike races. Fans would watch each episode with a burning desire to fill in the blanks about the intervening year—regarding both the protagonist's growing army of supporters and the enemies she was fighting against. The talk was that the scenario was geared toward discriminating viewers.

He's taking chances, Hitomi thought.

As the heroine grew up, the character designs would have to be made over, and all of the voice actors needed to be skilled enough to perform across a range from six years old to eighteen.

When Hitomi heard about that innovative setup, she felt unbearably jealous, but also fired up. If it were Hitomi, the fifth episode or so would be totally playful and feature a crowd-pleaser of a match. No, Oji, who valued tempo even more than she did, might go for that as early as the third episode—the premise provoked her soul as a creator and stimulated her imagination to no end.

The opening sequence ended, and after a commercial break, the story began. A pair of soft-looking twin ponytails swung across the screen. "Hey, si-iis!" called a young voice. The accouterments—a tiny pair of rain boots, an umbrella, a tricycle—conjured up everyday life, and the screen even warmly conveyed a tranquil girlhood's sense of the seasons. Presumably, the tricycle was meant to foreshadow the motorbike that would play a major role in the series. But how could a little girl's unsteady legs possibly ride a big bike?

This is good, Hitomi thought. *Too good. I can't stand it.*

She was filled with envy, but also with helpless excitement.

Right now, watching this in real time, Oji's fans had to be thrilled out of their minds. Watching this had to be nothing but pure joy for them. That made Hitomi jealous but, at the same time, inexpressibly happy and proud.

She worked in the same business as the person who was making this.

Instead of just sitting in front of her TV set and stewing in resentment, she could challenge him to a battle. She didn't need to stand impotently by, unarmed. She could charge in, weapon in hand.

She wondered where Oji and his team were watching this debut episode tonight. Studio Edge wasn't a very large enterprise, and it seemed as though Oji, the director, and Arishina, the producer, and the rest of the staff got along well. Hitomi hoped that all of them were together right this minute watching this broadcast.

The heroine, Jyuri, appeared on the screen.

When she made her entry, Hitomi felt like a wind had blown from behind the screen. The six-year-old protagonist was riding a bicycle. Eventually, the little girl would be trading it for a motorbike, in a stirring scene. That premonition made Hitomi's heart pound hard.

I can't lose, she commanded herself.

Her own show, *Sabaku*, would begin airing on Saturday night—less than forty-eight hours from now.

◆

Soundback: The Singing Stone
A Special Advance Screening of the First Episode
Date: April 6th (Saturday)
Time: Doors open at 3:30 p.m.
   Event at 4 p.m.
Place: Tokei Cinema, Hall A

Hitomi cast a sidelong glance at the handbill stuck on the entrance to the studio and then began to climb the stairs, feeling vaguely betrayed. The moment she entered the conference room she demanded, "What's up with that?"

Yukishiro was already inside, and he turned to face her. "Good morning to you, too," he said easily. He was wearing an expensive-looking gray-striped polo shirt with a small appliquéd logo in the shape of a fox on one side of the chest. Hitomi didn't recognize the fox symbol, but she could tell that the shirt was a designer brand. As usual, Yukishiro's fashion sense was almost maddeningly good.

Hitomi took a breath and said, "That handbill for the screening. I just thought we were going to do things a little more... quietly."

Still wearing a sunny smile, Yukishiro answered in a soothing tone, "Don't worry, it isn't costing us any money. Those makeshift posters were made here in the office, on the color copier. Surely there's no harm in sticking a few up on the day of the premiere? I mean, we have to do something to gin up interest."

The viewing circumstances of their handiwork's debut varied among studios and companies. No doubt some staff members eagerly watched every single episode in real time, while others didn't even bother setting their DVRs. Because a grueling rush to the finish was the rule rather than the exception for anime series, many production outfits probably didn't take the time to make a fuss and preferred to jump right into preparing for the next batch of episodes.

Even so, there was something special about a series debut, and the emotions it aroused could be exceptionally strong.

That was why Yukishiro was determined to have a public screening of the first episode of *Sabaku*. They'd recruited guests from across the general populace through notices in anime magazines and on internet message boards, and the plan was for the staff to watch the first episode at one of Tokei's affiliated theaters together with fans. Hitomi had heard that the director and the voice actors were to greet the crowd, and while she was hardly enthusiastic about it, she'd tried to accept it and move on.

She hadn't heard anything, however, about slapping up posters and making a big deal out of it. As if to deflect Hitomi's undisguised chagrin, Yukishiro introduced a new topic.

"That reminds me, yesterday was the first episode of Studio Edge's *Ryder*, right? I took a look at Kayako Arishina's official Twitter account for the show, and apparently the staff got together and celebrated the launch in a very informal way. Apparently, she and some other female staff made rice balls and fried some chicken at their studio in the middle of the night. What a cute gathering, I envy them."

There was not a trace of envy on his faintly smiling face.

An in-house premiere party was like a pep rally where, now that the thing was on, they exhorted each other to do their best. It was the pre-launch counterpart of a wrap party. She imagined the Edge staff gathered around a TV screen in the studio, sharing a friendly toast, and thought, *That must have been nice. Yes, that really, really sounds like fun. If it were up to me, I'd much rather do something simple and cozy like that.*

"So Mr. Yukishiro," she said, "what Oji and his team are up to seems to be very much on your mind."

Hitomi had been trying to keep her facial expression neutral, to hide her true feelings, but before she knew it those petty words had slipped out. Yukishiro was a producer with a slew of hits to his credit who had tasted "anime supremacy." She didn't mean to question his decisions but couldn't help noting that everything looked so different to the two of them.

Giving no sign that she had ruffled his mood, Yukishiro answered calmly, "Look, it's not as if I don't care at all, but I wouldn't say they're on my mind."

"About Ms. Arishina. I've heard that she was a legendary production manager—if she dropped by, the genga got done in time with 100% certainty."

Whether or not Kayako Arishina herself was aware of it, Hitomi had heard the rumor around the anime circuit.

People asking to have her sent to their workplaces just to get a chance to interact with Studio Edge's woman producer; her mere arrival making them perk up, as if to say, *Oh, she's the one we've heard so much about.* Arishina supposedly wasn't just good-looking but praised the work of animators and had an infallible sense of the right thing to say. Moreover, completely unaware of her status as an object of desire, she was hopelessly inept at romance. That just drove male animators wild, or so Hitomi had heard, though she couldn't begin to tell how much of it was hyperbole.

Hearing all this, Hitomi had felt somewhat repulsed, but the actual woman that she came to encounter a few times was kind, gracious, and brimming with love and passion for anime, including Hitomi's own work. Kayako Arishina was remarkably lovely, to be sure, but that wasn't her only appeal. Hitomi ended up thinking, *Ah, now I get it.*

"Of course a woman would be at an advantage," Yukishiro said with a wry smile in response to Hitomi's remark. "When a guy mentions that he hasn't slept in days, the response will be 'Big deal—welcome to the club,' but if it's a woman, some men will get all motivated and swear, 'Okay, I'd better finish this work, just for you!' I'm really quite envious. When push comes to shove with *Sabaku*, could you please encourage the male staffers that way?"

"I don't think I'd have the same effect."

"No need to be modest," Yukishiro said, laughing. Hitomi felt like he was making fun of her and clammed up.

Recently, her life had been so hectic that there were days on end when she didn't have time to take a shower, much less do laundry, and it showed in her untidy hairstyle and shabby, crumpled clothes. It was all she could do to occasionally stop and wipe the grime off her eyeglasses, and as for her attire, every morning she just went to the closet, grabbed the first things that came to hand, and threw them on.

Just as she decided to forget about the premiere and concentrate on *Sabaku*, Yukishiro asked, "That reminds me, would you like to see a fashion stylist the day after tomorrow?"

Hitomi couldn't believe her ears. She thought he must be joking, but he went on in a perfectly natural tone of voice, "My wife has a friend who's a fashion stylist. This friend does a lot of work for women's magazines and might be able to introduce you to a hair stylist, too."

"…No, I'm good." *I bet I'd be expected to pay for everything out of my own pocket*, she wanted to add, but instead just let out a deep but soundless sigh.

There was no sign that anyone had overheard this conversation, but later that day, as Hitomi was preparing to head home, an episode-supervisor colleague named Ouchi came up to her and said, "It must be rough. I mean, working with Mr. Yukishiro can be grating, right? He's the kind of person who doesn't even bother trying to remember people's names, and he likes everything to be flashy and glamorous. I don't know—there's just something kind of over-the-top about him."

"I'm not sure that's true," Hitomi replied, swallowing the multitude of things she felt like saying. "Everything's fine. He's doing a lot for the project."

After work on *Sabaku* began, a number of other people had made similar comments. In this case, Hitomi suspected that

Ouchi—whose name Yukishiro had forgotten once upon a time—was projecting his grievances onto her. Ouchi had made that sort of comment on more than one occasion, though, and because Hitomi had suffered similar slights while working on *Pink Search*, she understood how he felt.

He looked as though he wanted to say more, but Hitomi quickly summoned up a smile and told him, "I'd best be on my way," before leaving the studio.

◆

The day of the special public screening of the first episode was here.

The theater was already packed full of people to the point of overflowing, and Hitomi felt an urge to ask Yukishiro whether he'd even been listening to Oji at that press conference.

Anime belonged to the fans, but bigger didn't mean better. Why couldn't they go about pumping themselves up in a more modest and sincere way like Studio Edge?

After Yukishiro mentioned *Ryder*'s Twitter account, Hitomi had checked it out to confirm that Edge's whole staff had gathered together to watch the first episode to have a great time cozily following tweets and live-discussion message boards. On the latter, Oji and Kayako had posted official comments like *Many thanks for watching*, which had gotten the fans talking among themselves. *Dude!! Is this post the real thing?* And, *How tough are they to be accepting raw feedback as they work?*

By comparison, Hitomi's *Sabaku* was premiering in front of three hundred people, the majority of whom were there to watch their beloved voice actors take the stage. The crowd probably included guests who had been hired to applaud and to ensure that all the seats were filled—which they definitely were.

"Couldn't we have found a way to do this a tad more quietly?" complained Hitomi in a gentle tone, still unable to let it go.

"Anime belongs to the fans, you know," countered Yukishiro, his face a model of cool control. "Don't worry. Just because we're staging a big public event doesn't mean that I'm planning to go 'shallow and wide' with this show. The ideal scenario is to get every fan to make the maximum investment: the 'deep and long' strategy, so to speak."

In essence, Yukishiro's plan seemed to be to siphon off as much money as possible from the fans by capitalizing on the popularity of the voice actors, but Hitomi once again kept her thoughts to herself.

There was actually another reason for her stressed-out state.

Anju Mimatsu, whom Hitomi had driven to tears at a post-recording session the other day but apologized to afterwards to defuse the crisis, had muttered a stiff "Uh, good…morning" at the sight of the director and bolted out of her chair as if she were running away. Hitomi didn't know whether Anju's behavior was intentional or not, but she wished the actress would act more natural. Some of the other voice talent seemed to have heard about that incident, although it might have not been from Anju.

It was a hassle responding to everyone who came up to tell Hitomi, "I heard about what happened. That must have been awful," or "I'm sure Anju just wants to do her best, but I know it wasn't easy for you, either." Aoi, who had witnessed the incident first-hand, wasn't behaving any differently than usual, which felt refreshing and much more amicable.

The plan was to send the two male voice actors up on stage first, followed by the five women who'd played breakout roles in *Mermaid Nurses*. Finally, after screening the first episode, the director, Hitomi, would greet the audience. The main attraction was the voice actors, no doubt, but Hitomi still felt heavy-hearted and apprehensive about having to go on last.

Of course, she had absolute confidence in the content of the show itself. She'd have been happy just to have people watch the anime. Ever since last night, her heart had been racing non-stop.

Sabaku was a major undertaking, indeed.

How would an audience respond to her vision of a robot

that transformed when a magical stone was infused with actual sounds? The name of the protean robot was Soundback, and the protagonists were able to ride in it and control its movements.

Even at the early planning stage, when Hitomi suggested that the robot could appear in a different form depending on the infused sound in each of the twelve episodes, the appalled staff had questioned her sanity. But she had persisted, and her idea had made it into the final script. She was well aware of the selfishness of her directive but obsessed with filming it. She wanted to share her vision with everyone.

Industry-leading mecha designers who'd worked on numerous robot franchises at the venerable Tokei Animation would handle three episodes each, with four of them on board. The anime magazines picked up on this and ran splashy stories with headlines like "Clash of the Mecha Designers!" As if galvanized by those articles, the four designers threw themselves into the project with gusto, each determined not to be outdone.

An unknown like Hitomi could never have made that happen on her own.

Generally speaking, all titles were vying to be featured on the cover of major anime magazines. It generated a palpable scent of excitement that a project was hot. However, during the twelve-week run of any program, there would only be three chances to adorn the cover of a monthly magazine. That didn't come to pass unless reporters had an eye on a series in advance and believed that it had something going for it.

Sitting in the green room, waiting for the event to begin, Hitomi clutched the hem of her one good dress and took a long, deep breath. Ever reluctant to impart any impression that she was trying to be stylish, she'd remembered to throw on a collared jacket.

While she was waiting, she heard Yukishiro call, "Director Saito," and she went to greet the editor of the major monthly *Animaison*. He and Yukishiro appeared to be on extremely good terms. *Sabaku* was going to be on the cover of the issue hitting the stands in June, when the final episode was scheduled to air.

"Thank you very much for everything," Hitomi said. "We're

really grateful to you for giving us the cover story."

The editor looked at her with an embarrassed grin. "On our side, too, whenever an issue you're in charge of comes out, you're pretty nervous that month. It's also a big responsibility in terms of sales." Looking Hitomi straight in the eye, he added, "So I'm rooting for your show, all the more. I'm looking forward to it."

Yukishiro had given *Animaison* an exclusive on the news that *Sabaku* was being assigned four big-name mecha designers. The cover treatment for the issue going on sale in June was almost certainly *Animaison*'s expression of gratitude for that scoop. Antagonizing other publications was always a concern, but Yukishiro was incredibly adept at that type of delicate diplomacy.

"Mr. Yukishiro, can I borrow you for a minute?" another person came up and interrupted their conversation, and Hitomi, too, was accosted and asked, "Director, we'd like your time, too." She received business cards from a number of editors requesting that she appear in their publications the next time.

This scrum was only one of the things that made Hitomi realize what a big deal it was to be given the Saturday-evening time slot. It had become a sort of brand because shows scheduled for it in fact tended to become hits. While the strategy of late-night anime was to ignore viewing data and expect to profit later from Blu-Ray and other post-broadcast packages, that didn't apply to *Sabaku*, which couldn't afford to ease up on pursuing real-time ratings. No wonder Yukishiro was working so hard to drum up excitement.

With so many anime being shunted off to early-morning and late-night time slots, Hitomi also got a clear sense of how adamant the producers on the TV side were about not surrendering this fort of theirs. If the viewing numbers were poor, the brand time slot would lose its brand and no longer be dedicated to broadcasting anime. If worst came to worst, the network might even pull a show before all the episodes had finished airing.

Just as she was starting to wonder exactly how many people she'd greeted, the beginning of the event was announced over the PA system. While everyone other than Hitomi and the principal staff members proceeded to their seats in front of the screen, Yukishiro spoke in her ear, "I'm getting ahead of myself, but let's rent a bigger hall and do another screening for the final episode, with even more public participation. By then, *Sabaku* should have taken off, big time."

"So you're admitting that some of the people here today are hired seat-fillers."

Hitomi expected Yukishiro to be upset, but he just nodded unabashedly and said, "Yeah." Then he apologized, "My words didn't come out right, sorry."

Applause drifted in from the main hall. The monitor in the green room showed the voice actors taking the stage. Amidst the sound of mostly female cheers for the two leads, Yukishiro said, "Let's go," and Hitomi stood up. She'd seen the first episode many, many times, but since she had the chance, a proper viewing on a big screen with an audience was something she didn't want to miss.

"Hey, everybody! Hello!"

Ohhh, a cry of appreciation went up from the male fans, and even though Hitomi was still in the corridor, she could tell that Aoi and company had taken the stage. Mixed in with the escalating chorus of cheers, she could hear the voices calling out the names of the characters each actress had played in *Mermaid Nurses*.

"Okay," Aoi began, "today, we mermaids—no, we're actually here for a new program. All five of us are really happy that we got to work together again."

"Hold on," the emcee asked, "is it 'mermaids' or 'nurses'? I heard people have different views about the right abbreviation, so which is it going to be?"

Mermaids—nurses—mernurs, low voices bellowed separately before another of the voice actresses chimed in. "Anyway! That show was really something special, and for the five of us, getting to be a part of it was the treasure of a lifetime."

"Hey, we're not nurses today, we're here to talk about *Sabaku!*" interrupted Aoi, smoothly enough, before turning to face the audience. "*Soundback*—or *Sabaku* for short. Let's all get on the same page this time!" she bothered to explain. "Form a consensus, please."

The hall was engulfed in a great wave of laughter and applause.

Shortly after the voice actors climbed down from the stage, the house lights went dark. A giant image of a television screen was projected onto the theater screen.

Every time a ubiquitous ad for a carmaker or a beverage company appeared, Hitomi wanted to groan, *Ugh, again?* She felt her blood pressure rising.

5:00, white numerals flashed in the top-right corner of the screen, and the opening sequence of *Soundback* began.

The theme song was an original track by a rock band Hitomi liked. One day, when she happened to mention casually that she was a fan of their music, Yukishiro said, "Oh, they're friends of mine," and subsequently brought them to meet her. Thanks to that, the group's singing now adorned her anime, and she would never get tired of taking in these moments.

Hitomi liked watching anime openings in general.

A tight condensation of an anime's aspects, in under two minutes, that made you wonder what was about to unfold—*please*, she prayed, *let the delight I derived from all the quality anime I've seen over the years, some of that essence, be reflected here even a little bit.*

The title appeared.

The Soundback that the protagonist was riding sped through the air before landing on the ground with an intense thump that seemed to convey its weight and solidity. At that moment, the hero's friends lifted their faces toward the sun.

The opening was immediately greeted with applause. Hitomi breathed a little more easily, but she knew the crucial test was yet to come.

The story proper began.

The sound that the Singing Stone absorbed in the first episode was knocking. To repel a mysterious midnight-black robot from parts unknown that suddenly attacked Earth, the hero and his friends frantically pounded on a small box in which the Singing Stone lay sealed.

Over and over, with all their might, unafraid of crushing the bones in their hands, they kept knocking on the box. Finally, as if in response to the sound, the lid slowly started to open.

In the hushed theater, the screen went silent for several seconds—a length of time secured by the producer in negotiations with the station and just short of what viewers might worry was a technical glitch, it was the calm before the storm.

As the box opened with a wooden creak, the transformation began.

A voice boomed out stating the terms of the bargain: "Can you pledge your sound, your voice, and your song to me?"

Without hesitation the hero cried, "I'll give you anything!"

That was where the first episode ended.

Just when the transformed Soundback filled the screen, the image was replaced by an ad for a new product from a candy maker. The preview of the next episode and the ending theme were yet to come, but people began to clap like a cup overflowing with water.

A round of applause spread through the entire screening hall like waves lapping against the seashore and continued for a long time. Voices could be heard saying, *I can't wait till next week!*

Holding her breath, Hitomi looked around the hall. From her seat in the last row, she noticed that while the room was supposedly full, some seats appeared to be empty. Had they been that way from the start, or had people left early? That was a worrisome thought, but when she leaned forward to get a better look, she realized that those seats were occupied—by children. Some of them appeared to be talking to the motherly-looking individuals sitting next to them. Hitomi thought she heard one childish voice exclaim, "That was cool!" and her heart swelled with emotion.

She felt a strange tingling in her sinuses and quickly turned away. Next to her, Yukishiro said, "That went well, don't you think? I always knew it would."

The applause died down as everyone focused once again for the ending theme. The words "Directed by Hitomi Saito" appeared on the screen.

"You're up," Yukishiro prompted, and Hitomi nodded wordlessly.

◆

Hitomi wished people could just go home cradling their enthusiasm, but something unexpected happened as she greeted the audience from the stage. She had rarely stood in front of a crowd and hadn't even been interviewed that often, but the audience cheered, "Director Hitomi!"

Her surname was one thing, but being called by her first name, she just didn't know how to react. When some people even hollered, "So cute," she went beyond shocked and could only stand there rooted to the stage. The voices were both male and female.

She somehow managed to regain her composure, but it took everything she had to make a simple speech.

"Thank you very much. I'm Hitomi Saito, and it's my honor to be directing *Soundback*."

It was met with the loudest cheers yet.

In the corridor on the way back to the green room, Hitomi was waylaid by the editor of *Animaison* with whom she'd exchanged greetings before the screening.

"Let's talk soon about doing another special feature," he said. "This was incredible. I swear, the cheering was louder for the director than for those voice actors."

"No, I didn't think so," Hitomi protested. Besides, even if that was true, it was only because people had just been treated to the work. They simply hadn't come down from the elation of watching the first episode.

Mindful that the female voice actors might be within earshot, she wanted to move on from that topic as soon as possible. Her plan for the rest of the day was to go back to the studio to check the artwork for the fourth episode and beyond.

"There's a car waiting," Yukishiro said, popping up to rescue Hitomi with inadvertently perfect timing. His face wore a complicated expression: part happiness, part consternation. "I think we should have someone pick you up and drop you off for the time being. A bunch of your fans are waiting outside."

"What?" was all Hitomi could manage. Her voice seemed to be stuck in her throat.

And that was when she heard someone say, "Hmph. So now she gets an official escort? Well, isn't that just peachy."

As those words hung in the air, Hitomi felt a chill run down her spine. The urge to see who had spoken tangled briefly with the desire to turn a blind eye, and curiosity won out. When she looked around she saw Aoi Mureno, who had comforted her the other day at the studio, starting to head for the exit with an expensive-looking leather jacket slung over one shoulder.

"I'm jealous. You're like an idol now," Aoi groused. Facing Hitomi, who was momentarily at a loss for words, the voice actress said breezily, "See ya. Please treat me well when we start dubbing again next week, director."

"Um...yes."

Aoi's just being her dry self—Hitomi wanted to believe it, but the woman wasn't smiling, and her eyes only grew colder and stonier the moment she took them off of Hitomi.

Aoi's beautiful legs, flashing white under her miniskirt, turned the corner and vanished from sight. As the voice actress left, all alone, she seemed to be rejecting even Hitomi's impulse to ask her to come back so they could chat.

The director stood stock still, perplexed, when Yukishiro passed by speaking urgently into his cell phone: "No, but the thing is, that's why..." Seeing how he was avoiding prying eyes and making a beeline for the far end of the corridor, a senior producer named Negishi accosted Hitomi.

"That call is probably from Director Michino," he whispered. Michino was a veteran director affiliated with Tokei Animation like Hitomi. He'd been the overall director for *Pink Search*, and he and Hitomi, an episode supervisor for the series, had engaged in more than a few borderline-homicidal arguments along the way.

"He's pairing up with Yukishiro on an anime this fall," Negishi went on, "but right now the director's behavior is a trifle over the top. Everyone knows a producer can't be expected to focus on only one project at a time, but Michino is being unbelievably possessive."

"Possessive?"

"Ms. Saito, maybe you've reached a level where people are starting to resent you," Negishi said with a smirk. "Just the other day, Michino was yelling at Yukishiro, 'Don't you think you're being a little impure, two-timing and three-timing people?'"

"He got yelled at by Mr. Michino?"

Two grown men, who were nowhere near young—Hitomi was appalled that they'd had such a spat but also felt like she understood. A director faced an endless onslaught of withering, lonely tasks. It didn't seem unreasonable to want at least the producer to be looking out for your interests at all times.

Even so, Yukishiro didn't have it easy.

"Michino must have heard about today's screening, and that's the reason for his call," Negishi speculated. "From what I gather, they were hanging out together till late last night so Michino could lay out his ideas, and it's pretty intense to be accusing his producer of two-timing or whatever when they're both guys. Couldn't Yukishiro handle things a little better, though? Back in the day, when I used to pair up with Michino, nothing like this ever happened."

Unsure how to react to Negishi's fed-up tone, Hitomi blurted out, "I guess it's because Mr. Yukishiro is so popular."

The producer laughed again. "When you try to please and be liked by everyone, it gives rise to misunderstandings. By the way, aren't you tired?" he expressed his concern for Hitomi. "I mean, you had to get up on stage and greet all those people today, and you've been paraded around all over the place—there are quite a few people in the company who've been worried that his approach might be too much for you. Ideally, the project producer should be the person the director can trust and rely upon the most, but at the moment there only seems to be cacophony."

Hitomi didn't reply, and decoding her silence as he pleased, Negishi added, "If anything happens, please don't hesitate to say something, anytime. We're all part of the same company, and my colleagues and I are here if you ever need us."

"Thank you very much." Even as she nodded, Hitomi had a lingering feeling of doubt as if a thin fog had settled over her heart. This debut-screening day should have been full of joy, and she felt guilty about succumbing to gloom.

She still had so many problems ahead of her.

◆

The day after the screening was a Sunday, and Hitomi took a day off for the first time in a long while. The storyboard needed tweaking and she had brought some other "homework" as well, but just being able to perform those tasks in her apartment and not go into the office seemed like a rare treat these days.

She cleaned her apartment, which had been little more than a place to sleep during the past months, and whipped up a simple pasta dish for lunch. The only things she added were anchovies and sausage, but even so, when she took the first bite of homemade pasta, hot off the stove, it tasted almost unbearably delicious—especially compared with her everyday fare of bento boxes and random sweets someone had brought to the workplace. Hitomi had a fondness for cooking, but with her current job situation she never knew when she might get home at night, so the only groceries she kept around were items with a long shelf life. She knew better than to buy fresh meat or vegetables.

Before Taiyo and his friends from the same apartment complex who'd found and entrusted Zakuro to Hitomi could arrive, she washed the cat in the bath. Normally a placid, sedentary creature, on this occasion Zakuro resisted like her life depended on it, but Hitomi somehow managed to use the shower on her before capturing her under a towel and scrubbing her head and belly. The reply that Hitomi had stuck through the newspaper slot had disappeared, so she assumed that Taiyo had taken it.

She brewed a pot of tea, laid out some sweet snacks, and, with the soundtrack of her own anime playing in the background, got down to work. Afternoon shaded into evening, and still there was no sign of Taiyo or his crew.

They were probably just busy. Kids these days had terribly full schedules even on weekends, what with outside lessons and cram school.

"What's taking them so long, Zakuro?"

The cat had been grouchy thanks to getting washed, but apparently time erased that unpleasant memory, and she was dozing peacefully on the sofa next to Hitomi, who was still working. Hitomi was beginning to wonder what she ought to do about dinner when the phone rang. Just as she stretched out one arm to pick up the receiver, the ringtone changed to the whine of an incoming fax.

The anime business generated an overwhelming volume of email and data, but among staff members who preferred old-school methods, faxing was fairly common. Hitomi waited until the transmission was complete before getting up. She felt certain that it was related to *Sabaku*, but when she saw the pages the machine had spewed out, she gave a small gasp.

The sender was Office Lagoon. There was a two-page form along with a note requesting that Hitomi fill in and return the document at her convenience. On the cover sheet was a handwritten message: "If contacting you via your office email would pose problems, we would be grateful if you could let us know your private address."

The form in hand, Hitomi gazed absently at it for a while. She didn't feel like filling it out right away, and as she stashed it in a nearby clear plastic folder, her cell phone rang. She didn't recognize the caller's landline number but answered anyway.

"Yes, this is Saito."

She would be glued to her workplace for a while on account of *Sabaku*. The other party understood this. Promising to meet on a certain day the following month, she hung up.

Hitomi heard a quizzical *meown*, and glancing to her side she saw Zakuro facing the balcony with her forepaws against the window, batting at the glass with obvious annoyance. Thinking the cat might have spotted Taiyo, Hitomi joined Zakuro at the window and peeked out, but there was nothing below except the empty alley sprouting the shadowy stripes of evening. There wasn't a soul in sight.

◆

Sabaku's second episode was the talk of the town. Hitomi first heard this news from Yukishiro at the Tokei Animation studio, the day after the episode aired.

"God genga?"

"Yes, everybody's talking about it," Yukishiro nodded.

She was in the process of checking over some of the art with the animation director.

The images in anime were made up of *genga* and *doga*, the original pictures and the moving pictures, respectfully. Genga turned the storyboards drafted by the director and various assistants into polished drawings, while doga connected the still pictures and made them move. For example, in a scene where a character runs and raises her hand as she goes, the doga filled in the interstitial images between a genga with the hand lowered to another genga with the hand raised.

The majority of animators broke into the business by working on doga (that is, the animation process) and moved on to creating genga. After accumulating sufficient experience, some of the more talented individuals eventually progressed to animation director. Together with the director and supervisors, he or she ensured that all the cuts connected smoothly and formed a worldview in a natural, coherent manner.

"God" as an adjective expressing the highest degree of praise had arisen on the net and, like the phrase "anime supremacy," was being used in the anime world. People spoke of a great anime as being "god anime," or of a "god ep."

"In the second episode, there's a sound that the Singing Stone absorbs, right?" the producer said. "The sound of ice cracking as it's beginning to thaw."

"Yes."

A story that Hitomi had happened to hear when she went location scouting had given her that idea. The people in that area, where the snowfall was heavy, eagerly looked forward to the advent of spring. They said the sound of the ice covering the frozen ponds and rivers finally beginning to crack heralded spring.

"You know the opening scene on the road to school—the one that lays the groundwork for that sound?" continued Yukishiro. "The cut where Mayu and Towako hold hands against a backdrop of rice fields. Off to the side, the first fissures appear in a frozen pond."

"Right."

In terms of production values, she hadn't thought they were creating anything exceptionally artistic. To be sure, it was a charming, feel-good scene, but *Sabaku*'s selling point was the robot transformations. Normally, the transformation scenes, which shows relied upon to drive ratings and spur toy sales, would be able to recycle some of the same images from week to week, but in the case of *Sabaku,* the robot needed to morph into a different form every week. Not being able to reuse a single illustration ate up a lot of the budget, and that drew frowns from the brass.

Yet...

Hitomi replayed the road-to-school scene in her head repeatedly. Mayu and Towako walking by a cracking sheet of ice and holding hands in the sunshine—Hitomi retained a vivid mental picture of those soft little hands and definitely remembered thinking it had turned out better than expected.

"Ah, yes. That shop does really good work," said Goto, the animation director. "They're called Fine Garden," he named the genga studio that had been commissioned to produce the scene.

Anime genga required a colossal number of images, and Tokei Animation, too, subbed out a substantial amount of illustration work to independent studios.

"Also, isn't that studio located in Niigata? Even in the same town where *Sabaku* is set?" asked Goto.

"Oh, they're in Enaga?" When Hitomi raised her eyes, Yukishiro nodded.

"Yup," he said, "they all used to work for an anime-production company in Tokyo, but the genga team broke away and set up an independent company."

The number of anime studios located outside of Tokyo had grown by leaps and bounds. You also heard a lot of stories about the production company itself going bankrupt, and just the animators who belonged to it starting up a smaller company specializing in genga or CGI.

Hearing the name of the Niigata studio jogged Hitomi's memory, belatedly. In fact, in the third episode, which was scheduled to air this week, there had also been a scene in an incidental cut that she'd found quite beautiful.

"I don't know whose work it was, but wasn't there an incredibly meticulous rendering in the lunchtime scene in the first episode, as well?" she asked. "Where the twins stick straws into their bottles of milk and drink it with obvious enjoyment?"

"Oh, right," Goto said with a big nod. "Yes, that section was farmed out to Fine Garden, too. At a guess, I'd say those two scenes were probably done by the same illustrator." Turning to Yukishiro, he suggested, "Shall we try to find out who drew them? People are all over the god genga on the net, and I read a number of shrew posts. They're speculating that it might be the same person whose name appeared in the credits for last week's eps of

Ryder and *Sepia Girls*. Whoever it is must have a distinctive way of drawing fingers."

"Ah, I see. It's the fingers!" exclaimed Hitomi, louder than she intended.

At that point, Yukishiro butted in to tell his excited colleagues, "You're a couple of maniacs." A wry smile played over his face. "Since they were calling it a god genga, I assumed they were praising a transformation scene. Aren't you a wee bit disappointed that they seem to be overlooking the main element we're hoping to showcase?"

"But the freedom to focus on whatever happens to strike your fancy is one of the great things about anime," Hitomi said.

"That's true," Yukishiro granted. "Still…"

To be sure, they had poured a vast amount of time and money into the robot designs, and it wasn't as if Hitomi couldn't see Yukishiro's point of view. Even so, fans discovering an unexpectedly dazzling gem in another corner of the anime, and going crazy over it, made her very happy.

Yukishiro blew out a long breath. "Okay, so I understand that there's an insanely talented illustrator. In my experience, though, when viewers start making a huge fuss about god genga and the like, that's usually a sign that the anime itself isn't particularly good. People tend to start obsessing about obscure details when they aren't finding any other compelling elements. In my opinion, truly good anime are the ones where the quality of art is balanced and consistent across the board."

"I don't think we're talking about anything that narrow," Hitomi retorted.

She didn't appreciate being told that there was no compelling element, even if it had just been a manner of speaking. Yukishiro must have picked up on her bristling tone because he gave an exaggerated shrug.

"Well, anyway," he said, "when it comes to making use of god genga, I think it might be better to sprinkle them evenly throughout every episode rather than abruptly turning the spotlight on one. Okay, I get it. I'll try to track down that illustrator from Fine

Garden."

Yukishiro shot Hitomi a look that seemed to say, *I lose*, then quickly averted his eyes. She, too, fell silent and returned to the pages she'd been working on, using tracing paper to mark the necessary revisions on a batch of recently completed illustrations. The chief director made corrections in yellow, while the animation director used light blue, and when the drawings required a lot of notes, they could end up with a whole sheaf of overlaid sheets.

Just as Yukishiro said, it was Anime 101 to adjust the drawings of the various artists to create a pleasing balance.

This middle section, from episode four on, was going to make *Sabaku* or break it. The fate of many anime series seemed to be to start strong and finish with a flourish, while somehow managing to neglect the crucial middle stretch—which, everyone agreed, was disturbingly easy to do—but Hitomi didn't want to risk losing any viewers. These days, quite a few shows simply gave up on the middle section's quality for the broadcast and instead implemented major modifications for the Blu-Ray and DVD packages. That option wasn't open to *Sabaku*.

In order not to lose Saturday evenings for anime, its ratings needed to be kept up to the end. For the first two broadcasts, Hitomi had secured numbers comparable to other shows that had aired in the same time slot, but there'd been a slight dip from the first to the second episode.

Hitomi's task was to make that number rise by the final broadcast.

◆

Once an anime series began airing, it was like boarding an express train. No matter how much the workplace rattled and rolled during the journey, there was simply no getting off before the end.

The dubbing session for the sixth episode was underway, and the most shameless flatterer wouldn't have called the atmosphere positive. On this day, no one was absent, and Hitomi stood in front of the full cast of twenty-plus voice actors.

"I'll be most grateful for your cooperation," she said, bowing her head. "Thanks to your hard work, the first episode received a great deal of attention, and now here we are, already on the sixth installment. This is the episode where Takaya finally reveals to his parents that he is the Soundback pilot."

Several performers—including Yutaka Haruyama, who was playing the role of Takaya—chimed in with comments like *Ah ha* and *At last!* Hitomi appreciated the spontaneous chorus, which was the voice actors' way of getting everyone at the workplace fired up. Needless to say, teamwork was important where a crowd of actors had to stand in front of the mic and drop back in turn. It wasn't hyperbole to say that it took the whole first half of the series to regulate the flow and warm up.

But now, Aoi and Anju, who had been so playful and high-spirited for the dubbing session for the first episode, hardly spoke at all when they weren't performing. When a normally vivacious person like Aoi was being uncharacteristically silent, workplace morale declined accordingly. Hitomi, feeling far more tension than was constructive, had been dispirited since morning.

"This is troublesome," Yukishiro said. He didn't seem to be blaming Hitomi, but he sighed in apparent frustration.

The recording session was going smoothly on the surface. Both Aoi and Anju gave the impression of having fully grown into their characters over the past five episodes, but the problem now was a certain lack of will.

"Oh, wait, I forgot to act out the surprised reaction just now," Yutaka Haruyama noticed. "Could we record it please? It's on page twelve of the script—the part where Ryuichi collapses."

"Got it," Hitomi said, thumbing back through her copy of the script. When the screen in front of the mic stand showed the corresponding segment, sure enough, along with Ryuichi's lines in that scene, the figures of Takaya and Mayu were visible in one corner.

Through a combination of experience and instinct, voice

actors developed a sense for their characters' beats and saw the need to insert ad-libbed lines into the script based only on unfinished storyboards and rough-draft genga. Even when another character was doing the speaking, actors might judge that since their characters were also in the picture, their voices or gasps also needed to be included.

When an omission of this kind was in danger of being overlooked by the director and other supervisors, the actors would raise their hands, confirm if their input was required, and breathe life into their characters.

Rookies, especially young voice actors, tended to let their enthusiasm get the best of them or tried to grab the spotlight and often ended up whiffing. Anju was one such girl. During the first session, Yukishiro had remarked to Hitomi, "I think it might be a good idea to make her understand that her character's presence in a particular scene doesn't mean she always has to be saying something," and in turn Hitomi had instructed Anju, "We actually don't need to hear your voice here."

But the current situation was a different matter entirely.

"Anju, could we please have you put Mayu's voice in, too, synced to Takaya's reaction?" Hitomi asked politely.

"Oh, I see. Sorry I didn't notice," replied the voice actor, who was playing Mayu. She turned and looked in Hitomi's direction, then stood up with her head bowed.

Hitomi felt like sighing. Perhaps Anju had noticed but not been able to speak up. Since the day Hitomi made her cry, Anju's verbal participation in the creative process had diminished considerably.

"Director, Towako doesn't show up in the picture, but we know she's there, too, off camera. But I guess it's fine if I don't say anything?" asked Aoi, raising her hand. She was another headache, in her own way. Unlike Anju, Aoi didn't shrink from voicing her opinions, but ever since the incident at the public screening, she'd been openly grumpy and standoffish whenever she spoke to Hitomi.

"No, I apologize for the insufficient notations, but if you

could, please do add your voice. It would be perfect if you could just convey the impression that you're catching your breath."

"Got it. I'll do the same from the next part as well."

Aoi was playing one of the girls, Towako, who was as much of a protagonist as the two boys and thus appeared in many scenes. For some time now there'd been a distinct lack of communication, and she'd been getting up silently and inserting her additions unbidden instead of raising her hand first. Today was better than usual in that she'd stated her view, at least. She was good at what she did, no issues there, but was giving off a terrible vibe.

After almost three hours' worth of dubbing, they recorded a twelve-second preview of the next episode, a ringtone you could download from a cell-phone website, and the built-in vocalizations for the robot toy that was going on sale. A session that had taken all day was finally coming to an end. One by one, the voice actors who had finished their work departed until, at the end, only the two male leads remained.

When she thanked the pair and went out into the corridor, Hitomi overheard a veteran voice actor and his manager, who were still in the lobby, conversing with Ouchi, one of the episode supervisors.

"So Director Saito went to X University?"

Hitomi felt her stomach contract into a tight ball at those words. She'd overheard similar conversations here and there in the past, so she had a pretty good idea of what was coming next. *Why work in anime when you have a degree from X University? Ah, maybe that explains why she's so inflexible.* And so on—people said all sorts of things about Hitomi, and she often couldn't tell from the baseless remarks whether she was being extolled or slandered. The "bit of a genius" line Yukishiro liked to throw around was perhaps one example.

She didn't want to listen anymore, but as she started to withdraw into the soundproofed studio, a voice reached her ears again as if it were pursuing her.

"I'm sure Mr. Yukishiro has a complex about his lack of an academic pedigree. His wife graduated from a four-year college and so has more schooling under her belt than he does. Dealing with Director Saito must be complicated for him."

Back in the studio, Hitomi found Yukishiro in the middle of a meeting. In order to be able to check the scenes showing the Soundback, which had merchandise tie-ins, the staff had been giving priority to the parts where *Sabaku*'s robot made an appearance. In today's postrecording, too, those segments had been dropped into the whole already complete.

Yukishiro and the toy manufacturer, who had stopped by to monitor the progress, were verifying the nitty-gritty details together in the studio. Hitomi shared responsibility for the anime's content, but when it came to contracts and revisions necessitated by toy tie-ins, sometimes it was better if the director didn't directly partake in the negotiations. Hitomi had left all of that to Yukishiro.

He gave no sign of noticing that Hitomi had returned. As she idly watched them working away, she felt as if she didn't belong there, either.

Maybe the coast was finally clear outside. Surely that conversation would have ended by now.

Quietly getting up from her chair, she cautiously ventured into the corridor again. She didn't hear the voices anymore. It was perfectly quiet as if no one else were on their floor.

Breathing a sigh of relief, Hitomi poked her head into the lobby, thinking to buy something to drink, and then—froze.

She'd been sorely mistaken in thinking the place empty. There was someone standing in front of the vending machines. That person seemed to sense her presence and lifted his head.

"Hey," he called to Hitomi, "long time no see."

She stood dumbstruck while he cocked his head and gave her a quizzical look. "What, you don't remember me?" he asked, and she could only shake her head awkwardly in denial.

How could she possibly not remember? She'd recognized the person in the lobby the moment she laid eyes on him.

It was Chiharu Oji, the director of *Fateful Fight: Ryder Light*.

As always, he looked like some illustrator's fantasy of an

ageless schoolboy, and he appeared to be loitering aimlessly by himself.

"You don't remember me?" should be my line, Hitomi thought. She'd never dreamed that *he* would remember *her.* A while back, they'd exchanged formulaic greetings, but she didn't think he had even registered her existence.

The words "What are you doing here?" hovered precariously on the tip of her tongue.

The Tokyo Telemo Center was a place where people from various companies mingled. In fact, it was here that Hitomi had met Oji's current producer, Kayako Arishina, for the first time. However, there had been no indication that any shop aside from Tokei Animation had booked the facilities for dubbing or post-recording on this day. Hitomi was quite certain she hadn't seen any mention of Studio Edge or *Ryder* on the whiteboard at the building's entrance, either.

"I came here thinking I might get to see you, so this is great—you're here." What Oji said now was even more stunning, and Hitomi's eyes went wide with surprise. "Where's Mr. Yukishiro?" he asked, his lips curving into a wry grimace. "It could be a problem if he shows up."

Oji scanned the corridor beyond the lobby. Still feeling as if her soul had taken temporary leave of her body, Hitomi nodded and said, "Don't worry, he's tied up in a meeting for a while, at least."

"Really? Lucky me."

"Do you have some kind of issue with our Yukishiro?"

"Actually, yes," Oji said calmly. "In the past, I caused him a whole boatload of trouble, and I don't ever want to see him again, because I really hate to apologize."

Looking at Hitomi, he cut to the chase.

"So, I watched the first episode of *Soundback.*"

Spurred by a mixture of anxiety and excitement, Hitomi stood up straighter. The desire to hear his impressions intertwined with an equally strong urge to clap her hands over her ears. Before she had time to brace herself, Oji spoke again.

"I enjoyed it."

Hitomi's breath caught in her throat. It wasn't an exaggeration; she was unable to breathe. Gooseflesh sprouted up and down her arms.

I enjoyed it. His voice seemed to echo inside her. Her feet suddenly grew warm, and she shook.

"You were kind enough to watch it," she said.

"I've been asked to do this. Offer you support, I mean. It's hardly in character for me, actually."

Offer me support? Hitomi was mystified, but Oji just continued talking.

"Thanks to you, I got to see something good, so I came to tell you just to return the favor. Ms. Saito, it must be rough dealing with the sirens."

"Huh?"

"The sirens," Oji repeated. "The idols from *Mermaid Nurses*."

"Ah," she replied, a beat late. She hadn't expected to hear that name.

"I'm friends with them," Oji said. "Though I'd never use them professionally because they'd be quite a handful."

"Why…"

She was about to ask how he knew about her recent discord with the voice actresses but trailed off after the first word. The anime industry was insular, so he'd probably heard something over the grapevine. Or since he was close to them, perhaps he'd gotten the story directly. When she thought about that possibility, she felt uneasy all over again.

As if to save Hitomi's mood from descending any further into an abyss of anxiety and distress, Oji gave his head a resolute shake. "Of course, if you haven't had any problems with them, that's great. But still, it must be a challenge, even if the payoff can be big with popular performers in the right project. For me, I got too close to Aoi, so I don't ever want to cast her again as an actor."

At that last, offhand revelation, Hitomi felt an impulse to ask exactly how close. But Oji quickly changed the subject as if he were putting up a smoke screen. "Do you ever read those girls' blogs, or follow them on Twitter?" he asked out of the blue.

"No," Hitomi replied, still feeling a bit overwhelmed, to which Oji said, "You ought to. Their vocal performances are important, but I like to keep tabs on actors through their blogs and appearances on radio. Those five really aren't bad kids at all. Seriously, if you have a chance, take a look at them on social media."

Then his face turned suddenly serious. "Look, I totally understand the desire to keep the workplace free of schoolyard politics, so to speak. This may be out of line, but I can't help wondering whether you, Ms. Saito, might be the type of person who found that kind of female society disconcerting and simply avoided it. If I'm mistaken, I apologize, but to me it looks as though not wanting to be lumped in with the kind of girls who crowd together in cliques made you hunker down and study and now drives your work."

"...That *is* rude," Hitomi barely managed to croak out, indeed annoyed. It wasn't just rude toward her but to Aoi and the other women.

"Sorry," Oji said with unexpectedly good grace, then added, "If you're going to work with Aoi, at least use her properly. You'd be wise to make an ally of her. That's all I wanted to say."

"Seriously, what are you, anyway?" the words slipped out before Hitomi had a chance to think. If he and Aoi were so close, maybe the actress had been filling his head with stuff—trash about Hitomi, that is. And Aoi must have been the one who told him that there was a recording session here today and that Hitomi would be on hand.

I'm an adult now, Hitomi thought, *and just want to be able to do my work properly without being expected to behave as if I'm still stuck in junior high school.*

"Hm?" Oji turned to face Hitomi, and as she looked at his beautiful, neat-featured face she felt a surge of despair. *Damn, this person is ever so much better suited to working with women than I am.*

"What are you, Mr. Oji, to know so much about girls when you aren't one?"

"I might not look it, Ms. Saito, but I've been an expert on magic girls for some ten years now," the man answered with a nonchalant laugh.

A breeze seemed to blow past Hitomi's ears.

"Just kidding," Oji muttered. He pretended that it was a joke, but it was the truth, and it sank into her with a force that shook her whole being.

This guy was a pro.

He may not have been the main author on most of his projects, but he was her senior in the directing trade and had been working in this industry for some time.

"Well, I'll get scolded if I don't get back soon."

Just as Oji spoke those words, the entrance door opened and in walked Kayako Arishina, holding a smartphone in one hand. She looked surprised to see Hitomi and Oji together, but she just gave a little bow and said, "Oh, hi! How's it going?"

Approaching Oji, she demanded, "So you meant it? You just wandered off mumbling that you wanted to cheer Ms. Saito on..." Turning to Hitomi, she said, "I'm sorry for the inconvenience. I hope our director hasn't been making too much of a nuisance of himself."

"Oh, no."

"That's harsh. What kind of rep do I have, anyway?"

Ignoring Oji, the producer turned to Hitomi with a big smile. "Oji was invited to be a guest on a radio station behind this building. Right now he's waiting for his cue."

"Ah, I see."

After the first episode of *Sabaku* aired, Kayako had sent such a thoughtful and painstaking email of her impressions via the company's PR section that Hitomi felt grateful to the point of indebtedness.

To say that Hitomi was "penned" like some animal would be going too far, but any email addressed to her reached her only after a stop at the admin department, where it was screened. This practice, common among large companies, was designed to prevent employees from moonlighting. Because of that policy,

Hitomi had also refrained from responding to Kayako's email.

However, she realized something. Kayako must have been the one to prod Oji to watch *Sabaku* and connect with Hitomi like this.

"Um, thank you very much for that kind email." Given her tendency to be shy around people she didn't know well, Hitomi had no sense of whether what she'd just said had come out right. "I'm sorry I haven't been able to reply," she quickly ploughed ahead.

What she really wanted to talk about was something else entirely: how she watched *Ryder* every week, and her impressions of it. There were so many moving directorial touches and surprising developments, but there were also points that she might have handled differently...

Hitomi was dying to talk about all those things, but now that she actually had Oji standing in front of her, words failed her. She had no idea where to begin, so she ended up not saying anything at all.

"It's okay, I know how busy you must be." Kayako shook her head as if Hitomi were crazy to be apologizing. Then the producer added, with sparkling eyes, "I'll be looking forward to every episode," and Hitomi felt certain Kayako was speaking from the heart.

As Kayako slipped the smartphone she'd been holding into a pocket, Oji said, "Hey," as though to stop her. "You haven't by any chance been tracking me via GPS, have you? I noticed something suspiciously map-like on the screen just now."

"Well, we'd better be on our way." Ignoring her director once again, Kayako took his arm and pulled him along.

"Um," Hitomi called to their backs. When they looked around, she said, "Please keep on watching *Sabaku*. All the way to the end." Her voice cracked. "Me, too, I'll look forward to *Ryder* till the very last episode."

Oji gave a faint smile. At his side, Kayako's eyes went wide. She looked overjoyed.

"Of course!" her voice filled the empty lobby.

◆

It was the week that *Sabaku* was slated to appear on a magazine cover, and the workplace was in chaos. Even in the world of anime, where frenetic, sleep-deprived days were commonplace, pulling two all-nighters in a row took a palpable toll on their bodies. Their minds grew blank and feeble, and as if it were distorting their vision, everything they saw before them appeared to be coated with a thin, gelatinous film.

In addition to her usual hands-on work, for a while now Hitomi had been called upon to participate in the type of meetings and managerial sessions Yukishiro had previously handled alone. There were times when she complained that she didn't think she needed to, but Yukishiro stubbornly refused to budge.

"Even if it's just once, please show up so you'll have an idea of what it's like. It's essential for you to lay the groundwork for talking to toy manufacturers and sponsors."

But Yukishiro would assume control at all those meetings while Hitomi just sat and took in the general flow, lamenting all the work time she was losing. She hadn't been home in days, and the lack of sleep combined with an irregular meal schedule was giving her a persistent stomachache and a meager appetite.

Once, when she had run to a convenience store to pick up her favorite cup ramen and was slurping the noodles at her work desk, she suddenly became aware of someone's eyes on her. "What is it?" she asked, facing up.

"Nothing," Yukishiro answered with an appalled look. Narrowing his eyes, he said, "Ms. Saito, do you have any friends outside of work to lunch with? And if not, may I introduce you to some people I know?"

"That's really none of your business."

Yukishiro had made his offer as if he were steering her to a fashion or hair stylist, Hitomi noted with some bitterness. She felt like she was being upbraided for missing things during those recording sessions with the VA idols she couldn't get along with, and could only sigh.

She turned away from Yukishiro, who seemed ready to say more, and focused her attention on inhaling the remainder of her noodles.

It was the second month since the show had begun to air. The story was approaching its climax, and the time had finally come to start working on the final episode.

For a title like *Sabaku* that involved big-name mecha designers and a lot of money, extra care was taken not to compromise on quality, and as a result the project was perpetually behind schedule.

The team had finally finished editing the seventh episode two days before it was scheduled to run, and the last-minute insertion of sounds and images had been completed at 7 a.m. on the morning of the broadcast.

"I'll be off, then!" Yukishiro stashed the freshly completed data in his briefcase and stood up. While Hitomi and the rest of her colleagues were slumped in front of their monitors like a bunch of zombies, the producer put on a sports jacket to head to the TV station.

To ensure that no scenes were unsuitable to be broadcast, he would be showing the data to the person in charge at HBT. Even if problems were identified, it was already too late to correct them, so Yukishiro's final task for this episode was to foreclose any such discussion. The fact that his jacket hadn't a single wrinkle made him look terribly out of place in the studio, but it probably meant that he was being quite considerate in his own way.

"Are you going to be all right? I can go with you," Hitomi called out after him. Yukishiro, too, hadn't gone home in a while. Letting him go alone in his seriously sleep-deprived state seemed unfair, but he just replied, "I'll be fine." After shoving some personal items into his briefcase, he patted one pocket to make sure he had his car keys.

"But—" Hitomi protested.

"Your most important job right now is to get some sleep. Thank you for your hard work. You should be free until this evening so please use that time to get some rest."

With that, he left the room.

No doubt about it: Hitomi's eyes were burning from having been in constant use, and her entire body felt heavy as lead. Her whispered "Sorry" couldn't have reached Yukishiro's ears. She tried closing her eyes, and the darkness behind her lids was so heavenly that she felt as though she might never open them again.

She'd fallen asleep before she knew it, and what woke her up were the bickering voices of Yukishiro and a sub-producer handling promotions under him, a man by the name of Koshigaya.

Yukishiro actually sounded angry, which was rare. "Why didn't you tell me?!"

"I couldn't inconvenience the staff, could I?" the still fairly young Koshigaya answered in a reedy, shrill voice. "The highest priority is getting the episode ready to air—you're the one who's always saying that's the basic rule. *Animaison* is hoping for someone on the level of animation director. Their first choice is Mr. Goto, who handled the character design. But he wouldn't have had the time, right?"

Hitomi realized right away that they were talking about the cover.

Yes, she'd heard that it was coming up. In a flash, she was wide awake. She remembered the occasional reminders that the *Animaison* cover was due soon, but finishing the seventh episode had taken precedence over everything else.

"Are we not going to make the deadline?" she asked. When she sat up, still swaddled in the fluffy terrycloth blanket that some considerate coworker had draped over her, the two men looked over at her with a gasp. On the table between them was a photocopy of what appeared to be a *Sabaku* genga.

Koshigaya caught Hitomi's eye and, with a slight shrug of his shoulders, mumbled his answer. The guy was younger than her and looked like a delicate fawn. "The deadline was actually yesterday, so we already sent this over."

"Without even bothering to run it past the producer or the director," Yukishiro added in an uncharacteristically gruff tone.

"Show me, please." Flying over to where the two men were standing, Hitomi picked up the piece of paper they'd been examining. Her breath caught in her throat.

The three protagonists were facing forward, with the robot standing behind them in the light of morning. The kids' faces, however, were sparkling to a bizarre degree.... Their straining eyes were so much bigger than they appeared to be in the anime proper that even Hitomi, who thought of all the characters as her own darling children, wanted to ask, *Who in the world are these people?*

The quality was poor.

The design's cutesy, pandering impression might only have taken slight liberties on any given detail, but the overall disparity was nothing short of shocking.

"W..."

Why? she wanted to ask, but barely swallowed her question. She already knew the answer. The schedule for the current episode had been so tight that they hadn't dared to impose on her with other tasks.

As a rule, artwork appearing on any designated pages of an anime magazine, whether it was the cover, a "pinup," or just an article, had to be created "for this time only" and couldn't have already appeared or be scheduled to appear in the series. Sometimes an editor at the publication even outlined the layout for the order and expressed a preference for a certain artist as well. Most specific requests were for the animator in charge of character design or the animation director, but in any case, they hoped to snag core staff, the more skilled the better.

"The *Animaison* editor just got in touch with me," Yukishiro said, furrowing his brow and turning to face Hitomi. "He told me in this mild-mannered way, 'It looks like Mr. Goto wasn't able to draw for us,' but he was checking in to see if I didn't agree that the quality is unacceptably low. The illustrator is one of our in-house animators that Koshigaya here and Mr. Goto settled on between themselves."

Yukishiro waxed apologetic. "I'm sorry. This happened because my supervision was too lax. It's my fault for not asking who'd been given that assignment."

"I did get Mr. Goto's approval," Koshigaya raised his voice to give his excuse. "He said, 'This will do,' so I simply assumed that both of you had signed off on it too."

The promotions producer handled requests for copyrighted genga, that is, made-to-order artwork for magazines and merchandising outside of the series itself. His job involved conveying, to an insanely harried crew, that there was an order for six original pieces of art for "Um, K Publishing's calendar," for instance.

Amidst all that, Koshigaya, who was in his fifth year with the company, had made a point of telling Hitomi: "Of all the titles I'm handling, *Sabaku* is my favorite." He seemed to be growing into his job enough to be able to enjoy it, and perhaps he was feeling more confident. Hitomi did once happen to overhear other staff lament, "He talks the talk, but when he isn't sure about something or can't follow up, he won't come out with it, which causes all sorts of problems."

Well, this took the cake...

The blood drained from Hitomi's face, and she felt as though she might collapse.

She really couldn't blame Yukishiro, or Koshigaya. If only there were a bit more breathing room in their schedule, things might never have reached this point. Of course, the one who was responsible for operating so close to the deadline was Hitomi himself. The magazine had requested another animation director if Goto wasn't available, but both of them had been working nonstop for days with virtually no sleep.

The piece of paper Hitomi was holding in her hands didn't seem real. Before she even noticed, she uttered, "I'll draw it."

Huh? Yukishiro and Koshigaya seemed to gasp in surprise.

"I'll do it myself." Hitomi could feel her lips trembling. "Mr.

Goto is already swamped with work for the next episode, and there isn't enough time to ask anyone else to do it over, right? I feel like if I drew it, it'd be better than what we have here at least. Please let me."

She wondered how much of an extension they could get, given that the cover art had been due yesterday. Hitomi was the type of director who did a large number of highly detailed illustrations in the course of a project, and she had drawn the protagonists any number of times while she was storyboarding. She didn't have any experience creating actual genga but thought she could produce something that was closer to the original.

"Oh, in that case..." Koshigaya had been wearing a hangdog expression, but now his face lit up. "If Ms. Saito does the drawing, I think the folks at *Animaison* will be overjoyed. I'm sure it would generate lots of buzz, too."

"Yes," Hitomi agreed.

Could she really do it? She honestly didn't know. Taking on an unfamiliar task at this point would probably be tough. For better or for worse, the cover of an anime magazine had a large impact, but just being on there wasn't enough.

That's what Hitomi was thinking when she was startled to hear a voice say emphatically, "No, that won't work." She looked up in surprise, and her eyes met Yukishiro's serious gaze. "In that case, it would be better to turn down their cover-story offer. Director Saito can't do an illustration."

"But..."

Yukishiro curtly shook his head. "Creating a genga isn't something to be taken lightly. You're a director, and you may very well be the creative force behind this anime, but that doesn't mean the art that is such an essential part of *Sabaku* belongs to you. Your job is directing, not drawing pictures."

He spoke so sternly that Hitomi winced. She was struck dumb, but Koshigaya cried, "Then what are we supposed to do?" He sounded close to tears.

"I'll figure something out," Yukishiro said. "For starters, I already negotiated a deadline extension with *Animaison*, so we have till tomorrow at noon. We'll restart from scratch." Then he looked at Hitomi and said, "It's going to be okay. Please just leave it to me."

"What do you have in mind?" she asked, having cooled down a bit from her previous fervor.

"I'm going to get in touch with Ms. Namisawa at Fine Garden," Yukishiro replied. "If she does it, there shouldn't be any complaints."

At first, neither Hitomi nor Koshigaya had any idea who Yukishiro was talking about. A moment later the penny dropped, and Hitomi remembered where she'd heard the name "Fine Garden" before. It was the studio that employed the artist who drew the god genga.

Hitomi reflected briefly on Yukishiro's use of "Ms." and "she" and asked, "So it's a woman?"

"Yes, she's called Kazuna Namisawa. Remember I promised to track her down, a while back? Well, I did." Yukishiro caught Hitomi's eye and nodded.

Yukishiro contacted Fine Garden, the genga studio located in Niigata Prefecture's Enaga City, but when he placed a rush order for the cover art and explained that he wanted to come and pick it up in person, he was told that the creator of the god genga, Kazuna Namisawa, was currently on vacation and had presumably gone back to her family home in Tokyo.

While Hitomi stood next to him, anxiously eavesdropping on the phone conversation, Yukishiro said calmly, "That's actually perfect."

"She told us she was going to meet up with a friend—she seemed really happy about that," the person on the other end objected, but Yukishiro responded in an almost coercive tone, "Please give me her cell-phone number."

Next he called Kazuna Namisawa, who, as it turned out, was in the middle of a sightseeing tour of Tokyo Skytree.

"Right now I'm on a date with s-somebody I like," she stammered. Her voice sounded timid and weak, but even so, Hitomi got the sense that the artist was doing her best to resist.

Undeterred, Yukishiro just kept saying, "I'm really sorry" in an obviously rote way. Then, ramping up the pressure, he sealed the deal by declaring, "I'll come get you right now."

Hitomi waited with her heart in her mouth, but an hour and a half later, Yukishiro returned to the Tokei Animation studio with Kazuna Namisawa in tow.

She was a petite girl with glasses. Hitomi was the last person in the world to be playing fashion police, but she couldn't help noticing that Kazuna appeared to be completely lacking in style or sophistication. Even though she'd supposedly been on a date, she didn't seem to have put any particular effort into choosing an outfit. She was casually dressed in jeans and a hoodie, and her long hair looked unkempt, carelessly caught up in a scrunchie.

Hitomi liked her right away.

When she was around the gaggle of ultra-cute voice actresses, or the glamorous producer, Kayako Arishina, Hitomi often felt overwhelmed and outshined, but this newcomer looked as if she would be easy to get along with.

Apparently Kazuna Namisawa didn't pick up on the positive thoughts because she just muttered, "I resent this." She was teary-eyed. "What's the deal here? I went to all the trouble of taking a vacation day and coming to Tokyo, and now—seriously, what's the deal anyway?"

"I can't apologize enough," Yukishiro spoke the words he had doubtless been repeating over and over in the car on the way. "We need your help."

"It really isn't fair to put me on the spot like this."

Yet, even as she said so, Kazuna reluctantly allowed herself to be guided to an unoccupied animator's desk, where she took a seat. They showed her the *Animaison* layout, and as she listened to a description of the general feel that the cover was supposed to evoke, her expression gradually morphed from tearful to solemn.

"Oh, I'm late with the introductions, but this is *Sabaku*'s director, Saito," Yukishiro introduced Hitomi.

The artist turned to look at her. Flustered, Hitomi lowered her head, while Kazuna nodded and said, *Ah*, perhaps recognizing the director from the public screening or some article. Recalling Aoi's remark—"You're like an idol now"—Hitomi braced herself, but Kazuna abruptly chuckled.

"So it's you. You're the mother of those kids."

"What?"

"I'm really grateful to you for creating Takaya, and Towa, and the rest. Although Ryu is my personal bias." Kazuna dropped her head in a respectful bow, then turned back to her desk. After taking a quick visual inventory of the art supplies, she declared, "Well, then, I'd better get to work."

To an outsider, that brief exchange might have seemed frivolous and insignificant, but it meant a great deal to Hitomi. She didn't know how to express the emotions that were coursing through her, so she simply bowed deeply, a beat behind Kazuna, and said, "Thank you very much!"

So, there was somebody in the world who talked about the characters she had created as if they were actual friends. There was someone who even called Hitomi their mother.

"Oh, one more thing," Kazuna said, turning once again to look at the rest of the group, and Yukishiro in particular. Maybe she wasn't accustomed to maintaining eye contact with people; her gaze seemed to waver a bit. "I'm willing to take on this assignment, but I do have one condition."

"And what might that be?" asked Yukishiro.

"This is a rush job on a super-tight deadline… I'm having to work at an unfamiliar desk with tools I haven't used before, so if the piece needs to be signed, please don't put my real name on it. I have a pen name for situations like this, so I'd appreciate it if you could use that instead."

Kazuna lowered her eyes apprehensively. "When I'm not able to get a good enough feel for an assignment, I request that as a favor. I also use my pen name when I'm working on too many series in a given season or when I take on an independent job that hasn't come through the company."

The practice wasn't uncommon in the anime world.

Animators were craftspeople. Their vocation featured low pay and working conditions that were far from ideal, so in the end all they really had was the pride they took in their work. Subject to time restraints in a trade where the remuneration was also limited, their dilemma was understandable when artwork that they felt they could improve on got yanked out from under their hands. No one enjoyed submitting work that they weren't satisfied with.

Hitomi was about to nod her assent to what seemed like a reasonable request, but Yukishiro said, "I'm afraid that won't be possible."

Kazuna probably hadn't expected them to refuse. Her eyes widened in surprise. "Why not? I promise I'll do this right. Keeping my name out of it shouldn't be too much to ask, considering that you practically dragged me here."

"The reason we asked you to do this job is because you're Kazuna Namisawa. You're being talked about these days as an animator who draws god genga. Did you know that?"

"What?" A look of blank astonishment crossed Kazuna's face.

"Please lend us your name."

This time it was Hitomi's turn to stare dumbfounded.

"I truly am sorry that we ruined your vacation day," Yukishiro continued. "What we want here, though, is your amazing work, of course, but also your name. For *Sabaku*'s magazine cover, we need your signature. We need you, in name and in fact, not just for the content but for the credit."

Yukishiro didn't actually get down on his knees, but he came close, bowing from the waist at a ninety-degree angle. "Please help us out," he begged.

"Ack! Just stop it, okay?" protested Kazuna, embarrassed, but Yukishiro just glanced up at her and repeated, "Please help us." He evidently didn't intend to stop bowing until she yielded.

Stunned, Hitomi just stood there watching.

Finally Kazuna exclaimed, in a voice that sounded both worn down and fed up, "Argh, fine! I get it. I get it, okay?" The moment he heard those words, Yukishiro stood up straight. This time he just said, "Thank you very much," accompanied by the slightest of bows.

"I hate this. I bet you're being sarcastic. I won't forgive you for this," Kazuna grumbled unhappily. She glared at Yukishiro through eyes once again wet with tears.

After a wait of several hours, during which Hitomi kept continually busy with tasks of her own, Kazuna Namisawa was done—and the finished drawing was indeed worthy of the accolade "god genga."

Even Hitomi, who should have been accustomed to Kazuna's art, found herself gulping. Takaya wore a gallant expression, Ryuichi's eyes brimmed with good cheer, and Towako's face was suffused with kindness. Although the *moe* quotient was subdued, the girl's soft, sweet nature was beautifully conveyed.

Thank goodness we got her to do this.

When Hitomi looked up again, the woman in question was hanging her head and still moping in the same tone as before.

"Can I go home now? It's already too late to return to Skytree, but since my trip to Tokyo turned out like this, at least let me go back to Niigata. In the future I guess I should forget about love and dreams and just hole up and lead a bleak, dreary life. You're even using my real name."

"What are you talking about? You just created something absolutely wonderful," Hitomi praised.

"You're awfully adept at flattery."

And you're entirely too modest, Hitomi wanted to shoot back, but Kazuna really seemed to believe that it wasn't anything special and refused to listen.

"I'll take it to be colorized now," Koshigaya said, picking up the genga, and Yukishiro called after his departing back, "Apologize."

Completing the basic drawing was the first step. Next, color would be applied, followed by a few other refinements, and then the picture would finally be finished.

"Give *Animaison* our best regards," Yukishiro elaborated. "Tell Mr. Yasuhara, especially, that you're sorry to death for all the inconvenience. I'll give him a call in a while, too."

"Will do," Koshigaya said. He may have had some complaints of his own, but he just nodded and walked out the door. At last, the rigmarole since that morning finally seemed to come to a close. Collapsing at her work desk with her head on her arms, Kazuna murmured with a soul-deep sigh, "I'm so tired."

Thanks to everyone's efforts, Hitomi had been able to devote the day to checking a freshly completed script and working on the storyboards. Looking back and forth between Yukishiro and Kazuna, she wondered how best to express her gratitude, when the producer's eyes met hers.

"Thank you for your hard work," he said, including Hitomi too. Then he turned his eyes to the cover of the previous issue of *Animaison*, which he had brought in for reference. Out of the blue, he asked Hitomi, "Are you thinking, 'After he was so critical of god genga'?"

"No, nothing of the sort."

Yukishiro's surmise, in fact, wasn't that far off the mark. Seeing how he'd bowed his head to Kazuna to beg, "Please lend us your name," Hitomi realized that as a producer he was all about brands and PR benefits rather than artistic skill. At this point, though, she didn't see that as a bad thing. Adorning a high-quality cover with Kazuna Namisawa's name was indeed a big deal.

A fleeting smile rippled over Yukishiro's tired face. "They go by the 'in-charge' system. At *Animaison*."

"Sorry, what?"

"For each work, editors raise their hands if they want to be in charge of it, and that's how they decide who'll take on which titles. Mr. Yasuhara, whom I introduced you to the other day, is someone who's been following your work. If the anime project an editor's been promoting lands on the cover and that issue doesn't sell, he's held responsible. After Mr. Yasuhara's given us so much support, we can't make him lose face, now, can we?"

So saying, Yukishiro heaved what sounded like a sigh of relief.

Hitomi was about to reply, but at that moment Yukishiro's cell phone rang. Without bothering to excuse himself, he picked up the call.

"Yes... Ah, sorry I haven't been in touch. I'll drop by to see you tonight, for sure." His voice echoed around the room as he headed toward the door, and the caller was probably someone with no connection to *Sabaku*. Watching the retreating back of the producer, the jealousy magnet who'd been accused of being a faithless two-timer or even three-timer, Hitomi chewed on her lower lip. She, at least, had managed to squeeze in a brief nap earlier, but it looked as though Yukishiro would be attending to someone's needs again tonight.

It was just as he'd said: thinking of *Sabaku* as hers was wrong-headed.

True, she did deserve credit for creating its universe in the first place, but she, too, was just one member of a large staff. Her title may have been "director," but she was still just a cog in the machine.

◆

The workplace tsunami finally began to recede, and the next night, Hitomi was able to return home.

Will I get there in time, for once? she thought as she headed to the Mister Donut in the station building. But no: on this day, too, the shop's lights had already been turned off, and an employee was getting ready to lower the metal shutters.

Hitomi caught a glimpse of the French crullers in the show window and fought back the impulse to implore, "Can you please sell me some, just this once?" Her mouth filling with saliva, she trudged up the stairs.

The sprawling "bed town" where she lived was dominated by row upon row of housing complexes and apartment buildings as far as the eye could see. Since the residential areas and business districts were sharply separated by rezoning, she walked home on quiet streets punctuated only occasionally by the lights of road-side vending machines.

When she arrived at her home, she let out a deep, quiet sigh.

A young boy with a knapsack on his back was crouched there, with his back to Hitomi's door, his head buried in his thighs.

"Taiyo—?" she squeaked out.

The backpack, a snazzy shade of turquoise, was soiled and covered with wrinkles as if it had seen better days. In Hitomi's time, school knapsacks came in precisely two colors—red or black—but current trends seemed to favor a vast spectrum of pastel hues. She was fairly certain that Taiyo was in fifth grade. He was outgrowing the choice of turquoise that might have suited him when he first started school.

In response to Hitomi's voice, he slowly lifted his head. As soon as she saw the boy's expression, she caught her breath.

His eyes were dark and gloomy as if he was about to burst into tears and hadn't meant to let her see his face. His bangs stuck to his pale forehead with sweat, and his thin lips were cracked and flecked with blood.

When his eyes met Hitomi's, he blinked twice in rapid succession as if in surprise. She got a sense that he was deliberately adjusting his expression to banish the darkness lurking in his eyes.

"Hello," he said.

"What's going on? Isn't your house in Building B?"

There were three separate towers in the apartment complex, and Hitomi and Taiyo's flats were in different ones. She had adopted Zakuro partly because it was touching that the boy would come to her tower as well in search of someone to care for the homeless cat.

Taiyo didn't reply. He just sat silently, with downcast eyes.

Just as Hitomi was about to ask "What's going on?" again to nudge him, Taiyo grabbed both his kneecaps as if he were trying to dig his nails into them. She couldn't help noticing the uneasy trembling of his fingers.

Hitomi lacked the adult ability to ease herself into other people's circumstances on occasions like these.

"Did you come to visit Zakuro?"

This time, her question provoked a reaction.

Abruptly lifting his head, Taiyo spoke through chapped, barely moving lips. "Would that be okay?" he asked in a faltering voice that bore no trace of the self-confidence he'd shown on previous visits.

While Hitomi was unlocking the door, Taiyo murmured something about this being one of the three evenings a week he commuted to cram school. She turned to look at the boy, whose eyes were still glued to the floor, and he added in an even smaller voice, but more articulately, "I just didn't feel like going tonight."

The solemn tone was very him.

"Would it be all right if I hung out at your place until they're closed?" he asked. "If I went home now, my mom will know I bailed."

"Sure," Hitomi said, more because she didn't know how to refuse than out of kindness. She saw Taiyo's shoulders relax in relief. There weren't even any convenience stores in the immediate area, so where else could he have gone? This was a fairly safe and peaceful area, but he was just a schoolboy.

"Did you have a fight with your friends or something?"

Asking him that question wasn't bad at all for Hitomi, but Taiyo only mumbled a terse "Mm" and cast down his eyes.

She hadn't been home much of late, so her apartment was a horrendous mess. Even if the guest was only an elementary school kid, she hated the idea of having anyone witness her negligent housekeeping.

"Zakuro!" The moment he stepped inside, the boy spotted Zakuro reclining on the sofa and made a beeline for the cat.

It had been quite a while since boy and cat had seen each other, and Hitomi was a bit worried. Zakuro, however, remained calm and unruffled even when it was enveloped in a hug by the boy, merely turning her head and glancing at him as if to say, *Oh, you're here?* Evidently content to go with the flow, she submitted to the visitor's embraces without the slightest resistance.

After his initial exclamation, Taiyo didn't say a word. He didn't offer an explanation as to why he hadn't shown up that

Sunday afternoon, after they'd agreed to meet, or why he was cutting his cram-school class tonight. He just went on playing with Zakuro, in silence.

He did give an affirmative nod when she asked if he was hungry, so she began putting together a snack from the few supplies she found. She whipped up a batch of hotcakes, minus the egg and with water substituted for milk, and although they came off the griddle looking more squashed than fluffy, once she put some jam on top and paired them with sausages and ketchup, they looked quite presentable.

It occurred to her that between the hotcakes and the Milo-brand hot chocolate, anyone would have thought she was serving breakfast, but carrying the plates, she announced, "Here you go." She and Taiyo sat down facing each other across the table, and even for such a paltry, makeshift meal, he bowed his head, brought his hands together briefly, and told her, "Thank you for the meal. This looks good."

He certainly knows his manners, Hitomi thought. She was concerned that the menu might not be enough for a fifth grader in the middle of a growth spurt, but Taiyo ate with apparent relish while saying little.

"I hope you won't mind if I do some work," she spoke to him. "I can stop anytime if you'd like to talk."

Using one hand to open a requisition form for the anime's soundtrack that she needed to return to the composer by the next morning, Hitomi continued eating her hotcake with the other. Zakuro, Taiyo, and herself maintaining their individual distance and sitting there as if each of them constituted a point of a cozy triangle felt pleasant to Hitomi.

After a while, she sensed that Taiyo was laughing. "What's funny?" she asked, looking up.

"You're supposed to be a grown-up, but you're weird," he said, his eyes softening a bit at last.

Hitomi assumed he was calling attention to her ungraciousness in shuffling papers during a meal, but then he held up his mug of Milo and asked, "How come you have a cup from *Timaj*?"

Time Magic (or "Timaj" for short) was one of Tokei Animation's showpiece anime series. An enormously popular boys' manga serialized in *Weekly Kick* magazine, *Time Magic* had been turned into an anime while Hitomi was in high school, and through the years since then it had never surrendered its place at the top of the world of anime as well as manga sales-wise. Having nailed down a Sunday-morning time slot, its base of support among children was also strong, and it was a so-called national anime.

Hitomi had never told Taiyo that her job involved anime, nor that she worked at Tokei Animation. "I just like it," she answered him simply with a little smile. In fact, she only used it because she'd received it from someone at the office as a sample.

Surely Taiyo, like any other kid in his age group, was a fan of *Time Magic*. Thinking that she wouldn't mind giving the cup to him in that case, Hitomi asked, "Do you like the series too, Taiyo?"

To her surprise, his face clouded over in a scowl. "Not really," he replied quietly, still wearing the same stiff expression and plunking the cup down on the table.

"You don't like it that much?"

"Mm-hm."

Oh well, Hitomi thought, *I guess it's just a matter of taste.* Shrugging off the exchange, she murmured, "I see," and was about to return to her paperwork when Taiyo, perhaps fearing that he'd angered her, added in a flustered tone, "Sohei and Junta are huge fans, though. They know pretty much everything about it."

Sohei and Junta were the two classmates who'd found Zakuro together with Taiyo. They didn't live in the apartment complex and went to a different elementary school, but Hitomi remembered hearing the boys explain how they'd all become friends at their cram school.

"They won't buy me manga at my house."

Ah! An intense flash filled Hitomi's head.

Averting his eyes as if in embarrassment, Taiyo went on, "I don't know anything about manga, and I don't like it. I can't join in when my friends talk about it."

Hitomi understood what he was trying to say. At the same time, she found herself unable to reply, and amidst that vexation, the truth dawned on her.

Anime was a minor hobby in the world of adults to which Hitomi belonged, but for kids in elementary school it was ultra-major, mainstream culture. Rather than being a kind of existential rescue for a small number of attentive fans, the medium entertained the most visible kids who were at the center of classroom life. You only discussed it like you owned it if you were able to record anime and had the original manga bought for you.

Suddenly, Hitomi remembered her own childhood: how she never had magic-girl wands and manga volumes bought for herself; how she couldn't even switch on the TV freely because it was a waste of electricity; how the elegant girls who talked about those things seemed to shine and to belong to a different world. In those days, ashamed that she couldn't join in when everyone in class was discussing some anime, she felt hopelessly behind the times and out of the loop. Back then, anime culture didn't give Hitomi succor, and even wounded her.

"So, Taiyo, at your house you aren't allowed to buy manga?"

"Uh-uh. Not just manga—I can't have any fun books at all."

"What about novels?"

"Nope, they're forbidden, too. When I borrow books from the library, I'll get scolded if it isn't, like, an illustrated encyclopedia. I only read the manga in my 'correspondence seminar' books, but my parents get all worked up about even those, saying, 'What are comics doing in a book for studying?'"

That struck Hitomi as rather extreme, though she could still relate to his experience. Unlike in her case, it wasn't that Taiyo's family was poor. At this rate, watching anime on TV was no doubt off limits for him as well.

Chagrin bubbled up from deep in her heart. Of course, Taiyo's parents must have their own circumstances, and views about education. Perhaps they'd managed to traipse along this far in life without ever feeling the need for a little aid and comfort from popular culture.

But even so, to Hitomi, it was simply unfathomable.

She herself was a late bloomer who only discovered anime in college, but after the worlds created by the director Tsutomu Nonozaki served as her gateway, marveling at and being rescued by that whole realm was the only life she'd known.

"If it's just TV, isn't there some way you could watch secretly, without your parents finding out? You could even watch later, on video. Unlike buying manga, you won't need any money."

Taiyo stared at Hitomi in obvious amazement.

I want him to watch it, she couldn't help thinking. *I want this boy to watch* Sabaku. *From now through the final episode, if I don't create a work that kids like him can look forward to, then what I'm doing is a lie.*

An anime for boys that wasn't adapted from a manga had a chance. Wasn't any child being able to watch the point of public airwaves? She wanted kids to enjoy her work and have it on mind.

"There's a robot anime called *Soundback* that's on every Saturday evening at five, on HBT," she told him. "It's super fun, so you should watch. Find a way somehow, okay? Even if you jump in now, you shouldn't have any trouble getting into it."

"Uhh," Taiyo said, gazing doubtfully in her direction, "Junta has the card game from that series… Is it really that good?"

"It is," Hitomi assured. She'd never made such a clear-cut declaration even at work. When she realized what she'd just done, a wry smile flitted across her face.

While she was at it, she decided to go ahead and say it, even if she might not get through to him. Taiyo's face had regained some life thanks to the cup of Milo, but under the room lights it still looked far too pale.

"Taiyo, the world we live in isn't a sensitive place."

She'd used the word "sensitive" wondering if he would understand, but he didn't seem to mind.

Labeling whatever doesn't contribute to academics as a waste, dismissing such things as having no use in real life; people who spend money in an ostentatious way getting admired; and people getting ostracized for not being into mainstream culture: this world wasn't a place that picked up on every sensitive aspect of him.

"But even so," she continued, "once in a blue moon you'll come across someone who will maybe help you, or understand you. Sometimes you might also watch something that makes you feel understood."

Relief that they'd made it in time for the *Animaison* cover suffused Hitomi now for some reason, and she lightly bit her lip.

It seemed like Taiyo couldn't yet even imagine how anime and manga might prop him up someday, and he simply nodded and grunted, "Huh."

Hitomi wasn't sure her message had gotten across. When the boy looked in her direction, however, it was to say, "I'll try and watch. Most Saturdays my mother stays out till late in the evening, so I think I can."

"Okay."

Suppressing the urge to say *Thank you*, the director exhaled quietly.

◆

Work on the final episode was already underway when *Animaison* sent someone to interview the director for a special feature.

Yukishiro had a scheduling conflict and there was no way to move his other meeting, so his boss, Negishi, took his place as Hitomi's minder.

"It seems kind of irresponsible of him not to be here for this after he's dragged you all over town for promotional purposes," Negishi remarked.

"No, no, it's fine," placated Hitomi, not sure if he was joking. "Honestly, it doesn't bother me at all."

"You really are a good kid, Ms. Saito," Negishi said to that with feeling. While he indeed was quite a bit older, his patronizing tone bothered Hitomi a little.

Just then, several minutes ahead of schedule, the magazine's editor, Yasuhara, and the writer for the article strolled into the small conference room where Hitomi and Negishi had been waiting.

"We're getting a ton of positive feedback on the cover," Yasuhara announced. "Not to mention the robot, the three protagonists look so dignified—it's really incredible. That wasn't Mr. Goto's work, was it? The mood comes through spectacularly."

"The animator who did the cover is Ms. Namisawa from Fine Garden. I'm certain she's going to become more and more popular from now on," Hitomi said.

The interview with Yasuhara, the magazine's point man for the series, proceeded at a nice tempo. Just as Yukishiro said, the editor had clearly done his homework and seemed to be familiar with all of Hitomi's previous work. Talking to him couldn't have been easier.

"I wondered how a woman would go about expressing schoolboys' desire to ride in a giant robot," he said. "To be honest, at the beginning I was a bit worried. But the actual feeling I've gotten watching the series so far is that I shouldn't be discussing you, or Ms. Namisawa, just from the viewpoint of a female sensibility. Young boys aren't the only ones who want to ride in a robot."

"It's a huge relief to hear you say that."

His words made Hitomi happy because, in the past, she'd taken part in any number of interviews that tried to frame her work as a "woman's" in a facile manner. Yasuhara's interview, which lasted for about an hour, went so smoothly from start to finish that there was really no need for Negishi to be there.

They set a date to check the galleys, and as they were saying their goodbyes, Yasuhara asked with an apologetic smile, "I don't suppose there's any hope of getting a photo of you, is there? We'd really like to include a professionally taken picture of the director, for her fans. I'm guessing there's no chance of that?"

While grateful for the tentative wording of the request, Hitomi turned it down flat. "I'm sorry. It's not that I'm opposed to showing my face, but I want the characters and the mecha to be the face of the work as much as possible."

"Yes, yes, of course. I totally understand. Sorry for putting you on the spot," the editor said embarrassedly, relenting.

After he and his colleague took their leave, Hitomi heard a tongue click behind her. "Give me a break," Negishi muttered with a sigh.

It was never a good feeling to see someone getting angry. When Hitomi turned around, Negishi spoke again, louder, so she could hear him for certain. "That was seriously out of line. Thanks to Yukishiro presenting you to the public the way he did, people end up feeling free to say stuff like that. Poor you."

There was an uncomfortable sensation in Hitomi's chest, like sand shifting. She still hadn't replied when Ouchi, the episode supervisor, waltzed into the conference room and said, "I'm hoping that went well." A story meeting was scheduled to begin shortly, in the same room.

Perhaps he had overheard the earlier exchange. Ouchi's expression went still, as though he'd noticed something, as he looked at Hitomi and Negishi in turn. "Ah. Is this about Mr. Yukishiro, by any chance?" he probed somewhat gleefully.

Pushing his long hair away from his face, he asked again, "Did something happen?" Hitomi was pretty sure she wasn't just imagining that his eyes were sparkling.

The story editor, Yuuki, and various other staff members came straggling into the conference room on Ouchi's heels. Even as they spoke to one another, their attention seemed to be on the director and the producer. Unfazed by their gazes, Negishi said, "That reporter who was here wanted a photo of Ms. Saito. It's not like she's an idol or something."

"He wasn't pushy or aggressive. It was a very matter-of-fact request, and when I refused, he understood right away," Hitomi hurriedly followed up, but they weren't listening.

"He really is a piece of work, but what else is new?" commented Ouchi. It was by now common practice among the staff to refer jokingly to Yukishiro as a problematic character. "He's such a mindless fan of any attention he can muster. And he hardly ever bothers to remember anyone's name."

"That's because he started out on the promotions side as a producer," Negishi said. "Ultimately, he's just too concerned about appearances and what other people think. His approach may get results, but when it comes to the all-important matter of content, the anime he produces seem kind of hollow, more often than not."

"Oh, you mean that one, from year before last."

"I still have no idea why it was so popular. When it comes down to it, he's still just a PR man. He doesn't get the creative side and production, at all." Negishi gave his head an exaggerated shake. From where she was sitting, Hitomi could see a missing button on his shirt—which, unlike anything Yukishiro would ever wear, was entirely devoid of flair. "His meeting today is probably the same old story," he pointed out. "He went to nail down a partnership with a magazine or something, didn't he? I sometimes wonder about the value of that type of thing, but having a lot of connections is supposed to be his strong suit or something."

"If it generates talk about our projects, where's the harm?" asked Hitomi. She saw nothing wrong with a bit of networking on behalf of a work. Yukishiro was out trying to do what he could.

But Ouchi shook his head in disagreement. "Director Saito, you're being far too kind. Like just now—don't you hate being used?"

"I never felt for a minute that I was being used."

"If that's the case, I have to say that your approach to risk management leaves something to be desired," Negishi warned. "He's just feeding on you and *Sabaku* to gild his résumé. Watch your back, director."

The man laughed and clapped her on the shoulder in an overly familiar manner as he called her by her title. She felt, ever so slightly, that she was being pushed, and that was when.

Ptunk, some cord seemed to snap inside her head.

It was no exaggeration: she heard the sound, loud and clear.

Hitomi feigned an amiable smile, but the corners of her mouth were stiff. Wearing that contrived expression, she blurted out, "Um…"

"Yes?" Negishi said.

"Before you go accusing someone of feeding on a work, why don't you guys go and make something worth feeding on?"

Wha? an inarticulate sputter leaked out of the pair—or so Hitomi imagined. In fact, all she'd perceived were two men rendered speechless gaping incredulously at her with their mouths hanging open. She couldn't hear well thanks to a weird sensation that water was boiling deep inside her ears. The scene before her eyes seemed very far away.

The other staff members paused abruptly in mid-conversation and stared in her direction.

But Hitomi went ahead. She couldn't stop herself.

"Mr. Yukishiro…" she began. And she realized that she was angry—downright furious, and unforgiving. She couldn't refrain from exploding. "He's feeding on me fine, isn't he? If my work and I become edible as a result of what he does, I haven't once felt disgruntled about any of it. When did I ever complain, or say I didn't like it?"

"No…"

"Yeah, but—"

The two men stammered, but she had no intention of letting them get a word in edgewise.

Osamu Yukishiro was her producer.

"The only person who's allowed to badmouth Mr. Yukishiro is me. No one's getting tossed about by him more than I am, and no one's been causing him more headaches than me. But that person, me, trusts him, so there's nothing anybody can do about it, is there?"

Ah, right. She could admit the truth only now that she'd put it into words: Hitomi trusted Yukishiro. More than she did anybody else.

"You say he doesn't bother remembering your name? Well, no wonder. He judged that it wasn't worth remembering. That's how he was back when I was an episode supervisor, when I was an assistant director. He'd refer to me as 'that female supervisor' or 'the kid who did the fifth episode.' I'm sure he couldn't have picked me out of a lineup, either."

Yukishiro wasn't some fanboy. It was because he was profoundly aware of the value of a name that he put the kibosh on having her handle the *Animaison* cover art as an attention-getting gimmick.

She looked straight into the face of Ouchi, who was offended that his name didn't get remembered. Nobody said a word.

"Do you know how proud I am that he remembers my name now? Can you even imagine?"

The man seemed to be at a loss for words and just stared at Hitomi, goggle-eyed.

"He calls me 'Director Saito,' and I work with him now. I feel very fortunate to be working with him. There's no reason whatsoever for anyone to 'Poor you' me."

Huffing her shoulders to take a breath, Hitomi excused herself and headed for the door. She was supposed to attend the upcoming meeting but wasn't so stouthearted as to be able to stay.

Having said what she wanted in one go, Hitomi opened the conference room door and was about to slip out, when she paused. Her heart skipped a beat.

Apparently back from his meeting, Yukishiro stood there with his briefcase in one hand. He, too, wore an expression of bug-eyed astonishment.

Maybe he'd heard every word. The thought made her gasp, and her ears instantly began to burn with embarrassment.

Voices that sounded even more awkward came from inside the room. With an *ah*, Ouchi and Negishi froze, gazing at Yukishiro. The other staff members' eyes wandered as if they didn't know what to say.

On the surface, at least, Yukishiro gave no indication of being perturbed. In a jovial voice, as if to dispel the tension in the air, he smoothly got out the words, "Ah, the whole gang."

Negishi quickly looked at the floor, but Yukishiro gave a slight bow in his direction and said, "Thank you very much for today. It was enormously helpful to have you accompany Ms. Saito for

Animaison's reporting. I'm sure I'll need to ask for your assistance again, and I'll always appreciate it."

"Uh huh," Negishi replied weakly.

After gazing at his former mentor for a moment, Yukishiro turned to face Hitomi. "Director Saito, did you give your thanks?"

"My thanks?"

"Yes. Have you thanked Mr. Negishi yet?" Yukishiro's voice sounded calm, but its tone left no room for argument. He peered into Hitomi's face anew. "You'll continue to rely on him for your work. You should express your gratitude, past and future. And if you can, thank Supervisor Ouchi as well."

Given that Ouchi, too, had been mentioned by name, further resistance was futile. If Yukishiro had told Hitomi to apologize, she'd have balked at listening to him, but she found herself replying, "Yes."

You could lose your temper, but your workplace wasn't going away today, or tomorrow. Her colleagues giving her the cold shoulder wouldn't serve Hitomi in any way going forward.

"Thank you very much, Mr. Negishi, Mr. Ouchi," she said, bowing her head. Before they had a chance to respond, Yukishiro preempted in a bright voice, "So, let's get started, shall we?"

As if nothing had happened, he took his seat at the conference table, pulled a sheaf of papers out of his briefcase, and lined them up in a row.

"We're heading into the final episode. Let's make it good," he said, making eye contact with the whole room.

After that day's brainstorming session, the story editor sidled up to Hitomi and said, "You were awesome."

Not wanting to revisit the topic of her childish temper tantrum, she just replied, "Oh, really?"

At this, Yuuki cackled, heartily entertained. "I like Mr. Yukishiro a lot, too," he added. "People badmouth him a lot, but I've put my trust in you and him. So there's nothing anybody can do about it, is there?"

Hitomi wondered if being lumped together with Yukishiro

meant that people badmouthed her a lot, too. She almost started to feel despondent but put on a serene front and parried, "Thank you very much."

It was as if the words she'd shoved at Taiyo had come bouncing back at her.

The world we live in isn't a sensitive place.

For that very reason, the joy of meeting a kindred soul was immense.

◆

When Hitomi said, "Would you like to join me for tea?" she fully expected her invitation to be turned down.

For one thing, they were busy people, and for another, probably the last thing they wanted to see during their time off was the face of somebody from work. Hitomi had steeled herself for rejection, but when she showed up at the appointed place in front of the train station, there they were, not even conversing and perched on either end of a bench with enough space between them for another person to sit down.

Aoi, in sunglasses and a hat, was smoking a cigarette, while Anju was staring down at the book she was holding.

"Sorry I'm late."

Hitomi had had trouble getting away from work, and when she arrived, five minutes late, the two women raised their faces in unison. Aoi looked at Hitomi with cool, aloof eyes then stubbed out her cigarette in a pocket ashtray and stood up. Uncertainly, but sounding very much like a voice actress, Anju articulated a clear "Hello~" and bobbed her head.

This suburban station, best known for the large hospital perched up high on a mountaintop, was a forty-five-minute train ride from the center of Tokyo. To those in the know, this "holy site" was the setting for *Mermaid Nurses*, the work that became a breakout vehicle for Aoi and the other girls.

Earlier that week, when Hitomi issued the invitation to tea and gave the name of this station, Aoi and Anju chorused, "But why there?"

Hitomi replied, "I'd like to walk the pilgrimage course for *Mermaid Nurses*. Won't you please be my guides?"

Of course, she didn't make that request with the intention of poking fun at their roots, much less of making them feel like fools. She wasn't trying to curry favor with the actresses, either.

Not too long after Chiharu Oji's recommendation, Hitomi had looked at the blogs and Twitter accounts of Aoi and Anju. After a deep dive into the archives, she ended up wishing she'd read all those posts sooner.

Though bundled together as "idol actresses," their origins, tastes, and stances toward work all differed. Oji had said that he checked out the women's unfiltered voices along with their performances, and Hitomi finally saw why.

Both Aoi and Anju cherished the projects they'd been involved with. What they were reading after being chosen for major roles in *Mermaid Nurses*. Their thoughts about the comments and advice they received from staff and fans. Their interactions with the local government that hyped the so-called pilgrimage. The blogs were a compilation of that history. The fan events continued even after they recorded the final episode of *Mermaid Nurses*, with Anju posting any number of entries about how happy she felt to meet up with her fellow cast members.

How all five of them having cared deeply about *Mermaid Nurses* was their treasure. How proud she felt that the same members were together again working on *Sabaku*.

"In the anime, the five characters often got together at this coffee shop," Aoi remarked as they walked, "so the owner gives us the royal treatment whenever we visit. Shall we? They might be surprised if we turn up out of the blue, but the employees recognize us, too."

"Today is meant to be a private outing, so we could skip it if you're not in the mood. It's a rare day off for all of us, and I imagine you must both be tired." Hitomi had already made a selfish request and dragged two popular voice actresses out to the suburbs.

Anju let out a small laugh then, for the first time. "We… The thing is," she said, "Aoi is definitely popular, but the rest of us aren't all that busy. True, we're very proud of the work we did on *Mermaid Nurses*, but without any significant roles outside of it, people say that we're just clinging to a past project, and we know it."

Her frank declaration took Hitomi by surprise.

"Um, I'm sorry about the other day, I really am," Anju offered a low-key apology. "Since we were always together, including for events, whenever I had to do more retakes than the other girls, I constantly worried how I might be the only dud in the group. On set, too, and not just for *Sabaku*, I burst into tears a lot around that time."

"Hey, Anju, isn't that a little bit too much information? Stop with the negative talk, okay? It's probably awkward for Ms. Saito, for starters," Aoi chided, expelling a sigh.

"No," Hitomi mumbled, seized by regrets of her own. The two young women were much more thoughtful than she'd assumed. New stars were born overnight and summarily snuffed out, the turnover was brutal, but they understood the severity of their situation perfectly well.

Even their voices sounded different here on a sloping road in the airy suburbs than they did in a closed studio. "We probably won't be able to go inside…" warned Aoi. They started up the mountain road leading to the hospital to get a look at the exterior, at least. The scenery was just like the anime's worldview, with the said route coming into sight as soon as they passed through the shopping district.

"You probably haven't seen *Mermaid Nurses*, but this road—"

"I have," Hitomi interrupted.

She'd read their blogs and their tweets and then finally watched every episode as if she were carefully receiving what they held dear. Some of the supporting VAs gave the impression that it was nothing more than a job to them, but the five stars' passion seemed genuine—whether they were acting their parts well or poorly or somewhere in between. Their raw will and determination to value their gig and turn it into an accomplishment came through in their heated performances.

Aoi nodded with satisfaction at Hitomi's reply and said, "Back in the days when the last episode was broadcast, this road was teeming with fans who made a special trip here to take souvenir photos. But the events ran their course too, and after some time, it seems the pilgrimages here came to be seen as a fail and also as a cautionary tale."

"Why is that?"

"It was too glib, apparently. The town even rolled out merchandise with *moe* designs from the very outset and just hustled too much, so now it's totally become a thing of the past. Of course, our star power wasn't up to it, either."

There was a softness in Aoi's eyes that Hitomi had never seen in the studio's dubbing booth. Shafts of sunlight filtered down through the canopy of fresh green foliage. As the hospital came into sight, the façade of the major medical institution was quite overwhelming.

Next to Hitomi, Anju asked, "Are you ladies ready to tackle a bento?" with a merry laugh.

Eyeing the large basket and thermos that Anju held, Aoi muttered, "Yikes, you really outdid yourself." Then she told Hitomi, "When we have fan events, Anju bakes cookies from scratch and passes them out to every single person. You'd think she just buys them at some bakery, but nope, they're really homemade."

"Well, I have tons of free time."

"In that case, study acting or take voice lessons. Or watch some anime."

"I watch them, okay? But today, since we were coming here, I just thought there wouldn't be many decent restaurants..."

There was a little park behind the hospital, and at this time—noon on a weekday—it was almost deserted. Beyond the swings was a vast, grass-covered, gently sloping hill where Anju spread out the picnic cloth she'd brought and opened the basket. When

Hitomi accepted the rice balls, each of which came neatly encased in plastic wrap, she was moved to see that the surface was carefully sprinkled with salt. The salmon filling, too, had the taste of fish that's been properly grilled at home with the perfect degree of scorching.

"Delicious," praised Hitomi, and Anju's cheeks almost seemed to melt as she said, "Yay."

They had a clear view of the town below the mountain where the "mermaid nurses" had seen action. As she gazed down, Hitomi hesitated a little before ultimately concluding that she wasn't able to choose her words like a skillful negotiator. She quietly put down the rice ball she'd been munching on.

"I've been meaning to apologize to both of you."

Unexpectedly, this declaration drew blank looks from her companions, who exchanged a glance and slowly swiveled their heads to stare at Hitomi.

"Anju, even if I was just trying to give you some direction, I could have put things better. And Aoi, you ended up having an unpleasant experience at the public screening."

"Omigod, you've been stewing about that?"

It was Aoi who'd spoken. Looking surprised for real, she continued in her candid tone, "That was me just being petty. Please don't give it another thought. I was jealous that they were sending a car to pick you up, that's all."

"I guess I'm simply not used to people 'just being petty' like that. I don't have many female friends, either."

"Ah, I can see that," Aoi remarked. Her straightforwardness actually felt pleasant, so when Anju cautioned, "Hey, Aoi," in a whisper, Hitomi only smiled awkwardly and said, "It's fine, it's fine."

"You can be pretty vexing, Director Saito, when someone else is in a foul mood," Aoi continued. "If you just left them alone, they'd snap out of it on their own, but it's painfully clear that you feel like you have to do something about it."

"Ah, true, there, you might be right," Anju agreed haltingly and a bit sheepishly. "I could tell that you were trying to apologize to me, but I was to blame. That made it hard to say sorry."

"You've been busy, haven't you? These last few days. In spite of that, you were nice enough to invite us on this outing today," thanked Aoi.

Nearly buckling under her unwavering gaze, Hitomi blurted out, "Um, so, I read your blogs."

"Our blogs?"

"Aoi, you really, really like anime, don't you?"

Classics, recent releases, works unrelated to her job—she'd seen far more of them than Hitomi, and among them was *Butterfly*, directed by Tsutomu Nonozaki, whom Hitomi had wished to surpass.

Aoi wrote unsparingly about the dilemma of working up the fortitude to watch a favorite director's work when she'd flubbed the audition or never got invited to any. It was from an honest place that she described how she gnashed her teeth upon finding Oji's *Ryder* highly enjoyable.

Hitomi came to understand why the two actresses were so popular.

It made her want to work with them, going back to square one and beginning anew, from here.

"I do like anime," replied Aoi, once again casually. "We might have that in common, director. I love anime." She narrowed her eyes against the downpour of dazzling light. Then, as if to hide her embarrassment, she placed one hand on the brim of her hat and murmured, "I'm kinda worried about getting sunburned."

"What are some fun anime from the old days?"

Anju's easygoing voice seemed to slip smoothly over the green grass, and to fall into place. As though embarrassed by her own ignorance, she stuck out her tongue and mumbled, "I'll study harder."

Hitomi blinked, taken aback by the stereotypically idol-like gesture, but she felt as though a huge weight had been lifted from her shoulders.

Thank goodness, she thought. *I can count on these kids.*

◆

The preorder numbers for the first DVD were due to be announced just before the team buckled down to work on the final episode.

Hitomi was staying overnight at the studio more and more even as she felt the suspense so acutely it was almost palpable. Having lined up three folding chairs and laid down across them for a brief catnap, she opened her eyes a while later to stumble back to work, but her wrists felt strangely cold.

Huh? When she tried to stand up, baffled, her legs, which should have made contact with the floor, wobbled. There was virtually no sensation of stepping, as if the floor had disappeared and given way to a dark, gaping pit. She cringed. Her body felt completely devoid of strength.

This can't be good. Even as Hitomi formed that thought, her vision suddenly went all blurry and then, as if her body were being pulled from behind by some unseen force, she toppled over backward. The folding chairs she'd been using as a makeshift bed collapsed, and the metallic noise seemed to fill and reverberate in the core of her brain.

"What happened?!" she heard someone shout, running up to her, and when she tried to reply, "It's nothing—I'm fine," no sound came out of her mouth. She felt like throwing up, and she thought with perfect objectivity, *Oh, I'm anemic.* It was just that she hadn't been eating properly. A minor problem, easily sorted. But when she tried to explain this, the words didn't come out in a comprehensible way. Smarting like mad from having been open for countless hours, her eyes would barely stay open despite her short nap.

Just then, Yukishiro walked in. Seeing Hitomi lying prone on the floor, he gasped, then announced, "We're going to the hospital. You look pale." He helped her to her feet and gave her his shoulder to lean on.

"But," Hitomi was able to utter.

Yukishiro gave her a piercing look and said, "Please take a break until tomorrow."

They went to an internal medicine clinic near the studio, where Hitomi was diagnosed with anemia, given an injection via an iron-colored syringe with a needle as thick as an IV's, and allowed to leave. She thought Yukishiro would simply put her in a taxi and send her home, but to her surprise they went to the studio's parking garage, where he bundled her into his BMW instead.

"My house is a lot closer than yours," he explained.

"But—"

"I'll be going back to the studio, but I called ahead a while ago and my wife is at home, so please just rest up there for a while."

His tone brooked no argument, and Hitomi closed her eyes in the backseat of the swaying car. There were any number of more appropriate things to say, but she heard herself remark, "You must be a real workaholic to even live so close to the office."

She could sense him forming a grim smile as he drove. "Some people claim that their work quality suffers," he told her, "without the last train at night as a stopping place. Me, I want to work until the very last minute and still go home and sleep in bed."

When they arrived at the tall apartment building, Yukishiro's wife was waiting for them in the basement parking garage. Hitomi had often heard her described as a beauty who used to work as a flight attendant, but this was the first time they'd met.

Mrs. Yukishiro's softly waved, shoulder-length hair was a shiny black with no trace of henna; she wore an understated V-necked cardigan; and she didn't look like a woman who was the very picture of femininity, contrary to Hitomi's expectations. For the moment, that came as a relief.

"Are you all right?" the lady asked, running up to the car and offering her shoulder.

Hitomi wasn't wearing any makeup and hadn't had a chance to take a shower, much less a bath, since the day before yesterday, and when she remembered that, her boss's wife seeing her face was kind of depressing.

"You don't look well at all. I'll bet Yukishiro pushed you too hard," the woman said, glaring at the producer. Hearing her refer to him just by his last name, rather than calling him some version of "my husband" or even by his first name, made a favorable impression on Hitomi.

"By the way, we didn't meet at a mixer or anything," Yukishiro told Hitomi without being asked as he delivered her to his wife. "There seem to be some rumors floating around, but we've known each other since we were just students, long before she became a flight attendant. It's not like I used my travel-agency connections to attend one mixer after another."

"I really hadn't heard anything that specific," Hitomi demurred, though what reached her ears might have been similar.

Mrs. Yukishiro responded to the exchange with a look of incredulity. "What on earth are you jabbering about at a time like this?" she asked her husband. "First of all, she needs to get some rest, and then I'll find out what she'd like to eat."

Leaning on the woman's shoulder, Hitomi noticed a soft fragrance. It didn't smell like perfume, but more like fabric softener and a sunny day, which Hitomi found relaxing, and no sooner than she did, sleep engulfed her as if she'd fainted.

When she opened her eyes next, her hostess asked, "I made some rice porridge. Do you feel like eating?" Taking in Mrs. Yukishiro now, Hitomi saw how exceptionally slender and pretty she was. Her almond-shaped eyes gave her face an old-fashioned cast. *She's like those actresses who play men's roles at Takarazuka*, Hitomi mused, and the realization made Yukishiro's wife seem even cooler and more attractive. She was also different from the VA idols that Hitomi had encountered.

Getting up sluggishly, Hitomi went to take a bath. She heard the mistress of the house say, "I'll leave a change of clothes here for you," and Hitomi got dressed in an outfit belonging to her boss's wife, as daunting as that was.

In a room whose black-and-white décor reminded her of something in a model home, Hitomi gradually began to get a sense of the Yukishiros' daily life, and felt weird about it. *So this is what he comes home to.*

The borrowed shirt and jeans were both a trifle long on Hitomi, but she was relieved to find that the size difference wasn't really noticeable. Using a brush, she tamed her tangled hair. When she glanced at the mirror over the washbasin, she saw that her cheeks had regained most of their natural rosiness.

Making her way through the lingering steam, she made her way down the hall and found herself back in the living room. The air was filled with an assortment of delicious aromas. Mrs. Yukishiro shepherded Hitomi to a seat at the dining table, where a home-cooked meal was already laid out, and explained, "Yukishiro will be coming home for dinner this evening, so please join us. Help yourself to whatever seems appealing."

"Thank you so much. I'm really sorry for imposing on you like this."

"Oh, no, not at all. This happens quite a bit, so please don't worry about it. Though I have to say, this is the first time he's ever brought home a female colleague." Her bemused smile didn't seem to be lying.

Perhaps it was partly to take care of his staff in this manner that the producer lived so close to the studio. The thought suddenly made Hitomi feel bad all over again for letting herself succumb to their goodwill and be spoiled.

Shortly after, Yukishiro came home for dinner.

"How are you feeling?" he asked, and Hitomi responded, "I'm ready to go back to work."

"That's not what I was trying to get out of you," Yukishiro said with a sigh.

A bowl of the same rice porridge had been placed in front of his seat across from Hitomi's, and they began to eat. The tablecloth, the soy sauce decanter, and the dishes and spoons which appeared to have been carefully selected one by one, showed almost dizzyingly good taste, and Hitomi couldn't help thinking that Yukishiro was just the same at home.

Perhaps out of consideration, his wife, who had been busy in the open-plan kitchen adjoining the dining room, had casually vanished from sight before Hitomi even noticed.

As they sat facing each other silently dining on the porridge and a tofu salad, Yukishiro asked all of a sudden, "How soon are you hoping to leave Tokei Animation after you're done with *Sabaku*?"

A chill ran through Hitomi from head to toe. She raised her head with a sharp jerk and looked at Yukishiro. He quietly laid down his spoon, and there was no trace of either anger or sorrow in his eyes as he stared back at Hitomi.

"So you knew?" she rasped.

"I do. Never underestimate my social network or the speed at which information reaches me."

At last, Yukishiro smiled. *He really isn't mad, then*—Hitomi felt so relieved for now that she almost started shaking.

Many directors who started their careers at Tokei Animation ended up leaving the company. Whether it was Tsutomu Nonozaki, whom Hitomi revered, or Chiharu Oji, for better or worse a big company like Tokei Animation tried to keep its employees on a tight leash. The salary structure was rigid, too, and many directors quit on less than amicable terms.

The year before last, when Hitomi hadn't been serving as director on an anime series, her savings had dwindled by nearly a million yen over a twelve-month span. She liked to send her mother some money from time to time and was still in the process of repaying her student loans.

Despite the common lament that animators, including genga artists, had trouble making ends meet, the opposite was true at Tokei.

Perhaps because it was an established, venerable shop, in-house artists were guaranteed a certain level of income. It was the supervisors, who did the "invisible" work, who got the short end of the stick and didn't get paid much. Without the compensation that kicked in for heading a title, directorial staff were forced to raid their savings, no matter how many endless scenario meetings they held.

"You'll be going over to Director Nonozaki's Office Lagoon,

is that right?"

"...Yes," Hitomi nodded.

Her role model, Director Nonozaki, was making a new feature film that would follow up on *Butterfly*. Hitomi had been invited to join the directing team shortly before planning began for *Sabaku*.

Since she wasn't at a company that allowed freelance gigs, participating in Nonozaki's project meant leaving Tokei. It would be a lie to say that she hadn't agonized over it, but in the end, she'd made up her mind.

"When you go to work for Nonozaki, will it be as an assistant director?"

"No. The discussion hasn't really gotten to that point yet, so I might be an untitled supervisor."

"It's really a waste, you know," Yukishiro said in a clear, ringing voice. His face was solemn. Hitomi had thought her decision was set in stone, but as she looked into Yukishiro's eyes, her resolve began to waver for the first time in a while. The pullback was so powerful that she felt momentarily disoriented.

"You've already reached a point where a project can go forward if you just attach your name to it," the producer told her. "And now, with *Sabaku* bolstering your reputation, you could easily direct a feature film on the scale of *Butterfly* yourself."

"I don't care if I'm not credited. I'm ready to dive into it as a freelancer for the time being to learn as much as I can from working with Mr. Nonozaki."

"Would I be wasting my breath if I tried to stop you?"

"I'm sorry, but I've made up my mind."

Hitomi gave her head a firm shake.

Without averting her gaze, she said, "I can never fully express how grateful I am to you for making my name mean something. I will never, ever forget the debt I owe you."

"Understood," Yukishiro noted with a nod. "Well, I guess that's that." Then his expression softened. "I won't try to stop you, but I do have one condition. I hope you'll find a way to satisfy it."

"What might it be?"

"Please leave Tokei Animation on amicable terms."

Hitomi looked up, and Yukishiro continued in an admonishing tone.

"Whether it's Director Nonozaki or Director Oji, when people quit the company under exceedingly unpleasant circumstances, it becomes impossible for me, as a Tokei Animation employee, to ever call on them. Please, find a way to depart amicably and peacefully and avoid getting into a fight with the brass—so that we might continue to work together."

"You'd still be willing to work with me?" asked Hitomi, making no attempt to conceal her surprise.

Yukishiro's lips formed a displeased, straight line before morphing into an unmistakable grimace. "Why not? You're free to go wherever you want, but can't we still talk about your future? When I asked you a while ago whether you had any friends, this is what I was getting at. Didn't you just go and make these decisions all alone, about quitting, and going to Lagoon, without discussing them with anyone? You work until you literally drop, and you don't have any friends you can just chill out with."

"Actually, I do have friends. I just made some the other day."

Hitomi had offered to give a guided tour of a section of the apartment towers where she lived when Aoi had professed her love for *Butterfly* and begged the director. Anju, just so she could come too, was going to borrow the DVDs of the entire series from her castmate.

"Well, fine, if that's the case." Yukishiro sounded slightly incredulous, but he let out a long breath and smiled. "You have a very real talent," he said. "Ratings, money matters, sales figures—people who do care about the numbers can take the summit. I love your stance, like the way you announced openly that you were aiming for anime supremacy."

Hearing this straight from the mouth of her producer, Hitomi felt as if an electric current had shot through her body from the tips of her toes to the top of her head. While she was stunned into silence, Yukishiro went on.

"Plus, you have a very strong sense of responsibility. No

matter how lavishly people praise someone as a genius, no matter how handsome he might be, I utterly disdain anyone who'd run away from work. I will never, ever approve of anything such a person creates even if it draws raves."

When Yukishiro pouted hatefully at that point like he couldn't get over it, Hitomi felt like suggesting that the genius issue aside, maybe handsome should have nothing to do with it. She held her tongue because she enjoyed the rant.

Being praised felt good.

"Please learn and absorb as much as you can," Yukishiro continued, reverting to a solemn expression. "It may be tedious for you, but after *Sabaku* ends and until you leave the company, I'll try to teach you as many things as possible, like how to deal with sponsors, those pesky numbers, and so on. I hope you'll continue to think kindly of Tokei Animation, now and in the future."

"I hope you'll do the same for me."

Even as she spoke her concise response, her breath was catching in her throat. Her chest hurt like it was getting crushed.

She hadn't expected this.

She hadn't expected to be told all this, when she was leaving.

"Thank you very much," she said, pouring as much of her heart into those words as she could. How vexing that her voice sounded a bit tearful and distorted talking to plain old Yukishiro.

"Let's win it all," she also said.

The producer nodded decisively and assured, "Of course."

◆

It was only for Amazon, but the online preorder numbers for the first volume were in, so he was bringing them over, Yukishiro contacted Hitomi a week later with the news.

She tried to parse his tone of voice, but it merely sounded as stiff, excited, or placid as she wanted it to be. Just a phone call should have sufficed, but he was bothering to come see her near where she lived. That seemed significant, and her mind rapidly grew alert even though she'd just woken up.

Even some staff members had felt that it would be over the top, but they'd included all the characters in the artwork for the first volume of the DVD. The animation director, Goto, had been asked not to compromise one bit, and he'd come through with a small masterpiece.

Yukishiro was already waiting in the park in front of Hitomi's building where they'd arranged to meet, and he muttered, "Huh, it's true that there isn't much of anything around here."

He gazed up at the tranquil apartment complex with interest. Compared to the glorious high-rise where he lived, the general ambience must have been different, indeed. Children on bicycles crossed the street in front of the park, calling out, "Hey, wait!"

Sabaku wasn't just for adults, and that was one of its strongest points. Unlike anime airing in the dead of night, it didn't need to appeal exclusively to grown-ups. If they could attract younger viewers, they would win, hence the five p.m. Saturday slot—that was what Hitomi and Yukishiro had said from the outset. It also meant that if the series somehow flopped, the damage from negative online campaigns would be immeasurable, but fortunately, the sales figures for the robots and other merchandise were "winning," as the industry would put it.

Sabaku only had three more episodes to air before the finale, and now, at last, a major secret about the protagonists had been revealed.

Sounds sealed in a box.

The robot transformed when some sound was fed into the Singing Stone. In the first episode, when they entered into a contract with the stone, they were asked: "Can you pledge your sound, your voice, and your song to me?"

Without hesitation the hero cried, "I'll give you anything!"

What came to light in the previous episode was that the commitment was real.

Every time a sound was sealed and the robot transformed, the sound in question vanished from the world—not from that of

Takaya and Ryuichi, who rode in the robot, but from the heroine Towako's, one by one, unbeknownst to anyone else.

One sound had been disappearing from her world after every battle. She realized this but kept it secret. If she told them, they might not be able to keep fighting.

"Why didn't you say anything?" demanded Takaya, but the sound that was confined in the stone that episode was his voice, and she could only shake her head in confusion after the battle at his silent cry.

She couldn't hear it, not anymore.

Neither someone's desperate knocking nor the cracking ice heralding spring, nor the voice of her beloved Takaya.

The remaining number of foes and robot transformations... Since the advance publicity had made it widely known that four mecha designers had designed three robots each, even adult fans were speculating online, "Two more sounds are disappearing from Towako's world for sure, right? How's that gonna work?"

Were they still going to fight when Towako was being robbed of sounds? Takaya and the others had to choose now.

"Even if I won't hear a thing for the rest of my life, even if every single sound disappears from my world, I won't regret this past year."

The other day, at the dubbing session for the final episode, Aoi, who played Towako, had given her all delivering that line, bravely facing forward even as tears streamed down her face. Suppressing her sobs, she'd said, "Towako is so strong, it won't do for me to be crying all over the place."

Anju and the other kids had rallied around to support Aoi.

Hitomi had heard it said that when art and reality aligned, a god anime was born. She didn't know whether that was true, but Towako's line perfectly expressed her own feelings. *Whatever I might end up losing, I absolutely won't regret these days when I was able to create* Sabaku. *Even if I burned out here and now, I'd be happy.*

"Oh, that reminds me—I hope you'll enjoy this," Yukishiro said, pulling something out of his briefcase. The moment she saw the bag, Hitomi gave a gasp of recognition.

It was all she could do not to shriek in delight.

"I really should have brought you something from downtown," Yukishiro apologized, "but it wasn't until I was driving past the station that I realized I was empty-handed."

It was a bag from Mister Donut, whose sugary treats Hitomi had been craving for the past few months. Taking the bag and opening it, she couldn't help letting out a long, "Aaah."

She'd never brought it up with him, and yet—the bag contained a French cruller and a Pon de Ring. These, these were what she'd been dying for.

"Thank you so much…"

She was too moved to express her gratitude with any words beyond those simple ones. She sat with the opened bag in front of her, overcome with emotion. Yukishiro peered into her face and asked, "Is something the matter? Don't you like Mister Donut?" She responded with an extra-vehement shake of her head. The sugar-glazed coating's sweet scent swirled around her face.

"And here's this," Yukishiro said, holding out a sheet of paper with the results.

As she balanced the Mister Donut bag on her knees and took hold of the folded piece of paper, Hitomi did feel nervous. Yukishiro's poker-faced expression offered no hints at all.

"These are just the results from Amazon. I'm glad for you."

What the producer's words signified hit her at the exact same moment she unfolded the piece of paper. Just as she tried to confirm the numbers and titles, however, she noticed some familiar faces passing by in front of the park. It was Taiyo and his cram school pals.

No sooner than she thought, *Ah*, she noticed that they were holding *Sabaku* robots. Each was a different color and shape. The scene was her exact ideal: the three boys together, holding toys with varying designs.

In that instant, a rush of tremulous joy rose from her ankles and coursed up past her back, and she felt like she needed nothing else.

God, she thought.

She didn't know whom to thank. Anyone would do, really, and thus: *oh God.*

She cast her eyes on the chart. Clapping one hand over her face, she reached out with the other to grab the hem of Yukishiro's shirt.

Uhhh, a small, muffled voice escaped her first, and then came a loud, unabashed sob.

In her heart, she shouted with her whole being.

God Almighty.

Thank you for giving me the gift of anime.

CHAPTER 3:

"THE ARMY ANT & THE CIVIL SERVANT"

"Why did you get into the anime business?" people would ask her from time to time. Sometimes they added a rude quasi-reproach, something along the lines of: "But it doesn't pay well, and the work is notoriously hard, and it's kind of dark and exploitative—isn't it?"

Kazuna would just smile cheerfully and murmur something noncommittal like "I guess that's true," even when she felt the urge to scoff, "Really? Is that your angle?" (Well, she would never say anything of the sort out loud.)

You'll never get rich. The work is tough. There's tons of pressure, blah blah blah. She really had no desire to talk to the kind of people who asked such superficial questions—or who needed to have everything explained to them in the most elementary terms.

I love drawing pictures.

And I want to get better at it. Much, much better.

It didn't matter if the work was difficult and stressful, or if she hardly earned enough to live on. She didn't care if she had to live her days as a geek girl or a female otaku, with no semblance of a "real" life.

She was never going to stand by and let anyone make fun of her job.

◆

Kazuna Namisawa was fast asleep at her desk, with her head tucked under her arms, when a voice assailed her from above. "Choose," it demanded.

Her glasses had slipped down her nose while she was napping. Pushing them back into place, she groggily raised her head and said, "Wha—?"

"You can have first choice of the genga you want to take charge of. Then you can go back to sleep." A piece of paper was shoved under her eyes.

Niigata Prefecture, Enaga City. The proper pronunciation of the city's name was "Enaga," but in the mouths of longtime residents, it sounded more like "Erunaga." The local accent had a slow, stretched-out timbre that somehow seemed to mirror the area itself. Enaga City was home to the independent anime studio known as Fine Garden, where the office layout featured rows of desks partitioned off to create cubicles.

The piece of paper that had been thrust into Kazuna's face by one of the senior animators was tickling her forehead, and she was still so drowsy that there seemed to be a wispy white cataract veiling her field of vision. "Okay, okay," she mumbled, answering in a cheeky way that might have been plucked from an anime script. She probably wouldn't have gotten away with such an informal response at some offices, but it was perfectly acceptable at Fine Garden, where the atmosphere was relaxed but also laidback. Without raising her body from the desk, Kazuna picked up the piece of paper and, still in that indecorous position, took a look. It was a recent order in the form of a work-distribution chart for genga.

The client was a currently airing anime called *Summer Lounge:*

Sepia Girls (*Sepia Girls* for short), and the order was for the ninth episode. The chart was divided into blocks showing how many frames each artist would be responsible for.

Kazuna, still half asleep, said, "I'll be happy to choose after Fujitani." She handed the chart back to Seki, the chief animator. "I'm not all that attached to any of the characters in *Sepia Girls*, and I know you and Fujitani probably have certain characters you'd like to draw. I'm fine with taking whatever's left over."

Of course, even within the same anime, the genga-drawing assignments ranged from "relatively simple" to "labor intensive." At Fine Garden, there was a quota system for the number of sheets each animator handled in a month. To ensure an equal division of labor, every artist worked on a "combo set" that balanced the more complicated, time-consuming genga with less difficult pictures that would be faster and easier to draw.

The twelve in-house animators would get together and talk things over, then choose their own assignment packets in a process not unlike the grab-bag promotions in department stores. In addition to the basic criteria of degree of difficulty plus complexity, there was another, more subjective factor: when a certain anime was particularly popular around the studio, special combo sets would be created by character. The more coveted characters would be combined with others that weren't so highly desired. It was a positive development for an anime when its characters inspired animators to say, "I really want to draw this kid."

"Are you sure? Thanks, Namisawa."

"No worries," Kazuna said. "I think Riko and Akina will come to life much more vividly if they're drawn by someone who's genuinely fond of them."

Sepia Girls was what's commonly known as a *moe bishojo* anime.

Set at a seaside town in the near future, the story featured a group of high school girls and chronicled their summertime adventures at the local yacht club. For the last few rounds, animators who had been assigned characters had also handled the close-ups of the dolphin logo that adorned the yacht's sails, which naturally took less time to complete. Kazuna had already drawn that dolphin more times than she could count.

"Well, since you insist, I'll take Rikorin," Seki said, using the fans' nickname for the character. "But to be honest, I think Riko's fans would be happier if you drew her. It's great to see you getting a rep for god genga." As he spoke, Seki rubbed one hand over the unshaven stubble on his chin. The colorful, gaudily patterned aloha shirt he wore seemed far too bright to Kazuna's newly awakened eyes.

Hearing the words "god genga" was almost suffocating, like someone was actually choking her throat, but Kazuna managed to respond, "Not at all. Look, I've been telling you this all along, right? People are always craving something new to talk about, so they just choose some random person's work to make a fuss about. They happened to notice my drawings, for some reason, but it could just as well have been anyone else's."

"But recently you've gotten quite a few work orders where projects asked for you directly, haven't you? That's awesome. At this rate, maybe someone will offer you an animation director gig next season."

"Well, I don't know about that."

In the old days, only the cream-of-the-crop animators ever got the opportunity to advance to the position of animation director. However, thanks to the anime industry's practice of throwing a massive number of people at series that were cranked out in rapid succession, the demand for talent had outstripped the supply. These days, when it wasn't unusual for genga artists to be promoted to animation director before their skills were entirely up to that challenge, hearing your name being bandied about for the job wasn't necessarily an occasion for unalloyed rejoicing. Not only that, but the production credits at the end of recent anime often listed as many as ten names under the "animation director" section.

It was all very well for Seki to label rumors of Kazuna's possible promotion as "awesome," but he was surely aware of the circumstances. Depending on the project, being tapped to direct the animation on a series was an honor but also like some form of calumny.

Fine Garden, the enterprise Kazuna was affiliated with, had originally been a sub-department of a larger anime company called Studio Milky Candy. That company eventually ran into financial difficulties, and when things reached the point where its anime productions weren't generating enough profit to sustain the business, an employee named Koizumi gathered a number of animators from Milky Candy's creative department and struck out on his own. He was now the president of Fine Garden Studio, and Kazuna's boss. The town of Enaga City, in Niigata Prefecture, was his hometown. When he invited Kazuna to join the mass exodus from Milky Candy, he told her, "There are hot springs, and it's somewhat of a tourist destination, too."

Kazuna had never even heard of Enaga City before, but after arriving she quickly realized that "somewhat" was, in fact, the most pertinent part of that description. The area had apparently once been a popular hot-spring resort, but that was many years ago, before the bullet train came along and made it so much easier for travelers to get to other prefectures instead. After that, the tourist trade fell off to almost nothing. In this small town, where the bulk of the population was either aging or moving away, there was an abundance of unoccupied buildings, including abandoned schools and phased-out hospitals.

When President Koizumi moved back home to open Fine Garden Studio, he engaged in some successful negotiations with the local government and was able to rent some of those unused buildings for a song. The studio's main offices, where Kazuna and her colleagues worked, had once been an intermediate school, while the employees' dormitory was a converted sake brewery. The conversion process must have been minimal, because a faint aroma of sweet malted rice sometimes wafted into Kazuna's room, reminding her of sake and soy sauce.

It was often said that working as an animator was a hardscrabble, hand-to-mouth existence, but Fine Garden only charged a modest maintenance fee for the dormitory lodgings, so the rent was practically free, and utilities were relatively inexpensive as well. Word got around about the new venture, which the media labeled "the local, community-based anime company," and requests for information and interviews with the president poured in, not just from anime magazines but from hard-news outlets. Koizumi had gone back to his rural roots to start a business while he was still in his thirties and had succeeded in short order. That compelling story line, along with his youth and personable, soft-spoken demeanor, soon made Fine Garden's president a media favorite and resulted in a great deal of positive attention.

From Kazuna's point of view, Koizumi's friendly, gentle affect sometimes appeared a bit too soft to the point where he sometimes seemed gay. It certainly made him recognizable, however, and the media loved that.

He often said, "Even though we pay essentially the same wages as companies based in Tokyo, our employees will end up with significantly more disposable income than their urban counterparts." Kazuna believed her boss, but one time, when a TV station sent a crew to report on the Fine Garden success story and came poking around the dormitory with their cameras, she really didn't know what to say.

After that program aired, apparently some people said, "So this company sets up shop way out in the sticks and keeps their employees close at hand while also saving on labor costs. Tell me, how is that any different from moving your factory to Southeast Asia?" It made Kazuna feel all the more uncomfortable.

She was currently drawing genga, but when she first started working in the business, as an animator, her drawings generally paid between 180 yen and 1,000 yen apiece. However, back then she only received the higher rate for occasional large-scale work to be shown in theaters; she couldn't hope for assignments like that on a regular basis, so her average pay was around 250 yen per piece. This worked out to an income of somewhere south of 100,000 a month.

Nonetheless, Kazuna wanted nothing more than to be a full-fledged animator who got to draw pictures all day, and she poured all her efforts into meeting her monthly quotas. When all was said and done, she thought of herself as nothing more than an army ant in an industry that relied on large headcounts.

The directors and producers who created highly lauded anime got to go around talking about the works' technical artistry, cultural significance, and underlying philosophies. If those people at the vanguard of the profession were like the queens in an anthill, then she was a worker ant toiling diligently away to carry food to the communal nest. She had gotten into this line of work of her own free will, but no one could keep at it without first accepting that fact.

I really don't have any complaints, she thought. *I love to draw, and it's probably the only thing I can do.*

There was never much conversation around the Fine Garden office. Everyone just worked away drawing their pictures, and the hours passed in a steady, matter-of-fact way.

The animators had gone independent together, and by no means were they not on good terms. Strangers in a strange land, they went out drinking occasionally as a group, but since they saw each other constantly at work and at their digs, talking to each other simply out of consideration was something they did less and less in the five years since their arrival.

Seki had finished making the rounds with the work-distribution list, and now he sat down next to Kazuna.

"So how was it?" he asked. "Tokyo, I mean. I heard from our prez that while you were trying to enjoy your hard-earned holiday, apparently the producer of *Sabaku* tracked you down and put you to work? That's awesome. If it was for *Sabaku*, does that mean the producer was Yukishiro, by any chance?"

"Why do you have to bring that up?" Kazuna asked back without so much as a glance in Seki's direction, her eyes on her computer screen and keyboard. The truth was, she didn't want to be reminded of that incident. Even now, thinking about it made her feel like crying.

Her tone of voice must have been chillier than she intended. Seki hurriedly shrugged his shoulders and said, "Ah, okay. If you don't want to talk about it, that's fine." Kazuna was grateful for his perceptive reading of her reply and for seeing that they ought to steer clear of each other's sore spots.

"About the work on *Sepia Girls*," Seki went on, "well, the rest of us will be doing the lion's share of that, so when orders come in for *Sabaku*, I'd like to ask you to handle those as your first priority. Thanks in advance. Oh, by the way, you really did us proud, but I have to admit I was surprised. I had no idea you loved the local stuff so much."

Local stuff?

When Kazuna stared up at Seki with narrowed eyes, wondering what on earth he was talking about, he evidently misinterpreted her bewildered expression as a scowl. Looking away of his own accord, he immediately turned to the junior animator on his other side and asked her, "Have you seen the poster in front of the station? I hear they're planning to put some more up inside, too. It's really amazing." Kazuna still had no idea what Seki was talking about.

Jamming her earphones over her ears, she blocked out the voices of her colleagues. After cueing up the soundtrack from one of her favorite movies, she cranked up the volume but only high enough so that no one else would hear the music.

◆

Kazuna's "hard-earned holiday" in Tokyo—was a date.

The other person was someone she'd liked for quite a while. She'd often dreamed of going out with him someday, but this was the first time they had ever been together, just the two of them. She was well aware, almost to the point of being reluctant to use the word "date," that her romantic feelings were almost certainly unreciprocated. For Kazuna, even admitting the truth to herself—"I like him"—took quite a fair amount of courage.

If he finds out I like him, it'll probably just seem like a nuisance, she thought. In the past, with other crushes, even if her heart pounded a mile a minute, no matter how attractive that person seemed, Kazuna would end up realizing that her feelings were only puppy love or something akin to a *moe* crush on an anime character, not the kind of grown-up attraction a person living fully in the real world—a "realie"—might feel toward someone of the opposite sex.

Chattering about boys and fashion had never been Kazuna's thing; she wasn't good at that kind of banter, so she had always avoided those topics. And now here she was: twenty-six years old, and she still didn't have a boyfriend.

Watching anime, reading manga, playing games. She had enjoyed those solitary pastimes, perhaps too much, and felt timid and awkward around people who were easily able to socialize and find actual three-dimensional boyfriends.

While born and raised in the original downtown district of Tokyo, Kazuna never had very much in common with any of her classmates who got together to have fun at the traditional local festivals. Ever since she began working and then having moved up to Niigata, she hadn't kept in touch with a single acquaintance from the old days. According to her mother, back home in Tokyo, most of Kazuna's former schoolmates were already getting married and having children.

"Really? Are you serious?" asked Kazuna in a voice pitched higher than normal, but her mother just said, in an exasperated tone, "I don't know why you're acting so surprised. Those are just the things normal people do when they get to be your age."

Kazuna passed her days at the studio, keeping busy drawing pictures one by one, then, later, happily spotting her own work in various anime. That kind of talk about marriage and babies was just too dazzling to think about, and too distant from her own reality.

Sometimes she felt envious of people who were getting to live out those "normal" scenarios, while other times she just felt mildly disgruntled.

That idea of life, and being satisfied with it and forging ahead with it, had made feel Kazuna envious, discontented, and, truth be told, a bit frightened for a very long time. She was fully aware that there seemed to be no place in that world for someone like her.

Getting back to her date: the man she met was called Tetsuya Osato, and he worked in the anime industry, broadly understood.

He was only twenty-nine but already headed the planning department for Blue Open Toy, one of the leading producers of anime figures. He was cool-looking and fashionable, complete with a pair of jauntily framed spectacles. Kazuna loved men who wore glasses, so that was a major plus.

Osato had initially struck Kazuna as the type of person who would be right at home living a completely fulfilling real life, in the real world, among other well-adjusted people who were just like him. So she was floored when, at their first meeting, he had looked at her with sparkling eyes and asked, "Are you *the* Namisawa?"

Osato happened to be in Niigata on other business and had apparently gotten in touch with President Koizumi and arranged to stop by to check out the studio. Unlike the big companies capable of producing anime from start to finish, Fine Garden was a relatively small specialty shop that only undertook animations and original drawings. The fact that someone like Osato would go out of his way to drop in on such a minor enterprise was unusual in itself, but as it turned out, he was a hard-core anime fan and had seen a lot of the work Kazuna had done. Perhaps because he wasn't involved in the day-to-day creation of anime, but rather with the peripheral business of manufacturing and marketing figures, he retained a wide-eyed, innocent enthusiasm for the medium that seemed to have been lost by a lot of people on the production side.

"I'm a huge fan of your work," Osato told Kazuna that first day, looking into her face, and she had to admit—that didn't feel bad at all. On the contrary, it made her so happy that she didn't sleep a wink that night.

I'm so glad I've been doing this work, she thought.

When Osato learned that Kazuna's family home was in To-kyo, he said, "Really?" in a jubilant tone and added, "If you go home for a visit and have some extra time, we should meet up and grab a drink." Right then and there, he handed Kazuna one of the business cards that had his cell-phone number on it. Seeing how the handwritten numerals were so tidy and precise that they might have been printed out digitally, Kazuna felt an oddly tight sensation in her chest.

After Osato left, Kazuna found herself craving even a tiny morsel of additional information about him. Jumping online and searching his name, she was amazed to learn that apart from his day job as director of planning for Blue Open Toy, he had also designed a number of figures on his own. And there they were, displayed on her computer screen: a cute female character strik-ing a slightly sexy pose, a hero from one of the popular "fighting manga" in his trademark stance. As Kazuna scrolled through the images, her heart beating faster than usual, she even came upon some of Osato's figures that were based on characters from anime she'd been involved in. When she realized that she shared a con-nection with him through the same characters, she found herself squirming in her chair with a kind of exquisite agony. She had never experienced anything like it in her life, and it threw her for a loop.

Maybe it was because Osato somehow didn't seem raw and had the look of an anime character himself. For the first time, an actual human being was the object of an infatuation and fondness that Kazuna had, until now, only felt toward anime characters. Seeing Osato's work made her want to draw more, and more, and more. Looking at the figures he'd created, with their lively, lifelike expressions, made her vow to draw even better than before.

Convinced that the things he'd said were just social niceties, she couldn't bring herself to text or call him, but soon after his de-parture, he sent her an email. Her eyes were glued to the message.

To be honest, lately, ever since you started getting famous as a genga goddess, my mind hasn't been at ease
for a single day. Half of me is saying, "Her work has always been great, but people are only catching on now?"
while the other half is lamenting, "Oh, drat, I thought
Namisawa's work belonged to me, and me alone." It's
totally selfish, kind of like feeling lonely when you've
been following a certain pop star from the very beginning and then they suddenly get their big break, and
all you can do is wish them luck. (Sorry, I'm not trying
to creep you out.) Anyway, long story short, I'm really
glad I met you yesterday.

I'll try contacting him, Kazuna thought.

She needed to draw around thirty cuts a month to meet her
quota, so taking even one day off would make her fall behind, but
she didn't want to combine seeing Osato with one of her regularly
scheduled trips home. Rather, she thought it would be better to go
down to Tokyo for the express purpose of getting together with
him. Of course, she realized that his feelings toward her probably
weren't the same as the usual boy-meets-girl type of romantic interest. She thought she really did understand.

Yet, so uncharacteristically of her, she'd allowed herself to
dream.

A boyfriend who could talk about anime and whose eyes
didn't glaze over when she talked about her work. Great-looking,
moreover, and not only a lover of figures but a creator of them.
They were so well matched—who else could she talk to so freely
about work and hobbies? Nobody, that's who. She would never
meet anyone else so perfectly right.

*If the day ever comes when I can go out with someone like
that, I will happily die*, Kazuna thought. She could have gone on
dreamily fantasizing forever.

Ever since she'd resigned herself to the fact that she would
never be a realie, she had decided that it was foolish for someone like her to make an effort to improve her appearance (and

besides, she was sure the harder she tried, the more pathetic she would look). She deliberately distanced herself from any thoughts about makeup or fashion trends, and from then on she felt too embarrassed to do anything but dress in a way that suggested she had discarded her feminine side entirely. Jeans and a T-shirt: that was her uniform. One time she bought a new, horizontally striped T-shirt and later, when she noticed a faint line of pink lurking amid the other colors, she actually hesitated to wear it. That was the bravura extent to which she rejected any traces of femininity. She believed that if she had any charm or appeal at all, it resided solely in her work, and she clung to that thought as a last bastion of hope.

Being loved by someone like this eccentric guy who's totally crazy about my work is the only hope for me.

And so...

Her despair that day was very deep, indeed.

The Tokyo Skytree complex was located in the same general area where Kazuna grew up, but she had never once visited it. Construction had started right around the time when she was moving to Niigata, and she'd seen the completed structure from afar on her occasional visits home, but never from up close.

"Isn't Skytree enormously tall?" she wrote offhandedly in an email to Osato, and he responded, "Would you like to go and take a look?" He explained that he often went to Skytree on business because there was a mall called Solamachi ("Skytown") next door, and one of the shops there was selling Blue Open Toy's figures.

When the appointed day finally arrived, Kazuna didn't want to give the impression that she'd made a special effort, so as she waited for Osato in front of the station she was dressed as if for any old day at the studio, in jeans, a T-shirt, and a hoodie. She sometimes wished she could go back to that day and slap herself, hard. "Go to one of the boutiques in Solamachi and buy yourself a whole new outfit!" she wanted to yell at her past self.

But no, even if she had done something like that, the outcome would still have been the same. Worse, actually, because she would surely have felt even more pitiful. When she pictured herself decked out in an unbecomingly fashionable outfit, it seemed so ludicrous that she felt like bursting into tears, even though that scenario only existed in her imagination.

Like, how did all those girls running around town manage to look so put-together, when their crisply pleated skirts seemed likely to become irreparably crumpled after a single wearing? How did they know how many bracelets to wear, or where each bangle should be placed? When did all the stylish girls learn such things—and who taught them? Kazuna really didn't have a clue.

When Osato appeared, he didn't show any signs of being put off by Kazuna's get-up—or maybe he simply didn't care what she chose to wear, one way or the other. He laughed pleasantly and said, "I'm really grateful to you for spending some of your valuable time with me," then beamed at her.

Osato was dressed in a polo shirt embellished with checked fabric around the inside of the collar, and his trousers (more formal than jeans, Kazuna noted) were short enough to show his ankles at the bottom. A brown-and-pink-striped belt encircled his waist, and the whole effect led Kazuna to conclude ruefully that not only did he have an excellent fashion sense, but on this day he looked cuter than she did, by far.

He'd gone ahead and bought tickets for both of them before Kazuna arrived. When she protested, he said, "No worries. Since I'm with you, I can expense it, and my company will reimburse me." And then he laughed, showing all his teeth.

As they were walking toward the elevator that would take them to the observation deck, Kazuna happened to glance at Osato's willowy arm, which looked exactly like the appendages she'd drawn on any number of impossibly handsome anime heroes. Almost trembling, she thought, *Is it really okay for me to be so happy?* She had rarely experienced this kind of attraction to a real-world man, and she felt like she wouldn't mind coming into contact with so slender an arm.

But then…

As Kazuna was dreamily floating along, half in a trance, Osato stopped suddenly and muttered, "Oh!" Then, staring straight ahead, he called out, "Ms. Marino!"

Kazuna glanced up, and caught her breath in surprise.

An unbelievably beautiful woman was standing in front of them.

"Oh, Osato," she said. While Kazuna watched, frozen in mid-step, the woman turned to look directly at Osato.

She's just like Princess Kaguya. That was Kazuna's first thought.

The woman's long, lustrous black hair was layered shorter on the sides, and she really did bear an uncanny resemblance to the fairy-tale princess as seen in a hundred picture books. Kazuna couldn't even begin to figure out what was going on above the woman's almond-shaped eyes; she only knew that she'd never before seen such perfect double-folded lids, with creases so deep they could have been carved by a sculptor.

And her costume! A T-shirt of the genre known in Japan as "rock taste"—that is, rock 'n' roll style, with silver letters on a black background. A pink scarf patterned with skulls. High-heeled red shoes decorated with tiny cats.

On second thought, Kazuna revised her initial impression, *she's a Dark Kaguya.*

Feeling overwhelmed by her presence, Kazuna looked away. Her heart was pounding to the point of discomfort, and she suddenly felt terribly out of place.

Meanwhile, Osato was approaching the woman, and Kazuna had no choice but to follow timidly in his wake.

"What are you doing here?" he asked. "Were you off today?"

"No, I'm going into work early this evening. One of my friends is doing a fashion exhibit near here."

Kazuna's heart was beating even faster now. She wished she could pull out her smartphone and pretend to be looking at the screen, but the timing would have been weird and unnatural. As the pair continued to talk, taking no notice of Kazuna, she couldn't help thinking that they looked stylish and made a good picture.

Then she recalled something Osato had said, a few moments

earlier: "Ms. Marino." *Wait,* Kazuna thought, *did he just address that woman as "Marino"?*

She was seized by an unpleasant premonition, and as she was sheepishly glancing from one of them to the other, and back again, Osato finally remembered her presence and said, "Oh, sorry, Ms. Namisawa. I'll introduce you now."

He gestured toward the stunning stranger. "This is Blue Open Toy's figure-sculptor, Kaede Marino."

Kazuna's mind went completely blank.

The newly introduced Marino was looking at her curiously, seemingly wondering who on earth she might be, but said, "Hello."

Kazuna was shocked to the core. Kaede Marino was Bluto's number-one sculptor. No, not just Bluto. Right now, Marino was the most popular sculptor in the entire animation-figure industry. So many makers of anime and video games wanted her to create their figures that she was booked up several years in advance.

Kazuna knew Marino by reputation. In fact, the figure that she kept on her desk at the studio—that of the main character of an anime supremacy-nabbing title from last year—had been created by Kaede Marino.

All this time Kazuna had been thinking of that figure as *"his* work." She had never dreamed that the artist might be a woman.

Moreover...

Kazuna was so dumbfounded that she completely forgot her manners and just stood staring at the other woman, mesmerized by her exquisite face and spectacular appearance. So this was Marino: this living doll, this impeccably turned-out fashionista. The startling new influx of information whirled around and around in Kazuna's head. In a matter of seconds, Osato had been transformed from someone who seemed to be right next to her into a person who was very far away, with a multitude of hurdles in between.

"I know," Kazuna barely managed to reply. "I know. I even have one of your figures." Her lips seemed to have gone numb, and she hardly even felt like she'd spoken those words.

Without so much as a token smile, Marino nodded her head almost imperceptibly and said, "Oh, really? Thank you."

So Dark Kaguya was a cool beauty, too. The fact that Marino hadn't bothered to muster up the requisite smile threw Kazuna's mind into an even greater uproar of insecurity.

Out of the blue, she remembered an anime she had watched a few years earlier set in the research lab of a university's science department.

In one scene, a female character who was clearly meant to be perceived as neither cute nor pretty was gazing at the male protagonists with upturned eyes and begging them to give her some chores to do. And then the narrator's voice kicked in, saying jauntily, "There aren't very many girls in STEM fields, so the ones who aren't that attractive can still have an active social life!"

Kazuna's objective impression had been that it was an insulting way to portray a female character that bordered on discrimination and sexual harassment. Yet, the scene had also given her a ray of hope.

In a profession with few women, I have a chance, too.

But now...

"Are you guys on a date? Sorry for interrupting," Marino said in a frivolous tone, without altering the expression on her lovely face the tiniest bit.

To which Osato hastily replied, "No way, no way," repeating himself and shaking his head.

So even in our male-dominated field, regardless of the skill level, there are gorgeous women.

Whatever it was that had been swelling in her heart abruptly lost its footing, tilted crazily to one side, and collapsed into a heap.

She mustered up an awkward smile to conceal her shock. Osato went on.

"No, it absolutely isn't a date. Calling it that would be rude to Ms. Namisawa. Oh, Ms. Marino, this is Kazuna Namisawa. Have you heard of Fine Garden, up in Niigata? It's the up-and-coming anime studio that handled almost all of the art in *Raia* and the movie version of *Hikimori*. And Ms. Namisawa here is doing phenomenally well these days, too—getting a lot of attention for drawing god genga."

Marino responded with a muted "Huh," which made it clear that she didn't know anything about Fine Garden, much less about Kazuna's own work.

Not having heard of a particular staff artist at a small studio best known for being reliable was hardly a crime.

The genga for an anime, however intricate and charming they might be, could never be stand-alone works of art. For any production, they were no more than one part of a whole, and the anime ultimately belonged to the director.

No matter how hot a topic she became online or how many people praised her as a creator of god genga, Kazuna had consciously tried not to let it get to her head. But when she saw that Marino didn't have the foggiest idea who she was, Kazuna realized that she had allowed herself to be swayed by the attention, after all. Her shoulders felt like they were on fire at that mortifying insight.

"Sorry 'bout interrupting you guys," Marino said to Osato, in a more familiar tone than before. Was this the way she normally spoke to him? Kazuna felt as if her heart was being torn apart by this evidence of intimacy.

Marino turned to bow shallowly in Kazuna's direction, and at that moment the fateful call came in. It was from Yukishiro, one of the top producers at Tokei Animation.

Kazuna's phone was usually silent aside from occasional message alerts. When it began to ring shrilly and didn't stop, Kazuna thought impulsively, *Saved by the bell.* Sadly enough, that was what she thought.

Covering her mouth, she went over to stand close to the wall. "Right now I'm on a date with s-somebody I like," she mumbled in a voice that was almost a whisper. It wasn't until much later that she had second thoughts about having picked up a call from an unknown number without a moment's hesitation—or about not having turned off her phone while on a date.

"We'd like to ask you to draw the original *Sabaku* genga for

Animaison." That was the request, but why her? And why today, when she was in the middle of a long-awaited day off? None of it made any sense, and Kazuna seethed with resentment. However, on that day, her heart was already in shreds. She should have just refused the job offer and ended the call, but instead she ended up telling Osato about it.

Holding her phone away from her and cupping her hand over the speaker, she explained, "There seems to be some kind of issue having to do with the genga for *Sabaku*. They want me to draw the cover art for *Animaison*, and it sounds like they're in a big rush."

Upon hearing this, Osato took a quick, sharp breath.

Kazuna had shared this new development lightly, without taking the time to think things through, and she realized that it had been an impetuous and self-aggrandizing thing to do. She was basically flaunting her own status, saying, *See? I'm a pretty hot commodity, and people value my work so much that they'll go to the trouble of tracking me down on my day off, all the way from Niigata.* No doubt about it: that had clearly been the subtext, and the intent.

She expected Osato's face to light up again, as it had on their first meeting, and as a serious anime fan himself, she thought he might say, "Wow, Tokei Animation asked for you directly?" or "Whoa, *Animaison*?!" But instead of reflecting the childlike jubilation Kazuna was hoping for, Osato's face abruptly took on a severe, almost grim expression that left her feeling thoroughly befuddled.

Talking unnaturally fast, she continued, "Oh, no worries, I'm going to refuse. I mean, I'm taking today off, and—"

"Surely you aren't planning to turn them down?" interrupted Osato.

"Huh?"

There was a reproachful undertone in her companion's voice. Their eyes met. "Of course, you ought to go. I'm sorry, I messed things up by inviting you here today. Will you be heading to Tokei Animation, then? It's actually closer by subway than by taxi. Do you know where to change trains? Or actually, I can go with you, if you like."

"Oh, no, that's—" Kazuna rushed to shake her head, then blurted out, "The producer was saying that he'll come and pick me up, but..."

"Would that producer be Mr. Yukishiro, by any chance?"

"Um..." The name she'd seen on the screen when she picked up the call hadn't rung any bells, but it was possible the producer was someone well known. When she didn't elaborate further, Osato nodded to himself.

"Please tell the person on the phone that we'll be waiting in front of Kinshicho station. I'll take you that far. The less time you lose, the better."

"Oh, oh, okay."

In the blink of an eye, the date somehow came to an end before it got started. Kazuna glumly pondered this turn of events as she headed toward the JR station in a taxi, with Osato by her side. Through the window of the cab she could see Skytree, its sightseeing summit still unscaled, receding ever further into the distance.

After they arrived at Kinshicho station Osato said, "Since you'll be going to work from here, we'd better get something into your stomach," and led her into a family-style chain restaurant. They sat down facing each other and ate a meal together, and that, at least, seemed a little bit like a romantic outing.

The conversation wasn't exactly lively, though.

When Yukishiro met them in front of the station, Osato bowed and said, "Ah, just as I thought, it's Mr. Yukishiro."

The producer smiled and said to Kazuna, in a sly echo of Osato's remark, "Ah, so you were with our friend from Bluto?"

Yukishiro was tall, lean, and well dressed, and you couldn't say he wasn't good-looking. But when she first saw him standing there, waving at her, Kazuna let out a long, silent sigh and thought, *I'd much rather look at Osato's nicely bespectacled face, any day, than at a guy with just an aura of handsomeness.*

While Yukishiro went to fetch his car, Osato said, "I'm really sorry our time today was so short. Let's try again sometime." He extended his arm for a handshake and, timorously, Kazuna got to fulfill the desire that had consumed her since morning at last: to feel that beautiful, long-fingered hand in hers. As their palms touched, she didn't dare raise her head.

Osato's voice turned serious. "It's really amazing that Yukishiro singled you out for this assignment," he said. "I respect you a lot, Ms. Namisawa."

"Oh, really?" she responded lamely, in a voice that was more like a long exhalation, just as Yukishiro's car pulled up.

She climbed in, and as the car drove away she couldn't bring herself to look back for one last glimpse of Osato. If he'd still been standing there, seeing them off, that would have been great. But what if he had already rushed off to get back to the office as quickly as possible? Or what if he was busy fiddling with his phone, exchanging texts with Kaede Marino? Kazuna really, really despised herself for indulging in that kind of futile, gratuitous speculation, but she couldn't help it.

Yukishiro started the conversational ball rolling. "So, did you get together with our friend from Bluto for work?"

Kazuna had clearly mentioned on the phone that she was with someone she liked, but perhaps the producer had already forgotten? *Ah,* she thought, *there really are people like this in the world—the kind of insincere opportunist who doesn't give anything a second thought unless he has a personal interest in it.* She felt disgusted, but at the same time that selective forgetfulness seemed like a saving grace.

"Oh, well, you know," she said vaguely, but on reflection she thought Yukishiro's assessment might not be that far from the truth. For Osato, maybe meeting up with her today had just been part of his job. Maybe Osato, who had unambiguously urged her to take this job, was just another workaholic otaku. Beyond her genga-drawing persona, he didn't see anything in Kazuna at all. Being respected wasn't the same as being liked or loved—not even close.

Okay, she admitted to herself. *I loved, and I lost.* She felt like having a good cry, but she couldn't very well do that with

Yukishiro sitting next to her. Her infatuation had been so minor, so insignificant, that she couldn't even weep over its demise in front of another person.

When they arrived at Tokei Animation's headquarters, Kazuna was still in the depths of despair. She felt as though she'd passed the point of caring about anything, and she wasn't even certain that she would be able to draw a decent picture in her current state. And then, while she was mired in that dark frame of mind, she met Hitomi Saito for the first time.

The moment they were introduced, Kazuna's mood seemed to grow brighter, and calmer. It was almost uncanny.

Oh, it's this person, she thought, feeling immediately at ease, and she had a clear vision of what she wanted to create, right then and there. As if for the first time since she'd started working on *Sabaku*, she had a solid sense of her role in the process: she understood whom she was drawing for, and why.

"So it's you. You're the mother of those kids."

"What?"

"I'm really grateful to you for creating Takaya, and Towa, and the rest. Although Ryu is my personal bias."

Director Saito was almost as diminutively built and scruffily dressed as Kazuna. Saito evidently hadn't had a full night's sleep in recent memory, and the proof was on plain display under her eyes, in the form of dark smudges that she made no attempt to conceal. Her clothing was rumpled, and while the sweatpants she wore weren't entirely unbecoming, they were undeniably dowdy.

In the first moments after they met, Kazuna suddenly understood the connection between this anime director and the pictures she herself gave birth to at her desk in Niigata. *I'm an army ant*, she thought, *but this person isn't just someone who feasts on the food I carry back to the nest. She is truly my queen ant. I'm so glad I had a chance to meet her.*

Kazuna's mind, which only moments earlier had felt crumpled and creased, was now as calm as a windless sea. *I can draw*, she thought. *Those kids this director gave birth to? I'm ready to draw them right now.*

"Well, then, I'd better get to work," she said. She felt extremely fortunate that this assignment had landed in her lap when her feelings were at such a low ebb. Having a fixed task to tackle was a lifesaver, and having that task be something she wanted to do was icing on the cake.

That day's fateful encounter eventually led to her receiving any number of commissions for posters and important genga for *Sabaku*.

More than anything that day, though, it was some words from Yukishiro that gave her the will to carry on.

"For *Sabaku*'s magazine cover, we need your signature."

She'd been told that her art meant something.

Some days later, she received a cheery email from Osato as if nothing had happened. No—for him, in fact "nothing had happened" at all. Kazuna had just wishfully misread the signals.

> I saw the *Animaison* cover. It gave me goosebumps. Later, when I thought about the fact that we'd been hanging out together just a few hours before you created that genga, I felt honored, as one of your fans. One of these days, by all means, let's give Skytree another try!

Even though Kazuna had once liked the figure Marino designed so much that she displayed it atop her cubicle, now she took it down and stashed it in her locker. She sat perpendicular to the desk with her face resting in one hand, staring at the parade of robust, unclouded words in the email on her computer screen. Finally, without composing a reply, she quietly closed the browser window.

And then, straightening her posture, she went back to drawing genga.

◆

Kazuna's stomping grounds in Enaga City were limited to the studio, the company dorm, a large shopping center near her digs, and a branch of the Tsutaya bookstore chain located alongside the national route. The Enaga train station was at the far end of town, on the south side.

Kazuna seldom went all the way there since it was nearly half an hour away by car. In addition, the train from Enaga to Niigata City made all stops, and that trip took a full hour.

The whole area in front of Enaga station was lined with more or less deserted souvenir shops and hot-spring inns. There was also a cozy shopping street where the town's young people congregated, but Kazuna felt no connection whatsoever to the center of Enaga City.

She hadn't been so accustomed to urban life that she could say she'd grown tired of it, but in the five years since moving up from Tokyo, she'd carved out her own way of life in Enaga. She mostly just went back and forth between the dorm and the studio, but she occasionally patronized the branch of the Tully's Coffee chain in the nearby shopping center. There was also a movie theater, although it only showed popular Hollywood blockbusters and family-friendly anime.

When the pressures of work drove her to her wits' end, Kazuna also enjoyed cycling along the wide, sprawling roads picturesquely lined with rice paddies that went on and on, as far as the eye could see. The area was quite safe, so it was good for cycling at night.

There were hardly any streetlights so most of the time the road was dark, but one late-summer night, gazing up at the festival fireworks blossoming high in the sky quite far away, Kazuna had startled herself by exclaiming, "Beautiful!" She realized then, for the first time, that when people were impressed they really did say something out loud, even if there was no one around to hear.

Kazuna had grown up in Tokyo's old downtown district, and she expected to find country living inconvenient, but she actually felt so comfortable in this rural area that at first it seemed strange, even to her. But when she thought about it, maybe it wasn't that surprising, after all. Whether she was in Tokyo or Enaga, as long as there was a cinema, a bookstore, and a café or family restaurant where she could take an occasional break, that was all she needed.

She was completely at ease with the fact that aside from her work colleagues, she didn't know a soul in the area. Fine Garden's president, Koizumi, was originally from Enaga, and he had been actively networking among the local business community since returning home. Kazuna, however, hadn't made a single friend or even a nodding acquaintance during the five years she'd lived in the area. Fortunately, that suited her just fine.

As she walked from the company dorm to the bus stop, her eyes were dazzled by the brilliant expanse of sky, with its scattering of flat, thin clouds.

She was heading for the train station, by bus, because she needed to buy a bullet train ticket for her next trip home to Tokyo. Her cousin, who was a year older, was getting married, and Kazuna had been invited to the reception.

Summer was fast approaching, and while this hot-spring area was relatively deserted, there were still some tourists milling around at the station. This year, for some reason, the visitors seemed to be predominantly young people, and when Kazuna passed one such group, she averted her eyes and stared at the ground to avoid making eye contact.

She joined the queue at the ticket window, and when she faced straight ahead, she glimpsed a flash of vivid color out of the corner of her eye. At the same moment, she overheard a conversation.

"Thank you very much! We're really grateful that you put it up in such a prime spot."

"Oh, no worries. You can put one up at Soba-An, too—that's my family's noodle restaurant. I'll give my grandmother a heads up."

"Would that really be okay?" The young, enthusiastic male voice rang out across the station. "Thank you so, so much!"

Idly, Kazuna turned her head and glanced in the direction of that vibrant voice—and then her face froze.

In the most prominent place in the station, facing the ticket gates, a poster had been mounted.

It was Kazuna's own genga for *Sabaku.*

Her eyes widened, and she gasped. A sound—"Heowaa?"—that she herself couldn't decipher escaped from her mouth. *Hey. Hey!* Confused, shaken, she stared at the poster and blinked repeatedly.

She gave up her place in the ticket line and took a step toward the poster. Her eyes hadn't played a trick on her: it really was her art.

The poster read:

Welcome to Enaga City—the "Soundback" Town

Play It! Find the Stone's Sounds

In one corner of the poster, along with a credit for Tokei Animation, were the words "Tourism Section, Enaga City, Niigata Prefecture," along with information about a stamp rally built around *Soundback: The Singing Stone,* to be held at various locations around the city from the following month on.

It was broad daylight, but the world went dark before Kazuna's eyes. Her drawing—her own unmistakable renditions of Takaya, Towako, and Ryuichi—was on display in her adopted hometown's desolate train station.

Looking gallant and brave, the three protagonists were standing proudly in front of the "Sabaku" robot, and unrolling in the background was the same road between the rice paddies that Kazuna walked on a regular basis. There was an elementary school she remembered having seen, as well, tucked away toward the back of the picture, on the right.

These were the streets, fields, and houses of Enaga City.

But why? she wondered, her heart pounding a mile a minute. She had no idea.

The genga that Kazuna drew basically consisted of the characters and sometimes the robot. In some cases the background artist would draw the robot, but at any rate, when she finished drawing, Kazuna had only the vaguest sense of the backdrop to be added. For this piece, she had only heard that it would be a country landscape but had never seen the completed piece. After she submitted her genga, they were worked on by color designers and colorists, subcontracted out for some finishing touches, and redelivered to Tokei Animation. Adding the background art was the next step after that.

Oh, now I get it. As she stood staring at the poster, Kazuna realized for the first time what its purpose was. The local tourism bureau was trying to turn the area into an anime-pilgrimage destination.

She flashed back to Seki's remark in the studio, and finally understood what he meant. In the course of talking about focusing on orders for *Sabaku*, he'd said, "I was surprised. I had no idea you were so into the local stuff." In other words, the kind of thing shown in this poster.

Kazuna had watched *Sabaku* sporadically, as the episodes aired. As a busy animator, it would have been nearly impossible for her to follow every anime she'd had a hand in creating. To be sure, there had been times when she'd noticed that the backgrounds in *Sabaku* looked very similar to the scenery around this mountain town. However, there were rice fields all over the country, so it could have been almost anywhere. She'd never dreamed that the show had actually used this area as a location.

Her initial reaction, when her mind began to work again, was intense denial: *Give it a break.*

Her plan for today, after buying the train ticket, had been to stop by Tully's Coffee, where she'd buy something to drink and read a modest bit of the latest installment of one of her favorite manga that Amazon had just delivered. After that she intended to go back to the studio and work until late at night. At the very least she'd hoped to be able to savor these priceless moments of free time...

It was supposed to be an oasis of stress-free tranquility, during which she could forget about anything related to work, or anime, but now she'd been subjected to this humiliation play. A wave of heat suffused her cheeks and then engulfed her whole face.

It isn't anything to put up in such a slow and peaceful place.

Kazuna couldn't bear to stay there for a moment longer, and she was just wishing she could make herself invisible when an old woman passed by.

"Huh? What's this about? Mr. Munemori, is this a manga?"

The man who had put the thing up turned at the sound of the elderly woman's voice. He was holding a thick cylinder of rolled-up posters in one hand and appeared to be planning to post still more.

"No, granny, it isn't a manga. It's an anime."

Since the woman had addressed the man as "mister," he was almost certainly not her real grandson, but he spoke to her as if he was.

He was a big, broad-shouldered guy. He appeared to be quite a bit older than Kazuna, but he might be younger than he looked. His sporty crew cut was a bit too short, making his hair stand up a little. He had twisted and rolled up his sleeves so far, exposing deeply tanned arms, and Kayako found herself wondering, *Why would anyone want to do that?* It was a look that even elementary school students would have shunned. He was wearing work pants with his T-shirt.

Kazuna had a sudden feeling that the man was about to turn and look at her. Hurriedly averting her gaze, she made a mad dash for the exit.

As she emerged from the station, she began to feel dizzy again. She wandered along in a daze until she found herself in front of a souvenir shop, where the same disturbing poster was on display. Feeling genuinely unable to stay there for a moment longer, she turned tail and ran to the bus stop, hanging her head in shame.

By the time she realized that she'd neglected to buy her train ticket, the bus had already left the station far behind.

◆

The next time Kazuna saw Shuhei Munemori, the poster guy from the station, was three days later.

This time, though, the encounter took place on her home turf—the Fine Garden studio—rather than out in the town. The company president had called out to her: "Namisawa, can you come here for a sec?" She'd responded sleepily, "Mmm-hmm," as she stumbled toward the reception area. When she got there, she saw a seated visitor.

He immediately leapt to his feet and greeted Kazuna warmly.

"How do you do? I'm glad to meet you!"

She recognized him right away as the man from the other day. His overly clear, crisp speaking voice seemed to resound in her head.

"I can't apologize enough for taking up your precious time!"

"Um, it's fine."

"Mr. Munemori, you don't need to keep standing up like that every time. Anyway, this is our Namisawa—the artist we were talking about earlier. Namisawa, won't you please have a seat?"

"Yes, of course…"

She had no idea what was going on, but as she was mentally scratching her head, President Koizumi explained, "This is Mr. Munemori, from the Enaga City Tourism Section."

Despite having been advised that it wasn't necessary to get up, the visitor sprang to his feet once again, standing perfectly straight, before bowing to Kazuna.

"Please treat me kindly!"

His posture was so impeccably correct that it made Kazuna wonder, *What is he, anyway—a soldier or something?*

Here in the studio, where the majority of her colleagues could be described as the "herbivorous" type, it was rare to hear such a loud voice. Kazuna found his high-volume exuberance oppressive.

"I'm Namisawa, from Fine Garden," she said at last.

So he was a city employee. Today, again, he was wearing a T-shirt and dark gray work pants. Short hair, deep suntan, rolled-up sleeves. Certainly not bespectacled. There wasn't a single thing about this man that she felt comfortable with, and she felt certain she never would. With his aura of robust health and excessive forthrightness, he was like someone from a different world. Unlike President Koizumi, who fit right in with his trendy glasses frames and long hair, this visitor seemed completely out of place in an anime studio.

"Namisawa, did you know that *Sabaku* used Enaga City as its location?" her boss inquired.

"Yes."

To be precise, the production side was identifying Enaga City as "the site that served as a model for *Sabaku*," although Kazuna only learned that later, when she researched the matter on her own. The story told in the anime didn't take place in Enaga City per se. That clarification seemed typical of Director Saito's fastidious approach, which Kazuna approved of.

Kazuna had assumed that her drawing was being used without her permission, but that was a misunderstanding on her part, because she didn't have all the pertinent information. After she'd worked on the cover for *Animaison*, Fine Garden had seen an increase in orders from *Sabaku* for so-called copyrighted art, genga that wasn't for the series proper. The option of using those images for posters had been stipulated in the contract. Kazuna had accepted the job as an honor, never dreaming that they would get plastered all over her very own town.

Koizumi nodded, evidently satisfied with Kazuna's affirmative answer.

"As you know, these days there's a big craze for anime pilgrimages. It seems that in the very beginning, the *Sabaku* crew had no plans to publicize the fact that they'd used this area as a location, but with the final episode coming soon, I heard that they decided to alter that policy and ramp up the local angle a bit. They're working with some officials here, and Enaga City will now be mentioned by name. The Lily of the Valley Railway Line will be featured, as well."

"Oh, really? Is that true?"

The Lily of the Valley Railway Line was a local route connecting

Enaga City with a number of far smaller, more secluded villages deep in the mountains. It usually had only one car and didn't run often. When Kazuna first arrived here, she and the rest of the Fine Garden team had ridden that train just to have a story to tell. It had been an exceedingly windy day, and everyone aboard was seriously worried that clustering on one side might unbalance the car and make it topple over. That's how decrepit the line was.

"Yeah, it's true. And also, I gather the tourism section wants to hold a stamp rally, but they say they've been having trouble finding places to set up. Namisawa, do you think you could give them a hand?"

"Huh?" *Why me?* she added silently, and that thought was apparently visible on her face.

"Tokei Animation is asking for you, tha~t's why," Koizumi answered in a fey, affected manner. "I already mentioned this earlier, but I've heard that at first the director was opposed to working with the local government here. When she finally changed her mind, it was very late in the process to add a new wrinkle. You might call it a delayed departure. Normally, if an anime wanted to promote the fan-pilgrimage aspect, they would start putting up announcement posters in front of the station before the series began to air. In Enaga's case, though, they're just starting to spotlight the local connection toward the end of the series."

"I see."

Kazuna wondered whether Saito's change of heart was due to her workdays becoming less frantic with the end of the series in sight and the numbers indicating a bona fide hit. Preorders for the first volume of the DVD had only just begun, but they suggested that *Sabaku* had a good chance of winning the anime-supremacy stakes.

Remembering her impressions of Hitomi Saito, whom she'd met for the first time the previous month, Kazuna wasn't surprised that the director would have been opposed to the pilgrimage angle at first. An outside entity—Enaga's municipal government—getting involved with the production to revitalize the local economy would surely have felt like an attempt to exploit her precious creation.

"Look, as we all know, Enaga is very far from Tokyo," Koizumi continued. "I gather the production side came up here a number of times to scout locations, early on, but now they're in the thick of broadcasting, on a super-tight schedule, and they simply don't have enough staff to send people all this way."

"But I still don't see why they're asking us," Kazuna said.

A face flashed across her mind, even though that person hadn't yet been mentioned by name even once: Yukishiro, the producer who had dragged her away from Tokyo Skytree.

Wearing a look of feigned ignorance, Koizumi said, "I know, right? It's a real hassle." His perplexed tone didn't sound very convincing. "They're asking whether we could help them out just this once, since we have an animator right here on staff—that is to say, you—who's familiar with the details of *Sabaku*. I did tell them it would be a major inconvenience since our Namisawa is so busy and in such great demand."

From the seat next to Koizumi's, the visitor spoke up. "We'd like to start the stamp rallies next month, to coincide with the beginning of summer vacation. I heard that the last episode of *Soundback: The Singing Stone* will be broadcast at the end of this month. Excitement about the show should be peaking right about then, so we've been thinking we should launch our rallies immediately after the finale airs. We've already started on the prep work."

Without relaxing his sitting posture, the civil servant Munemori faced Kazuna.

"Ms. Namisawa, when I heard that you were the person who drew the art on the poster, I was very impressed. It's embarrassing to admit this, but until recently I thought that all the images in anime were machine-drawn. I simply couldn't believe that such beautiful pictures were actually drawn by human beings. And then when I found out that the artist was someone from a studio right here in Enaga!"

"...I see."

Kazuna felt as though a cold blade had been run against the

surface of her heart. Intellectually, she understood that he meant to praise her, and was no doubt expecting a happy, flattered response. She honestly wished that she were capable of letting the matter go.

However, she simply couldn't. Those well-meaning remarks had pushed all Kazuna's buttons in the worst possible way.

Beautiful like they'd been machine-drawn—that was among the very last things any animator ever wanted to hear. If the point was that animators made use of tools and mechanical devices, that much was certainly true, but being praised by someone who clearly had no clue about the basic fundamentals of anime was never going to fill Kazuna with joy.

Evidently noticing that Kazuna was slow to react, Munemori doubled down on his compliment.

"I really respect you."

The instant she heard those words, a voice she thought she'd forgotten sounded in her ears.

"Ms. Namisawa, I respect you a lot."

When Kazuna recalled how uplifting it had been for her when Osato, who'd watched and loved innumerable anime, singled out her work for praise, she felt so empty—all the more because her elation until a few days ago was still fresh.

She knew it was unreasonable to feel resentful toward this person, but right now she wasn't happy at all.

An amateur would find it difficult to spot the subtle differences among anime or specific genga. Munemori would probably heap the same kind of praise on any number of other artists and their work, too.

Kazuna figured that to his untrained eye she was just one among many, and her drawings could have belonged to anybody.

"It's been eons since I watched an anime or read a manga," Munemori confessed. "Maybe it's because of that, but I don't really have what they call an artistic sensibility. Even so, I totally respect you."

Kazuna fished for an innocuous question she might ask and managed to find one. "Was the stamp rally Tokei Animation's idea?"

"No," Munemori said, shaking his head. "We came up with the idea on our side. They agreed to provide the stamp designs, and they're in the middle of creating them right now. Why do you ask?"

"No, it just seems a trifle commonplace."

Why did people love stamp rallies so much? Whenever local governments tried to come up with events for pop-culture pilgrimages, the very first thing they proposed was a stamp rally, but as threadbare concepts went, it wasn't so much a rehash as a three-hash. To put it bluntly, a stamp rally didn't seem like a very bright idea.

Kazuna had thought it was unlike a tried hand like Yukishiro, and sure enough, she was right. Tokei Animation probably wasn't too committed to this anime-pilgrimage project.

In Kazuna's head, a picture of what was going on began to take shape. The municipality was raring to go, while Tokei Animation wanted the locals to go ahead on their own and was merely hoping to benefit in the unlikely event that it somehow caught on. That's why, rather than dispatching any of their own people, Tokei was leaning on Fine Garden to act as liaison.

Oblivious to the sarcasm in Kazuna's remark, Munemori just wore a befuddled expression before standing up perfectly straight once again. "We'll be very grateful for your help," he said, bowing.

"Yes, Namisawa," Koizumi echoed, "many thanks for helping out. Look, you're a very popular artist, and under normal circumstances I wouldn't dream of asking you to upend your schedule like this. However, we have our business relationship with Tokei Animation to consider, and I'm going to pay you something extra, too. We can also reduce your monthly page quota while you're working on this."

The conditions were so sweet that Kazuna realized something. *Dammit, there's some money-related stuff going on behind the scenes.* President Koizumi had probably struck a deal with Tokei that would benefit Fine Garden in some way. It was already a fait accompli, and getting her on board was just the final step.

"All right, I understand," she said with a reluctant nod. "Though I'm not sure I'll be of any use—"

"Thank you very much!"

Popping up again before Kazuna could finish, Munemori executed a bow with impeccable posture.

◆

Seichi junrei.

In Japanese, the word *junrei* ("pilgrimage") originally referred to the practice of traveling around visiting and worshiping at temples and shrines, usually on a predetermined itinerary. As for *seichi* ("holy sites"), that could denote any place with a significant connection to a person's belief system, and heading out to them was a *seichi junrei*, a pilgrimage to holy sites.

The derivative and colloquial use of "pilgrimage" referred to the practice, increasingly popular among fans, of visiting the places where anime, manga, and light novels were set. Striking their favorite characters' signature poses in front of the places and buildings featured in the productions and taking pictures, for instance, the "pilgrims" basked in the knowledge that "*they* had been here too"—that's what it was all about. It was similar to the "location tours" for live-action dramas and films.

The earliest anime pilgrimages were spontaneous jaunts privately organized by the fans themselves, but in the last five years or so the trend had spread rapidly, spurred by a great deal of media coverage, and local governments recognized the economic benefits of becoming a destination. In collaboration with production companies, local manufacturers created licensed thematic goods to sell at inns and in souvenir shops—for example, showcasing the characters from a certain anime on the packaging for regional specialties such as sweets. They worked together to generate hype. Tourist bureaus also installed "comment books" at train stations to encourage fan interaction and invited voice actors and directors to participate in local events. If the effects were lasting, the financial windfall could top a billion yen.

However.

The more Kazuna heard from Munemori about her role as designated helper with the stamp rally, the more convinced she was that this situation was a result of Tokei Animation trying to take the path of least resistance. The Enaga City Tourism Section had made the proposal, and all Tokei had done was to give their approval.

That wasn't surprising. Kazuna heaved a sigh of resignation.

Enaga City was simply too far away from Tokyo as a pilgrimage destination. Getting here was inconvenient, too, because visitors needed to change trains twice after disembarking at the closest bullet-train station. The fact that it wasn't a feasible day trip from the metropolis would surely be an insurmountable hurdle for most fans. Indeed, until now, the majority of successful holy sites had been in the Kanto area around the capital. Kazuna wondered why *Sabaku* had chosen Enaga in the first place.

As she walked with Munemori along rough roads that wound through the vast, unshaded rice paddies, her shoulders slumped and she felt as though she'd been trapped in an onerous situation. It was only the day after Munemori had come to Fine Garden, and she was already being made to help. He was in work clothes and a T-shirt today, too, and once again he wore his sleeves rolled up like he'd never heard of sunburn.

"What do you think about putting a stamp table next to one of the rice paddies around here?" asked Kazuna, more out of boredom than anything else. "Those kids walk along this road pretty often."

After she learned that *Sabaku* was set in Enaga, Kazuna binge-watched all the episodes of the show that had aired so far. She recognized the road the kids took to school—a national route, although, contrary to the grand-sounding name, it had very little traffic. The surrounding scenery was superb.

Munemori, who was walking along next to Kazuna, lifted his

head. "Oh, when you say kids walking, you mean in the anime."

He nodded. "The children in *Soundback: The Singing*—"

"Uhm," Kazuna interrupted. She had been wondering since the day before whether she should say something but couldn't hold back anymore. Munemori looked at her.

"It's not *Soundback*," she explained. "It's *Sabaku*. The *Singing Stone* part is the subtitle, so we basically don't use it when we talk about the work. Please don't use the formal title every time, okay?"

When she spat out all that, Munemori blinked. Just as Kazuna was starting to think she might have gone too far, he nodded and said, "Got it. I'm sorry, I guess that would be kind of tedious and irritating, when you stop to think about it."

Kazuna quickly looked away from him and gazed at the viridian rice paddies that stretched far and away on both sides. The early-summer breeze rustled softly through the unripe rice plants.

The thing that annoyed her was not so much Munemori's habit of using the entire title, although that *was* tedious. Every time he said "*Soundback*" in a clearly unaccustomed tone, she sensed acutely that he didn't understand anime, at all, and that was painful for her. She felt certain that if it weren't for the circumstances, Munemori would have never even watched an anime, much less become involved with promoting one.

"Mr. Munemori, have you watched many anime?"

"Well, when I was a kid I watched *Dragon Ball* and *Fist of the North Star*, but not since then. I was always the type who enjoyed playing outdoors."

"I see." As Kazuna delivered that rote response to the entirely predictable answer, she thought, *Ah, I bet he looks down on me.*

The type who enjoyed playing outdoors—for as long as she could remember, she'd felt ill at ease with them. That formulation automatically conveyed that he viewed people who enjoyed anime and manga as the "otaku minority" who spent all their time indoors. That wasn't necessarily true these days, but he seemed not to have gotten that memo.

Hah, this realie, she whispered under her breath.

"Sorry, did you say something?"

"No, it was nothing," she fibbed.

"About the stamp booth, I think it'll be difficult to set one up here. This rice field is Mr. Nagasaki's private land. He's a nice old guy, but he probably doesn't know the first thing about anime."

Evidently the landowner was an acquaintance of Munemori's. Hearing the easy familiarity in his tone, Kazuna felt weary and dejected again. "But the fans will definitely want to see this road," she persisted. "So we need to guide them here, somehow."

"Well, there's no elementary school around here to begin with, so this isn't really a school route."

Kazuna sighed, but didn't reply.

Munemori must have heard because he hastened to add, "In the anime, they used the middle school on the other side of the station as the model for the elementary school."

He seemed to know the rough outlines of the plot, at least.

"Sure, because it's fiction," Kazuna deadpanned, and Munemori nodded.

"Right. As I watched it, I was thinking a story like that could never happen in Enaga, in a million years."

Kraaack. Kazuna seemed to feel something snapping inside her head, almost audibly. Did it really matter whether the story could take place in real life? There was no point in enlightening this guy, so she swallowed her objections and remained silent.

"Whew," Munemori said, looking up at the blue sky, "it's a hot one today. But anime's amazing, isn't it? Our tourism section has helped with live-action movies and dramas in the past, but this is our first anime. Things that would be impossible in live action due to the cost would be free and feasible in anime, so it's got a good deal."

"Riiight." Once again, Kazuna was forced to give an anodyne response even as she thought, *You... Some incredibly talented people designed that robot, and I reckon all the CGI and special effects were extremely expensive, too.* She had a lot of other things to say but simply didn't know where to begin.

Just then, Munemori exclaimed, "Oh!" Shielding his eyes with one hand, he peered across the rice fields, then bent down and pointed into the distance. "Speak of the devil—it's Mr. Nagasaki," he informed Kazuna.

Bewildered, she craned her neck and asked, "What? Where?"

Munemori was already calling out, "Mr. Nagasaki!"

Behind her glasses, Kazuna narrowed her nearsighted eyes. Then, surprisingly, from quite far across the rice field, a relaxed, rural-sounding voice responded, "What is it?"

Even after hearing the voice, Kazuna went on scanning the sun-splashed landscape for a human form. *Huh? So someone's actually there?*

"It's a long shot but I'll go and ask if we can put a stamp table here," Munemori said and broke into a run.

"Wait a sec—" she called after him, but Munemori was already gone, first sprinting between the rice paddies, then threading his way down a farming road so skinny you could hardly tell it was there.

Mr. Nagasaki didn't let them put a stamp booth on his land. However, it wasn't because the old man was obstinate or because he didn't understand anime.

His reason made perfect sense: "If you put it in this wide open spot without so much as a roof overhead, it'll get wrecked by the wind and rain before you know it."

Kazuna was out of breath after chasing Munemori, even at a light jog. It had been years since she had last run like that—not since gym classes in high school. Still panting, she stood next to Munemori, whose arms were folded across his chest in obvious disappointment.

"Oh, shucks," he said. "I guess you're right, though."

"But even if you do this stamp-rally thing, will those tourists come all the way up here?" Nagasaki was thin and sinewy, but the arms that he folded as he spoke were a deep reddish brown from years spent toiling in the fields. He stared at the younger man with a skeptical expression.

Munemori nodded. "They'll come. They'll definitely come. And I've heard that the fans who travel for anime are a lot better behaved than the ones who come to ski." He said this with such a startling degree of conviction that Kazuna, listening at his side, was flabbergasted.

While generalities like that were definitely floating around, she wanted to jump in and say that anime fans probably ran the gamut. However, she didn't have the self-confidence to make that assertion in front of someone she didn't know.

"Ah, that so," Mr. Nagasaki swallowed it whole for his part.

Then he asked, "Hey, do you guys want these?" The elderly farmer bent over, and for a brief instant Kazuna hoped they might be about to receive some delicious seasonal fruit. *That would be lovely, a perfectly countrified kind of social exchange*—but when she saw what he was holding in his hand, she doubted her own eyes. It was a bag of snacks sold at any convenience store: puffy, deep-fried rice crackers flavored with sweet soy sauce. He had probably been planning to munch on them during a break. But why? Why go out of his way to share his Kabuki Krisps?

I could just buy them on my own instead—Kazuna's expression had grown stiff, but Munemori said, "Are you sure? Thank you very much," and stretched out his hand to receive the gift.

"Here," Nagasaki mumbled, handing Kazuna, who hadn't even spoken up, not just one but two crackers. He sent the visitors on their way saying, "Keep up the good work."

As they traipsed back along the narrow agricultural road, Kazuna felt obliged to make conversation.

"Too bad that didn't work out."

"Can't be helped," Munemori responded, nodding. "We'll just have to think of something else."

He was already tearing open the wrapper on his Kabuki Krisp. *Do you really have to eat it now?* Watching him devour it with loud crunching noises, Kazuna's mind brimmed with silent questions again.

They had left Munemori's official vehicle (which had "ENAGA CITY HALL" emblazoned on the sides) parked on the shoulder of the national route. On the way back there, Kazuna asked, "How did you know the visitors are well behaved?"

"Oh, from the reconnaissance tours," Munemori replied right away. "When *Soundba*—I mean, *Sabaku* approached us, I went around to other municipalities to see how they handled something like this. I talked to the people in charge, and they told me that the people who go on anime pilgrimages are very respectful toward the sites and have very good manners."

"Where did you go?"

"To T City in Ibaraki Prefecture, and E Town in Kanagawa, and also C City in Saitama Prefecture, for instance. Everyone was really nice about sharing their experiences, and I learned a lot."

So apparently he wasn't going into this completely cold without having done any research about anime at all. The places he named were so well known, and so closely associated with certain popular anime, that Kazuna could give the titles off the top of her head. As pilgrimage sites went, they were pretty much the cream of the crop.

"Those were good choices," she couldn't help but admit.

Looking somewhat bashful, Munemori replied, "Actually, I know someone who's very knowledgeable about anime and such. He was ahead of me in high school, and he's living in Tokyo now. When I was kind of floundering around with no clue how to even start learning about anime, I called him up and asked for advice. He suggested going on a reconnaissance tour and gave me the names of some municipalities that have been successful with this kind of thing."

"Oh, I see." *So at least he has a friend who's an anime fan*, Kazuna revised her view of Munemori. Still, it seemed quintessentially real-worldish to consult with someone within his own extended community and call it a day. She thought it must have been daunting for that friend to try to explain his hobby to someone with absolutely no knowledge about the subject, and she felt a small pang of sympathy for the anime fan in Tokyo.

Sure enough, Munemori confessed, "That person told me I shouldn't dream too big, though. He said it would be a grave mistake to assume that just because a certain area appeared in an anime, you could automatically expect fans of that show to turn up in droves. He actually got mad at me for being so naïve, saying it was essential for an anime to be interesting and enjoyable in itself, and to become must-see viewing on its own merits."

"True," Kazuna said, but she was thinking, *That other guy sounds like a true anime fan. He knows what he's talking about.*

There was no way of knowing how much of his friend's wisdom had actually hit home, but the piece of advice was solid.

"Yes," Munemori nodded almost gullibly. "So I'm absolutely certain they'll come."

"Huh?"

"*Sabaku* is interesting and enjoyable, so I'm absolutely sure they'll come here."

Having tossed into his mouth and ingested one cracker, Munemori ripped open the wrapper of his second Kabuki Krisp.

Why now? Why scarf down another one? Kazuna found his behavior baffling, but at the same time she felt a teensy bit impressed.

Munemori's evaluation was rooted in ignorance, so it couldn't be trusted, by any means. Kazuna was scornful of rank amateurs who knew hardly anything about anime and, for that very reason, formed an irrational emotional attachment to the only shows they'd seen, throwing around words like "god" and "masterpiece" like so much confetti. Even so, hearing him say that a project she'd worked on was interesting made her happy.

◆

On that same day, Munemori took her to see one more candidate for a stamp-rally station.

Located at the far edge of a deep forest, the limestone cave was one of the area's most famous tourist spots and appeared in *Sabaku*. Indeed, the story's key item, the Singing Stone, had resided there.

Although the cave was within Enaga's city limits, it would be

Kazuna's first visit. When she told Munemori she'd never been there before, he was surprised. "Are you still able to draw a place without having seen it?" he asked.

"No. I only draw the genga," she explained. "The backgrounds are drawn by artists in another section." She wasn't confident in his ability to understand the details of animation, so she only gave a perfunctory explanation. Perhaps he didn't even realize that the images in an anime were made up of layers. With a sigh in her voice, she continued, "I mostly get around on a bicycle, so I tend not to roam this far away."

"Ah, the president of your company was telling me that most of the staff commute by bike."

For starters, the limestone cave was nearly an hour's drive from the center of Enaga City, and it wasn't as if fans who came by bus or train could casually stop by. Kazuna felt dejected even before she'd given the place a visit and crossed it off the list of possible stamping stations, but Munemori told her, "If you take the Lily of the Valley Train, the cave is right near a station. The train company is one of our sponsors, so we actually want a few locations that people can't get to without using the line."

"Oh, so it's a bottom-line thing," Kazuna took his meaning.

Summer vacation hadn't yet begun, and there was just a scattering of tourists, mostly middle-aged or older, at the cave. Souvenir shops flanked the path leading to it, and the elderly men and women tending those stores called out, "Ah, Mr. Munemori!" as he and Kazuna passed.

He responded to each greeting with a simple "Hello" and a respectful lowering of his head. Seeing this, Kazuna felt like asking, *Are you personally acquainted with every single person in this city, or what?*

At the entrance to the cave was a miniature shrine that also served as a ticket office. Inside sat a middle-aged woman whose face, with its plump, puffy cheeks, bore an extraordinary resemblance to folk-art masks of the Japanese goddess of mirth, Okame.

"Oh, Shuhei! Welcome, welcome!"

As she watched the auntie smiling at Munemori, Kazuna's

eyes went wide. For some reason, the woman was wearing the traditional red-and-white costume of a shrine maiden.

"Is this place operated by a shrine or something?" Kazuna asked Munemori in a low voice, but before he could reply, the older woman answered, "Nah, it's cosplay," smiling at Kazuna as easily as if they'd known each other for years. "Rena in *Soundback* is a shrine maiden, so it's with her in mind. I'm actually just working part-time for the tourism section."

"Wha?"

This day was turning out to be a continuous parade of surprises. Seeing Kazuna's baffled expression, Munemori laughed in obvious delight. "Auntie has been pretty cooperative—and by the way," he said, "this is Ms. Namisawa from the Fine Garden anime studio. She's helping me with the stamp rally."

"Oh, isn't that nice. She sure must be helping you plenty." *Heheh*, the woman chortled, her shrine-maiden costume oddly becoming on her thanks to her uncanny resemblance to Okame.

"Please take good care of our Shuhei. He was just behind my son in high school and has always been a good kid. When my troublesome and selfish boy announced that he didn't want to go to school anymore, Shuhei came by to pick him up every morning... It's all thanks to him that my son was able to graduate."

"I see." There was that local-network angle again.

An unseasonably chilly wind came wafting out through the dark, gaping maw of the cave entrance. They paid the cosplaying auntie three hundred yen per person for admission, and she lent them each a well-worn miniature flashlight in the shape of a candle. The handle was covered with rust and felt moist.

When they stepped inside, Kazuna found herself unexpectedly impressed. *Wow*, she thought, *it's the same.* The mood was remarkably similar to that of the cave portrayed in the anime. Numerous white stalactites hung from overhead like icicles, and cold water seemed to be dripping somewhere nearby. The air of sublime solemnity lived up to the work.

"It'd be great if we could set up a stamp table inside here, maybe along with life-size cutouts of the characters," Munemori's voice sounded behind Kazuna as she took in the place's grandeur.

She answered reflexively, "What? I don't think so."

She had assumed that the stamping station would be placed outside. Munemori, his big frame hunched in the cave, turned around and said, "Oh, is that a bad idea?"

"No, I mean, bringing anime cutouts into someplace like this with its otherworldly atmosphere would kind of ruin the scenery—don't you think?"

She remembered the disconnect she felt at her own artwork adorning the mundane train station.

Kazuna was convinced that the pleasures of something like anime were ultimately personal. The idea of imposing upon sightseers who might be visiting purely to see the limestone cave didn't sit well with her. *Doesn't he get that when he works for the tourism section?* she wondered.

"It indeed might not be a good idea from a safety standpoint," Munemori nodded and agreed for a completely different reason. "In fact, when I saw how this cave was being used in the anime, my first thought was, *Whoa, if a lot of fans came here, that could be a mess. It's dark, and somebody could get injured.* Deeper in, there are some places that aren't properly fenced. Before we start attracting more visitors, we need to put up some rudimentary fencing, at least."

"...For municipalities, I guess it's always safety first."

The city just had a different perspective from the production side, which didn't give any consideration to actual visitors while location scouting. In the darkness, Munemori exhaled a white cloud and nodded again. Unlike with live-action works, we weren't consulted in advance. Sometimes, the other municipal staff and I have ask to each other, 'Hey, where is this?' only after we're provided with the art, and then turn pale when we realize that, say, it isn't all fenced."

"Anyway," Kazuna said, "we're getting things backward if we end up spoiling the original scenery just so we can put up the anime material. Fans will fill in the blanks and provide the worldview on their own if we simply point them to the location. Not changing things can be just as important."

Kazuna spoke those words without pausing for breath, and Munemori blinked slightly. The beam from his faux candle bathed his cheeks in golden light. Plunging ahead, she spoke a word too many.

"Unlike with live-action works, what anime fans see won't be this actual place, but the landscape inside their heads. The real location is only a screen for projecting that." She stopped to take a breath and continued, "You might not get what I'm saying… For people like me, though, the reality of what we see isn't everything. Inserting actual 'things' like standing cardboard cutouts in reality will only backfire. The moment there's even the slightest hint that we aren't respecting the work, it's over."

When she took a breath, she felt a cold sting in her nasal cavity even though they hadn't been there all that long. A light layer of gooseflesh sprouted on her arms.

"Let's get back outside," she said.

Munemori drove her back to Fine Garden in his government-issued car.

Kazuna thought her comments back in the limestone cave had been sharp-tongued to the point of rudeness, but perhaps they hadn't sounded that way to the stolid Munemori. He didn't show any outward signs of being bothered and just began talking again in an even-keeled tone.

"I'd like to find a way to include *Sabaku* in the upcoming Kanaga Festival."

"Oh, is that the one where they set off fireworks?" Kazuna had seen them in the distance as she rode her bicycle along the road between the rice paddies, on her way home to the dormitory. Naturally, festivals and fireworks shows would be the tourism section's business. Munemori appeared to be slightly surprised by her ignorance.

"There are fireworks the evening before the festival, but the main event is the boats traveling downriver. In the course of one day, a whole bunch of them are sent down the Enaga. It's quite rapid, and there are rocky stretches, so it's rare for a boat to make it all the way downstream without getting smashed up. Every year, everybody comes out to watch and see how far each boat will go, and it's always exciting."

"Isn't it dangerous for the people on board if the boats get broken up?"

"Huh? No, the boats are unmanned, so it's fine. You've never seen it? The chamber of commerce, regional banks, and other organizations with some link to Enaga team up with craftsmen and spend almost the whole year building these wooden vessels that look like large versions of bamboo-leaf boats."

Evidently, it was a famous event. "You didn't know about it?" he asked, perplexed. Kazuna heard the unvoiced subtext: *After living here for five years?*

She replied huffily, "No, I didn't. I'm sorry."

Munemori said, "Oh, I see," and immediately let the topic go. "Anyway, after talking it over with the tourism section, I proposed that at the festival this year we could hold a little ceremony and issue proofs of residency to the characters in *Sabaku*."

"Uh, no. I don't think that will pass."

Proofs of residency! she screamed loudly inside her head again. *Not cool. Not cool. Not cool at all.*

Didn't these people have any idea that a work had a finite lifespan? It'd be different for characters from so-called national manga that ran continuously for over a decade, but weren't they afraid that residency for characters from an anime series might turn out to be pretty transient once the boom died down?

When it came down to it, government bureaus everywhere fell into the same trap. They didn't breathe the air of the times and didn't have the foggiest idea what would appeal to fans and make them happy.

"You're right," Munemori sighed, not sounding offended in the least. "Tokei didn't approve the residency idea. That's why I was wondering whether you might have any other suggestions. I hope you'll help us out."

Swallowing the urge to tell him, *Well? How 'bout not trying to mix the anime up with your festival at all,* Kazuna just answered with no pretense of enthusiasm, "Sure, if I can."

When they arrived at the studio, she tried to make her escape with a quick "See you," but Munemori leaned out the driver's-side window and called after her, "Um, Ms. Namisawa?"

Reluctantly, her sole desire to be liberated from this ordeal, she turned around and asked, "What is it?"

Munemori was pointing in the direction of the parking lot reserved for bicycles. "Does that bike over there belong to you, by any chance?" he inquired.

"Huh?" Kazuna followed his gaze.

"It's just that they're low on air. Your bicycle tires."

Finally comprehending, Kazuna said, "Ah," and nodded her head.

Still, the bicycle was quite far away from the car, and even when she narrowed her eyes and squinted through her prescription lenses, she couldn't discern the tires' condition. *This guy really has good eyesight,* she thought. That was a characteristic seldom encountered in the anime world where the detailed work and eye-straining hobbies made for a largely bespectacled population.

Kazuna hadn't put much thought into the purchase of her current bicycle. She had simply gone to the shopping center and bought a so-called granny bike that would be convenient for commuting. She'd never done anything in the way of maintenance beyond fixing an occasional puncture.

As long as the bicycle was functional, that was all she cared about. And when it reached the end of its useful life, she figured she could just go back and buy a cheap replacement.

"My uncle has a bicycle-repair shop, so if it's okay with you, I can take it over there and air up the tires, then return it. It'll fit in the back."

"No, really, that's okay."

If he'd been driving a truck, that would have been another matter, but surely there was no way to jam a bicycle into the trunk of a normal automobile.

However, Munemori wouldn't be swayed. "I'll just put air in

the tires and bring it right back," he said, as if it were no big deal. "Proper inflation makes a big difference in the comfort level—you'll be amazed."

With that, he hopped out of the car, opened the back door, and folded down the rear passenger seats to create a flat surface. In no time, Kazuna's bicycle was safely stowed inside just as he'd promised.

"When will you be getting off work?" he asked.

"I think today it'll probably be after midnight..."

"Oh, perfect. I'll have it back here by then, for sure."

Munemori straightened his posture, almost as if he were about to give a snappy salute. Then, bowing deeply to Kazuna, he said, "Thank you very much for today."

◆

Back at the Fine Garden studio, Kazuna sprawled out across her desk, heaved a massive sigh, and moaned, "I'm so exhausted."

Perhaps because she almost never walked around outside during the day, her cheeks felt tingly from the early-summer sunburn she'd picked up. The earthy smell of the farm road and the chilly dampness of the limestone cave seemed to have permeated her entire body, and she wasn't able to simply brush them off.

"You've had a long day, Ms. Namisawa." Seki, her section chief, stood up from the desk in front and looked at Kazuna. His voice sounded sympathetic, but there was a glint of amusement in his eyes.

Kazuna replied with a simple "Thanks."

"It must be rough, having to work a second job on top of your main one."

"You can say that again. Especially since this extra work isn't my cup of tea."

"Oh well, what can you do? We'll all try our best to support you as much as we can."

Seki laughed. Kazuna took a long deep breath and thought, *Ah, home at last.* The safe familiarity of the studio felt like an embrace. The smell of paper—her lovable indoor job.

Glancing at the corner of her desk, she noticed a drawstring gift bag filled with sweets that, she was quite certain, hadn't been there when she left that morning. When she picked it up Seki said, "Oh, that's from the civil-servant guy. Apparently he brought it when he came to see the president yesterday."

"Gee," Kazuna said dryly. "Somebody certainly has good manners."

Picturing the face of the man she'd just said goodbye to, she fiddled with the drawstring pouch. The label read "Mochi Chocolant."

"So, how was it?" asked Seki, with the same gleam of humor in his eye. Kazuna found her boss, who could see how she wasn't in the most chipper of moods and who bugged her anyway, annoying but somehow hard to hate.

Feeling weary and defeated, she replied, "Today, in just a few hours, I feel as if I got to know Enaga City much better. Even if I feel like I was forced to." In a single day, she'd visited several places she had entirely ignored during her five years here.

In the car on the way back, Munemori had said, "Since we're already out and about, won't you have dinner with me? I'm going to be more and more obliged to you, so it'll be my treat." But Kazuna had politely refused the invitation.

Until now, when it came to eating out in Enaga City, she hadn't gone anywhere beyond the restaurants in the neighborhood shopping center, and Tully's Coffee. The place Munemori wanted to take her was one of his favorite spots, an *izakaya* pub specializing in yakitori located in the station-front shopping district where Kazuna had yet to set foot. Apparently, it wasn't part of any chain but was run by the ex-girlfriend of his buddy from kindergarten. Just hearing about such ties made Kazuna's head spin, and even though Munemori assured her that the food was "pretty darn good," she didn't feel like going.

Today, she'd been continuously hearing about people he

knew—the high school friend and his cosplaying mother, and so on—but kindergarten? That left her speechless. And he even knew that old friend's ex-girlfriend. *Oh, these people,* she thought. Surely when they fell in love it was with someone local, somebody they'd known since they were little kids, and it would be smooth sailing for them to get married and build a family. Thinking this, she spat the word "Realies!" And of course country folk tended to marry young, too.

As Kazuna hung her head, Seki interrupted her dour reverie.

"That civil-servant guy's the same person who got into an argument with Director Saito at the initial meeting, right? I heard that's the reason the preparations haven't exactly been running like clockwork."

"Huh? Is that true?" This was news to Kazuna, but she had simply been dragged into the president's office and strong-armed into going along with the plan, so Seki, who had stayed in the studio, probably had a better handle on what was going on. "Um, by the way," she asked, "would you know why they chose Enaga City as the location for *Sabaku*, even though it's a major hassle to get here from Tokyo? Is this the director's hometown or something?"

Pop-culture pilgrimages weren't always limited to sites that appeared in the work and could be made to the actual hometowns of anime directors or manga writers. Of course, some authors used their own alma maters as models. In order not to create problems for the school or family home, there'd been cases where fans had been asked to exercise restraint and skip those sites.

In addition, if a municipality got wind of the fact that a certain celebrity originally hailed from the area, they'd try to rope her into giving lectures or appearing at local events. Thinking about this, Kazuna felt concerned and tacked on another question. "So getting involved with local matters might have been troublesome for Director Saito?"

Seki shook his head. "No, that wasn't it. Director Saito is actually from a completely different part of the country. Enaga was just a place she remembered visiting with her parents when she was little. Somehow it left a lasting impression, and from what I hear, she chose Enaga when the time came for location scouting."

"Whoa…"

Unlike live-action films, anime didn't shoot actual footage of scenery, but location scouting was still conducted to draw backgrounds. *A-ha*, Kazuna thought. The whole time she'd been wondering, *Why an out-of-the-way place like this?* Now at last she understood.

"Originally the director just happened to choose this place, and I gather she had no intention of revealing the location and making a big deal about it in public," Seki explained. "But I guess the producer picked up on it and tried to get the ball rolling for some kind of collaboration with the local government. This was early on, while *Sabaku* was still in the conceptual stage, but evidently both sides took a look at the content and concluded that there was some potential for a mutually beneficial partnership."

"And the director got angry about that?"

"No, it seems the municipal office told her it'd be unnatural not to include the festival and sent her unsolicited info—but I don't know if that's true."

"Ahh…"

Most likely it was true. Munemori had gone on today about the Kanaga Festival. He wasn't a bad person; he just wasn't very good at reading situations.

Seki continued with a wry smile, "Well, from the city government's point of view, that festival is a famous local event, so of course they'd want to see it showcased. I can totally understand how they feel. But what Director Saito wanted to make wasn't a PR video for Enaga."

"Oh, is that event really so famous? The Kanaga Festival, or whatever it's called?"

"Huh?" Seki had been talking a blue streak, but now he stopped abruptly, and Kazuna saw a familiar expression cross his face. It was the same look Munemori had given her earlier that day under similar circumstances. *Oops*, she thought, but it was too late.

"You must at least have known it existed? You know, watching boats flow downriver," reminded Seki.

So the festival was something everyone knew about, plain common sense. Kazuna felt like she was being laughed at for her utter ignorance about anything that didn't fall within her sphere of interest, so she fibbed, "Oh, of course I do. The chamber of commerce and regional banks providing the boats, and all."

"Right, right. We're always swamped with work so I've never been able to go watch, but as long as we're living here in Enaga, I'd like to see it live at least once."

"Uh huh."

In truth, Kazuna didn't have the slightest desire to, even now that she knew it existed.

This wasn't about being an otaku or not. She was the kind of person who had absolutely no interest in anything that went on beyond the borders of her own little world, she realized in third-person mode. But then, what could she do?

Being surrounded by the things I like, and being able to draw: that's what makes me happy. Her world might appear narrow and trivial to others, but she was a small person who felt comfortable there, so what could she do?

That night, when she finished work and went out to the parking lot, she found that her bicycle had been returned, just as Munemori promised. At a glance, she didn't notice anything different. However, after she climbed into the saddle, kicked off with her right foot, and started pedaling, she abruptly exclaimed, "Oh!"

Her line of sight was slightly higher, and the pedal action felt more fluid. Compared to that morning's commute, the bicycle went much further with each revolution of the pedals. Munemori had said he wouldn't do anything beyond airing up the tires, but the bike appeared to have received a complete tune-up.

She noticed some distinct improvements in the brakes—they engaged quickly, with no play at all, and no longer made the usual metallic screeching sound—and realized that they must have been in rather bad shape all this time. The headlamp had evidently been cleaned, and it now shone so brightly that the dark road appeared both wider and straighter. The night wind felt suddenly cool against her ears as the bicycle and its beam of light cut through the muggy early-summer air.

Until now Kazuna had seen this cheap bicycle as something she had casually acquired and never formed any attachment to it, and her plan had been to discard it as soon as it became unusable and to replace it with another, equally disposable model. But now, as she chased the moon across the night sky, it occurred to her for the first time ever that you could take care of it.

◆

Unexpectedly, Kazuna didn't hear a peep from the Passionate Civil Servant (her nickname for Munemori) for one week after their field trip.

It gave her a chance to concentrate on her normal work. Sometimes she felt a twinge of anxiety, since she knew the stamp rally was supposed to begin the following month, but she felt the ball was in his court and that she was under no obligation to get in touch with him.

That was her official position and she stuck with it, telling herself over and over, *Don't worry about it. It's no big deal.*

When she finally capitulated and reached out to him, it wasn't because she was concerned about his welfare or because she wanted to offer her assistance. Rather, after considerable stewing and reflection, she judged that getting things rolling now was preferable to waiting until just before the stamp rally and coping with a crisis.

Making endless excuses to assure herself that it definitely wasn't because he was on her mind, she sent Munemori an email.

It was true that her bicycle was in such good shape after his maintenance that she looked forward to riding it every morning.

Even though jocks like him weren't her type, she somehow ended up spending half a day on the email: writing, deleting, writing, deleting again, taking particular pains to make the wording as curt and indifferent as possible.

The whole process was mortifying, but she finally finished and sent it off.

—*It's Kazuna Namisawa from Fine Garden. How about Lily of the Valley Park as one of the stops for the stamp rally?*

She could thank him about her bicycle in person. Having it remain in writing somehow felt embarrassing.

It had taken her so long to send that simple message that she was startled to hear the *ka-jingle-clink* of her cell phone announcing an email (that was her alert, the sound of cascading coins) after what seemed like only a moment. There on the screen was a straightforward reply that showed no hint of awareness of her hours of agony.

—*Perfect timing. I was just thinking about getting in touch with you. Can you spare some time in the near future? Munemori*

The meeting place he suggested was the same rice field where they had spoken with Mr. Nagasaki the week before. The same city-issued vehicle was parked on the shoulder of the road. Kazuna got off her bicycle in front of the car, looked around, and let out a small gasp of surprise.

A small shed with a blue tin roof now stood in a spot that had definitely been empty the last time she was here. The lean-to, which appeared to have been built from used materials, resembled a street-food booth or one of those unmanned roadside produce stands sometimes seen in agricultural areas.

A colorful array of eggplants, tomatoes, and other vegetables, packaged in clear plastic, sat on a narrow table, with a basket for cash off to one side.

Evidently a form of commerce based on the honor system was still alive around these parts.

"Oh, she's here, she's here. Ms. Namisawa!"

Munemori and Nagasaki both looked in her direction and raised their hands in greeting. The younger man's voice was as loud as ever.

"Hello," Kazuna replied with a small wave and began walking toward the men. "What's going on here?" she asked.

"Mr. Nagasaki installed this for us. A friend of his had a produce stand in a more secluded spot, but they did some negotiating and moved it here."

"You guys are lucky it's summer," the farmer said. "If it wasn't the season for selling vegetables, my friend would never have let us move it. But he figures there'll be a lot more traffic passing by here and consented as a special favor."

Nagasaki mopped his brow with a towel that had taken on a faint brownish tinge from all the sweat it had absorbed. As he stared up at the searing sun, a new crop of perspiration was already starting to trickle down his face.

The thrumming sound of cicadas cascaded across the fields. The summer heat was abnormally intense by Enaga standards, and it was only the middle of June.

"Let's put the stamping station here, on this side, under cover. That'll take rain off our list of things to worry about," Munemori said with a laugh. "This is a private road that belongs to Mr. Nagasaki, but he kindly said we could use it."

"Just make sure lots of guests stop by."

"Yes, sir." As Munemori happily made this promise, Nagasaki whacked him on the back, hard.

Kazuna, meanwhile, stole a furtive glance at the produce stand. The small shed had obviously been exposed to the elements for years on end, and there were patches on the roof where the blue paint had worn off. The boards that formed the foundation had a sunbaked look and smelled faintly dusty. *So fans are going to stop here to get anime stamps?* she wondered, but today, for some reason, she felt as though that would be perfectly fine.

It seemed clear that after their last encounter, Mr. Nagasaki had done his utmost to find some way to help. He wasn't motivated by any benefit to himself nor trying to promote tourism as a local resident. Rather, the farmer saw that his acquaintance Munemori was struggling and wanted to lend a hand. It was as simple as that.

Even Kazuna, who specialized in seeing things through jaded eyes, found such kindness hard to deride.

The other day when they were just walking around, she'd seen how many people greeted Munemori, one after another, and had barely resisted the urge to ask snidely if he knew every single person in this town. And it wasn't because of where he worked; surely not every employee of the Tourism Section would have gotten the same reception. It was like an alien realm to Kazuna, but she understood one thing.

People trusted Munemori.

As they headed back to the car, Kazuna finally said, "About the bicycle—thank you very much."

For her, this was a heartfelt expression of gratitude, but Munemori no doubt extended similar considerate gestures to just about everyone. "Ah," he replied vaguely as if he'd already forgotten about it.

A moment later, he spotted Kazuna's blue bike by the side of the road and said, "It looks good. I'm glad."

The stamp-rally meeting was going to take place at the *izakaya* pub he'd mentioned the other night when she turned down his dinner invitation. She locked her bicycle and left it in the shade of the produce stand. Trusting that they wouldn't return to find it stolen was another bit of proof that honor among humans still existed, at least around here.

"Would you mind making two or three stops with me before the meeting? There are a couple of places I need to visit before the end of the day."

"Sure, that's fine. But where?"

Munemori opened the trunk. The space where Kazuna's bicycle had nestled not so long ago was now crammed full of cardboard boxes. Munemori placed his hand on them happily and said, "The cider finally arrived."

"Cider?"

"Yes, we asked Tokei Animation and made some '*Sabaku* cider,' the first in a line of anime-themed local goods."

On the side of each carton was the name of a soft-drink manufacturer that wasn't one of the major national companies. Each box also bore a color illustration of Towako that had been drawn by someone other than Kazuna.

She knew it was an unreasonable reaction but somehow got a prickling sensation in her chest.

In the case of licensed goods like this, the assignment usually went to an animator with superior skills who had an established relationship with the production company. Kazuna herself had received many orders for DVD packaging, posters, and such for *Sabaku.*

She wasn't the only animator working on the show. Of course there would be instances where someone else handled the copyrighted art. Yet she still couldn't help but think, *My real work isn't running around town helping out with some stamp rally. It's this, drawing.*

Munemori, seemingly unaware of her mixed feelings, continued his explanation in an exuberant voice. "When the manufacturer said they couldn't break up the order and deliver it to various places, we decided to take care of distribution ourselves. So the boxes were brought to city hall, and I've been delivering them. These are the last ones. Would you mind going with me?"

"No, it's totally fine," Kazuna assured offhandedly.

In contrast to her offhanded assurance, what Munemori engaged in was nothing less than heavy labor.

Their itinerary included two stations on the Lily of the Valley Line that were ridiculously far apart, and a kiosk by the precincts of a shrine that was one of the city's best-known sightseeing spots. At each stop, he had to deliver the weighty boxes of cider.

The shrine, especially, posed a particular challenge because it was located at the top of a narrow mountain path that didn't allow vehicular access. After parking the car in a lot at the bottom of the hill, Munemori said, "Please wait here."

As he began to hoist a heavy carton onto his shoulders, alone, Kazuna asked, "Are you going to be okay? Sh-Shall I give you a hand?" Even an animator who would rather die than perform physical labor couldn't remain silent and not feel guilty. *Eek*, she thought, all but trembling in trepidation. *What if he says yes?*

But Munemori gave his head an easy shake and said, "Nah, it's much too heavy. Please just stay here. I'll be fine. Though actually, there is something—" He put down the carton and rummaged around amid the chaos on the back seat until he located his satchel. Extracting a clear file folder and handing it to Kazuna, he requested, "While I'm away, if it isn't too much trouble, could you please take a look at this? I've been thinking a lot this past week, and I also watched *Sabaku* again, several times."

"Hm?" Kazuna saw the words on a sheet inside the folder and caught her breath.

THE ENAGA FOREST — A *SABAKU* MAP

The map's starting point was Enaga Station, and its surface was sprinkled with countless black dots, each indicating a point of interest. Under each mark were annotations explaining which *Sabaku* scene, in what episode, took place at that location. Pictures, screenshots of the actual anime, had been supplied as well.

"This..." When Kazuna looked up in tongue-tied astonishment, Munemori launched into his explanation with a serious expression.

"Please tell me if you see any problem areas or things that need improvement. The anime pictures are just some that I took with my smartphone directly from the screen, so they haven't been authorized by Tokei Animation, but if this looks okay to you, I'll go ahead and request the actual images. I might have overlooked something, and also, I'd like to set up the stamp-rally course around the points on this map, so I'll be grateful for your feedback."

"So this map would be distributed to fans?"

"That's right." Munemori nodded. "We can't include every site in the stamp rally, but a map will guide people to the other ones, too. I think it'll be more efficient than putting up signboards.

Actually, when I went on the recon tour of other municipalities with holy sites, they all had maps like this one at train stations and elsewhere."

"But making this must have been so much work."

As she studied the map, Kazuna gave a sigh of admiration. There were some locations she hadn't even been aware of herself, and she found herself learning new things at every turn. *Ah, so there was something here, too!*

There were probably websites on the internet where diligent fans had done the research and posted this type of information, but even if Munemori had consulted them, his map was beyond detailed.

"This is my home turf," he noted, as if reading her mind. "I've been seeing all the places regularly ever since I was a kid, so I pretty much know what's where without even being told. And whenever I see a familiar place on the screen, it makes me happy. Well, I'm off."

With that, carrying a heavy box, Munemori started up the sloping path.

Inside the car, the air conditioner noisily worked overtime, making a whiny, windy sound that was almost like a cry. Even though the afternoon was teetering on the brink of evening, it was still scorching hot outside the car. Holding his map in her hand, Kazuna watched as Munemori, clad in work clothes stained with sweat, trudged up the hill.

Twenty minutes or so later, he returned, dripping with perspiration.

"Sorry to keep you waiting," he apologized, breathing heavily with his shoulders. The minute he was back in the driver's seat, he rested his forehead on the steering wheel, saying, "Oh, air conditioning. I feel alive again."

"Well done," praised Kazuna. "Are you sure you're okay, though? Do you really need to deliver all the boxes today?"

"Well, for both of the train stations, I can practically drive up to the door, so it'll be fine. And also, all the other shops have already had their cider delivered, so the remaining ones not having them just won't do." He forced a smile. "The topography around these parts is a little problematic. Especially for the shrine and the limestone cave, roads are narrow and you can't get very close with a car."

"Have you been out delivering since morning, by any chance? The cider, I mean."

There's no "by any chance" about it, she thought. *Hey, Tokei Animation, you're shirking your duties!* Something about this whole arrangement definitely didn't feel right.

"Why can't the manufacturer deliver the boxes to more than one place?" she asked. "They ought to get them out to the shops themselves."

"No, we secured the orders on our side to have it made, so that wasn't an option. The shipping charges would have been too high if they'd done all the individual deliveries."

"Still, this isn't the kind of work city employees should be doing. It seems like a job for a freight company."

"Nah, it's very much ours," Munemori said in an easygoing tone, lifting his head from the steering wheel and fishing a handkerchief out of one pocket. While Kazuna sat silent, at a loss for words, he repeated with a laugh, "It's part of my job—although if I could make one small request, I'd be grateful if the next batch of cider could be in plastic containers or paper cartons instead of glass bottles."

"I doubt it. They need to be in cans or bottles to be collectibles. Also, paper cartons and fizzy drinks aren't exactly a match made in heaven."

Kazuna couldn't budge on that point, and Munemori wiped away the sweat that was still streaming down his face and made a show of slumping his shoulders. "How strict of you," he muttered. "Either of those would be heavy."

Hearing him, Kazuna chuckled. "Yup," she said, looking at Munemori and nodding.

En route to the shopping district where the yakitori bar was located, Munemori started talking about the necessity of getting the chamber of commerce involved in the planning.

"The chamber of commerce?" echoed Kazuna, turning to her companion from the passenger seat. The small air conditioner was still doing its noisy best to spew out cold air.

Munemori nodded without taking his eyes off the road. "Right now, we're having to make cider with the city government as the broker and Tokei Animation paying out of their own pockets, but that approach will only result in one or two tie-in products at most, and the effect will be minimal. The ideal solution would be for the local chamber of commerce to realize the anime's potential and to take the initiative in negotiating with Tokei. There are some small businesses right here in Enaga that make sweets and beverages."

Ah, Kazuna thought, *that makes sense*. Since Tokei Animation was half-hearted about the pilgrimage, they would almost certainly balk at spending any additional money on local licensed goods. "So in other words, if local manufacturers could produce the goods on their own, Tokei Animation and the city government wouldn't need to shell out any cash."

"In fact, Tokei would profit from the licensing fees."

Kazuna was impressed. Actually, the licensed goods created for other anime-pilgrimage sites must have owed to a similar system. The other day, she'd been appalled that the municipality side was so focused on "things," but they did pay attention to safety and financial considerations much more than she'd realized.

"If all goes well, then the chamber of commerce will take care of applications for licensing and so on, and the tourism section will be freed up for other things. That would release me from this kind of extra obligation, but for now it's just part of my job to run around delivering cider." Munemori laughed ruefully. "The directors at the chamber of commerce are mostly in their fifties and sixties—old masters, so to speak—and they don't have a clear sense of how anime can bring profits. Enaga's out in the boonies, of course, and even if you try to explain that something is hugely popular in Tokyo, they won't really get it. To persuade them, we need actual proof like the cider we supplied selling well, so they can feel it. We've got a lot riding on this."

"I wish I could have drawn it."

"What?" Munemori whipped his head around to stare at her.

Kazuna was no less surprised that the words had slipped out of her. She hadn't even realized she was harboring such thoughts. She would never have talked like this to her colleagues, for fear they might perceive it as arrogance, but somehow she felt comfortable confiding in Munemori.

"The packaging, for the cider you're betting on..." she said haltingly, getting stuck on her words. "I wish... I could have drawn it."

After hearing this, Munemori's face brightened immediately. "Thank you very much," he told her with a wide smile. "You're pretty amazing, Ms. Namisawa. I can't even imagine what must be going on inside your head, to be able to draw the way you do."

"Oh, well, it's my job," Kazuna returned. "Drawing pictures is completely normal—it's just like any other work. Actually, if you make too big a deal of it, some people might take it the wrong way. I mean, if somebody went on about your astounding ability to hand out people's family registers at the service window, you'd have some mixed feelings about that, right?"

"Well, I've never worked in the family register section, so I don't even know how."

"No, that's not what I meant."

They were still on completely different wavelengths.

Kazuna frowned slightly and heaved a sigh, but she felt only a small fraction of the irritation that had consumed her at their first meeting.

It was just a few minutes past six o'clock, but several groups of customers were already ensconced in Munemori's preferred hangout, and the air was thick with yakitori smoke. When Kazuna and Munemori entered through the *noren* curtains that partially covered the entrance, a number of ruddy-faced older men who were sitting at the bar glanced up at them.

"Welcome!" caroled a voice from the back, and a moment later a woman appeared behind the counter. When she saw Munemori, her face relaxed into a smile. "Ah, Shu. Welcome," she addressed him by the first syllable of his given name.

"Hi, Asami," he said. "Listen, I'm sorry to ask this, but is there a table in the back we could use?"

"Yes, I kept it open, and it's all yours. Please stay as long as you like."

After one glance at the proprietress's clearly delineated facial features and slender, shapely body, Kazuna thought, *She's pretty.* And then, in an odd flash of insight: *She's the type of person who can run her own restaurant.*

When the older men who were seated at the counter called out an order—"Asami, bring us another round!"—the woman laughed and responded, "Yes, coming right up! Are you guys trying to set a record today, or what?" A moment later, in a flurry of gracious efficiency, she was carrying a fresh round of drinks to them.

It wasn't a particularly large establishment. Besides the bar counter up front, there were only three low tables in a tatami-matted area in the back. The hand-lettered "Reserved" sign that sat on one of the tables was made from thick drawing paper folded so it would stand on its own, and it gave a sense of the homemade aesthetic in its fullest flower.

"Is this your first time here?" asked Munemori.

"Well, this is the first time I've ever actually visited this shopping street, although I've seen it when I was passing by."

"Oh, really?" Munemori seemed surprised, but the truth was that Kazuna had never dreamed she might someday set foot in a place like this, so vibrantly redolent of local flavor.

One of the red-faced men sitting at the counter peeked into the back area and, with no trace of manners or self-restraint, said, "Hey, Shu, who's the girl?"

Kazuna felt her shoulders stiffen, but Munemori turned around and replied, calmly and politely: "Someone who's being tremendously helpful with work."

Asami, the owner, let out an exasperated laugh and scolded, "Don't bother them, gramps!"

I don't belong here, Kazuna thought. They had only just arrived, but she already wanted to leave, a bad habit of hers.

Munemori said, by way of explanation, "That man used to run a rice store, but he's retired now," then asked solicitously, "Is beer all right?"

Behind the counter, a male cook was silently tending to the yakitori skewers sizzling on the grill and assembling a variety of side dishes while Asami bustled around the restaurant in perpetual motion, making and serving drinks. Coming to the back to take their order, she said familiarly to Kazuna, "I'm sorry it's so noisy," which made the first-timer a bit glad.

"Mr. Munemori, you certainly know a lot of people."

"Oh, well, that's just because I've lived here, like, forever. There are quite a few people in these parts who really love it in Enaga and have no desire to leave, even though it's way out in the sticks. Most of my classmates from middle school and high school are still living around here."

"Wow…"

"A lot of my soccer buddies got married and had kids, and there was a stretch when they were too busy to go out and have fun, but we've been getting together again and will be playing futsal this weekend, too. So yes, I'm never short on friends to hang out with."

"Mr. Munemori, are you married?"

"I'm single. They often tease me for being footloose and fancy-free, as the saying goes."

Somehow it was a relief to Kazuna to hear that, contrary to her assumption, not everyone in rural areas married young.

But when Munemori asked, "What about you, Ms. Namisawa?" she let out a strangulated *ghk*.

"Wh-Why would I have anyone?" she stammered hastily. *What a question to turn back on me*, she fumed, but Munemori didn't even seem to understand why she should feel so flustered. He tilted his head and commented, "Are you serious?"

"Thanks for waiting!"

Glancing at the beer and hors d'oeuvres that arrived, Munemori thanked Asami. Then, peering into Kazuna's face, he said, "Shall we have a toast?"

"Oh, yes," she said, and as they lightly clinked beer mugs, they told each other, "Good job today."

Having spent the entire day schlepping heavy boxes under the blazing-hot sun, Munemori drained half his beer in a single gulp, announced, "That really hits the spot," and crumpled towards the mug like some weary dad. Picking up a bite of one of the appetizers—dried, shredded daikon radish reconstituted in a piquant marinade—he posed a question to Kazuna.

"From your perspective, how do you feel about *Sabaku*? For me, as an amateur, it seems certain that it will win a lot of fans, but I'd be very interested in hearing the thoughts of an insider who works in the field."

"It's doing really well. I'd say it's definitely one of the favorites to walk away with anime supremacy this season."

"Supremacy?"

Oh, he wouldn't know, and he'll be even more at sea if I go into too much detail. With that thought, Kazuna explained succinctly, "It's a sort of unofficial title bestowed on the biggest hit of the season. Does that make sense?"

"Cool, sounds like *The Romance of the Three Kingdoms*." Munemori looked satisfied and continued, "In the beginning I didn't understand how anime worked at all, but I learned later that anime series don't always take off while they're being broadcast. For pilgrimages and such, the crunch begins after all the episodes have finished airing. Anyway, in my newbie's ignorance I thought we needed to hurry and get the ball rolling for merchandising and stamp rallies as soon as possible, while the series was still going. When I first talked to Tokei Animation in a panic, though, I got scolded and was told to hold my horses."

"Yes, right now that's how it is. In the case of *Sabaku*, the sales of toys aimed at kids are a significant source of revenue. The buying habits of child fans versus adult fans aren't in synch, but anyway, an anime can't become profitable from broadcast proceeds only. I believe the moment of truth is when a series comes out on DVD and Blu-Ray."

In fact, whether a show won the "anime supremacy" title ultimately came down to those sales figures. The Amazon ranking, the Oricon ranking, the total preorders—now that the industry concept of "supremacy" had caught on among anime fans, there was even a designated site where you could get quick updates on those stats.

For the current crop of anime, that site showed that *Sabaku* had the largest number of preorders so far for the first DVD. Next, in the number-two position, was a continuing series from the previous season: an anime with a campus theme, based on a light novel, called *I'm Saying I Love You, So You Can't Say You Want to Die* (a.k.a. "Love Die"). Then in third place, leading among a number of shows that were bunched together, was Studio Edge's *Fateful Fight: Ryder Light,* directed by Chiharu Oji.

Among those, Kazuna received work orders from *Sabaku* and *Ryder* and was actively engaged in drawing genga for both projects. Now, in early June, the series that began airing in April were heading into the final stretch. *Sabaku,* in particular, was getting a lot of attention for a heroine who had "lost her sounds," a plot point that was pretty heavy for children to handle. Since the director was Hitomi Saito, the fans who frequented internet message boards were confident that there would be some respite and that the sounds would be restored to the girl.

"To be honest, whether people decide to buy the entire series on DVD has a lot to do with whether they liked the outcome in the final episode. So the most crucial period for the current crop of shows will be through the end of this month and into the next, when all the finales will be airing. Of course, even if *Sabaku* doesn't end up being ranked number one in the final stats, I don't think there's any doubt that it's already a bona fide hit."

"Oh, really?"

"By the way, is the person you've been talking to at Tokei Animation named Yukishiro?"

"No, it's Mr. Koshigaya, the producer for promotions."

"I see." Kazuna nodded, but she was thinking, *No, actually, I don't see. That doesn't sound right, at all.*

Sabaku was Yukishiro's project, wasn't it? No matter how lukewarm Tokei might be about the pilgrimage, since they'd made it official and were working with the municipality, Yukishiro needed to be taking responsibility, especially if he was so surpassingly capable. Kazuna felt a rising swell of irritation compounded by her grudge against the producer who'd barged in and wrecked her date at Tokyo Skytree.

Just then their yakitori orders arrived, and Kazuna exclaimed, "Oh, that smells delicious!"

"It *is* delicious, guaranteed," Munemori said. Then he adjusted his posture, tucking his legs under him so his upper body was resting on his heels. Suddenly wearing a serious expression, he said, "May I ask you something before we're too drunk?"

Kazuna was reaching for a skewer of yakitori, but she paused with her arm extended in midair, surprised by his formal manner. "What is it?" she responded, bracing herself slightly.

"You keep on using the word 'realie' with me, and I was just wondering—is that a way of suggesting that people like me are stuck in reality and have nothing else?"

The instant she heard those words, Kazuna's lips parted, then froze in place before she could say so much as "Huh?"

Her mind had stopped working.

Munemori's face was the very picture of solemnity, without a ghost of a smile. Seeing his rigid, unyielding expression, Kazuna felt as if all the blood were draining from her body.

The first thought that came to her was: *Oh, no, he heard me?* But she realized on brief reflection that of course he would have. She'd constantly been muttering, *You realie,* or *Damn realie,* when it was just the two of them.

She'd been lulled into complacency by Munemori's cheerful temperament and stolid air and taken him far too lightly.

Next, a beat or two later, came confusion. *What shall I do, what shall I do, what shall I do?* Kazuna feigned bewildered misunderstanding and gulped down her saliva. When she spoke, her voice was thin and tremulous and she sounded like she was on the brink of tears.

"Reality and...nothing else?"

The term "realie" meant leading a full, active life rather than having "nothing else."

"Oh, I'm sorry," Munemori said quickly. "I'm not angry or anything. It's the truth, so if people want to say those things about me, there's nothing I can do about it."

His face relaxed, and that simple change was enough to make Kazuna feel an incredible sense of relief. But then, noticing how her heart was pounding loudly in her chest, she wondered if it had stopped beating for a while along with her breathing.

Kazuna was good at writing, and at analyzing other people from the shadows, but she was desperately unaccustomed to being confronted point-blank. She lacked the mental fortitude to conduct such conversations.

"Unlike me, people who are involved with anime, including you, lead such rich lives," Munemori said.

Kazuna stared at him, momentarily speechless. *Rich*. The word echoed in her ears. *Rich*.

"What do you mean?" she asked at last.

"Well, I only have this one actual, everyday reality, but creative people like you have other, rich—how to put it? Fertile grounds that have been tilled deep?"

Kazuna was gobsmacked. She had never expected to be told such a thing, and found herself unable to exhale the breath she was holding in her lungs.

"When you said it the other day at the limestone cave, it made me think," he went on. "People like me are obsessed with actual results and facts, but people who care about anime somehow aren't seeking the same things. That's why I tried making that map."

"The map is absolutely wonderful," Kazuna rushed to say, and she was speaking from the heart. "You're totally on the right track with that. I'm sure everybody will love it."

"I hope so." Munemori gave an awkward smile, clearly feeling shy about Kazuna's praise. "I know I just said realistic stuff like tangible results aren't the be-all and end-all, and this is going to sound contradictory, but..."

"Okay?"

"It's a first for me—doing work that leaves behind something with form and substance."

"What do you mean?"

Munemori took a small sip of beer as if to wet his whistle, then stared at Kazuna.

"From the point of view of directors and producers, this whole project may seem like a nuisance and nothing more than self-satisfaction on our part. But the thing is, our regular work at the tourism section doesn't leave anything tangible behind. Whether it's prepping for the festival or enticing skiers to visit during the winter, even though we give it everything we've got, when the season or the event ends there's nothing left—no evidence that something lively took place."

"Yes, I think I understand, somehow," Kazuna said, imagining the desolate hush after a festival.

Munemori smiled pensively. "With anime, however, Enaga City will live on in the work. So that's a kind of lasting form, and it makes me very happy. It feels like a worthwhile thing to be working on."

Silently, Kazuna gazed at Munemori.

"This is something my friend who knows a lot about anime told me up front," he continued. "He said that pilgrimages don't work if the municipality expects the anime to carry all the weight. He scolded me saying that both sides need to keep on working together, even after the last episode airs—that's how a city cooperates. And I totally agree with him."

Munemori straightened his spine, then bowed his head in Kazuna's direction. "Forgive me, I've been blathering on about mundane things, and I'm sorry if it's been boring or unpleasant for you."

"S-Stop it please," Kazuna stuttered, not sure what to do. Still holding the bow, Munemori looked at her with upturned eyes.

"We want to do everything we can to make people watch *Sabaku*. I'm just a realie, so it's probably only natural for you to assume I don't understand these things."

"Wait, wait—hold on a minute!" Kazuna had heard enough, and she shook her head rapidly. People weren't supposed to denigrate themselves with that word. It just sounded weird. "Mr. Munemori, I'm sorry, I get the feeling you don't understand the term, and you've got it all wrong. It's not supposed to be a bad thing, and it's not a word to apply to yourself when you're being modest. In fact, using it to describe yourself could even be gross and off-putting."

"Oh, is that so?" Munemori looked perplexed. "I thought it was a term of contempt for sure, like calling someone a shallow, empty guy."

"Oh, no, not at—" Kazuna started to issue an automatic denial but couldn't. She wasn't able to muster a smile, either.

An epiphany struck her like a ton of bricks: she had uttered those words multiple times—*damn realie*—to disparage him. Yes, it expressed disdain. Why? Because, without a doubt, people who immersed themselves in local human networks, who were loved, who fell in love, and who hung out with each other, were her enemies.

In this world, there were those who needed fictional stories, including anime, and those who didn't. To Kazuna, the people who were able to live without fiction appeared to be carefree denizens of a different universe. Blissfully clueless about anime, they always seemed to walk on the sunny side of the street. It had never occurred to her that they might feel hurt by whatever a dweller in the shade like her said.

I took him for a fool.

She believed using her head was one of her strong suits, but she also knew that she had a tendency to get hung up on troublesome, solipsistic thoughts—to the point where even when she went on a date with someone she had a gigantic crush on, her toxic self-consciousness was so disruptive that she couldn't even bring herself to put together a nicer-than-usual outfit. To her, "realies" came across as carefree and happily devoid of anxiety or worry. She even saw the people who got all dressed up and put on makeup and fell desperately in love as shameful, somehow, and that was why she'd made up her mind not to indulge in that sort of behavior herself.

It was just as Munemori said. In her vocabulary, "realie" wasn't a compliment; it was a put-down. Because she was afraid of people she couldn't understand, she pretended to be craning her neck to see them when in fact she shoved them and looked down on them. Since she herself wasn't a realie and hadn't been blessed with a fulfilling youth or with romantic love, she had decided that those deprivations gave her the right to scorn anyone who had enjoyed such things. She preened her feathers and congratulated herself for seeing the world so much more deeply, for all her faults.

All these years she'd been telling herself that as long as she could enjoy the modest happiness of being able to draw, that was the only thing she needed. But to anyone else, the very act of drawing for herself alone, while feeling superior to and distancing herself from others, was a form of happiness that was fairly arrogant.

Munemori had picked up on that.

"No," she said now, "That isn't it, at all." She wanted to apologize to him but didn't know where to begin, so she just lowered her eyes.

"Thank goodness," Munemori said, with a long, heartfelt sigh. "If I didn't annoy you or make you dislike me, that's a huge relief."

"Dislike? No, I mean…"

"It isn't that I don't respect it," Munemori said. "When we were up at the limestone cave, you said that if the fans found out that we didn't respect the work, it would be over. But the thing is, I have nothing *but* respect for *Sabaku*. If my approach was somehow wrong-footed, I can't apologize enough. Watching that show and seeing how carefully and evocatively the pictures are drawn, I've gotten gooseflesh more times than I can count, and I'm even moved. I'm truly grateful that they chose to make this area the backdrop for the story."

"…Okay." Kazuna didn't want Munemori to notice that she was feeling down, so she raised her head and mustered a weak smile. But the man, showing no outward signs of unease, just gestured toward the platter of yakitori and urged, "Please, have some while it's still warm."

Now, though, Kazuna knew better than to mistake his easygoing nature for any lack of sensitivity.

Perhaps he had seen right through her, but out of consideration, forgiven her as well. Kazuna felt so mortified about her own snobbish behavior that she wished she could just disappear.

It was sheer conceit to think that she was the only one who cared, or understood. She had looked down on Munemori for his ignorance about anime and otaku culture, but what about her? By the same token, she'd been entirely clueless about a famous local festival and hadn't even recognized its name. And she had taken virtually no interest in the minutiae of real, everyday life, such as the fact that simply airing up the tires could make her bicycle so much more comfortable—and pleasurable—to ride.

It was the same with the stamp rally. Now that she thought about it, all she had done was to pour cold water on his ideas, one after another: *No—I don't think so. No—I doubt it.* She felt her entire body grow hot with shame as she remembered how she'd been.

I'm so sorry, she thought, feeling a fresh wave of regret over her inability to say it out loud. In her heart, at least, she bowed her head and apologized to him over and over again. She felt herself teetering on the brink of tears.

I'm sorry, Mr. Munemori.

"On another topic, there are some practical things we need to discuss." Munemori leaned across the table and extracted a clear plastic file folder from his satchel. In addition to a copy of the map he had given her earlier, it contained a tourist brochure for Enaga City. The cover couldn't have been less anime-esque. It showed some rough-looking men in happi coats clustered next to a boat decorated with dragon motifs, which appeared to be on the verge of setting off down a fast-flowing river amid a shower of white spray.

KANAGA FESTIVAL, read the caption.

"Oh, this is the festival you were talking about?"

"Yes. Starting at nine in the morning, various groups launch their custom-made boats at one-hour intervals, and lots of local people and visitors come to watch. Most of the boats end up running aground or breaking up on the rocks before they make it all the way downstream, but watching the grand crack-ups is part of the fun. Though my residency idea went over like a lead balloon..." Munemori paused with a rueful smile and continued, "I started thinking, *What if we could launch a* Sabaku *boat?* You know, decorate it with pictures of the characters and the robot and have the fans watch it flow down the river. Every year, we expect somewhere around a hundred thousand visitors for the festival, and TV crews always come too, so it would definitely generate some publicity."

Kazuna almost said "Ah!" out loud.

The scene popped into her head. An admiring crowd surrounded a boat completely covered with *Sabaku*-themed designs.

Munemori continued with his explanation. "Almost all the boats end up being destroyed, but the fragments of those wrecks are said to keep you safe, sound, and healthy for the next year, and the custom is for visitors to take them home as amulets. So even after it gets smashed, people will be treasuring the boat in a way."

"I like that idea." Nodding, Kazuna repeated, "I really like that idea."

In her mind's eye, fans were still eagerly surrounding the boat, pointing out various details and snapping photographs. And she thought:

If they'll let me, I want to draw the images on that boat.

"Oh, really? It wouldn't be weird to propose that to the other party?"

"It wouldn't be weird at all. I think a *Sabaku* boat would be a big hit, and if it ended up getting some TV coverage, that would be beneficial for the Tokei Animation side, and for the work itself."

"The problem is the cost." Munemori's face clouded over. "The boats have to be made by professional artisans, so they aren't cheap, by any means. It will all depend on whether or not Tokei will be willing to underwrite the cost."

"Well, anyway, let's try proposing that idea. If they say no, we can revisit it then. Together we'll—" Kazuna stopped in the middle of her last sentence, surprised by what she heard herself saying, but finished, "Together we'll be able to think of something."

Having spoken the words, she thought, *Wow, I'm starting to feel a genuine desire to do something. I really want to help make this happen.* Until now, her involvement had been forced upon her by her boss and by this guy. However, that had been a supremely selfish and uncool way of looking at it.

Toting the heavy cartons of cider, a task that surely wasn't listed under his official duties, Munemori had told her that it was his job. Compared to his attitude, what a pain she'd been, grumbling and quibbling and dragging her feet wherever they went.

Helping out with the anime pilgrimage was an authentic part of her job.

And this job, she thought, *is mine.*

◆

The final episode of *Soundback: The Singing Stone* was scheduled to air toward the end of June, approximately two weeks before the stamp rally launched.

That episode included a great many drawings that Tokei Animation had commissioned Kazuna to do, and she participated in numerous conferences with the show's animation director regarding the backgrounds for each scene. She didn't travel to Tokyo for any face-to-face meetings, but for the most part, Skype was sufficient for their needs.

But even Kazuna didn't have any inside information about the core part of the screenplay: how *Sabaku* ended. Normally a show's primary director or the director of animation would drop a few hints here and there, but in a case like this, where she'd grown attached to the anime and wanted to learn the story's conclusion by watching the actual, real-time broadcast, she went out of her way to avoid picking up any major spoilers from the staff at Tokei Animation.

"Would it be all right if I joined you?" Munemori asked when Hitomi mentioned that a number of the animators were planning to gather in Fine Garden's lobby to view the final episode together. When the day arrived, he showed up with a hefty supply of locally brewed sake and craft beer and received a rousing welcome from the group before they all settled in to watch the show.

Purely as work, it went without saying that Kazuna loved every anime equally, and this was the first time she'd ever formed such a strong emotional attachment to a project that featured her genga.

When the episode started, her heart began to race. From time to time some of her colleagues wandered by, apparently thinking they might drop in and out during brief breaks from work. But when they saw Kazuna and the others sitting perfectly still, staring fixedly at the TV screen in front of them, the would-be casual viewers invariably turned and tiptoed away, and eventually stopped trying to pop in altogether.

While the episode was airing, neither Kazuna nor Munemori spoke a single word—not even during the commercials.

Would Towako, the heroine, miraculously regain all her lost sounds? That question had been a hot topic on online message boards.

Not daring to miss a second of the action, they watched the protagonists waging their final battle.

When the ending theme song came on, the familiar first section was followed by a second verse, heard today for the first time in the series' run.

The images under the credits were different, too, and looked back on *Sabaku*'s most memorable moments.

The song came to an end.

As if to bring the transported viewers back to reality, a trailer for the next season's anime series came on, and the high-pitched voice of that show's main character filled the air. In that instant, Kazuna felt the long-accumulated tension drain from her shoulders.

She almost wanted to scream out loud.

Director Saito, she whispered the name of that diminutive woman in her heart instead, with a sigh. *Director Saito. What an amazing thing you've done.*

Kazuna thought the final episode and the way the story ended couldn't have pleased everybody. However, what clearly came through was that the director had no regrets—the series had run its course with no trace of compromise, as the story she wanted to tell. No matter who might bash her or criticize her, she hadn't wavered.

When Kazuna happened to glance up, she noticed that Munemori was sitting with his back to her. Without looking around, he said, "I'm just going to buy some drinks," and exited the building.

This seemed odd, since there was a vending machine right there in the lobby, and the table was still covered with the alcoholic beverages he'd brought.

She felt a trifle concerned. Personally, she had found the final episode brilliant, but she realized that it might be difficult for an anime newbie like Munemori to accept the absence of a clear-cut happy ending. Impelled by worry, she quietly followed him.

He was standing on the road in front of Fine Garden, bending backwards and staring up at the sky. As he took a deep, long breath, Kazuna saw that his eyes were a little moist.

At the sight, she said to herself: *Ah, I get it.*

Just because he was new to the world of anime, that didn't mean he objected to the ending. In fact, his very dearth of exposure might have caused him to be affected even more profoundly than Kazuna and her colleagues.

After hesitating for a moment, she stepped out and walked

toward Munemori. This time of year, just after the summer solstice, the luminous light of sunset spread across the landscape from the western sky, painting the distant mountains and the vivid green rice fields at their base with a rosy glow.

This is a beautiful town, Kazuna thought.

Right now, she had the distinct sense that those *Sabaku* children really had fought to protect this place, and her heart felt full to overflowing.

"That was good, wasn't it?" Munemori noticed Kazuna approaching, and flashed her a bashful smile. "Those kids really gave it their all. It makes me feel very proud to think that they fought their battles right here in my hometown."

"Yes, I know."

Kazuna gave a firm nod. She was proud and happy to have had a part in bringing those kids to life until today.

A week had passed since the broadcast of *Soundback: The Singing Stone*'s final episode.

Due to scheduling reasons, the final episode of *Fateful Fight: Ryder Light*, directed by Chiharu Oji, aired a full week after *Sabaku* went off the air.

Kazuna had been commissioned a large number of genga for *Ryder*, as well. Yet, even though she had received at least as much info beforehand for the series, the finale left her shell-shocked.

Unlike Saturday evenings, which had been *Sabaku*'s time slot, the midnight hours were prime working time for animators, so a much larger crowd was gathered around the television in Fine Garden's lobby.

"Incredible," Chief Seki could be heard murmuring midway through on the wings of a seemingly unconscious sigh. No one else uttered a single word. The lobby, that summer night, was enveloped in perfect stillness.

There were several scenes that Kazuna had drawn based on explanatory storyboards. Even so, what she saw on the screen took her breath away.

The backgrounds, and the music, and the characters: the whole was so much greater than the sum of its parts and seemed to swallow the viewer whole. It almost seemed like the small screen, the TV screen, had grown many times larger. The characters were alive and moving around on it as she watched.

The quality was so high, it was scary.

"It may be a good many years before anyone else dares to try their hand at the magic-girl genre," murmured President Koizumi, who had been watching silently from the back of the room. When Kazuna and her colleagues turned to look at him, their boss nodded. "I guess that's what that director is capable of. Quite a few outfits will be stealing from his direction starting next season. We need to be ready, too."

Then he added, "This season's supremacy goes to Director Oji's determination. From now on, anime will never be the same."

◆

The spring-season anime continued to air their final episodes, one by one, and in the second week of July the time finally came for the Enaga City stamp rally.

It all begins today, read the text message Kazuna received early that morning. Unable to sit still for a moment longer, she ventured out into the town.

It was Saturday.

The rainy season had just ended, and the clear sky was gloriously illuminated by the crisp, refreshing morning sun. Reflecting its rays, the rice fields in the distance, still knee-deep in rainwater, glittered brightly.

The stamp-rally tables that Kazuna and Munemori had run around setting up in various locations numbered ten in all.

Anime pilgrims who returned to the "goal line"—the visitor-information center in front of the train station—after having acquired five stamps would receive a special *Sabaku* picture postcard, while those who completed the entire ten-stamp circuit would be rewarded with an original *Sabaku*-themed towel, in addition to the postcard. Kazuna had designed both items, and receiving those coveted commissions from Tokei Animation had been a dream come true.

Please, let the stamp rally be a success! And please make people buy lots of things—especially the cider that a certain person worked so hard to deliver.

Those were the thoughts running through Kazuna's mind as she rode her bike along the national route, flanked on both sides by rice paddies.

And then, with a delighted and incredulous "Whoaaa," she stopped and caught her breath.

On the road ahead, which had been all but deserted as recently as the previous day, she saw a fair number of people. Walking along in separate groups rather than as a mob, they were all clutching copies of the map Kazuna and Munemori had collaborated on. The majority of clusters seemed to be made up of young people—probably high school or college students—but there were also some couples and parents with children in tow. "Mama! I think it's that way," called out one kid, who might have been in elementary school, pointing in the direction of the produce stand old Mr. Nagasaki had provided. Kazuna's heart seemed to quiver gently in her chest. She was so happy that she had to grit her teeth.

Another kid of about the same age was shouldering a backpack with the upper half of a *Sabaku* robot sticking out through the top.

We did it!

Kazuna exulted, striking a celebratory "guts pose"—fists balled up and hoisted in the air—all by herself. A moment later she was firing off a text message to Munemori. She wanted to share this tableau with him.

—I just got to the national route, and the turnout is good. Mr. Munemori, where are you today?

No sooner had she hit "Send" than her smartphone sounded its message alert. It was from Munemori.

—I'm up on the national road. The turnout is really good. Ms. Namisawa, where are you right now?

Somehow, they had texted each other at the exact same moment, and their messages had crossed in midair.

When Kazuna read the words and looked up from her phone, she spotted a figure that looked like Munemori, far ahead down the long, straight road. Hopping on her bicycle, she pedaled furiously in his direction over the sunbaked asphalt. He'd evidently just read Kazuna's text, as well, because he glanced up from his mobile phone just then.

"Mr. Munemori!" called Kazuna when she was a few yards away.

"Ah! Ms. Namisawa." His face breaking into a broad grin, he bowed and said, "Good morning."

"We did it."

"Yes," Munemori agreed, facing up again. "Today's the first day of the stamp rally, but ever since the final episode aired, we've heard that quite a few pilgrims have been visiting Enaga. To be honest, it's beating our estimates. Tokei Animation kindly posted the info on the official *Sabaku* website, too."

Seemingly overcome with emotion, Munemori looked into Kazuna's eyes. "It's all thanks to you, Ms. Namisawa," he said. "Thank you so much for all the advice, inspiration, and motivation. Going forward, I hope you'll give me lots more guidance and encouragement!"

"No, no, it's not me, but the strength of the work itself!"

Munemori's expressions of gratitude were as stuffy as ever, but somehow that sort of thing no longer bothered Kazuna as much. Besides, she was busy watching people enjoying the stamp rally, which made her happier than anything.

In the days since *Sabaku* ended its broadcast run, the orders she was receiving for copyrighted genga related to the series had increased, rather than the opposite, even apart from the stamp rally. All the signs seemed to indicate that *Sabaku* had made a name for itself.

"But what's up with this bonus towel?" asked Munemori. "It

has Takaya, and Towako, but not Ryuichi?"

The "*bonus*" *towel?* The wording threw Kazuna off, but Munemori lifted one end of the one he wore wrapped around his neck so she could see. *Ah*, she realized. He meant the *Sabaku* original towel handed out at the goal point.

As he innocently showed off his sample, several people who were tromping past at intervals clearly took note. They didn't make a big fuss, but there was a quiet hum of excitement as passing fans nudged each other and pointed at the towel, saying, "Look, that's it!"

"Oh, during the broadcast, it was mainly Takaya, Towako, and Ryuichi," Kazuna began, then paused to suggest, as an aside, that it might be best to keep the towel out of sight. Getting a preview could deprive people of the pleasure of seeing their prizes for the first time at the finish line. "Anyway," she continued, "for some reason, after the series ended, the orders often started to be for Takaya, Towako, and one of the twins, Nobu. I even received orders for two-shots of Takaya and Nobu, and Towako and Nobu. Sadly, my personal bias is Ryu, but I just have to give them what they ask for."

It seemed Nobu had caught on with viewers after the last episode aired. That type of shift was reflected mercilessly by the orders she received.

"In that last episode, Nobu did look cool, for sure. He was quite brave," Munemori said. He went on in a sympathetic tone, "Only, it seems kind of unfair to Rena, the other half of the twins. I feel sorry for her, being left out in the cold while her brother gets his face on all kinds of goods. I mean, they were always together, in almost every scene where they appeared."

"That's right—that's exactly right! I'm like, *Hey, think about how Rena feels not getting drawn!*"

At any rate, the genga orders were still pouring in even after the series went off the air, and Kazuna was happy to have the chance to continue drawing the characters she'd come to love.

She was glad, too, that she could talk about those characters with Munemori, bandying the names back and forth as if it were the most natural thing in the world.

Just behind them on the road, they heard a voice saying, "Since this is the Hokuriku region, you kind of have an image of snow country, but during the summer it doesn't seem to be cooler than anywhere else, huh?"

Kazuna and Munemori quietly looked around. The other half of the visiting couple—they appeared to be around college age— replied, "True, but it really feels good to be out walking in the summer sun."

Hearing them, Kazuna thought, *Oh, those kids must have come all the way from Tokyo or some equally faraway place.*

"We're getting overnight visitors, too," Munemori whispered, gazing at the students' receding figures. "The Inn Association is over the moon—they're saying it really livens things up to have young guests. Most of the inns have gift shops, and apparently they're going to start carrying that cider."

"It'll be great if the cider takes off." If the sales were robust, the chamber of commerce would be willing to get involved in the anime pilgrimage. That would take some of the workload off Munemori's shoulders, and then perhaps he could relax a bit.

"Yes," he agreed. His face muscles seemed to tighten as he continued, "On Monday there's going to be a meeting at city hall with the chamber's directors, and that'll determine what happens from here on out. They're a sponsor of the September festival, so I'll also be bringing up the possibility of having a *Sabaku* boat this year."

"What time does that meeting start?" Kazuna didn't have any urgent genga deadlines for Monday. Occasions like meetings were quite high on her list of things to avoid—and anything hosted by city hall sounded excruciatingly formal—but if they were going to be talking about the boat...

She pulled out her smartphone and was about to check her calendar when Munemori said, "Wait, what?" in a surprised voice. "Ms. Namisawa, you don't need to go out of your way to come to the meeting. I can take care of everything."

"But if the chamber of commerce ends up doing some licensed merchandising on their own, Fine Garden might be able to get commissions for original art, and besides, I'd like to be in the loop if it's going to involve the festival. Would it be better if I didn't go?"

The truth was, if they were going to launch a *Sabaku* boat during the Kanaga Festival, she badly wanted to be the one to draw the pictures on the vessel. She had a feeling mentioning that wish now would seem shamelessly assertive, so she kept it to herself. Much as she disliked meetings, she thought it might be a means of getting a foot in that door.

In addition, she and Munemori had been talking about putting on some kind of *Sabaku*-related event the day after the festival: maybe a talk show featuring the director and some of the voice actors, or a live concert by a band that would sing the main songs from the show. If they could pull off something like that, more visitors might stay overnight, for the *Sabaku* event the following day. Kazuna had advised Munemori that it was definitely worth trying to negotiate some kind of arrangement with Tokei Animation.

"Well, the meeting starts at ten in the morning..." he informed her hesitantly—almost apologetically. "But I promise, I'll be fine by myself."

"The meeting can't last more than an hour or two, can it? I'll go with you." Kazuna began to smile. "Sounds like fun."

"I hope you're right."

Munemori smiled, too, but somewhat weakly.

The expression seemed to be tinged with gloom or dread, which was unlike him, but at the time Kazuna didn't give it a second thought.

◆

It was Kazuna's first visit to city hall since she'd gone there to file her notification of residency, five years earlier. Both the former middle school that Fine Garden rented for its offices and the converted brewery that served as a dormitory for the company's employees were structures of a certain age, but the building that housed Enaga's city hall was far older than either of those. The concrete walls had evidently been white from the start, but while they had probably been repainted from time to time, the flaws were hard to miss. There were numerous uneven patches of color where the pigment had worn off, and the surface was riddled with cracks.

Kazuna's first thought after stepping inside was: *It's so dark.* They were probably trying to conserve electricity. On top of the lack of sufficient lighting, it was swelteringly hot because the air conditioning wasn't on.

On the first floor, just inside the entrance, there was a row of service windows, and the clerks who sat on the other side all had their sleeves rolled up and were attempting to cool the air around their faces, at least, with an assortment of hand-held implements: mostly folding fans or the round paper versions.

Kazuna took a quick look around and didn't spot any *Sabaku* posters like the ones she'd seen at the train station and in the shopping district. With a sudden sense of having strayed very far beyond her comfort zone, she went to find the tourism section. A directory signboard in the lobby told her that it was located on the second floor, at the top of the stairs. As she climbed the staircase she could hear the sound of cicadas seeping in through the open windows, and the rivulets of sweat that had been streaming down her neck all day seemed to be on the brink of merging into a full-blown river.

Kazuna peeked through a door that bore a plate reading "ENAGA CITY TOURISM SECTION" but Munemori was nowhere to be seen. A bit nonplussed by this unexpected complication, Kazuna went inside and called "Excuse me?" across the counter.

"Yes?" answered a young woman, standing up and approaching the visitor. At a guess, she was probably a bit younger than Kazuna, and her face was prettily made up.

"Is Mr. Munemori here? I'm Namisawa from Fine Garden, an anime studio, and I'm here for the meeting with the chamber of commerce."

"Oh, it's *you*," said a voice, and Kazuna saw that the speaker was a man seated at a desk in the back. In appearance, he was an exact match for the image that would have sprung to her mind upon hearing the term "civil servant": a middle-aged man with glasses wearing a dress shirt complete with necktie, despite the fact that his colleagues all seemed to be sporting short-sleeved polo shirts in keeping with the "Cool Biz" initiative.

"Ah, Section Chief," the young woman said diffidently, ceding her position up front. The section chief ambled slowly up to the counter, then addressed Kazuna.

"You must be the one from the manga company Munemori's been working with."

"Umm…"

"*You*"? Kazuna's cheek twitched at the man's mode of address; she'd introduced herself by name. Plus, it was anime, not manga.

Unlike the ground floor, this office did at least have one of the "*Sabaku* Stamp Rally" posters (featuring Kazuna's drawing) on the wall, although it wasn't displayed in a particularly prominent place.

"If you're looking for Munemori, he's in the conference room down the hall. Right about now the retiree brigade is probably raking him over the coals, big time."

"Huh?" Hastily, Kazuna glanced at her watch. There was still quite a bit of time before the meeting was scheduled to begin. "I thought it started at ten…"

"Well, it's certainly slated to, but these old guys have handed over their shops and businesses to their kids to run, so they have nothing but free time. They wake up very early, and if you tell them 'ten o'clock' they'll usually start to wander in an hour before that."

"*Usually*"? *Yikes, how can that even be?*

Kazuna was momentarily speechless. On reflection, though, it fit with what she knew about the habits of elderly people. She was about to hurry and ask where the conference room was, but then she paused.

"What do you mean 'raking him over the coals'?"

"Eh?"

"And won't you be in attendance too, Section Chief? This meeting."

If the festival was as famous as everyone said, it had to be a big deal for the tourism section. However, from where she stood, it looked as if nearly all of the staff were at their desks. The only visibly absent person, as far as she could tell, was Munemori.

"Ahh. I knew there was gonna be trouble when Munemori went there first to talk to the elders about manga. So we'll be joining them later, right?" the man said, looking at the young woman standing next to him.

She forced a smile and said, "Yes," but appeared distinctly ill at ease.

Something about the section chief's oppressively arrogant way of speaking, coupled with the way the girl was staring anxiously at Kazuna with upturned eyes, felt unpleasant.

Nursing a sense that something wasn't right, she asked, "I've heard that the tourism section is handling the pilgrimage for *Sabaku*—"

"Well, technically, yes. Since the situation arose, we needed someone to step up and deal with it, so Munemori's taken that on."

Come to think of it...

Kazuna started to remember things. From the start, whether it was making preparations for the stamp rally or laying out the pilgrimage route, Munemori always showed up alone. Even when he stopped by Fine Garden to request their cooperation, that first time, he had come by himself, conspicuously unaccompanied by any of his superiors. Actually, since Fine Garden was going to be represented by its president, it should have been customary for someone in a position of higher authority to bring the request.

Something else was nagging at her mind, too. A moment ago, the section chief had referred to her as being "from the manga company Munemori's been working with." It sounded as though he saw the whole business as a nuisance.

Now he said, in a similar tone, "We told him not to get overly involved, but he somehow got dragged in and that's caused problems on our end. Oh well, at least it's just a short-term thing. That manga ended already, right? I gather hardly any people visited, after all."

"No, in the case of anime pilgrimages, the fans don't start to come until after the series ends. So, on the contrary, we're only just beginning to see the effects now."

Despite Kazuna's valiant attempt to inform him, the section chief just exchanged skeptical glances with his subordinates and murmured, "You don't say," in a lukewarm voice that couldn't have sounded less convinced. He snickered and added, "A 'pilgrimage,' eh? Seems like a grandiose term, in this case."

Kazuna's shoulders were shaking with indignation. Had he not seen the crowds of excited visitors walking around town for the stamp rally, this past weekend? Nothing she said seemed to be getting through, and she felt dizzy with anger and frustration.

"In other words," she asked, "Mr. Munemori had to do everything for the stamp rally and the anime pilgrimage all by himself, with no assistance or support?"

"No, we put up the money for the poster and had it made, so you can't say he didn't have any assistance at all. And at no point did we ever push him into doing anything on that project. Isn't that right?"

"Yes," said a new voice from the back of the office. "Munemori volunteered to be the point person." The young male employee who stood up appeared to be around the same age as Munemori but also a totally different type. Kazuna, who was accustomed to gazing at handsome 2D males, found nothing harder to look at than guys who weren't all that attractive wearing their hair long and dyed brown.

The young man continued, "When we first learned about this event, it seemed doubtful that there would be any upside or benefit for our office, so we were on the verge of rejecting the proposal, but then Munemori said, 'No, let's give it a try!' And that's how we ended up getting roped in. That guy may not look the part, but he's more of an otaku than you might think." He mumbled the last remark in an offhanded way, but Kazuna felt a chill run down her spine. She knew that people like him only used "otaku" in one way: as a put-down.

"Well, of course, it wasn't like what happens with a real movie," the section chief said. "There was no actual location filming, so we didn't have any actors or celebrities coming in here—oh, oops."

The man turned to Kazuna, who was at a loss for words, and his face twisted into a faintly annoyed expression. "Sorry, I forgot. You're from the manga company, aren't you?"

"I'm not from the production company—that would be Tokei Animation. I work for a studio here in town that's a subcontractor for anime drawings."

"Oh, I see," the section chief said, but his demeanor didn't convey any sense that he was making an effort to see, or understand. He just nodded, as if to keep things moving along. "And then, finally, Munemori was spouting some nonsense about wanting to have a manga boat in the Kanaga Festival, so it's only natural that the old-timers would have called him onto the carpet. We're counting on them to give him a good scolding and talk some sense into that stubborn head of his—"

"Where's the conference room?" Kazuna interrupted.

"Eh?"

"Please allow me to participate in that meeting."

Munemori had warned her, so she shouldn't have been surprised. Enaga was a country town, and no matter how many times you explained to the local folks that something was super popular in Tokyo now, they wouldn't really get it. So when the initial inquiry from Tokei Animation came in, probably the only person who had cared enough to watch the series in earnest had been Munemori. As a business, the anime pilgrimage wouldn't have a chance of succeeding unless the local community had faith in the power of anime in general, and the *Sabaku* project, in particular.

And if nobody around here, apart from Munemori, believed in that power…

Kazuna remembered now. He had also said, "We want to do everything we can to make people watch *Sabaku*."

Initially, she had been filled with outrage at the thought that "realies" and the local government were trying to exploit a work, but now that seemed like some ludicrously minor occurrence that had taken place in a parallel universe long, long ago. The way these people thought about anime—as something unfamiliar and troublesome, a foreign nuisance—was actually much more in line with the thinking of the "realie" world that she despised.

All the participants in this scenario—on the hand, Kazuna, the director, and the production side, who were primarily concerned with protecting the integrity of the work, and on the other hand, the municipality that had been approached about the pilgrimage project—saw themselves as the ones being asked to grant a favor. And thus, they saw their own positions as somehow above and more important than the other party's. No wonder things didn't go smoothly.

"To get to the conference room, just turn that corner there and go all the way to the end of the hall."

"Thank you," Kazuna said hastily, not even glancing at the man's face.

The section chief who had addressed her as "you," the young woman who stood next to him wearing a pasted-on smile, the male staffer who seemed to think "anime" automatically equaled "otaku": she could talk to them until she was blue in the face, and nothing would change at all. At the same time, she realized what genuinely good people Munemori, old Mr. Nagasaki, and the cosplaying auntie at the limestone cave, who got into the spirit of things by dressing up as a shrine maiden, actually were.

Munemori had gone all out, trying to make the pilgrimage a success all by himself, acting as a go-between between the local government and the anime-production side.

If Kazuna ever laid eyes on that boorish section chief again, she felt as though she might lose her temper and shout at him:

"You're all a bunch of fools, not to see what a stroke of good fortune—and, potentially, good business—it was to have your town chosen as a setting for *Sabaku*. This area isn't exactly a magnet for tourism, but when a major, first-class new attraction shows up on your doorstep, you turn up your noses and whine about the inconvenience? And you dare to call yourself the tourism section?"

And then she thought: *We don't need to depend on jerks like that for anything. In the end we'll be smiling at them in triumph. We will have a boat in the festival, no matter what, and we'll get visitors to come from far and wide.*

The door of the conference room had been left open, and as she approached, Kazuna seemed to feel a palpable air of tension even more intense than the contentious cloud that hovered around the counter in the tourism section. She was about to enter when she heard a voice inside saying, "Well, I'm against it," and her spine stiffened.

Kazuna took a deep breath. "Um, excuse me," she said, stepping over the threshold, and every eye in the room swiveled to look in her direction. Munemori was sitting in the chair nearest the door, and when he saw her he exclaimed, "Ms. Namisawa!" in surprise.

Kazuna had never felt so nervous in her entire life. Her heart was literally pounding in her ears, but focusing on maintaining a dignified expression, at least, she bowed her head and said, "I'm sorry I'm late." In fact, she had arrived ten minutes before the meeting was scheduled to begin, but inside the room the atmosphere was icy and fraught as if a goodly amount of debate had already taken place.

"I've been working with the tourism section. My name is Kazuna Namisawa, and I'm employed at an anime—a local company that produces artwork. May I sit down?"

When she looked around the room, it was just as she'd heard: the faces from the chamber of commerce were mostly quite old—sixty and up. There was a sprinkling of younger men, relatively speaking, but even they appeared to be in their late forties or fifties. The attendees numbered around twenty; they were sitting in chairs arranged in a horseshoe shape, and every face was set in an expression of grim severity.

No one made a move to reply to Kazuna's greeting. After shooting a collective glance in her direction as she entered, they had all quickly looked away.

"Please, have a seat." It was Munemori who guided her to the chair next to his. A bitter smile that said *Sorry about this* played across his face, and seeing that, she felt a wee bit more at ease.

He waited for Kazuna to settle into her seat and spoke. "All right, then. Is there really not a single person here who's willing to give us permission to launch a *Soundback* boat at the festival this year?" There was something sad and almost cruel about the way that relentlessly upbeat voice rang out in the silent room.

"Don't get us wrong, Shu—we're not just rejecting your proposal out of hand," said an old man whose snowy hair and long white beard gave him the look of a mountain hermit. He was sitting at the head of the table, dressed in kimono, and a triangular nameplate identified him as the chairman of the board of directors. "It's fine with us if you want to put on some events before or after the boats. However, it's a firm no on launching a boat of your own. We can't possibly give you permission to do something like that."

Another man who was sitting next to the chairman nodded his head. "We're talking about three hundred years," he said with a solemn expression. "The Kanaga Festival represents three hundred years of history. We can't just let some manga or anime or whatever intrude on that tradition, willy-nilly."

"Not only that, but you don't even have the financing confirmed, or any craftsmen lined up?"

"I was planning to negotiate a budget with Tokei Animation after this."

When Kazuna heard Munemori say that, and watched him sitting there with his usual military-grade posture, she was struck by how grand he looked in profile. Considering the circumstances, she'd thought he might be disheartened, but he appeared undaunted and completely resolute.

"As for the craftsmen," he went on, "some of the shipbuilding companies registered with the Kanaga Festival Preservation Society are already finished with their boats, so I think there's a good chance one of them would take this on."

"Yes, but still—"

"Is there any reason we couldn't wait until the vice chairman gets back, and revisit this then? Please?" Munemori suddenly jumped to his feet and got down on both knees on the bare wooden floor as if he were about to prostrate himself. But there wasn't a trace of subservience in him; rather, it resembled a martial artist's first greeting upon entering the dojo, an entirely proper stance.

"I've already explained about the prospects of using anime to attract tourists and sell locally manufactured products. Right now, the stamp rally and the sales of goods have only just begun, but over this past weekend there was a bump in the number of visitors. Needless to say, we could expect many more at festival time."

He inhaled deeply, then lowered his head and continued in a resonant voice that came from his gut. "Above all, I think the tourists will have a wonderful time here, and even after they leave, there will be a positive connection between our hometown and everyone who visits."

Munemori raised his head. "If those people go home with memories of Enaga as a nice place to visit, then even if the anime's popularity eventually starts to wane, they will keep coming back. The Kanaga Festival will be the key."

"Please stand up, Shu." The chairman, who really looked the part of a community elder, let out a sigh. "You say wait for the vice chairman to return, but…" He glanced at the seat next to his, with its "Vice Chairman" nameplate. That seat was conspicuously empty.

Even after being told to stand up, Munemori continued to kneel on the floor. "The vice chairman was supposed to be here for this meeting," he said, "but apparently his flight was delayed, and he hasn't yet returned."

"What, another overseas trip?" The chairman narrowed his eyes and stared at the vacant chair.

"Is there any chance he'll make it?" asked another voice.

"Make it"? You early birds decided to start an hour ahead of time! Kazuna came dangerously close to shouting those words in protest, but she bit her tongue and instead looked around intently. She had come in the hopes of providing a supportive presence, but there didn't seem to be anything she could do, and she felt impatient and fretful.

That was when.

It wouldn't be entirely correct to say that reinforcements had arrived, but at any rate, an interruption occurred. A voice was heard from the corridor, calling "How's it going in there?" A moment later the tourism section chief strolled into the room. While he had been distinctly unfriendly to Kazuna, he greeted the old men of the chamber of commerce with a face that was all smiles, which in itself seemed nasty and hateful to her.

"Oh, Section Chief!" called any number of voices, to which the new arrival replied, "I'm so sorry. I tried to stop him." He shot a half-exasperated, half-disgusted glance at his renegade employee, who was still on his knees on the floor, then turned back to address the group. "Look, how about this? Nothing's going to get settled right away in any case, so why don't we put a pin in the anime talks for the time being and go ahead with our regular meeting, as we do every year? Otherwise we could end up being here until the sun goes down."

"Hmm, maybe we should…" The chairman stared into space, seemingly deep in thought. Presently he asked, "Is that all right with you, Shu?"

"Yes," Munemori responded with a nod.

"Well, that's that, then!" said the section chief. He placed his bag on the chair Munemori had been using and plopped heavily down on a seat.

To Kazuna, every single word the man uttered seemed to sting as if it were studded with nettles.

Munemori finally stood up. Things hadn't exactly gone well,

but his eyes were still alight with what could only be called fight.

"We'll come back later," he said.

Kazuna followed Munemori out of the conference room, and they returned to the tourism section. Inclining his head slightly to his colleagues, Munemori deposited his bag at his desk, then turned to Kazuna and said, "Let's get out of here for a while."

He led her outside to the city hall parking lot and bought two cans of coffee from a nearby vending machine. Accepting her can, Kazuna asked, "What was that, anyway? I understand the significance of three hundred years of history, but aren't they being a little bit too closed-minded? I mean, just because something has been around for three centuries doesn't necessarily mean you need to keep repeating it in exactly the same way forever, does it?"

"The Kanaga Festival really is a venerable tradition," Munemori said with a wry smile. He sat down on the edge of the flowerbed in front of city hall and pulled the tab on his can of coffee. "I agree with you completely, but there's no way someone from my generation can say something like that to the chairman and the others. It would need to be somebody from their in-group, or at least someone as old as my section chief. Otherwise it would be difficult."

His face clouded over with an apologetic expression. "I'm sorry," he said. "I feel bad about making you experience something so unpleasant. I should have insisted on going alone."

"I didn't know."

"Huh?"

"I didn't realize you were doing all the prep work for the pilgrimage in such an isolated environment, with no support to speak of."

Munemori shrugged as if to say it was nothing he couldn't handle. "You don't need to worry about that," he said with a smile. "The section chief isn't a bad person, at all. As soon as some tangible results start to come in from the *Sabaku* relationship, the situation is sure to change. The fact is, while the question of having a boat in the festival is still up in the air, they've already agreed that we could stage a *Sabaku* event the following day. That's something, at least."

"What are you hearing from Tokei Animation?"

At this, Munemori's expression darkened. "They're saying their budget is maxed out, and they can't give us another yen."

"No..."

Kazuna was tempted to add that the show was a huge hit, so the company must be making money hand over fist. However, the truth was that she wasn't very knowledgeable about financial matters. She had heard it said that because the production costs for an anime were so colossally high, even if a show was a modest hit, it didn't come close to breaking even. The expenditures weren't fully recouped until after the final volume of the DVD set was released.

"The first hurdle is to get official approval for the boat, and if that falls into place, I trust Tokei Animation would be willing to consider our proposal. If not, there's a chance we might need to ask the chamber of commerce and the municipal government to think about paying for it out of their own pockets."

"After the way things went in that meeting, doesn't that seem impossible?"

They were already fighting over whether or not the boat would be approved, so it seemed hopelessly optimistic to think that the city side would somehow be persuaded to cover the costs.

Munemori nodded. "We just have to keep pleading with them to loan us the money. The idea would be to pay them back out of the tourism revenue generated by the anime connection. In other words, we would borrow the money using *Sabaku*'s popularity as security."

Once again, an apologetic expression crept across Munemori's face. "I'm really sorry," he repeated. "I've been going on about how to monetize a work of art and talking about nothing but practical matters. I'm sure you find that offensive."

"No, really, it's fine," Kazuna said, feeling somewhat impatient. She didn't think that was the most pressing problem at the moment. "From what I saw, I really don't think the people in that room would jump at the chance to invest or lend money if the collateral was something as intangible as a work's popularity."

She'd gotten an acute sense of the situation during the meeting. If you couldn't present those men with something visible, there was no way they would ever get on board. It was frustrating, but this was how things were in the world of business.

"In the first place," she went on, "we don't even know whether we'll even be able to enter a boat in the festival. Do you think there's any chance of getting permission for that?"

"I do." Munemori nodded his head with unexpected firmness, and Kazuna's eyes opened wide with wonder. "The vice chairman of the chamber of commerce wasn't at the meeting just now, but he's someone who actually understands the anime world to some degree, so I already asked him for support on this. Unlike the rest of those retirees, he's an active-duty CEO, and he's influential. If we could just get him on our side it would be—" Munemori stopped in mid-sentence and caught his breath. Eyes fixed on something behind Kazuna, he scrambled to his feet. "Speak of the devil," he said. "It's the vice chairman. Perfect—he made it."

Kazuna hastily turned to look behind her and she, too, let out a small gasp.

A bright red Porsche, incongruous on the country road, was gliding into the city hall parking lot. Kazuna knew next to nothing about automotive makes and models, but she recognized this one because she'd been called on to draw a Porsche for an anime series a few years ago. The car had belonged to the hero's affluent rival.

The red sports car came to a stop.

"Vice Chairman!" As if he couldn't bear to wait for the door to open, Munemori galloped toward the car, madly waving one hand above his head. The Porsche's steering wheel was on the left side, and when Kazuna saw the person climbing out of the driver's seat, her eyes opened wide.

"Hi there, Munemori. Sorry I'm late."

An undeniably gorgeous middle-aged man emerged from the roadster. As his feet touched the ground, he took off his sunglasses.

He was so strikingly handsome that Kazuna, wordless with admiration, wondered what on earth an apparition like this was doing in their little hick town. She had no problem whatsoever with the fact that the new arrival's longish hair, which he swept smoothly back from his forehead, was tinted a tawny brown.

◆

While most local sake breweries were either downsizing or closing up shop entirely, the splendid-looking vice chairman's *sakagura* was actually growing by leaps and bounds. He was in his early sixties but didn't look nearly that old.

"Nice to meet you, Ms. Namisawa."

His delivery sounded youthful as he greeted her, and he projected a completely different aura compared to the section chief who'd addressed her as "you" or the elders in the meeting who wouldn't even meet her eyes.

Kazuna even had a vague feeling that she'd seen him before somewhere, but that might just have been because he was good-looking enough to be on TV or in the pages of magazines. He could have outshone quite a few celebrities and entertainers.

The sake mogul was dressed in a summer jacket with a patterned scarf peeking out of the breast pocket. Gaping at his stylish outfit and his snazzy car, Kazuna almost wanted to ask whether he'd just stepped out of a photo spread in *LEON*, a fashion-and-lifestyle magazine for men over thirty. He was a totally different type than Munemori, but she would never have met anyone like either of them in her normal sphere of activity.

As the two men talked, Kazuna gathered that the newcomer was also pouring his energy into the business of exporting sake and had recently begun reaching out to other manufacturers and utilizing his overseas connections to wholesale their wares along with his own. The other local brewers were immensely grateful to him, and that was how he had come to hold the vice chairmanship of the Enaga City Chamber of Commerce.

"The truth is, they tried to get me to be the chairman, but I really wasn't up for taking on a role like that, with all the heavy responsibilities. On the other hand, I'm not averse to wielding a bit of power, so the vice chairman position was a perfect compromise."

During these preliminary explanations, Kazuna never stopped marveling at the sheer charisma of the man; he was so intensely dazzling that she almost had to look away. *Who is this richly layered character?* she asked herself.

"I might as well take it all the way and run for mayor," the vice chairman mused in his melodious voice.

"Vice Chairman, please don't say such things in the city hall parking lot," Munemori admonished playfully. "The current mayor might hear you."

"Right. Because if I did run, he'd get clobbered." Tossing off that radiantly self-confident reply, he looked at Kazuna and Munemori in turn. "No, but seriously, I'm sorry about this. If I really were the mayor or even the chairman of the chamber of commerce, you could have gotten your *Sabaku* boat without a hitch. You wouldn't have had to deal with these difficulties. And to top it off I was late today. So, where are the others?"

"They're already in the conference room. They've moved on to other topics."

"Ah, the same boring nonsense they discuss every year? I get the picture."

That was something Kazuna had been thinking but hadn't been able to say.

"Well, then, shall we go?" the vice chairman invited and started toward the building.

Watching his dependable-looking back, Kazuna stammered, "Um..." It was the first sound she had uttered since the initial exchange of greetings.

The vice chairman stopped and turned around. "Hmh?"

"Mr. Vice Chairman, I was just wondering whether you've watched it. *Sabaku*, that is." Since arriving at city hall that morning, he was the first person, apart from Munemori, who'd mentioned the work by name. Everyone else she'd met—the staff, and the members of the chamber of commerce—had only used vague terms like "anime" and "manga."

For a brief instant a baffled look flitted across the vice chairman's face, as if he were thinking, *You're asking me that now, at this late date?* Then he replied, "I did, of course. I was in Italy, but online streaming is really convenient these days. In the last scene, I couldn't help wishing my sake brewery had been destroyed in the battle as well. It would have been great fun to see my factory turned into rubble through Towako's valiant efforts."

And then he added something that left Kazuna agog. "I watched *Love Die*, too," he said, "and I thought it was hurt by a bad episode. Don't you agree, Munemori?"

"I don't know—I haven't seen that one."

"Really? It's quite good."

Kazuna had heard that the vice chairman was open to anime, but the reality was exceeding her wildest imaginings. *He's almost too young,* she thought. In terms of cultural age, he was definitely younger than Kazuna, who hadn't been able to get into *Love Die* enough to continue watching.

Suddenly serious-faced again, he turned to look at Munemori and Kazuna. "Even with my powers, such as they are, I'm honestly not certain how far I'll be able to advance your cause vis-à-vis getting a boat into the Kanaga Festival. It'll be a challenge, for sure, but please just wait—with a moderate degree of hope. Sometimes it's better to have a discussion like this among the immediate family, so to speak."

"We'll wait outside," Munemori said, bowing his head. "Whatever happens, we're very grateful for your efforts."

He didn't speak with the customary ebullience, and his ponderous tone somehow made Kazuna's heart ache. She could tell how strongly Munemori felt about this matter.

In a rush, she followed his lead. "I'd like to wish you the best of luck in there, too. By the way, I work as an anime artist myself." Although self-promotion didn't come easily to her, she continued,

"If we end up being able to launch a boat, I would like to draw the pictures that are used to decorate it." It was the first time she'd given voice to this desire, and she had a peripheral sense that Munemori was staring at her in amazement, but she just lowered her head in silence.

The vice chairman responded to their heartfelt pleas with a light "Gotcha. I'll see what I can do, so please wait a bit." He spoke in a clear, unyielding voice, then nodded as if to confirm his commitment to the cause.

The meeting, with the vice chairman in attendance, lasted well past midday. Kazuna and Munemori waited anxiously at the foot of the staircase in a state of suspense, unable to relax for even a moment. Finally they spotted the vice chairman on his way down the stairs, walking with the same spring in his step as before.

"Sorry to keep you waiting!" he called out as he approached. "Treat me to some soba in the cafeteria."

His fellow board members followed him down the stairs and then left the building together, shooting freighted glances as they passed as if there was something they wanted to say. Kazuna and her two companions headed for the employee cafeteria at the back of city hall as though to elude those prying eyes.

"So, how did it go?" she asked impatiently, begrudging even the time it took to pose that question.

"Oh, it passed," the vice chairman replied with a matter-of-fact nod.

"Thank you so much!" chorused Kazuna and Munemori, fairly elated, but then the older man added, in a measured tone, "However..."

The old city hall cafeteria and the dapper vice chairman might have been another bit of incongruity, but he seemed to know his way around, perhaps through previous visits. He appeared perfectly at home as he submitted a meal coupon. He sprinkled seven-spice condiment on his bowl of soba, topped it off with chopped green onions, and took a seat.

"As I was saying, permission to have a boat in the Kanaga

319

Festival has been granted, but all the same conditions will apply to you as to any other entrants. You'll need to participate in the usual lottery to determine what order you launch in, and there's a chance you'll draw some ungodly hour—incredibly early in the morning, or late in the evening—that will be tremendously inconvenient for the fans who want to watch. Are you okay with that?"

"Yes."

Just as long as they were allowed to enter a boat in the festival, everything else would fall into place somehow.

Slurping his soba, the vice chairman continued, "And then there's the matter of money. We can't give you any help at all with financing, so please bear that in mind."

Munemori and Kazuna were momentarily silenced by this revelation. They exchanged a wordless glance, and then Munemori nodded and said, "Understood. We'll find a way to manage that on our own."

"Yep. I'm sorry, but that was the best I could do. As for me personally, the Association of Sake Breweries has its own boat to get ready, so I'm afraid I can't offer anything in the way of funds or assistance, either."

"You've already done more than enough. Thank you very much."

"So, who are you going to get to be the boatsinger?"

When the vice chairman raised this question, Kazuna cocked her head in puzzlement. "Boatsinger?" she echoed.

"Oh, you don't know about that?" He glanced at Kazuna, then went on, "I guess you've probably never seen it, but before they launch each boat, someone performs a special chant with a very distinct intonation, relating the boat's lineage—who built it, and so on, describing all the hopes and aspirations it carries with it. It would be very difficult to deliver a chant without training, but there are still a few old grandmas around here who are experts, and they give lessons."

"Huh…" Once again Kazuna regretted having been uninterested in the Kanaga Festival for so long. It certainly sounded as though the traditional boatsinger's chant was a part of the launching ceremony that they would need to respect and include.

"I guess the top choice would be the director," Munemori muttered in a strained voice.

"No, wouldn't voice actors make more sense?" the vice chairman responded, quick as a flash. His knowledge of anime indeed wasn't just a superficial affectation. "The professional voice talent associated with any anime production—you ought to book *Sabaku*'s three main actors as soon as possible."

"Um, actually, that might be a bit tricky," Kazuna pointed out, hesitantly.

The voice actors who played Takaya, Towako, and Ryuichi were all in the top ranks of their profession. They were immensely popular and constantly busy. Nailing down a commitment from all of them now would be next to impossible. Having the actors at the festival would be a huge draw for fans, and Kazuna would have loved to see it happen, but the fact was that Enaga was quite distant from Tokyo. It wasn't the kind of request that could be made casually, especially given the need to practice the boatsinging technique in advance.

"What are you thinking about for the event on the following day?" asked Kazuna, addressing another of her concerns. Getting permission to launch their boat had been a major hurdle, but if the following day's event was lackluster, that might have an adverse effect on the pilgrimage's reputation.

Munemori's face wore a growing look of consternation. "I've been talking to Tokei Animation. I asked whether the director would be willing to give a lecture or do a sit-down interview, in talk-show format, but things don't seem too promising."

"Oh, really?" Kazuna said glumly. It was starting to look as though the road to the festival was only going to become rockier from here on.

Kazuna had met Hitomi Saito just that one time, in Tokyo, but the director hadn't struck the animator as the type who would welcome the chance to speak in public. On top of that, Director Saito probably still had mixed feelings about allowing her work to be used by the local government.

"At any rate, I'll touch base with them again," Munemori promised. "Perhaps they might come up with something when they hear we've gotten approval for the boat project."

"Is your contact person at Tokei still the promotions producer you mentioned the other day—Koshigaya, was it?"

"That's right." Munemori nodded. "He seems to be very busy with other work right now, so it isn't easy to get hold of him, but he's doing his very best on this."

"I see..."

This was changeover time in the world of series anime. Kazuna could only guess at what sort of person this Koshigaya was, or what his situation at Tokei Animation might be. However, she did know that he would be swamped with work this time of year juggling a number of new titles during the rollout period. She had doubts as to what "his very best" amounted to.

"Three hundred years," the vice chairman told Kazuna and Munemori after they'd finished their meal and were preparing to exit the cafeteria. He held up three fingers, for emphasis.

"They say the first Kanaga Festival was held 327 years ago. I support your participation completely, without question, but I only ask that you keep that tradition in mind and give it the weight and consideration it deserves. Otherwise I'll feel bad for the older members of the chamber of commerce."

"Of course, we understand that," Munemori assured with a solemn expression.

Kazuna felt the same way. Earlier that day, when one of the board members at the meeting had been going on about the ancient tradition, her reaction had been entirely negative. But now, hearing the phrase "three hundred years" from the vice chairman, she fully understood its significance.

"We promise to work hard," Kazuna said gravely, straightening her posture and bowing her head to him.

◆

If only I'd asked for their business cards, Kazuna thought, awash in remorseful hindsight. *Director Saito's, and Producer Yukishiro's.*

That messed-up day in Tokyo, she was so filled with resentment for having been dragged away from her Skytree date that she hadn't even bothered to greet them properly. In retrospect, she saw her petulant behavior as childish and ungracious, and regretted it immensely.

Sitting now in her room at the company dorm, she opened her browser and stared at a line of numbers on the screen of her PC. Then, making up her mind, she began tapping on the keypad of her smartphone.

The string of numerals she entered was the phone number of Tokei Animation's central switchboard. It was a primitive approach to getting in touch, but she had located that number on the home page of the company's website, under "Contact Us."

"Um, hello?" As she spoke into the mouthpiece after the call went through, she had already half given up hope. "My name is Kazuna Namisawa, and I'm with the anime studio Fine Garden. Would it be possible to speak with Director Hitomi Saito of *Soundback*, by any chance?"

Tokei Animation was known for tightly guarding its prize employees against possible poachers, so she didn't really expect to be able to reach Director Saito by way of the general line. She was already thinking about her backup plan: to call Producer Yukishiro. He might not be as helpful, but he would at least have the decency to listen to her...

That's what she was thinking during the interlude after the receptionist said, "Please wait a moment." Suddenly, she heard a voice on the other end of the phone.

"Hello. Saito speaking."

Kazuna let out a gasp of surprise. Could it really be this easy? "Hello," she said breathlessly. "This is Namisawa, from Fine Garden."

She could sense an immediate reaction, and when the voice on the other end spoke again, it was in a much friendlier tone.

"Ah, Ms. Namisawa."

Thank goodness, she remembers. A great wave of relief began in Kazuna's toes and surged upward until it engulfed her entire body. "Long time no see," she said. "Congratulations on the last episode of *Sabaku*. I know how busy you must be, so I didn't expect to be able to talk to you today. I never dreamed I'd get through to you so easily."

"Oh… Actually, this is a relatively calm period for me, so it was fine. And also, I…"

The director seemed to hesitate, then broke off without finishing her sentence. Kazuna wondered what she had been about to say.

Changing the subject, Director Saito asked, "So, what's going on? I mean, I'm happy to hear from you, but were you calling about anything in particular?"

"Well…"

And in that instant, the totally unreasonable thought that rushed into Kazuna's mind was: *You and Yukishiro have really treated me shabbily, you know that? I mean, if you have so much time on your hands these days that you can pick up the phone right away, you could at least have helped us out a little bit with our project in Enaga.*

What she said out loud was: "Is there any chance you might consider returning the favor from the other day?" Her voice sounded dry, and the words seemed to stick in her throat.

"I'm sorry, what?"

"I'm talking about the cover art for *Animaison*. I was at Skytree, taking a very rare break from work, when you suddenly called me in to do that job." Kazuna heard what sounded like a sharp intake of breath on the other end but couldn't stop herself. She wanted Director Saito and Producer Yukishiro to come to Enaga and was in desperation mode.

Anime production was basically an indoor job, and opportunities to see the fans in the wild were fairly scarce. Just one time—that's all it would take—Kazuna wanted the director and producer to actually see the delighted faces on people as they engaged in the stamp rally along the national route, some carrying toy *Sabaku* robots in one hand. She wanted the primary creators of the series to enjoy that wondrous sight as she herself had done.

"If you have any feelings at all about that day—gratitude, or remorse, or anything else—I'd like to ask you for a favor. Would you please consider coming to Enaga City? Right now there's a *Sabaku* stamp rally going on, and I've been helping out with that. There'll be a festival—"

There. I said it.

"There'll be a festival in September, and we were wondering whether you might be willing to lend your support to help us make it a success. We want to enter a boat, and we're working as hard as we possibly can—"

"I understand." Hearing the firm resolve in Director Saito's voice, Kazuna took a shallow, hopeful breath. The director continued, "I'm sorry, but this is the first I've heard about a festival. Could you please give me the particulars?"

After the merest pause, Saito added, "Of course, I feel a deep sense of gratitude and obligation for the work you did, Ms. Namisawa. You have my deepest respect, and I know we owe you a lot. If there's anything I can do, I'll be more than happy to be of assistance."

Those warm words seeped deep into Kazuna's heart and seemed to resonate there. She felt a prickling at the back of her sinuses, an unmistakable harbinger of tears.

As Kazuna briefed her on the various details, it became apparent that the director had heard next to nothing about the *Sabaku* pilgrimage project.

"I told Mr. Koshigaya some time ago that if, by chance, there was going to be a *Sabaku* stamp rally, I'd like to see the route map and any forms, and he said that as soon as anything arrived from the other party he would pass it on, and that's where things have stood until today," Saito explained.

Hearing that, Kazuna was speechless. It was unthinkable that the hyper-conscientious Munemori would have neglected to send those materials, so it was beginning to look as though the Enaga projects had never made it beyond the promotions producer's desk.

On the other end of the phone line, Director Saito sighed. "I'm so very sorry. The truth is, that kind of blunder happens a lot with him. In fact, this entire company seems to have a problem interacting properly with the outside world. I don't know whether it's a lack of awareness, but either way, I can't apologize enough."

"Is it really all right to be saying things like that on a company phone?" Kazuna asked out of genuine concern, but Director Saito gave what sounded like a rueful chuckle and shared something that struck Kazuna as truly terrible news.

"Well, I'm quitting."

Not for the first time that week, Kazuna's eyes opened wide in surprise.

"I've already told them," the director went on, "but I'll be leaving here before the end of the year. I'm not saying that gives me carte blanche to badmouth this company, but it's an objective fact that they're really poor at handling certain things, and this type of misunderstanding is the result."

"What are you going to do after you leave?" Even as she was asking that question, Kazuna realized something. *That explains it.* That was why Tokei Animation's operator had put Kazuna's call through so readily.

"I'll still be working in the anime world," the director replied. "I'm sure I'll be asking for your assistance with assignments in the future, so if it's all right, I'd like to get in touch with you after I've settled in at the new place." It was the perfectly polite, formulaic thing to say, but it sounded genuine. "But enough about me," Hitomi Saito went on. "I honestly had no idea that Enaga City had embraced *Sabaku* with so much fervor, and I hadn't heard that fans were making the trek up there, either."

"Young and old, female or male, they're all coming," Kazuna said proudly. "They look so happy, walking along the national route—the road the kids take to school in the anime. I've seen a boy trying to keep a bunch of *Sabaku* robots to himself and squabbling with his little sister..."

This is glorious, Kazuna thought. *Being able to share these lovely things with Director Saito is such an incredible honor.*

Down the phone line, the director seemed to be holding her breath. After a little while she said slowly, "I'd like to go. Regarding the festival, I'll have somebody who knows more than I do about such things give you a call. We'll need to talk about the costs again on this end, as well."

"That sounds great. Um, would it be all right to ask one more thing?"

"Sure, go ahead."

"If we do manage to resolve the issue of financing an entry in the Kanaga Festival, I wonder whether I might be allowed to draw the pictures on the boat?"

Kazuna knew she was being pushy and impertinent, but she couldn't help it. She wanted to draw those pictures, no matter what. "I know it's totally cheeky for me to ask when you have Animation Director Goto, but do you think you might be able to help me with this? I'd be glad to do it on a volunteer basis, so my work wouldn't even need to be included in the cost."

"That's a wonderful idea. I couldn't wish for anything better," Director Saito said. Then her voice took on a sterner tone as she added, "But Ms. Namisawa, regarding the business side, your proposal is completely unacceptable. Please don't ever say that you'd be 'glad to do it on a volunteer basis,' no matter what. You should never devalue your drawings or sell them short."

"But—"

"Thank you very much." That should have been Kazuna's line, but the director continued, "Thank you for loving my anime kids so much and for caring so deeply about *Sabaku*. I really can't thank you enough, for everything."

There are times when progress can seem glacial or nonexistent, but on the other hand, everything can race ahead at mind-boggling speed when you're working with capable people—such was the lesson Kazuna learned that day, in spades.

She had barely ended the call with Director Saito when her phone rang—only it wasn't the director with some afterthought but Producer Yukishiro.

The first words out of his mouth were "I heard the story. Regarding the financing, roger that. We'll let you handle the pictures on the boat, but please include the entire cast of characters. Don't leave anyone out."

"Tokei Animation is paying for it?" asked Kazuna, her voice brimming with hope, but Yukishiro replied with a flat "No."

"Huh?" she let out, deflated.

"I'm ashamed to have to say this, but the company can't spend another yen on these projects."

"So then—"

"So then we'll get the fans to buy shares for a certain amount apiece, and raise the funds that way."

Kazuna's mouth fell open, and her eyes opened wide. She had never even imagined that such an option existed.

"After I heard about what was going on, I did some quick research about the Kanaga Festival," Yukishiro explained. "Apparently they say that if you can retrieve one of the fragments after a boat has been smashed to smithereens on the rocks, you'll be guaranteed a full year of perfect·health and freedom from accidents."

Come to think of it, Munemori had mentioned something about that folk belief.

Yukishiro continued, "So, we'll collect and distribute those fragments among the fans who chipped in to share the costs of making the boat. And for those who aren't able to attend the actual festival, we'll mail their shards later as proof of their participation. Of course, the more shares someone buys, the more bits of the shattered boat they'll receive, so I think we can hope for some serious capital. Anyway, that's why I'd like to have you draw as many character pictures as possible, so that every single fragment will contain some illustration."

As Yukishiro spoke, Kazuna could feel a gentle surge of excitement spreading upward from her viscera all the way to her throat. She came close to blurting out, *You rock, Just the Aura of Handsomeness!* Curbing that impulse, she said, "Wow, that's a truly amazing idea, Mr. Yukishiro! I'm sure we'll be able to raise enough money that way—"

"Not only that, but a lot of fans will feel like they have a personal stake in the festival boat because they helped pay for it, and they'll want to see the launching in person. Attracting visitors to the event should be smooth sailing, so to speak. Please leave all the publicity to us. We'll get plenty of coverage from all the anime magazines we work with, and we'll promote it on the Tokei Animation website as well." And then he added, "I'm sorry. I'm really sorry to have neglected such a fun and promising item for so long."

Hah, this guy, Kazuna thought cynically. *He's probably way more concerned about the profit than the fun.* But the truth was that those remarks made her infinitely happier than the apology.

"Also, from here on out I'll be taking over responsibility for handling anything related to the pilgrimage, so please call me directly," Yukishiro announced. "Let's make these projects a huge success."

Kazuna couldn't see the producer's face, but she thought he was probably wearing a smug expression as he laid out his undeniably excellent plans. She wasn't thrilled about the prospect of watching him become even more self-satisfied than he already was, but she did feel hopelessly, helplessly relieved.

That Munemori's diligent efforts up until now wouldn't end up going to waste. That they were all going to have tons of fun working on this together.

The producer's reputation as an able hand had been no lie. Having Yukishiro join their little team gave her a sense of security she wouldn't have thought possible a few hours earlier. She felt a great rush of joy.

"Thank you very much," Kazuna told him.

The next morning, she got a call from Munemori. "The director confirmed that she'll appear at our event the day after the boats," he reported. "She said okay!"

Then, in a voice that sounded almost tearful, he added that Yukishiro had also been in touch with him the previous night to talk about financial matters.

"Ms. Namisawa, truly, I can't begin to thank you enough," he said, and she could tell from his voice that he was sincerely grateful. "About Director Saito," he went on, getting back to business, "she said she couldn't possibly give a solo lecture, but something in a talk-show format, with another person conducting the conversation, seems doable."

"Oh, I see," said Kazuna absently. She was remembering her conversation with Hitomi Saito the day before, and when Kazuna thought about all the helpful things the director had done soon after they hung up, she got a lump in her throat.

"It's all thanks to you," Munemori repeated. "Now that we have our ducks in a row on the practical stuff, we can start prepping for the festival."

"In retrospect, I probably should have tried calling them a little earlier. I'm sorry about that."

"No, no, don't be!"

"Anyway, let's give it our best shot from here on out," Kazuna said.

"Yes," Munemori seconded emphatically. "I'm going to give it everything I've got, with total respect for *Sabaku*."

And then the day after that, once again, Tokei Animation called with what seemed like downright miraculous news.

A voice actor had agreed to chant the boatsong for launching the *Sabaku* entry on the river: Aoi Mureno. She had voiced Towako in the series.

Aoi Mureno was in high demand, and the boatsinging job required a certain amount of practice, so Kazuna had thought the chances of her taking the assignment were slim to none. But not only had the voice actress accepted with alacrity, she had arranged to bring along a posse of four fellow cast members from *Sabaku*. They would travel to Enaga, and on the day of the boat launch, see it off together.

The quintet of women had become inseparable while starring in a recent series called *Mermaid Nurses*, which had made them all exceedingly popular. When Kazuna heard that the moment Aoi contacted the other four they had immediately rearranged their schedules, she was at a loss for words. *Are we really being allowed such a luxury?* she asked herself.

Apparently Aoi had even called Munemori directly and said, "I'd like to learn this boatsinging, but how should I go about it?" She also explained the situation with the other actors, saying, "The two male leads, Haruyama and Mikage, won't be able to attend because they have recording commitments, so I'm afraid it'll just be the five of us."

"Oh, please, it's unbelievable that so many voice stars are going to come all this way, and we appreciate it greatly," Munemori thanked humbly.

"We're no good unless there are all five of us," Aoi explained. "Just one of us, alone, probably doesn't make much of an impression, but we're not ashamed of having to come in a bunch. With the five of us together, you can safely count on a big turnout of fans."

Having to come in a bunch: that was a startlingly self-deprecating thing for a voice-acting idol to say about herself. Aoi Mureno sounded cool.

Hearing later that Aoi had spoken of Director Saito as a best friend, Kazuna was overcome with emotion. The staff that had worked together to create an anime that she loved being on such good terms in real life was almost too delicious to bear for Kazuna the fan.

"There's nothing we wouldn't do for Director Saito and *Sabaku*," Aoi had reportedly said. "It's our pleasure, and there's no need to thank us."

◆

The Kanaga Festival always took place shortly after the autumn solstice, during the fourth weekend of September.

On Friday night—which was known as Festival Eve—there was a fireworks display, and booths were set up in long rows. Saturday was the main event, the launching of the custom-made boats, and the following day, Sunday, visitors would be savoring their memories of the river while enjoying various events taking place on a special stage.

While the craftsmen made steady progress on the boat, the *Sabaku* stamp rally experienced a sizable surge in attendance once summer vacation began. That proved decisively that Enaga's location, far from Tokyo and other major cities, was not necessarily a drawback, as some had feared. Since it wasn't possible to complete the stamp rally or walk the pilgrimage as a day trip, bookings at local inns increased dramatically, with many guests staying for some time.

The soba restaurants, the cafés, or Asami's yakitori bar in the shopping district in front of the station were usually patronized exclusively by locals. But by the time August rolled around, the shops and eateries were all packed to the gills with visitors from out of town who had come to make the *Sabaku* pilgrimage.

One evening, when Munemori and Kazuna got together at the yakitori bar for a festival-planning session, they happened to overhear a local resident asking some tourists, "Did you folks come because of *Sabaku*, too?" to which one of the visitors replied, "Yes, this is our second time here this summer."

At that, Munemori interrupted his conversation with Kazuna and swiveled his head to see who was speaking. When Kazuna said, "This is so great," he turned back, his cheeks slack with glee. "It really is," he agreed. "The chief and others at my section are overjoyed, too."

Kazuna couldn't resist snarking, "Well, isn't that just dandy for them," but Munemori said, "You think?" with a simple, happy smile. Kazuna sighed. *This person really is too good to be true*, she thought as she munched on edamame.

In truth, she didn't feel all that bitter anymore, about anything. One of the things she'd learned from being around Munemori was that life was easier if you took things lightly, and looked on people kindly, and let the bad stuff go.

Some of the members of the chamber of commerce, who had initially acted as though anime were some dubious alien entity, had done a complete turnaround and begun eagerly requesting licensing permits for a variety of goods. "We'd like to make *Sabaku* cupcakes for the festival," they'd say, or "We're making plum wine, and we want to put *Sabaku* pictures on the labels."

Not only that, but everyone—even the formerly skeptical elders—had stopped referring to the series as "that manga, or anime, or whatever." They invariably called it *Sabaku* now, just like the younger fans.

"They're saying the boat should be finished sometime after the middle of next month, right before the festival," Munemori was saying. "We've asked them to make sure it's ready three days in advance, at the latest." He straightened his back and peered into Kazuna's face. "It's going to be a very tight schedule for you to try to draw all the pictures on the boat. Do you think you'll be able to do it?"

"I'll be fine. I'm practically counting the days—I can't wait to get started."

At the moment, Kazuna was making a relentless push to get all her other work done well in advance, to ensure that no other obligations would crop up during that three-day period.

It was very unusual for a festival boat to be decorated with original drawings. Usually the designs or motifs were carved into the wood, and even when pictures were used, those were nearly always copies in the form of transfer prints attached to the boat with heavy-duty glue. Bucking tradition, Kazuna intended to draw pictures directly on the wooden surface. Of course, the vessel was going to end up smashed to bits, but afterwards the pieces would be distributed among the fans who had bought shares in the project. She was determined to cover every inch of the boat with illustrations to convey the excitement of the day.

Yukishiro's inspired idea had borne fruit in a big way, and the funds needed for the boat project had already been raised by the presale of shards.

"There's something else I need to talk to you about," Munemori said.

"Okay, shoot."

"It's about the event on Sunday—the talk show with Director Saito."

"Oh…" It occurred to her that they hadn't discussed the talk-show event since the day Hitomi Saito had agreed to participate. In the immensity of their relief they must have been thinking of it as a done deal, but there were still some details to be ironed out.

"So," he ventured, "I was wondering—would you consider being the interviewer?" For a moment, Kazuna couldn't make sense of the words that seemed to hang in the air. She stammered, "Huh?" thinking it must be some kind of a joke, but when she looked at Munemori's face, she was surprised to see no trace of a smile. After a beat that lasted just a bit too long, she found her words.

"Whaaat?! No, no, no. No way, not in a million years. It's completely and utterly impossible."

"No? I think you'd be a perfect fit for that role."

"No way. There's no way in the world I could get up and talk in front of a bunch of people. For something like that you need a voice actor or some other kind of professional. Besides, if we want people to show up for that event, Director Saito and I are too much alike—we're not exactly outgoing or loquacious, and I'm afraid having the two of us in the lineup would be very drab and dull, so to speak."

"I don't think it would be drab or dull in the least, and words like that seem kind of insulting to Director Saito—so to speak."

"Oh, I didn't realize what I was saying. I'm sorry." Hastily, Kazuna apologized, and Munemori gave a dry laugh. Then he asked again, somehow seeming even more determined than before, "You really wouldn't even consider it? The thing is, the voice actors were barely able to rearrange their schedules so they could be here through Saturday, and they have to rush back to Tokyo the next day for a concert, or something. So there's no way we could ask one of them to stick around and host the talk show. I still think you'd be an ideal choice—you're an animator who was involved with *Sabaku*, and you live in Enaga, to boot."

"No, it's impossible. Really, could you please let me say no, just this once?" To show how completely serious she was, Kazuna turned to face Munemori squarely. "I'm very sorry to disappoint you," she said, bowing her head. "I'm somebody who works behind the scenes, and that's the way I like it. But also, *Sabaku* has a very distinguished animation director named Mr. Goto who's been with the project from the beginning. He and the director built *Sabaku* from the ground up, starting with the character design. In this or any other situation, for me to put myself out in front, displacing the person who really deserves the attention—that would make me incredibly uncomfortable, and it would also go against my core beliefs."

"Your core beliefs?"

"That's right." Kazuna nodded. She wasn't refusing to do the talk show solely because of her aversion to appearing in front of a crowd. There were some personal principles she wasn't prepared to violate, and this was one of them.

"The thing about anime drawings or pictures is that no matter how great people think those pieces are, or how much praise they heap on the artist, those elements are just a small part of the whole," she explained. "They should never be looked at as works of art that can stand on their own. And when people see some value in an individual drawing, that's entirely due to the charm and appeal of the overall creation. Not only that, but I think of working behind the scenes, and creating small details as part of a larger work, as the proud labor of an army ant."

"An army ant?" echoed Munemori, smiling.

Kazuna smiled back at him and said, "Yes." She couldn't believe she was able to respond to his question with such cheerful conviction.

That's how it was, though. When people said she created god genga, or whatever, they were isolating her work from the whole, and that's why compliments like that made her so uncomfortable. The true value of a genga artist's work lay in the way it melted seamlessly into the greater vision, fitting perfectly—and unobtrusively—into its own anonymous slot.

And that's why I want to remain an army ant, Kazuna thought.

"So anyway, because I'm a proud army ant, or worker ant, I just wouldn't feel right about sitting on a stage next to an ant queen. Let's try to find somebody more appropriate, okay? If the voice actors aren't an option, then—oh, wait," Kazuna interrupted herself in midsentence. "If the interviewer is a local female news announcer or someone who doesn't have any particular understanding of anime, I think that would make things difficult for Director Saito. I saw something like that on Niconico before the spring anime season—they were live-streaming a combination talk show and press conference, and it was kind of a train wreck, to be honest. I don't think that kind of arrangement would be good for anyone, including the fans."

"Oh," Munemori said, nodding. "I've seen something like that, too."

"You have?" Kazuna said, looking at him in mild disbelief. *Does this person really watch Niconico?* she mused, aware that it might be otaku snobbery to think so.

Munemori was staring into space. After a moment he said hesitantly, "I do have one idea, though it's probably a long shot. I actually know someone who pretty much fits the bill: he's very knowledgeable about anime, and he wouldn't be out of place sitting next to a queen ant, and seeing him on stage would almost certainly make the fans happy. The big question is whether or not he would be willing to do it."

"Surely you aren't talking about the vice chairman?" Kazuna asked with a half-smile, thinking to herself that the flamboyant sake mogul would definitely look right at home under the spotlights.

"What?" Munemori said. "No, no, not at all—though I can't say this person is unrelated to the vice chairman." He smiled cryptically, then continued, "I have a good friend who was ahead of me in high school. He knows a lot about anime, and he's been giving me advice about all sorts of things, including about the pilgrimage project."

"Oh, this must be the friend you mentioned once—the anime fan?"

"No." Munemori spoke in a low voice, and there was an undertone of reluctance in the way he shook his head. When Kazuna tilted hers suspiciously, he continued, "He isn't an anime fan. I mean, he loves anime, of course, but rather than being a fan per se, he's someone who works in the industry. He just finished a big project, so I thought there might be a slight chance that he would agree to help us out..."

The person whom Munemori had mentioned came home to Enaga in the middle of September, and she tagged along when he went to the train station to meet his "anime advisor." Actually seeing the friend standing nonchalantly in front of the *Sabaku* poster, Kazuna gulped.

Advance warning notwithstanding, this was the biggest surprise so far in what had been a summer of astonishments.

"It's hot! You're late! How long were you planning to make me wait, anyway?"

The person hurling complaints at Munemori, with his face twisted into a petulant grimace, was the anime director Chiharu Oji.

Fresh off the success of his comeback vehicle, *Fateful Fight: Ryder Light*—widely considered the leading candidate for anime supremacy for that season—Oji was the most talked-about person in the anime world at that moment.

Kazuna had only ever seen Chiharu Oji in magazines and on TV screens, and her sense of wonderment grew when she saw how easily Munemori approached the star director, with no sign of deference or hesitation.

"Hey, sorry I'm late," Munemori said.

"You're *extremely* late, Shuhei," Oji corrected with a childish pout.

"I know, and I really am sorry for keeping you waiting. Thanks a lot for agreeing to host the talk show."

"Nah, it's all good. Or should I say, my turn has come at last?" Oji let out a long, loud sigh. "My producer came up from Tokyo with me, but right now she's busy pawing through *Sabaku* goods on the shopping street. She was all 'Squee, we're on holy ground!'—I mean, seriously, she's so giddy about being here that she's acting like a total fool. She just left me high and dry and ran off to check out the shops."

Seeing the two men standing together, Oji, with his age-less-schoolboy face, looked younger than Munemori. Anyone would have thought the civil servant was the one who had graduated first, and not the other way around. Kazuna was stunned by the realization that Munemori was younger than she'd thought. When Oji was a third-year in high school, Munemori had been a first-year, so that meant the director was two years older.

As Oji, still wearing the same sulky expression, stood before her at this familiar train station, Kazuna suddenly thought: *Oh, of course. This person really does belong on the same stage with the Queen Ant. His surname even means "prince"!*

Kazuna hadn't known that Director Chiharu Oji was originally from Enaga City. She'd been working at Fine Garden all these years, but when she and her colleagues had talked about Oji or *Ryder*, no one had ever mentioned that fact. Not even the company president, who was supposed to be an Enaga native himself, seemed to be aware of it.

"Is that really true?" Kazuna asked Munemori skeptically at Asami's yakitori bar.

He nodded. "Yes," he replied in an uncharacteristically low voice to avoid being overheard by any anime fans who might be within earshot. "If Fine Garden's president didn't know, I think it's probably because they're from different generations. Oji didn't start working in anime until after he moved to Tokyo, and whenever he has to provide information about himself he always just gives his birthplace as Niigata Prefecture."

Munemori paused in apparent perplexity. He seemed to be racking his brain for what to say next, and how to say it.

"It's just—I think there must have been some conscious thought behind his choosing to give only the name of the prefecture. There aren't that many celebrities from around here, and if it became widely known that Oji is a local boy, I'm sure people like the mayor and the section chief would try to pressure him into giving lectures or designing the town mascot or whatever, just because he's famous."

"I'm sure that would be a very real possibility," Kazuna nodded, full of quiet admiration for Munemori.

She had often heard stories about famous directors or screenplay writers whose alma maters or hometowns became public knowledge and were descended upon by hordes of fans, which caused all manner of problems. Or else the celebrities would be pestered to act as tourism ambassadors or to perform other functions that had no connection whatsoever with their true work. In her heart, Kazuna had always sympathized with them.

In Oji's case, Munemori had been instrumental in keeping that type of situation from developing. As someone who worked in the tourism section, it would have been natural for him to capitalize on their friendship, but instead he went out of his way to protect Oji's privacy. The fact that until recently he had never given Kazuna the slightest hint as to the identity of his "anime advisor" was a striking demonstration of his character and integrity, especially considering how much time she and he had spent together on the project.

"Oh, but anyway," Oji rambled on, "I mean I was prepared for this, but still, the whole town is like wall-to-wall *Sabaku*, everywhere you look! It feels like—how shall I put this—a bunch of marauding barbarians came in and plundered my hometown. If I had to make this place the setting for an anime, my love-hate relationship would get in the way, and I just absolutely couldn't, but someone who isn't from here surely did a marvelous job of portraying the countryside. Really, it's amazing. I totally respect what they've done."

"Oji, your voice is a little bit loud." Munemori grabbed his friend's arm, and Oji scowled up at him.

"What's the problem?" the director demanded. "I've been looking forward to this. I mean, I refrained from saying anything to anyone while *Sabaku* was airing, and I feel like it was all for this talk-show extravaganza. There are loads of things I'd like to say to Director Saito—I'll be serving up a full measure of sarcasm mixed with appreciation, guaranteed. And I'm really grateful to you, too, for giving me a chance to grill the person who basically stole my hometown. I'm really honored. No, but seriously, thank you very much for giving me this awesome gig, Shuhei."

"Um…" Kazuna didn't see any graceful way to interrupt their easy banter, but when she voiced that timid syllable, Munemori and Oji both turned to look at her.

Munemori began to introduce her, saying, "This is Fine Garden's—" and in that instant, as Oji turned to face her, she saw what seemed to be a flash of recognition in his eyes. It didn't feel as if that was her self-flattering imagination working overtime. Or at least that's what she wanted to believe.

"So you're Kazuna Namisawa," Oji suddenly spoke her name. He took both her hands in his and shook them, literally. "Thank you," he said. "We owe you so much for your work on *Ryder*. I've often heard our animation director mentioning your name and talking about your stellar reputation. But I was surprised when Shuhei told me—I had no idea Fine Garden was located in Enaga, of all places."

"Oh, um—thank you."

"It must have been a huge hassle trying to decipher my storyboards to turn them into genga—for the second half, especially, they were kind of a hot mess. The thing is, I'm really not good at drawing, and I always feel bad about how difficult that must make it for everybody else."

"No, really, it was fine."

Now that the conversation had turned to a discussion of work, Kazuna began to relax a bit. But Oji was watching her with a curious look in his eyes, and this unleashed a fresh surge of nervousness in her.

Nevertheless, she continued gamely: "To be sure, storyboards that are put together by a director who doesn't normally draw pictures may be populated with stick figures and the like, but in your case, Mr. Oji, you still manage to show clearly what you want to do, and what you're hoping to create. To me, it's almost like receiving a challenge, and it always feels very worthwhile and satisfying."

"Huh." Oji made an ambiguous sound, and for a moment Kazuna was afraid she might have offended him. But then the director's face lit up with a genuinely joyful smile. "Thank you very much. I hope we can work together again sometime."

Oji was a famously volatile character, but when he smiled at her in that elegant, almost ethereal way, Kazuna could only think, *What a beautiful face.* She forgot everything she'd heard about his personality—flaky man-child, demonic at work, yada yada—and nearly got swept away by his handsome visage.

"So—what now, Shuhei?" Oji let go of Kazuna's hands and turned to Munemori.

Some of the travelers at the station—anime fans who had come to make their pilgrimage, from the looks of them—were showing signs of having recognized Oji. This made Kazuna feel uneasy until she noticed that the director seemed to be openly welcoming and even basking in the attention. He had just finished safely guiding a major title to the finish line, and the feeling of relief must have been absolutely colossal.

"When's the Tokei Animation team arriving, anyway?" Oji went on. "I mean, I'm really astounded that Yukishiro gave his approval to having me host the talk show. I thought he would have wanted to keep me as far away as possible from his precious princess."

"I heard that Director Saito said she'd be delighted to have you onstage with her," Munemori told him. "Apparently she was very surprised to learn that you're from Enaga. She's ready to submit to any slings and arrows you may want to fling in her general direction."

That was just the kind of grace Kazuna would have expected from Director Saito. She was moved, but she couldn't help noticing that Munemori's face wore an expression of mild anxiety.

"The Tokei team will be arriving on the morning of the first day," he said. "But Oji, are you really sure you're okay with this? I mean, having everyone find out you're from here?"

"Find out? It doesn't really matter. People who know already know, and it's not as if I was actively trying to hide the fact. As I was saying just now, I'm actually going to enjoy giving Director Saito a hard time about helping herself to my home turf." Oji let out a small puff of air, then added, "But it's really been hard, you know? They were using my hometown, so I wanted their show to be a hit. Shuhei here was laying on the pressure, along with my dad, so I did a bunch of things that weren't my style at all. Like visiting Director Saito on the front lines of her project, which was a little weird because I was creating my show for the same season. You'd think they'd support me, the homeboy, instead. Give me a break."

Just when it was starting to seem as though Oji's screed might go on all day, a male voice called, "Hey, Chiharu!"

Kazuna turned around and uttered a little squeak of surprise, an "eh" that had a hint of a "g" in it.

A red Porsche had pulled up in the traffic circle in front of the station, and the vice chairman of the Enaga City Chamber of Commerce was leaning out of the driver's-side window. "Oh, Munemori, too, and Kazuna." Hearing this, Kazuna's eyes grew wide, and wider still.

A-ha! she thought, as an entire jar of pennies dropped.

"Chiharu, welcome home," the vice chairman said.

Squinting in the direction of the car Oji nodded and answered, "Ah. It's good to be back, Dad."

The first time Kazuna had laid eyes on the vice chairman,

who was the epitome of a gorgeous older man, she'd had a vague but undeniable sense of having seen him before somewhere. Now that mystery was solved: his face was almost identical to that of Director Oji.

No more than a few seconds after the red Porsche's arrival, a tall, long-legged beauty came running up carrying paper shopping bags bulging with what appeared to be souvenirs. "Sorry to keep you waiting," she begged her pardon.

The newcomer stared at Kazuna's face.

Kazuna liked good-looking men, very much, but she saw beauteous women as her nemeses. She had trouble looking either in the face, and reflexively, she tried to avert her gaze, but the stunning woman was having none of that.

"So you're Kazuna Namisawa!" Planting herself directly in front of Kazuna, the lady echoed Oji's words from earlier, her eyes sparkling in just the same manner. "Nice to meet you! My name is Kayako Arishina, and I'm in the production department at Studio Edge. It's really an honor to meet you in person. You helped us so much with *Ryder*, I can't even begin to—hang on. Business card, business card…"

"Hey, come on, calm down," Oji chided. "Well, at least everyone's getting to see Ms. Arishina in full-on anime-otaku mode." He let out a huge, exasperated sigh. "Also, both my parents are here, so don't you want to pay your respects to your director's closest relations? You know, the 'I'll be indebted to your son for all eternity' or 'Your son is an unbelievable genius, but you probably knew that already' kind of thing."

"What? Oh, oh, oh! Please forgive me."

What on earth is going on with these people? wondered Kazuna, gaping at them.

Just then one of the rear windows of the Porsche slid down, and a face peeked out—a face Kazuna remembered very well.

"Hello there," came a laidback greeting. Kazuna recognized that voice right away, as well.

It belonged to the round-faced woman who had greeted her and Munemori at the entrance to the limestone cave when they were searching for sites for the stamp rally—the friendly middle-aged auntie who had, unforgettably, been wearing a full shrine-maiden costume in the spirit of cosplay.

Ah, Kazuna began preparing to issue the customary pleasantries, but stopped suddenly, bewildered. Why on earth was the ticket-taker from the limestone cave riding in the vice chairman's Porsche?

When Oji caught sight of this new face he said, "Ah," and gave another respectful nod. The car door opened and the woman stepped out. Today she was clad not in the vermilion culottes of a shrine maiden, but in a bright-colored summer dress made from lightweight jersey. Making a beeline for Kayako, she asked, "Are you Ms. Arishina, by any chance?"

Kayako nodded and said, "Yes."

"Oh, I thought so. I'm so sorry I couldn't have been more helpful the other day when you were having trouble getting into my boy's apartment. I'm Chiharu's mother."

Geh, Kazuna croaked and opened her eyes wide again.

She looked from the face of the vice chairman, who was still hanging out of the driver's-side window, to the beaming face of the woman talking to Kayako Arishina, and then back again.

What? How? These two are a married couple?

As she stood like a statue, trying to process this new plot twist, Munemori turned to her and said, "Oh, you didn't know? Sorry, I thought I told you. Both of Oji's parents are always helping us out through the chamber of commerce."

"That's right," the vice chairman chimed in. "There was a shortage of pretty girls to take tickets at the limestone cave, so we lent you our lovely Akiko part-time. Isn't that right, sweetheart?" he asked, grinning from ear to ear.

"Yes, that's right, dear," Akiko Oji said softly with a smile.

Seeing this, Oji growled, "Will you two please knock it off? I mean, spouting that kind of lovey-dovey stuff in front of people, and at your age, too." He wore an exasperated expression but didn't sound too annoyed.

Kazuna was very close to overdosing on amazement, and she

didn't even know where to start trying to get a handle on all the startling new developments. On top of everything else, today was also the first time she'd heard that the vice chairman was Oji's father. Almost tottering in her confusion, she put out a hand to brace herself against the nearest wall. Just then her smartphone emitted a *ka-jingle-clink*.

Watching out of the corner of her eye as the war of pleasantries between Kayako Arishina and Oji's mother escalated—"I'm *so* deeply obliged to you!" "No, no, I'm the one who's in *your* debt!"—Kazuna opened the email.

And then—she caught her breath, sharply.

"Long time no see," read the subject line.

The email was from Kazuna's Tokyo Skytree date—Osato from Bluto.

◆

Three days before the Kanaga Festival.

The boat was delivered, just as Munemori promised.

There was a longstanding organization called the Kanaga Festival Preservation Society that was dedicated to protecting and preserving every aspect of the tradition. Most of the members came from the higher echelons of local government and the chamber of commerce, so they were well equipped to negotiate and coordinate with everyone directly involved with the festival.

The Preservation Society held its meetings in a mountain cabin not far from the steep-walled river valley where the boat launch took place, and they had agreed to lend that facility to Kazuna as a workspace for the three days it would take to decorate the *Sabaku* boat.

The building was quite ancient and lacked any air conditioning, and Kazuna had resigned herself to the prospect of working in the sweltering heat. However, Munemori's car hadn't climbed very far up the primitive mountain road before the air temperature dropped so precipitously that it was hard to believe they were still within the city limits.

The cool wind blowing through the depths of the mountain reminded Kazuna of the chilly breeze inside the limestone cave.

Munemori gave Kazuna a ride to her temporary workspace, and the road took them through a forest filled with towering, thick-trunked trees that were like a completely different species from their shorter, skinnier counterparts at the base of the mountain. Even though this was technically part of Enaga City, it was impossible to reach the cabin without a car, so Kazuna had asked Munemori to act as her chauffeur, morning and night, starting today.

As they drove along he said, "This is from Oji's mom," and handed Kazuna a bundle wrapped in a *furoshiki* cloth patterned with a dainty traditional motif.

"What's this?" she asked.

"I gather it's some *ohagi* sweets. She was saying that since drawing pictures requires a lot of brainpower, you'll probably end up craving something sweet."

The car continued to make its way up the road, which gradually morphed into a trackless track. Peering through the windshield at the mountain vista unfolding before them, Munemori explained, "Apparently she got a lot of practice when Oji was living at home. From the time he was very young, he was always immersed in some passion project that had nothing to do with schoolwork, and his mother was constantly being pressed into making midnight snacks for him, so that type of cooking became a specialty of hers. I heard that tomorrow she's planning to make Inari sushi with wasabi and sesame seeds."

"That'll be a lifesaver. Once I'm up in the cabin, it would be rough to have to go all the way back down the mountain to buy food."

"If you need something, or if anything happens, just call my cell and I'll run up here right away." Munemori pulled his smartphone out of his breast pocket, then frowned. "Huh, I didn't expect this, but apparently there's no signal up here."

"Nothing we can do about that," Kazuna said. She checked her own phone and it, too, was displaying the "Out of Area" icon. "That's okay. I was prepared for this. I'll just have to concentrate on working hard until evening. We don't have much time in any case."

"I'm really sorry the boat was delivered so late. I was hoping against hope that it would be ready a day early, at least, but the shipwrights are true craftspeople, and they're very particular about every detail."

The boats would be reduced to debris by the end of the festival day, but—or, more precisely, *therefore*—the artisans poured all their skills and talents and pride into making sure the ephemeral vessels would shine as brightly as possible during their brief, extravagant turns on the grand stage. Kazuna thought it was a lovely tradition.

"It'll be fine," she said. "And besides, help is on the way, later today."

"Oh, yes, I really wanted to thank you for arranging that, too," Munemori said gratefully. The road had grown so rough that the entire chassis seemed to be one massive vibration. "Whether it's Producer Yukishiro or Director Saito, it's all thanks to your character and credibility."

"Oh no, not even," Kazuna protested with a self-deprecating moue.

At last the car arrived at the mountain cabin that would be Kazuna's studio for the next three days. She stepped inside the simple, one-storied structure.

The building resembled a high-ceilinged storeroom. Even though it was still the warm season, the air inside was downright chilly.

A plastic tarp had been spread across the middle of the floor, and on top of it sat the boat, covered by a white cloth.

The sight made Kazuna catch her breath. She had seen the boats from previous years in photographs and on video, but it was much larger than she expected. For someone of her small stature, it was almost overwhelming.

Without saying a word, Munemori gently removed the cloth covering. The boat was made entirely from raw, untreated wood, and the heady fragrance of freshly milled lumber filled the room.

Kazuna stood facing the boat, sizing it up, and after a long moment she said, "It's good. It's incredibly good."

The naked grain of the wood looked like a living organism. The boat gave the impression of having been carved from a single gargantuan log, and it was almost impossible to spot the places where sections had been expertly joined together. More than ever, Kazuna understood the meaning of the phrase she'd been hearing—"a festival rich in tradition"—and her heart was flooded with emotion.

The beautifully rounded contours of the boat were somehow reminiscent of the curvilinear landscape of a female body. This festival, continuously celebrated from olden times until today, was surely a way of giving thanks for the bounty of nature, as represented by the feminine form. No one had ever explained this to Kazuna, but she was somehow able to deduce it just by looking at the shape of the boat.

Here and there, some deliberate marks had been engraved into the wooden vessel. One, at the prow, was probably the first kanji of Tokei Animation's name (which meant "east"), enclosed in a triangle.

And when she walked around the boat she saw, incised into the stern, Enaga's official city emblem, which resembled a roman letter "L."

Kazuna took a deep breath and bit her lip, hard. "I guess I'd better get started," she said.

Munemori bowed his head. "Thank you so much for doing this."

Munemori climbed back into his car and drove away, and Kazuna stood watching until he disappeared down the mountain trail.

Alone now, she went back into the workspace. Even though there was no one around to hear, she said aloud, "Well, then, shall we do this?"

That was when she realized that a prior visitor was standing in front of the cabin.

Kazuna hadn't seen anyone earlier, when she and Munemori arrived, but now a small girl had emerged from behind the building. Startled, Kazuna let out an involuntary "Whaa?" The child stared back at her, eyes wide with surprise.

The little girl was very cute. No—make that super, ultra, mega cute. She appeared to be three or four years old and was dressed in a horizontally striped black-and-white top and a ruffled black skirt. The hem of the skirt was adorned with a row of closely spaced rhinestones that made their glittery presence known whenever the girl made the slightest move. A pochette-style bag patterned with biscuits hung from one of the girl's slight shoulders.

For an instant, Kazuna seriously thought the child might be a fairy or wood sprite.

This deep in the mountains, anything seemed possible. But no, probably not, since the little girl was decked out from head to toe in children's clothing from what even Kazuna could recognize as high-end brands.

"Um…so who are you?"

The child made no reply. With the same astonished look on her face, she began to back away, a few inches at a time. Kazuna had no idea who the little girl might be, but it didn't seem wise to let her wander off into the deep-mountain forest by herself. Hurriedly, she asked, "Do you belong to someone from the chamber of commerce? Did you come with your parents?"

Dealing with children was not one of Kazuna's fortes, but she was giving it her best shot. However, the child kept her mouth tightly shut and didn't say a word in response. She just stood quietly, staring at the strange grown-up.

Kazuna tried again. "Um, I wonder where your mother is. Do you have any idea?" she asked, but this question, too, went unanswered.

At her wits' end, Kazuna looked around, but all was silence in the forest with its lofty trees, aside from an occasional trill of birdsong and the distant sound of power tools being put to work. There was no sign of any other human presence.

"Let me see…"

This was a problem—a really major problem. The clock was already running on her limited allotment of working time, and every minute was essential and precious. In desperation, she asked, "Will you come into the cabin with me?" but once again there was no response. Kazuna found herself thinking that designer clothes notwithstanding, the child really might be a wood sprite or a mountain spirit.

"Well, I'll be in here, so if you need anything please come and find me, okay?" If this small person's parents or guardians turned up, surely they would notice the cabin and take a look inside.

Giving up, Kazuna turned and headed for the door. Despite having shown no signs of responsiveness until then, the little girl followed behind her at a safe distance. When the child entered the workspace, with its delicious smell of tree sap, her tiny mouth opened in an unvoiced "Oh!"

My goodness, I hope she doesn't want to touch it, Kazuna thought, but the child kept her distance, decorously sitting down on the floor next to the entrance without ever taking her eyes off the boat.

What on earth is going on with this kid, anyway? And I can't send Munemori a distress signal, even if I wanted to, 'cause my cell is completely useless here, and I have so much to do, and…

With those fragmented thoughts running through her head, Kazuna went ahead and got to work. First she spread out a giant sheet of the thick, coated paper known as imitation Japanese vellum, on which she had sketched the outline of her entire design after numerous discussions with Tokei Animation. Seeing that, the little girl's mouth once again formed a silent "Oh!"

Kazuna compared her design with the boat. Then, taking up a position on the right side of the vessel, she muttered, "Okay, here goes," and drew the first line.

Kazuna felt guilty about this in retrospect, but once she became absorbed in the task at hand, her concern about the enigmatic child gradually faded from her mind.

As many characters as possible. Facial expressions that are as lively and vivid as possible. The absolute maximum number of highlights for each character... Kazuna's arms moved as though she were making frantic gestures. The reluctance she felt at first to sketch directly on the sanctified wood soon vanished.

At one point, something abruptly derailed her trancelike concentration, and she stepped away from the boat for a moment. That was when she noticed that the little girl had crept up and was standing next to her, holding something in her hand while she looked up at Kazuna.

"Draw," asked the child.

It was the first word Kazuna had heard the kid utter. Looking more closely, she saw that the object in the girl's hand was a "doodle board," one of those toys where a magnetic stylus and iron sand are used to draw pictures that can be erased with a shake of the wrist. It must have been stowed in the girl's pochette.

With no change in her unfriendly, inscrutable expression, the girl repeated, "That's *Sabaku*, right? Draw it for me."

Ah, Kazuna thought. *I guess she isn't a wood sprite or a mountain spirit, after all. She's apparently watching Japanese anime.*

"Okeydokey," she said aloud, accepting the doodle board.

After Kazuna finished sketching Mayu, the character the mysterious little girl requested, she took a quick sip of her drink and then got back to work. The more she drew, the blacker her drawing hand became.

It wasn't that long, but the next time Kazuna looked around, the child had vanished. When could she have left?

Kazuna didn't even remember hearing the sound of the front

door opening, or closing.

Muttering "What? How?" she rushed around outside, looking for the girl, but the summer forest was as calm and tranquil as ever.

This is bad, she thought. *Maybe she really was lost. She might even be in danger right now.* But then, just as Kazuna was about to expand her search to the area beyond the cabin, she heard a voice saying, "Whew! We found it, at last!"

It was a voice she had heard before: a voice she couldn't forget even if she wanted to. Kazuna looked toward it, and her eyes met those of the speaker.

"Hello, Ms. Namisawa," Tetsuya Osato said. "Long time no see! Sorry we're late—we got spectacularly lost."

Osato's shoulders drooped under the weight of an enormous rucksack. And behind him, somehow managing to look cool as she pulled a wheeled suitcase up the mountain path, was the master figure-maker, Kaede Marino.

Ahhh. Deep in her heart, Kazuna let out a silent groan. She'd known there was a chance the helper Osato brought along might turn out to be Marino, and sure enough, here she was. Kazuna still felt some lingering discomfort from their last encounter, but a second later that feeling had vanished and been replaced by surprise.

Marino was wearing a long skirt, and behind her slim waist stood the little girl, staring at Kazuna with the same blank, unreadable look on her face. One small hand was tightly clutching the folds of Marino's skirt.

"I thought you might need some help," Osato said when he phoned that day, shortly after Kazuna received his email.

She had been at Enaga Station to meet Chiharu Oji and Kayako Arishina, and she was already in a state of mild shock from the nonstop parade of startling revelations even before Osato's email arrived saying that he wanted to talk to her about the Kanaga Festival.

"I'm sorry about sending a message to your cell, out of the

blue," he'd said over the phone. "I saw something about the boat for the Kanaga Festival on the Tokei Animation site, and that gave us—that is, Bluto—an idea, so we got in touch with Mr. Yukishiro. That's when I learned that you were going to be drawing the pictures on the boat. So I was wondering whether you might consider letting us lend you a hand."

Kazuna had always thought of Osato as a workaholic with an almost excessive love of anime, but this offer seemed to suggest that his passion for the medium was far greater than even she could comprehend.

She had answered his call that day with some trepidation, but even though it had been quite a while since they last spoke, Osato rushed through the usual greetings and got right to the point.

"How are you planning to handle the painting?" he asked. "I was very surprised to hear that you were going to try to cover the entire boat with images, all by yourself, in only three days. Excuse me for asking, but you don't usually do the coloring, do you? Not just that, but drawing on objects and painting them is very different from the genga process you're accustomed to. Won't you let our figure-sculptor help you out?"

Osato went on to explain the idea Blue Open Toy had proposed to Tokei Animation. What if, when the individual shards from the wreckage of the *Sabaku* boat were distributed among the fans, the package included a miniature model of the entire boat? Even if those bits of debris really did confer some mystical benefit, they wouldn't be complete pictures, and given the random patterns of breakage, there would be no way to ensure a fair distribution.

Couldn't they use Bluto in that case? That had been the gist of the proposal: *It'll be tight, but we figure if we can have three months, that should be enough time to make all the miniboats to ship along with the fragments. If participating in the event becomes a thing going forward, starting next year we can sell the figures of this year's boat at various marketplace events and at the festival itself.*

Long story short, Osato told Tokei Animation that he would like to check out this year's festival, accompanied by a figure-maker, and Yukishiro, who was famously fond of lucrative angles, agreed immediately. It was then that Osato learned about Kazuna's involvement with the boat project.

"When it comes to three-dimensional work, we're total pros," he told her over the phone. "If you'd allow us to give you a hand, you could concentrate solely on drawing the pictures. Or, at the very least, perhaps you could just let us help with the painting part?"

"I really appreciate the offer, but…" Kazuna was about to say, *I'll be fine on my own*, when Osato suddenly began to rattle off a litany of questions one after the other.

"Ms. Namisawa, what do you have in the way of painting supplies? Do you have lacquer? How about enamel? You might want to start by making sure you have all the equipment you'll need for that part of the process. And if you're going to be drawing directly on wood, won't you need to primer any grooves that were left by the carvers? Do you have any experience prepping surfaces?"

Kazuna was instantly silenced. She realized at the same time that her reckless insistence on drawing all the pictures all by herself might have seriously underestimated the scope of the job. She had, until now, been referring to one aspect simply as "coloring," while Osato called it "painting," and that disparity alone seemed to demonstrate that the task of applying pigments required a completely different set of skills. She felt shaken.

"I'll be up there anyway, with one of our figure-makers," Osato had said, as the phone conversation wound down. "Please let us help you with the boat."

"Sheesh," Osato spat as the little group filed into the mountain cabin. "I'm really sorry to be so late, especially after I talked such a big game about wanting to help you." The minute they were inside, he took off his rucksack and set it on the floor.

He was wearing a piece of hooded outerwear that Kazuna guessed must have cost at least twice what she had ever paid for similar items. The garment was designed to look like a racing jacket, but it was made from sweatshirt material, and Kazuna wasn't sure whether to call it a hoodie, or a parka, or what. While Osato was as stylishly dressed as usual, the rucksack, in contrast, had an old, weather-beaten, outdoorsy look that made her think it must be on loan from someone else. Certainly Osato must have needed to haul a lot of heavy tools.

"We took a cab from the train station but the driver said he wasn't familiar with the mountain roads, and he made us get out and walk the rest of the way," Osato explained. "We couldn't get a cell signal, and then on the way up, we lost sight of Beniha, and I really thought I was going to cry."

"Seriously, I was even closer to tears than Osato was," Marino said, but Kazuna found it hard to picture the ultracool sculptor crying over anything.

The woman, too, looked decidedly incongruous in this primitive, rustic space. Kazuna was flabbergasted to see that the sculptor had hiked up a mountain path wearing a long skirt and high-heeled shoes. Like the short, ruffly version worn by the little girl, the figure-maker's skirt had a line of rhinestones marching around the hem. The child, who until a while ago had been peeking out from behind that skirt, was now in Marino's arms. Kazuna couldn't help thinking that those arms looked rather frail, but they seemed to have no trouble carrying a child.

"I never dreamed you'd able to come, Ms. Marino," Kazuna said. "I'm surprised. I mean, you must be so busy." She still didn't fully understand the situation. Could one of the most popular figure-makers in Tokyo really just drop everything and travel all this way to do some incidental work?

Truth be told, Kazuna had been afraid that she might get depressed again if she had to cope with the woman's exceptional beauty and had been praying that it would be someone else.

The sculptor glanced at Kazuna, and just that slight interaction felt like being strangled.

"I definitely don't have much free time," Marino said, and her voice, at least, sounded somewhat more amicable than when they'd first met in passing at Skytree. "But we didn't get to go any-where this summer, so this is doubling as a sort of belated family trip to make up for that. I'm usually so busy that I don't get to be with her as much as I'd like."

"Wait, what?"

"Oh, Beniha is Marino's daughter," Osato explained.

Kazuna found this information so difficult to assimilate that she could only repeat, "What?" Gaping at the mother and child, who stared back with unfriendly looks on their exquisite faces, Kazuna felt thunderstruck all over again. "Whaaat?!"

"Yes, even if I lost track of her a little while ago," Marino said, her face perfectly serene. "Then she came back with one of your pictures on her board, and that's how we finally found our way to this cabin. Thank you very much."

Marino smiled for the first time. When a normally impassive beauty finally smiles, the impact can be earthshaking. And then, on top of that, she apologized.

"I'm sorry. I'm raising her as a single mother, and once again I've ended up dragging my daughter to work with me."

"No, please don't worry about that, at all," Kazuna told her. "Before you arrived, she just sat quietly and watched me working. She was very well behaved."

As she spoke, she was still trying to process the implausible fact that this glamorous person was a single mother. It just didn't seem real, somehow.

Marino smiled again, gazing into her daughter's face. "I'm pleased to hear that. She likes to watch people work. It was hard when she was younger, though. Making figures involves lots of minuscule parts, which children tend to like."

"Oh, of course. I can definitely see that."

"I remember this one time—it was an incredible mess," Osato said. "Beniha was sitting quietly in the corner of the studio, like a little angel, but when I went to check on her I saw that she'd stepped on a tube of adhesive and it was spread all over the floor. I swear, it looked like an impromptu roach motel."

At this, Beniha, who was still safely nestled in her mother's arms, cried, "Stop it! Osato," and reached out and slapped him in the face. Osato grabbed the tip of his nose and whimpered, "Ow!"

The way the little girl mimicked her mother and used his surname without any honorific was irresistibly cute, and as Kazuna watched that comical exchange, she felt a distinct sense of relief.

As of this moment, she would be able to converse normally with Kaede Marino, too.

In fact, her own assumptions about Osato and Marino's relationship—simply because the two happened to work at the same company and the latter was a beautiful woman—were embarrassing. Seeing everything through such a lens was just stupid.

"I wasn't sure whether Marino would be able to rearrange her schedule, but I'm glad we were able to come together," remarked Osato.

"Thank you so much," Kazuna said, and this time she spoke from her heart. "It's going to be a huge help having you both here. I'm sorry to ask for such a major favor."

"Don't be silly, that's what friends are for—oops, sorry... I went and called you a friend."

"Come on, it's a little late for that, don't you think?" Marino said, setting Beniha down on the floor and looking at Osato through narrowed eyes. "I mean, you go on and on about it at work. Whenever the conversation turns to *Sabaku*, you always start bragging about how Ms. Namisawa is a friend of yours."

"Well, I'm just proud," Osato admitted, laughing.

Kazuna took a deep breath. "Honestly, I'm flattered." The words came out much more smoothly than she'd expected.

The romantic hopes she was harboring around the time of their meeting at Skytree had long since been snuffed out, but she still remembered how awkward she felt when Marino had asked whether she and Osato were there on a *date*. Osato's chosen word—"friends"—sounded infinitely better to her ears.

I'm friends with these people.

We're the kind of friends who can support one another, each feeling proud of the work the others are doing.

Kazuna had never confessed her feelings to Osato, and now

she was able to happily accept that they were "just friends." It was ever so much better than having someone misunderstand their relationship and jump to the conclusion that she was his girl-friend, or lover, or whatever.

Beyond differences in our exact occupation or upbringing, our attractiveness or femininity, we're linked through working on the same thing.

"Well, let's do this," Kazuna said. "We only have three days. I'll be enjoying working with you."

"Same here!" chorused Osato and Marino, their easy infor-mality refreshing.

The *Sabaku* boat was finished on the morning of the day before the Kanaga Festival after an epic all-night work session.

The strong aroma of raw wood was gradually supplanted by the even more potent odor of enamel, and when the paint smell completely overpowered the fragrance of the lumber, they knew their job was nearly done.

As she watched Marino and Osato at work—carefully mask-ing off one area with a cloth, then applying paint with an air-brush—Kazuna thought, *This definitely isn't something an ama-teur could do.* It was frightening to think that she had originally believed she could decorate the entire boat by herself. As Marino layered color upon color, Kazuna's illustrations gradually began to take on the vivid depth of actual anime images.

As the project approached the finish line, Munemori joined her in watching the process. While they'd been holed up in the cabin, toiling away, a number of the restaurants and inns involved with the *Sabaku* pilgrimage had sent a constant stream of meals and refreshments, until the workspace began to resemble the scene of a banquet. And because Enaga City was known for its breweries, there were so many donations of bottled sake that it appeared the boat had received a bounty of christening gifts a few days early.

"We're done," Marino's voice rang out.

Dealing with a boat many times bigger than the anime figures she usually worked on couldn't have been easy for her. Peeling off the mask she wore to avoid inhaling the spray-paint fumes, she said, "Now we just need to wait for it to dry."

"Thank you very much."

Speaking for everyone in the room, Munemori bowed his head to Marino. Then, still bowing, he turned towards Kazuna.

"Ms. Namisawa, too. Really, thank you so much. I never dreamed that we would be able to go this far."

Raising his head, he gazed at the work of art in the middle of the room and added, "This boat really is magnificent. I can't wait to show it to Director Saito, and all the fans."

Kazuna was deeply moved by his sincere words.

On the body of the boat, Kazuna had drawn the Kanaga Festival.

She had done her homework, visiting the gorge where it took place, poring over videos of past festivals. Her design featured a picture within a picture: the characters from *Sabaku* ranged along both banks and were launching a festival boat on the river, and that boat was adorned with images of the twelve robots they had been riding in.

Symbolic renditions of the sounds that the characters had sealed—knocks, the creaking of ice, the sound of rain, Takaya's laughter—all of them were included in the background, along with the rice paddies the kids had fought so hard to protect in the final battle.

Now that boat was ready to go. The festival was about to begin.

◆

It was the morning of Festival Eve, a few hours after the finished boat had been left to dry, when the *Sabaku* team, headed by Director Saito and Producer Yukishiro, finally arrived on-site.

Many of the people in the group were visiting Enaga for the

first time, and the instant they stepped off the train a multitude of voices could be heard saying, "Wow, this is amazing!"

WELCOME TO SOUNDBACK TOWN: ENAGA CITY, read a large banner specially prepared for today. When Director Saito spotted the sign, she blinked in unmistakable happiness.

Even if you discounted that year's added anime-pilgrimage factor, the Kanaga Festival was famous throughout Japan. The attendance numbers bruited about by the tourism section—a hundred thousand visitors every year—didn't appear to be an exaggeration. From morning, trains jam-packed with travelers had been pulling into the station, and many of those people were getting off at Enaga. The roads around the area were also clogged with vehicles.

If the throngs were this large on the day of the festival eve, it stood to reason that even more visitors would descend on the area the following day, when the boats would be flowing downstream.

"There are definitely a lot more young folks than usual, this year," Munemori said excitedly. "I think that's the *Sabaku* effect."

"So many people," Director Saito remarked, sounding almost appalled.

Noticing the director, quite a few of the travelers who had come because of *Sabaku* were exclaiming in surprise. Some children even approached her, with greetings that ranged from a shy "Hello" to "Good job!"

"It's nice to see you again," Kazuna said when her turn came to welcome the director. Compared to their previous meeting, Saito gave an impression of having become somehow softer and mellower. In her jeans and striped jersey, she wasn't dressed fancily at all, but perhaps because her hair was tidily arranged, her entire look appeared far more polished.

The last time the two women had met, Saito had been in the middle of the broadcast run of an anime series. Now, though, she had just emerged from that long, drawn-out battle, and the current recess must have felt like a blessed interlude of calm before the next storm. Today, Director Saito, away from the fray, looked so much more serene and easygoing that she was almost unrecognizable as the person Kazuna had glimpsed on that frantic day in Tokyo.

"Thank you for inviting us," Director Saito said, smiling at Kazuna.

"No, thank you for coming," Kazuna replied. "Really, I can't apologize enough for calling you for my own selfish reasons and asking for such enormous favors."

"I'm sorry we weren't able to get away earlier. I never imagined it would already be such a madhouse here, though."

"Wow, business is really booming. Phenomenal."

Unlike Director Saito, who was parceling out her words one by one, Yukishiro stood with one hand on his forehead, shading his eyes as he scanned the vast wave of visitors stretching far into the distance. *Ah,* Kazuna thought, *his eyes are probably seeing all the people as one giant roll of banknotes.* She still wasn't entirely comfortable with the producer's modus operandi, but she kept her own counsel.

"We heard that Director Oji and the others will be coming directly to the launching site tomorrow," Munemori reported.

Yukishiro's face clouded over slightly as he responded, "Ah…" Clearly, he wasn't thrilled by this news. "Roger that. No, really, he's certainly up to it in terms of stature," he said, his grimace belying his words.

Facing the two leaders of the Tokei Animation delegation, Munemori said, "Producer Yukishiro, we need to go to the lottery that determines the launch time of the boats, if you don't mind." Then turning to Hitomi Saito, he asked, "Is it all right to have Mr. Yukishiro do the drawing, instead of you?"

"Oh, he should definitely do it, by all means," Director Saito said as they began walking. "He has much better luck than I do when it comes to games of chance, so he's sure to get us a good launch time."

"Not really," Yukishiro demurred, glancing back over his shoulder as he and Munemori strode along a few feet ahead.

"Also," Director Saito added sotto voce, for Kazuna's ears only, "another good thing about having Yukishiro do the drawing is that if he doesn't get us a good slot, he'll be totally to blame. It'll be much more relaxing for me, that way."

"You're unexpectedly vicious," Kazuna joked.

"I know, right?" Director Saito smiled knowingly. "Seriously, though, thank you again, so much. We received the images, and it really is a beautiful boat."

"The actual boat is even more amazing," Kazuna promised, puffing out her chest with pride. "We all feel completely confident about this work. The staff members from Bluto really helped a lot, too."

"I can't wait to see it!"

Shortly after, at the launch-time lottery, where the chamber of commerce and the preservation society were also present, Yukishiro drew a yellow ball.

The minute he caught sight of that color, Munemori jumped up from his seat beside Kazuna and struck an extra-triumphant "guts pose." At that, everybody realized that yellow must signify a positive result.

The number inscribed on the side of the ball Yukishiro drew was 13:00.

Since it was just after the noon hour, one o'clock was considered the best possible time. It would definitely be convenient for the fans.

"You did it! You really do have the magic touch, Mr. Yukishiro!" exulted Munemori.

"Nah, no biggie," Yukishiro said, climbing down from the lottery platform while Munemori pounded his shoulders with congratulatory slaps. The producer was clearly trying to maintain his usual cool façade, but he couldn't stifle a satisfied smirk. When he snuck a look at Director Saito, she didn't say a word and just gave him a soft, gentle smile and clapped. Kazuna, quietly observing the exchange, found that glimpse into their relationship dynamic fascinating.

A few minutes later Kazuna and Hitomi went on their way, leaving behind Munemori and Yukishiro, who needed to attend a briefing for festival participants.

As the women were walking down the street, a voice hailed them from behind.

"Ah, hey, hey! Young ladies!" They paused and turned around to see Oji's mother, Akiko, standing there. With light steps she approached them. Today she wore a traditional Japanese apron, no doubt because she was helping prepare food for the festival. Peering into Hitomi's face, Akiko said in her outgoing way, "You're the director, aren't you? Yes, you're the one who directed *Sabaku*. That's really impressive, when you're still so young."

"Oh, no..." stammered Hitomi.

"Anyway, this is perfect. Come to our house tomorrow morning to get kitted out in yukata. I hope you'll come too, Kazuna, if you can."

"Oh—"

"I really love them, you see." Akiko smiled, which made her already full, round Okame face look even softer and plumper. "Ever since I was young I've had a weakness for fine clothes, especially traditional styles, and I've amassed quite a collection of yukata, as well as semiformal kimono. I don't normally have many chances to take them out of the closet, so if you don't mind, I'd love to have everyone wear them for the festival. I can help you put them on, too."

"Oh, but, I mean..." Kazuna hemmed and hawed. She didn't know about Hitomi Saito, but for her, the very idea of wearing traditional clothing was an alien concept with no place in her life. She had simply ignored her invitation to her coming-of-age ceremony, for which the dress code was always kimono—a decision her mother still ragged her about even now.

Tokyo's historical downtown, where Kazuna grew up, was home to a great many local festivals, but to her, normal pastimes like attending one of those celebrations dressed in yukata fell into the same category as having a boyfriend or going on dates: luxuries reserved for a privileged class she would never be able to join. That culture, she thought, was just too different from hers.

Kazuna was about to refuse ("Oh, no way, I couldn't possibly" was her standard response in such situations), when Oji's mother said in a tone that left no room for argument, "Come by our house later on and we'll have great fun choosing which ones to wear. And if you know anyone else who might like to dress up, you're more than welcome to bring them along, too." Then, before anyone could stop her, she trotted off with a cheery, "See you soon!" and was swallowed up in the jubilant crowd.

"Um, Ms. Oji!"

Kazuna called after the woman, but the words just hung fruitlessly in the air.

Director Saito, who seemed to be at least as overwhelmed as Kazuna, if not more so, marveled, "What a character."

"She's Chiharu Oji's mother," Kazuna told her.

"What?!"

Hearing the incredulity in Hitomi's voice, Kazuna chuckled. *Yes,* she thought, *you're right. It is an astonishing thing, indeed.* And then she shrugged her shoulders.

◆

"Yukata? How festive."

Sent off with those words from Yukishiro that may have been sincere or just heartless, Kazuna and Hitomi headed to Oji's natal home that afternoon.

When they told the taxi driver their destination, he immediately nodded and said, "Oh, that's the house of the Oji Sake Brewery family. Yes, yes." He explained that while the factory itself was in a different location, the house was famous around these parts.

As soon as the two women stepped out of the cab and took in the splendor of the massive gate and the deep, lush garden beyond, they let out impressed sighs.

It was a spectacularly stately Japanese mansion. Set amid the well-maintained stands of pine trees and camellia bushes was a large lily pond, and they could see the quicksilver glimmer of carp. *So Director Oji came from a wealthy family...* As Kazuna and Hitomi stood there, stunned and staring, a voice suddenly issued from inside the house.

"Hey, if you guys are thinking Director Oji's a spoiled rich kid, try again, okay? That's the furthest thing from the truth. I've never once asked my parents for help since I left home."

"Oh!" Hitomi turned her head in the direction of the voice.

The sliding doors at the front of the house were open, and Oji emerged from the entry hall. Producer Arishina followed a step behind him with a "Nice to see you again."

"Mr. Oji," greeted Hitomi.

"Hey, Director Saito. I'm looking forward to the talk show day after tomorrow."

"So am I." A sheepish smile played across Hitomi's face. "I'm sorry. I had no idea Enaga was your hometown. I apologize for using it without asking for your permission first."

"No worries. My parents are really happy that you did." His voice sounded considerably calmer than it had the other day, when he was throwing a minor tantrum at the station.

Just then Akiko Oji emerged from the house, saying, "Come, come, come. Young ladies, please come in—I've got everything ready for you."

As they all filed inside, Akiko burbled, "For tomorrow, I've mobilized some of my friends who are good with kimono to help you get dressed, so really, please make yourselves at home and don't hold back at all. It's going to be such a treat to see you all re-splendent in yukata. But honestly, I never dreamed my son would be able to bring so many charming young ladies to our house... He's really grown up."

"Well, I may not have brought any girls home but trust me, I was plenty popular back in the day," Oji boasted. "But seriously, Mom, take it down a notch."

"Oh, that's such a fib—you weren't popular at all," Akiko teased.

"Yes, that's my impression, too," Kayako said, nodding sagely from the side.

At that, Oji exploded. "You don't have to agree with everything my mother says!"

Kazuna and Hitomi looked at each other and exchanged a spontaneous smile.

Director Saito wasn't the only one. Chiharu Oji, too, had weathered the storm of creating an anime series and was now enjoying some (relative) peace and quiet.

Akiko led them to a large parlor at the rear of the house, where she had laid out an assortment of lightweight summer kimono in decorative rows. There were some subdued hues, but most of the yukata were brilliantly colorful and adorned with pretty seasonal patterns: morning glories, fireworks, fringed pinks, lilies of the valley...

"This one is an antique," Akiko explained, holding up a yukata with an all-over print of swimming fish. "It originally belonged to the daughter of a seafood merchant."

"Wow!" chorused the three younger women.

"This obi and these zoris go with this yukata, so I'd like the person who wears it to wear them all, as a set. Oh, but on the other hand, those same accessories go really well with this other kimono, too."

"That obi would also look good with this deep color," Kazuna ventured. She might have been a complete novice in the art of kimono, but when it came to color sense, she was confident she could hold her own.

Smiling happily at Kazuna's contribution, Akiko said, "Okay, then, it's decided. We'll make those two a set."

"I'll put them together," Kayako volunteered. Briskly, she began to rearrange the yukata, coordinating each one with various accessories. Watching Kayako and Akiko bustling around, Kazuna thought they looked like the mother-and-daughter proprietors of a kimono shop. Or, no: since Kayako was staying at the Ojis' family home, maybe she seemed more like a daughter-in-law.

Oji himself, however, stood up and excused himself midway, saying, "Knock yourselves out."

"Kayako, you're tall, so a larger print might work better for you—maybe something like this, with the peonies?"

"Oh, Kazuna, I think you'd look good in that yukata over there—the one with the choco-mint color scheme—and a brownish obi."

"Director Saito, you should absolutely stick with the cooler colors. You'll look so distinguished."

Kazuna was surprised to find herself not only engaging in girlish chatter, which she'd always thought was not her sort of thing, but also enjoying it. As the three of them tried on different outfits and peppered each other with compliments like "That's so cute on you," she had to admit that she didn't hate it one bit.

A new batch of visitors showed up at the Oji mansion in the evening. Akiko Oji went alone to greet them at the entrance, and her voice could be heard exclaiming, "My word, what a bevy of beauties!"

At that, Director Saito said, "Oh," and rushed out of the parlor to join the welcoming party.

The new arrivals were the five voice actresses who comprised the so-called *Mermaid Nurses* gang. The group's de facto leader, Aoi Mureno, stood in front of the others. Taking off her sunglasses, she bowed her head politely and said, "It's nice to meet you. Thank you very much for your kindness."

Kazuna had seen all five of the women before on live video and TV, and in magazine photo spreads, but it was different to meet genuine VA idols in the flesh. They all had slender legs and impossibly small, pretty faces. Kazuna's lowbrow heart was thrilled by the sight of these pop-culture icons, and she was so impressed that she forgot to feel jealous and insecure.

An adjoining room was thrown open to accommodate the growing crowd, and the back parlor with all the yukata strewn around began to look exactly like the dressing room for a group of star performers.

A bit later, Kaede Marino and her daughter, Beniha, who had

spent the day touring all the local sights, joined the party. Once again Akiko's face split with a beaming smile as she told Beniha, "Don't worry, sweetie, I borrowed some child-size kimono, too. There aren't many designs to choose among, but I hope you'll find one you like."

I appreciate it," Marino thanked, and then, turning to Kazuna, she added, "It was very nice of you to invite us, too."

"Oh, don't mention it. I just thought the two of you—mother and daughter—would look amazing dressed in yukata."

As she spoke, Kazuna happened to notice that Beniha, who was clinging tightly to her mother's hand, was staring down at the floor. Granted, she had inherited a fundamentally blasé face from her mother, but even so, the child was clearly not in good spirits. Her cheeks were inflamed as if she'd been crying, and she was continually biting her bottom lip.

Kazuna was wondering what could be wrong when the little girl plucked at the animator's arm and complained, "It's gone."

"Huh? What's gone?"

"Oh," Marino answered for her daughter, "I'm sorry. She's been crying and acting out since morning because the drawing you made on her doodle board got erased."

Noticing now that the little girl was clutching the same magnetic-drawing board from the other day, Kazuna stared at the child, dumbfounded. Surely the basic premise of a doodle board was the ability to continually draw pictures, erase them, and start all over again? It was already going on four days since her first meeting with this child.

"She was being really careful not to erase the picture you drew," Marino explained. "But this morning, the maid at the inn where we're staying was tidying up our luggage and happened to touch the board by mistake. Beniha's been in a terrible mood ever since."

"Beniha, can you let me see the board for a minute?"

Nodding hugely without saying a word, Beniha handed it over. The picture of Mayu that Kazuna had drawn was half erased, but the remaining portion was perfectly intact. When she saw that little Beniha had somehow managed to preserve the drawing for all this time, Kazuna felt deeply moved.

"I'll draw it again for you," she said, bending down to look Beniha in the eyes. The child had seemed so unemotional. The thought that one of Kazuna's drawings could make this tiny person feel joy and even sorrow left the genga goddess at a complete loss for words.

"Because it's the real thing," Beniha said solemnly. "It's the real Mayu, that's why."

"Thank you," Kazuna expressed her heartfelt gratitude.

◆

On the eve of the Kanaga Festival, dozens of stalls were set up in front of the train station. There would be fireworks, too.

"Let's not waste this chance—why not wear them tonight, too?" Akiko had urged, so everyone was decked out in yukata as they walked en masse from the Ojis' house to the train station. The group's colorful costumes already made them stand out from the crowd, and they attracted even more attention as passers-by recognized the directors and the voice actors among them. However, none of the looks that came their way were of the unpleasant variety, and the general atmosphere was joyful and ebullient.

The voices of Aoi and her cohorts, half-jokingly calling out, "Prince! Be sure to hire us for your next title," intertwined with other light conversation. "Hitomi, that yukata is super cute on you," Anju, the actress who had played the role of Mayu, lavished Director Saito with compliments.

Being surrounded by such a dazzling cast of people was almost too much for Kazuna to handle. It seemed unthinkable that this was happening in Enaga.

The big street in front of the train station was completely transformed, lined on both sides with booths offering food, games, and souvenirs and festively lit by rows of round lanterns in red and white. The generators powering the food stands emitted a dull hum that made the summer air vibrate, and the aroma of the savory sauces for stir-fried soba and octopus fritters tantalized the olfactory senses of everyone walking by.

"I want to catch a yo-yo," Beniha told her mother, referring to a festival game where players used a hook to try to fish decorated balloons out of a tub of water without breaking them. The little girl was riding on Osato's shoulders, and the three of them were swallowed up in the throng around the yo-yo booth, just like that.

Director Saito and the *Mermaid Nurses* posse had been waylaid by a phalanx of fans and were being pestered for handshakes. Keeping one eye on that scene from afar, Kazuna continued strolling along between the rows of booths all by herself.

She wasn't accustomed to wearing a snug-fitting obi, and the pressure around her midsection made it slightly difficult to breathe. It was bothering her more and more, but she suppressed the unseemly urge to make an adjustment in public view.

Surely Asami must have set up a yakitori stand somewhere around here, she thought, peering into every stall she passed.

That was when it happened.

A voice called "Ms. Namisawa!" and Kazuna turned around.

Shuhei Munemori was standing there dressed in a *happi* coat emblazoned with the letters "KANAGA FESTIVAL."

"Ah, Mr. Mune—" she began, starting to look up at him, then abruptly froze when she remembered that she, too, was dressed in yukata. Because she had always thought of wearing one to festivals as a privilege reserved for women who were confident about themselves, she felt suddenly embarrassed and filled with misgivings.

Somehow thinking that she needed to apologize for her costume, she started to stammer an excuse: "Oh, um, this is just— Mr. Oji's mom just kind of forced us all to wear them, so—"

"Wow," Munemori interrupted, "you look absolutely adorable!"

Kazuna tried to say something along the lines of "Wait, what?" but the words stuck in her throat. Munemori closed the short distance between them, laughing happily. When he was next to Kazuna, he said with a grin, "I was really surprised just now. You look astoundingly, stupendously lovely and so very, very cute."

From far away came the *pom* of the first firework, and a cheer went up from the hordes of people around them. The sky grew bright, illuminating Munemori's face. But he paid no attention to the fireworks, because he was completely focused on gazing at Kazuna.

He's looking right at me, head-on, straight.

When she confirmed that fact, tears sprang from her eyes without any warning.

A hot torrent began to pour down her face, and there was nothing she could do to stop it.

"Erm…" This time it was Munemori's turn to be perplexed. "Um, Kazuna, what's the matter?" he asked, but she was unable to respond. The tears just kept coming, faster and faster, welling up and rolling down her cheeks. *This must be so distressing for Munemori,* she thought, but still she couldn't stop crying.

It was the first time anyone had ever called her cute.

No one had ever praised her looks right to her face like that.

A new round of fireworks blossomed brightly overhead, and everyone turned their attention to the night sky. Kazuna could feel the tempest of intense sound and brilliant light above her, and after a moment she felt something else: the warm weight of a hand placed—tentatively, timorously—on top of her head.

The gentle gesture was Munemori's. She looked up at him, and their eyes met. Once again, he said, "You really do look adorable tonight. You're beautiful, and amazing."

Hearing that, Kazuna plunged into full-blown sobs. He had said such sweet, kind things to her, and here she was, completely messing up her face with tears. That thought was so upsetting that she began bawling like a little child.

Thank you very much…

Her reply to Munemori came out in incoherent bits and pieces and hardly sounded like anything.

◆

September twenty-eighth: the Kanaga Festival.

One o'clock in the afternoon.

The *Sabaku* boat made its first public appearance by a stretch of gigantic boulders in the gorge where the launch would take place.

Aoi, who was in charge of the boatsong, stood mic in hand in front of the vessel. The other voice actors and Director Saito watched behind her, waiting. Kazuna, too, stood nearby, observing the scene.

Aoi Mureno's voice, chanting the boatsong, resounded through the steep-walled valley and merged with the sound of the flowing river.

Don't regret our days
Feeling hopeless, feeling numb
This is what we chose
The dear tomorrow we chose

As Kazuna had heard, the chant was performed with a distinctive melodic intonation reminiscent of a traditional folk song. There was no accompaniment, and Aoi's beautiful *a cappella* voice rang out through the valley, clear and bright.

The words were the lyrics of the opening theme that began every episode of *Soundback*.

An unvoiced hum of excitement spread among the fans as they recognized the song, as they shared thoughts.

Aoi hadn't been able to take lessons directly from Enaga's master chanters due to her busy schedule. However, sample tapes and written instructions had been dispatched to her in Tokyo, and she'd practiced the boatsong a great deal on her own for this day.

Don't regret our days
Fretting over what may come
That would be the easy way
I made my choice, I chose this road
You're right here beside me
Walking alongside me

Together, we will march along
We'll forge ahead, brave and strong
Our road is never lonely
And my heart is never sad

Aoi sang the words until the end.

Then, in a dramatic change of mood, she gazed around at the throngs of people gathered there: the directors, the other staff, the members of the chamber of commerce, and all the spectators who'd come from near and far. And of course, she looked at Kazuna, as well.

"When I say 'Ready, set,' can I get you all to shout 'Go'?"

Wooh!

A boisterous cheer went up from the spectators.

Spurred on by their voices, Munemori, Yukishiro, and members of the Tokei staff hoisted the *Sabaku* boat onto their shoulders like a portable Shinto shrine. Then they bore it toward the swirling rapids.

After seeing that the boat was on its way to the riverside, Aoi cried, "Okay, let's do this! Ready, set—"

That morning, while they were getting the boat ready, Yukishiro stood in front of the completed vessel in unmistakably high spirits and asked Kazuna a question.

"Amazing. But were Enaga City and Bluto considering this idea from a long time ago?"

"What?"

"No, if you've been secretly plotting this for a while, I'm not complaining. But that day at Skytree—Mr. Munemori was already in the picture, too, right? Along with Bluto."

Kazuna stared at him, wide-eyed.

"Oh, am I mistaken?" The producer didn't sound the least bit embarrassed. "I definitely remember what you told me on the phone that day, Ms. Namisawa. 'Right now I'm on a date with somebody I like.'"

Kazuna had assumed that the sharp and able Yukishiro must also be insincere and lacking in empathy—that surely he would have forgotten her Skytree remark.

But now, as she mulled over Yukishiro's question, which didn't seem to mask any hidden agenda, she nodded slowly. At the same time, she was wondering, *Do people normally ask acquaintances stuff like that?* She felt blindsided by his staggering insensitivity about a woman's feelings.

"Could be," she replied evasively.

It wasn't really an answer, but Yukishiro nodded and said, "I thought so," in the most indifferent tone. Looking at his profile, Kazuna reminded herself: *This person is not to be trusted, or believed.*

Yet at the same time, Yukishiro's odd query had forced Kazuna to admit something to herself for the first time. The realization came as a shock, but she could feel its truth deep in her marrow.

She'd never dreamed that anyone who seemed so clueless about anime would ever seem appealing to her.

—*Go-o-o-o-o!*

The tremendously loud cry of the gathered multitude overlapped and rose like an earthshaking rumbling from the bottom of the river itself, and the entire gorge seemed to pulsate with sound.

The sun was shining high in the sky.

All the hands that had been holding the boat now let go.

In that instant, Kazuna had another thought. It felt as if the surface of her eyes was trembling, and she couldn't keep them open in the dazzling light.

Mom, Dad, she found herself calling to her parents in her mind.

I was born a pure, dyed-in-the wool non-realie.

But please let me have this lovely illusion, just for today:

—My real life is so full.

Buoyed by the cheers of the crowd and bathed in the beautiful Enaga sunshine, the *Sabaku* boat began its journey downriver.

FINAL CHAPTER:

"THE WORLD IS A CIRCUS"

On the day Hitomi Saito left Tokei Animation, the cool autumn winds began to blow from evening on. It was the end of November, and the season was on the cusp of changing once again, from autumn to winter.

Hitomi was well aware of the company's tendency to give the cold shoulder to those who left—no surprise there. One by one she took the items she'd used in various projects from atop her desk, and from the shelves behind it, and packed them into the cardboard boxes she'd been given by the general affairs department along with grim glares. She stripped the overhead bookshelf of all its research materials and put them in a box.

The photo album from England was from the time she had to depict a palace for *Pink Search*.

The Edo-period document was used as a reference for kimono style when she was creating the in-game anime.

And the illustrations showing the characteristic movements of boys and girls were from working on *Sabaku*.

Leafing through, Hitomi remembered the day-to-day struggles with storyboards, when she had consulted this document so often that the pages became crinkled and smudged. These materials had been the building blocks of her career until now. And today, she would be leaving the company where she'd gotten her start, and paid her dues.

Hitomi was so immersed in her solitary task that before she knew it the sky outside had grown dark. Around the time when the light from the studio's fluorescent lamps began to be reflected in the glass window, she heard a voice behind her.

"Are you almost finished packing?"

She turned around.

Osamu Yukishiro was standing at the corner entrance to Hitomi's workspace, which lay behind a partition.

"Mr. Yukishiro."

"I'll bring the car around. I can drop those things off at your house."

"Thanks, but it's fine. I'm going to have them delivered, so please don't worry." She was planning to send some of the boxes directly to Office Lagoon, her next workplace.

Yukishiro seemed to get the message because he nodded briefly and said, "I see. If there's anything else I can do to help, please let me know."

"Thank you." Hitomi stole a quick glance at his profile. "About the spring supremacy—" she began.

"Sorry?" Yukishiro turned to face her.

He's keeping his expression purposely casual, she thought, quietly lowering her head. All the times she'd told Yukishiro, with supreme confidence, that she was going to win "this season's anime supremacy" was already the season before last.

"I'm really sorry *Sabaku* couldn't take the crown," she apologized.

Alas, the spring-season title with the highest sales, the winner of the "anime supremacy" stakes, wasn't Hitomi's *Soundback: The Singing Stone*.

It wasn't Director Oji and Studio Edge's *Ryder Light: Fateful Fight* either.

The anime that racked up the best numbers for that season was *Summer Lounge: Sepia Girls*. Known as *Sepia Girls* among the fans, the series was a slice-of-life tale of adolescence set in a girls'-school yacht club. It was a quality anime that delineated in great detail the protagonists' passion for yacht racing as well as their friendships.

Sepia Girls' remarkable feat of crushing far more highly touted titles was an unexpected outcome—both in the anime industry and among fans. While the series was running, it mostly seemed to be under the radar to the point where a lot of people in the business and fans had to start by asking, "Huh, *Sepia Girls*? What's that?"

The story's subject matter and inspirations were relatively simple, and since it seemed to be cut from the same cloth as any number of series that had gone before, it didn't receive much advance attention before it was broadcast. Promotion was minimal, with next to no buzz-generating events, but the creative passion behind the anime gradually managed to forge a connection with viewers. The series was the collaborative effort of a veteran director working alongside a much younger staff, with one aim: to take a conventional concept and render it extraordinarily well.

While it was airing, fans' voices that "It's kinda basic, but this season *Sepia Girls* is really good too," began to grow louder.

The girls in the anime were all cute, and the portrayals of emotional moments were vivid and full. In addition, the yacht-racing scenes were easy for amateurs to understand, and while the art was in a simplified anime style, the race dynamics retained a compellingly realistic sheen.

Thanks to all these factors, the show's ratings gradually began to rise. It lent itself to fanzines that presented the girls in flagrante with one another, and its popularity found a wide base through that summer's Comic Market.

Many fans started asking, "Is *Sepia Girls* really that good?" and rushed to buy the DVDs the moment they were released. Sales figures skyrocketed. The creators, meanwhile, seemed to feel they'd been the beneficiaries of a happy miscalculation.

Anime magazines and internet sites overflowed with headlines like "From Zero Advertising to Anime Supremacy," and reporters never tired of chronicling *Sepia Girls'* unexpected success through the eyes of the directors, producers, voice actors, and other contributors.

Ultimately, at least within the industry, "anime supremacy" referred purely to sales numbers: that is, the quantity of DVDs and such sold. There were no other metrics to quantify an anime's popularity.

Hence, *Sepia Girls* was declared the winner because it sold more in packaged content than any of the other series that aired in spring.

"Oh, that."

With a dry chuckle, Yukishiro looked at Hitomi.

"I never expected you to apologize, but it's fine—don't let it bother you. To be sure, our sales might not have measured up to *Sepia Girls*, but I look at it in a positive way."

"You mean it's because our show had good ratings thanks to its Saturday 5 p.m. slot. A lot of people watched *Sabaku* on TV, so they were probably less inclined to run out and buy the box set."

At least, from what Hitomi heard, the TV network—HBT—was pleased. And because so many children were watching faithfully every week, toy sales were robust, and the production costs ended up being offset by those proceeds.

"Still, I put it into words," Hitomi stated flat-out. "I did say that I wanted to aim for supremacy, that I wanted to win, so I thought I should apologize. I'm sorry."

"Well, we might have lost when it came to DVDs, but *Sabaku* took second place by a good margin. First runner-up, so to speak. And if we were allowed to factor in toy sales, our net profit would be higher than for *Sepia Girls*."

"But we still lost. And not just to *Sepia Girls*. Director Oji's *Ryder Light* beat us, too."

When he heard that, Yukishiro sucked in his breath. After a

silent beat that he carelessly seem to have allowed—which was rare for him—he replied, "We didn't lose."

However, his true feelings were betrayed by his facial expression and the timbre of his voice.

Together with Hitomi, the producer had kept a close eye on *Ryder* down to the day when the final episode aired, so the fact that they'd lost must have sunk into him by now.

In terms of sales, Director Oji's *Ryder* had finished behind both *Sepia Girls* and *Sabaku*. But if you asked fans which series had been the supreme anime for the past spring, the majority would probably point at *Ryder*. Beyond visible results like sales figures, the general consensus seemed to be that Oji's anime was wonderful, and innovative, and shocking.

To begin with, anime fans didn't follow the competition for a given season's "anime supremacy" from the viewpoint of results. After having enjoyed the offerings as they aired, when it came time to reflect on which title had been number one, people's memories were often rather vague.

Anime that created a lasting impression occupied a vastly larger place in their minds than whichever one had racked up the highest sales numbers. Even when industry insiders like Hitomi looked back on a certain season, the anime that they considered the victor wasn't always the one that had actually "won" at the time.

In the end, what drove anime supremacy weren't sales but individual tastes. Everyone was desperately chasing after "his" and "her" supremacy.

And in that sense, Hitomi thought, she'd lost to Director Oji as well.

◆

The event in September at Enaga City's Kanaga Festival.

Oji, who was serving as Hitomi's partner for an informal talk show, confessed, "I was floored."

Hitomi was happy to hear those words, of course, but she also felt a bit jealous that he could speak them with such aplomb. She realized that it was the flip side of his absolute confidence. It was precisely because he believed completely in *Ryder* that he could say so. If he genuinely believed that he had lost, he could never say such a thing outright.

"It's an honor to hear that from a genius," Hitomi tempered her response with a sardonic undertone, but Oji was unshaken.

Scrunching up his handsome face, he replied, "I get that a lot, but I don't think so. I'm not the genius, you are. People might get me wrong, but I'm merely brilliant."

He tossed off those remarks but didn't seem to be lying or offering lip service. His face grew serious, and he turned towards Hitomi again.

"Getting floored by your *Sabaku* isn't sarcasm or anything. I think a lot of the anime business is like a virtual-sex industry that delivers imaginary lovers to the world. They say you can forget about establishing any sort of supremacy in the business as it stands if you don't appeal to viewers' crotches or wombs, but *Sabaku* accomplished something nobody else could do so far. It's a wholesome work that doesn't offer an easy-to-digest cuteness. You pitched a straight-up ball game and won. It's MVP material. From now on, thanks to *Sabaku*, the rest of us will find it easier to get financial backing for productions that don't revolve around the *moe* quotient. Sponsors will sign on, and projects will be approved. What will change the anime world isn't *Ryder* with its *bishojo*"—its beautiful young girls—"but *Sabaku*."

Oji gazed over the audience of fans at the event. "Look at all the people your anime managed to attract to this godforsaken burg. Hey, it's my hometown so I'm allowed to talk trash about it," he said to laughter.

As always, Oji's presence alone transformed what could have been a low-key event into a show to remember.

Hitomi, meanwhile, was so stunned by his over-the-top praise that she didn't quite know how to carry on.

"You'll be the one who changes the anime world, Director Oji," she managed to say. Sounding like a mutual admiration society might have been unseemly, but she couldn't budge on that point.

"I think *Ryder Light* is a masterpiece that will go down in history as a work that pushed the anime world forward by a full decade," she praised. "Surely from now on everyone will start to change their directing style to try to match what you've created. To be honest, watching in front of the screen, I felt jealous. It'll be a very long time before anyone surpasses *Ryder.*"

"Happily, I've been hearing that a lot lately. Oh, okay, in that case—" Oji's eyes lit up as if he'd just thought of something fun. "Why don't you give it a try, Director Saito?" he continued. "The magic-girl genre that everyone is supposedly too intimidated to tackle now thanks to me. For your next project, why don't you show them they're wrong, and just crush it? If you don't, then I won't be able to make anything else either. How 'bout it?"

The audience roared its approval of Oji's suggestion. There, on the platform, surrounded by fans hollering, *Fantastic*, or *That's an awesome idea*, Hitomi's hands, wrapped around the microphone, began to shake. She muttered into it, audibly:

"...Pressure!!"

The audience erupted in laughter.

During the latter half of the talk show, Oji asked, "What was the most difficult thing during the making of *Sabaku*?" He was posing one of the questions for Director Saito that had been gathered beforehand via the internet. "Well, of course, making an anime can sometimes feel like a nonstop parade of problems, but what was the biggest hardship you experienced?"

"Hmm, hardship?" Lowering the mic, Hitomi thought for a moment, but she already knew what she wanted to say on this occasion. Gripping the microphone anew, she answered, "Of course there have been many hardships along the way, but now that the work has found its final shape, the broadcast run is safely over, and the problems have all been overcome, there's nothing particular that comes to mind. Although there's a tendency to focus too much on the difficult aspects of our industry—"

Her face broke into an irrepressible smile. In the front row were Yukishiro, who'd walked alongside her, and Kayako Arishina, Oji's creative partner.

"I still want to say that I think working in this business is fun. It's fun and worthwhile work, despite the hardships. I want people to feel attracted to the industry and for a steady stream of newcomers to enter it. I crave successors."

Oji laughed. "That's so forthright and you, Director Saito, I love that. But we're really a couple of chumps, aren't we?"

"Sorry?"

"Wanting to see an influx of new talent is tantamount to going out and recruiting a bunch of formidable rivals. We release our title and then some young Turk watches it and basically strips it for parts, repurposing our directorial touches, and we're hoping that will revitalize the industry. 'Not like that, nor like that,' we coach up our juniors, creating our own competition. Oh well, I guess it's probably the same in every business." Oji gave a dry laugh. "We just really like anime, don't we? We're crazy about it, so what can we do?"

When she heard those words, Hitomi's body was wrapped in an almost feverish warmth. "Yes," she nodded.

Delighted, she nodded again.

"I love anime, too."

◆

The reason Hitomi's *Soundback* fell short of "supremacy" in terms of both sales and impact or memorability had to do, of course, with the stiff competition, but also with the content of the show itself.

Many anime fans and reviewers zeroed in on the final episode.

The question on everyone's mind, going in, was: "Would the sounds that the heroine, Towako, nobly sacrificed for the cause be restored to her?" People went into the final episode expecting Director Saito to pull off a happy ending where what was lost somehow all came back to the girl. But on the point of whether or not that actually transpired—Hitomi had fudged and not given a clear picture.

So in the end, Towako didn't regain those sounds.

From the scenario-meeting stage, Hitomi's proposed conclusion was controversial. They said it wasn't very Hitomi Saito, it wasn't very boys' anime, and it wasn't very Tokei.

But as far as she was concerned, that was the ending she'd decided on from the start.

There were times in life when you needed to accomplish something even if you were going to lose something else, something important. You just did what you had to do.

For that thing to be simply and conveniently restored later wouldn't do just because the action was taking place in an anime. The risk had been taken, so Hitomi didn't want to peddle false hope. That would be like conning her young viewers.

Sabaku's opening theme lyrics, "Don't regret our days," made the same point. Hitomi had learned early on, during her own childhood, that life didn't suddenly turn around and do what you wanted it to do. It was probably no different for kids today.

She didn't think the protagonists who had fought through it all, and Towako, who'd been denied twelve sounds due to the robot transformations, were necessarily to be pitied. She wasn't going to let anyone tell her it wasn't a happy ending, either. On the other hand, she didn't intend to leave children feeling that it was a cruel and heartless story. She wanted to convey the positive, hopeful message that efforts have their proper rewards.

That's why Hitomi chose not to reveal in any way whether Towako regained her lost sounds after the fighting. The protagonists returned to Enaga City—the place they had protected until the end—and were welcomed by their families and friends. Emerging from the robot, the kids returned from sky to earth with outstretched arms and smiling faces.

Websites dissecting Hitomi's ending were still going up, and it remained a hot topic. Many of them were critical and accused her of having cut and run.

—*Towako's sounds should have returned. The rug was pulled out from under us after all that.*

—*So what happened afterwards? In the final scene they're smiling happily, and it even looks like Towako might be talking with Takaya. That means the sounds came back, right? Help!*

This type of reaction had been anticipated by Hitomi's colleagues, and the long script meetings had become even more frequent as the finale approached. Among the staff, there'd been a palpable sense of apprehension mixed in with some greed.

"Better late than never, let's just figure out some way for Towako to get her sounds back," they urged, but Hitomi stood firm, unwilling to budge: "The groundwork hasn't been laid for that, and we can't do anything so slapdash."

Even after adult fans found fault or felt let down by the finale, Hitomi never doubted her own conviction that the ending she'd chosen was the right one. People didn't need to get it right away, as long as they remembered and recalled it fondly some day. If the finale stayed lodged in someone's heart, that would be enough.

The only person who'd supported Hitomi's decision through all the resistance she faced was Yukishiro.

"Let's do what the director says," he finally called a halt to the long, confrontational script meetings.

"Okay, but we may miss out on supremacy if it doesn't even have a happy ending," one staff member sniped. Those sarcastic words seemed to slice through Hitomi's chest like a frozen blade, even though she'd been vaguely aware of that danger from the staff's reactions by then.

Unable to look up, she began furiously biting her bottom lip, but Yukishiro didn't lose his cool.

"That may be so, but we're a big, established outfit. We don't always have to compromise on the work's quality in pursuit of short-term profits. Instead of aiming for this year's supremacy, let's be thinking about making anime that will be talked about ten years down the line. It's the duty of venerable companies like ours to leave behind a masterpiece from time to time." Pausing to lock eyes with Hitomi, who had finally lifted her face, he concluded, "No matter what kind of ending Director Saitodecides on, we've come this far with her, so we should follow her the rest of the way in good faith."

Even so, the open-ended finale had probably hurt *Sabaku*'s chances of winning the anime-supremacy title. Hitomi had made such a point of wanting to aim for it and said repeatedly that she didn't want to lose, yet couldn't bring herself to compromise on the ending. That was pathetic, if she did say so herself.

At the same time, she felt rejuvenated. She had a very real feeling that she'd run all the way and never slowed down.

"Director Saito, are you free this evening?" asked Yukishiro.

"Huh?"

"Surely you don't mean to just go home alone tonight like always, when it's your last day," the producer teased as he helped her pack the boxes.

Hitomi, who didn't have any plans, snapped, "Is that bad?" She was a wee bit miffed. The company's pattern of coldness toward anyone who left was indeed nothing new.

"Just as I'd expected," Yukishiro remarked with a big sigh. Then, raising his face, he said, "If you don't mind, can we hit a nearby *izakaya*? Everyone on the *Sabaku* team is meeting there for drinks."

"Oh..."

"Everyone," the producer said, smiling. "It's your farewell party. Won't you come, please?"

"What would you have done if I'd already had plans for tonight?"

"Well, I figured it was a safe bet that you didn't." Yukishiro's expression was gentle, even though his words were rather rude.

"In that case, everyone would have just had a normal drinking party reminiscing about *Sabaku*, so don't worry."

"Thank you very much," Hitomi replied without thinking. Then she surveyed the piles of documents and supplies still waiting to be packed away. *Can I finish today?* she wondered. *If I don't, it would be so awkward coming in again tomorrow when they bothered to get together for a send-off...* But even while she fretted, her mouth began to curve into a smile.

"By the way," she said, "I heard about the spring-break theatrical feature you'll be producing for the year after next."

"Oh... So you heard."

"Yes, and I'm really looking forward to it. But it's a rather unexpected decision."

Frowning almost imperceptibly, Yukishiro replied, "Well, what can I do? At the end of the day, I'm just a salaryman. I'll give it my best shot, although I fear it will be even more hectic than it was with you."

He squatted down opposite Hitomi and began sealing up a cardboard box with packing tape.

After continuing to help her silently, he said abruptly, without looking up, "I know they say parents can't be objective about their own offspring, but for me, *Sabaku* had the spring anime supremacy by miles. *Sepia Girls* and *Ryder Light* were no match. When I heard the crowd cheering as the boat came out at the Kanaga Festival, I was so damn happy."

Looking down, Hitomi went on fitting reference materials into a cardboard box and pretended to be occupied with the task at hand. If she didn't, she felt as if she might burst into tears.

Everything that she'd managed to do with Yukishiro until today.

Everything that she'd learned during her time at Tokei Animation.

The fact that she would be leaving today.

"I was happy, too," she squeezed the words out in reply. She did her utmost to hold back the tears, but her voice was trembling like rippling water.

Somehow, they managed to finish all the packing that evening.

Even though Hitomi was exiting the building for the last time, she was rushing out in a remarkably familiar manner. In a flurry, she unlooped the lanyard that held her company ID from around her neck, handed it over to Yukishiro, and requested, "Could you please return this to general affairs?"

With an ambivalent smirk, he took it and said, "Sure. And thank you for all your hard work."

"Thank you for all your kind assistance," Hitomi reciprocated.

Outside the building where she had worked ever since graduating from college, the red paper lanterns that lined the adjacent shopping street were switched on here and there, illuminating the gathering dusk.

Hitomi and Yukishiro hastened to the pub, where nearly all the main *Sabaku* staff were waiting for them. They had booked a private tatami room in the no-frills, inexpensive *izakaya* that was mostly frequented by residents of the neighborhood, and someone had gone to the trouble of hanging several *Sabaku* posters on the wall.

A voice greeted, "Ah, they're here, they're here!"

"Sorry we're late," Hitomi said. Glancing up, she noticed that a banner had been rolled out above one of the posters, and her heart suddenly felt full.

GOOD LUCK, DIRECTOR SAITO, it read.

She looked around at everyone's faces. There were colleagues with whom she'd clashed about work and fought, and others who'd pled with her not to leave, but all of them were sending her off with a smile today.

It occurred to Hitomi that given the company's history of tumultuous partings, this might have been a first. Feeling a bit satisfied with herself, she lowered her head in a tiny bow.

She proudly told the assembled group, "I hope we'll meet again someday."

◆

Ever since spring season's *Fateful Fight: Ryder Light* completed its broadcast, Studio Edge's conference room had been doing double duty as a space for interviews with Chiharu Oji. Today's session was with *Extra-Fine Entertainment*☆, a magazine that focused primarily on live-action films and TV dramas rather than anime. The interview was slated to appear in the end-of-year issue, which would include a retrospective of the year's best anime.

While Oji was calmly fielding questions from the reporter, Kayako stood behind him, monitoring the interview's progress.

Sure enough, ten minutes in, the reporter raised *that* question. "These days the anime world is kind of a war zone to the point where there's even a term like 'anime supremacy,' but what do you think? Do you have any opinions about that, as the director who took the spring crown with *Ryder Light*?"

When she heard that, Kayako quietly sucked in her breath. It wasn't an unusual question, by any means.

"Ah yes," Oji said with a nod. There was no sign of an impending outburst; he simply replied matter-of-factly, "I'm sorry to contradict you, but *Ryder* wasn't the supreme anime. We didn't sell the most DVDs that season. I'm not the least bit concerned about that kind of thing, in any case."

"Really?" The reporter blinked as if in surprise, then flipped through his notebook. "What was the number one anime for that season? I apologize—I should have done more research."

Kayako followed up from her post behind Oji's chair. This wasn't unusual, either. "*Sepia Girls* was in first place, *Sabaku* took second, and *Love Die*, a carryover series still popular from the previous quarter, came in third. If you're talking strictly about sales figures, then we were fourth." Giving that answer, she didn't feel bad at all—quite the contrary, in fact. It was a bit crass to discuss sales and rankings so openly, but her mood couldn't be brighter.

"Oh, so that's how it was—again, I'm sorry. When I asked

around about which anime created the most buzz this year, everyone always mentioned *Ryder*, so I just kind of..." The reporter had clearly meant no harm, and he seemed to be sincerely apologetic.

"No worries," Oji said. "Really, I don't mind at all." It might have sounded like he was putting on a brave front, but his face was beaming with a confident, almost impudent smile—as if he couldn't care less, appearances be damned.

A full year had passed since that press conference, but Kayako could still hear Oji's voice clearly in her mind, spitting out "anime supremacy'" as if it were a dirty phrase.

The concept asked which title had been number one in a given quarter, but fans who kept an eye on such things didn't just focus on the top title. To the extent that they judged honestly and fairly which anime stood out the most, fans could be severe, but also generous.

While viewers kept watching Saito's *Sabaku* hoping that the lost sounds would ultimately be restored to the heroine, Towako, public expectations for Oji's *Ryder* were the complete opposite: savagery.

—*Sure, things seem peaceful now, but just wait. The calm is actually scary in itself.*

—*Well, it's Oji, so there has to be a bloodbath coming up.*

Nine years earlier, while Oji was directing his now-legendary anime, *Yosuga*, he had wanted to kill off his heroines, but Tokei Animation wouldn't let him. Although the story wasn't reported at the time, it had since become widely known, and expectations grew that Oji would take advantage of *Ryder*'s late-night time slot and end his current series with a scene of major carnage.

Kayako had netted the director by taking that approach at their very first meeting. She'd asked him, *Would you care to kill them with me?*

Ryder would be a no-nonsense project exploring how beloved heroines with strong fan bases might be killed off in a viable manner, as it were. Since the characters grew older by a year in each episode and would be turning eighteen in the twelfth and final episode, fans predicted that Oji would stage a "deadly graduation" in order to express the end of girlhood.

The shifts in design as the characters aged, from six to seven and so on, drew a lot of attention, and fans even voiced selfish views like *Jyuri was so adorable at age X!* and *Stop growing right there!* There was an established tendency for magic girls to attain popularity more easily if they had childlike physiques, and Oji might kill the heroine as if to satisfy such requests. *"I don't even want to see what she looks like as an adult?" Fine, then!*

In the last episode, however, the heroine, whose death had seemed like a foregone conclusion, didn't die.

Ryder's battle scenes took the form of motorbike races. No matter how many times they fell off their bikes, or had their machines destroyed; no matter if they suffered serious injuries, or got worn down to the bone; no matter how much they lost along the way, none of the heroines died, not a single one.

It was so excruciating that you could almost hear your own heart creaking painfully. Screwing up her face un-prettily, the heroine shouted at her adversaries—and the viewers:

Hey! I bet you want us dead, but too bad. I'm not dying.

That's old, spat Jyuri, the protagonist.

Nobody here is gonna cater to some musty notion that it's not a shining end unless you die in a blaze of glory. Just wait and see. Shamelessly, and even if nobody wants us to, we're gonna return from this place alive. And when we do, you might think us ugly— but own it and love us.

That "Own it and love us" promptly went viral. If there was a prize for best anime buzzword, it would surely have won. Fans were gleefully using the line in their writing and daily conversation.

And just as Jyuri warned, none of the protagonists died.

Moreover, even the enemy magic girls who didn't repent and stayed evil walked away alive from the protagonists. That put Oji's stubborn idea on full display: he wasn't going to kill anybody in his scenario.

Attached to "living" as if it were a fixation, the heroine, completely deprived of magic girls' customary prettiness and smiles and instead cast as a witch or ogress, spent an unprecedented ten minutes fighting and riding without any background music, accompanied only by the roaring engine and the sound of her own breathing, and when the score resumed, her beautifulness was overwhelming in contrast as she filled the screen—alive. "It's a beautifulness that is a slap across the face of fans who didn't want to see her grow," one reviewer wrote.

—Live. The only person in the world who can make you despair is you.

Jyuri's voice resonated like a thunderbolt cutting through the darkness. It was a poignant injunction "not to die" meant for viewers on the other side of the screen.

The girls Oji had shown were uncouth—and they had survived.

"Maybe I'm just getting old, but I felt like recognizing whatever it is that doesn't rely on easy show-stoppers like loss or death."

That's what Oji said to Kayako the day he returned, after a week's disappearance, bearing the storyboards up to the twelfth episode. She had just finished reading them all the way through.

His face, thinner and slightly haggard after his marathon writing session, also seemed to reflect his satisfaction at having finished.

"How was it?" he asked.

Kayako was choked up with emotion.

"I won't listen to feedback from anyone else, but you, alone, have the right to criticize my script." A fiendishly happy ending that didn't kill anybody off—that's what Oji had been hoping to present, even if it meant breaking their promise to start up a project that would kill off a popular heroine.

"You're sure about what you've done here?"

"Yup," Oji replied without a moment's hesitation. "I might change a few details, but that's basically what I want to go with."

"It's wonderful."

Oji finally took his eyes off Kayako and turned away, so he was in profile, but she could see him taking a quick breath. She drew in a breath of her own—a long one—as she prepared to speak. Her nasal cavities felt prickly and sore, and tears were starting to well up again.

"Good job. It was a wonderful read."

"I'm glad," Oji let out and plunked his head down on the desk again.

Tidying the sheets of the finished storyboard she'd just received, Kayako put both hands on top of the pile and bowed her head in gratitude.

And *Ryder*, on that day, was reborn as a series that would let its heroine live.

Chiharu Oji, who presented a clear-cut happy ending and was widely considered to have reigned supreme despite losing in terms of sales.

Hitomi Saito, who avoided a lazy happy ending and delivered an honest story to children but was denied supremacy despite superior numbers.

Kayako was proud to have worked in anime during a season that featured two such incomparable talents.

This world was an endlessly interesting place. You never knew what was going to happen. It fascinated Kayako like a circus you couldn't take your eyes off for a single moment or like a magical toy box filled with thrilling tricks.

At the end of the interview for *Extra-Fine Entertainment*☆, the reporter asked Oji, "What's on deck for your next anime project? Of course, I realize that after making such a major work you probably won't start thinking about the next one right away, but fans can't help wondering what you might be up to."

"I haven't decided yet," Oji replied, but he quickly followed that up with a grin. On the inside, he might have been a jumble of imperfections, but if you only looked at his face, it was alight with an exceedingly refreshing and beautiful smile now as he continued, "Also, in your article, please don't praise me too much, okay? If it's too over the top, I won't be able to shoot anything from here on out. I want to keep on creating, worthless rubbish included, so please cut me some slack. I promise I won't be making anyone wait nine years this time."

After the interview had come to a peaceful end, Kayako escorted the reporter and cameraman to the exit, then returned to the conference room. "Good work just now," she said.

"Oh, hey, thanks." The director was still standing there drinking tea from a paper cup as he turned to face her. "So I guess we're done?"

Gazing at him, Kayako trembled in happy disbelief. *Holy cow, Chiharu Oji just did an interview with someone who wasn't up to speed on anime, and he isn't in a foul mood. He's really grown up.* She thought she might cry.

"There's nothing else scheduled for this evening," she replied.

"Won't you come out for a little drink? I mean, seeing as we're both here and all."

"Sounds good."

There weren't that many bars and restaurants around the studio, and having spent so many nights holed up, working, she'd become a regular at practically every establishment and couldn't look forward to any surprises. Nevertheless, she felt sad that she was going to be accompanying Oji on his whim less and less frequently. *I guess I'm a masochistic producer, all right. Yeah, I'm pretty far gone.*

Taking just her handbag, Kayako left the studio with Oji. Following in the wake of the director, who was walking a pace or two ahead, she stared at his neck and spoke.

"So, I heard about your next project."

Oji glanced back and said, "Oh, you did?"

"Yes." Kayako nodded. "I was surprised. You, working with Mr. Yukishiro."

The project was a feature-length anime adaptation of a light novel by the popular author Koki Chiyoda called *V.T.R.*, as in the Japanese acronym for "videotape recording." It was being developed by Oji's old home, Tokei Animation.

He winced at her words. "I really had no choice. Chiyoda asked for me specifically, so I couldn't say no. But who told you, Ms. Arishina?"

"Mr. Kuroki from Daidaisha, when he took the time to call and say some nice things about *Ryder*."

In the anime industry, where there was an abundance of freelancing, it was considered basic etiquette not to discuss any parallel engagements even if you happened to be on the same team for the time being. Nonetheless, it was astounding news.

Tokei Animation and Daidaisha had embarked on talks about a film adaptation of Koki Chiyoda's *V.T.R.*, and it was the author who brought up the name Oji after watching the last episode of *Ryder*.

"I know there are all kinds of factors in play, but could we please have him direct?" Chiyoda pleaded.

There were indeed all kinds of factors, but Oji readily consented. *It'll probably be hard going back to my old workplace,* he admitted, *but I welcome the chance.*

Oji and Yukishiro sounded like a terribly disharmonious pairing, and it was hard even to imagine. To tell the truth, Kayako was a little jealous of her fellow producer. Beyond her chagrin, though, she was genuinely interested to see what a collaboration between the two would beget.

Chiyoda had requested Oji "to dismantle the original work completely and to start from there." Kuroki had added a condition of his own: "Keep my author out of the scriptwriting team this time."

"Hahaha!" Kayako laughed loudly when she heard that, because it sounded so exactly like them.

"I heard that Kazuna Namisawa will be the animation director."

"That one's still at the stage where the offer is on the table," Oji replied. "It's going to be a big project, so she would need to commit to staying in Tokyo for an extended period of time, and it's possible she won't come because she's madly in love with her boyfriend up there."

"What?! Kazuna has a boyfriend, in Enaga?" cried Kayako, more than a little surprised. "I envy her. Is it somebody at Fine Garden?"

Oji stopped in mid-step. "You're kidding," he said, turning around with his face contorted into a major-league scowl. For a long moment he stared incredulously at Kayako as if she were some strange creature.

"Ms. Arishina, you did go to Enaga with me, didn't you? Didn't you notice the way those two were acting during the festival? How could you see that and not know?"

"Wait, what? Her boyfriend was there, too? I wonder who. I wish I could have seen him."

Kayako was asking seriously, but Oji just tilted his head like he couldn't believe her. Feeling a little ticked off, she said, "What's the matter?"

Oji sighed deeply. "No, I was just thinking: no wonder you don't realize when someone's proposing to you."

"Wha... Oh, you mean Mr. Sakomizu? That was just—"

Interrupting her correction, the director yelled, "Nope, nope!!"

Leaving a flustered Kayako behind, he strode off at a brisk pace.

The same director who had been so preoccupied with not killing his heroine barked sharply over his shoulder, "You can drop dead!"

"Wait, wait," Kayako called, hurrying after him. "Mr. Oji!"

He turned around and said, "Yeah?"

At that moment, Kayako flashed on a sweet memory. She couldn't believe it was only a year ago.

They'd been returning from the press conference for *Ryder*.

Gazing up at the dark but clear winter sky, she'd wondered

what they would be up to next spring when the title was going to air. Oji would probably get mad if she told him directly, so instead she'd whispered to his back.

"I'm going to see to it that you reign supreme."

Now, with that same quiet determination, she asked him, "Would you be willing to work again with me, too, one day?"

Even after the end of the season that they somehow made it through together, they would be working day after day, without a break, on new titles with different partners.

They might go their separate ways for now—but until then.

I'm truly fortunate to be doing this work, she thought from the bottom of her heart.

Whether it was anime or figures, men or women, people who worked in and around this industry were, as a rule, vulnerable to "love." They were easily impressed and even moved when someone's behavior proclaimed, "I take pride in what I do" and "I really adore my work!"

Even after financial problems that couldn't be resolved by good feelings alone arose in projects launched amidst such excitement, even as everyone started feeling overwhelmed by the hellishly hard work and the endless complications—

When it came right down to it, people who worked in this industry were all vulnerable to love.

"Sure, why not?"

Oji was facing Kayako, who had called out to him. Quite unlike the time she'd invited him to work on *Ryder Light* a few years ago, he nodded quickly and smiled.

"By then, I'm planning to be a little bit more of a straight arrow than I am now, so relax."

With that, the director swiftly turned around and began walking a few steps ahead of Kayako again.

"Ms. Arishina, let's go," he said impatiently.

"Right!" she responded, loud and clear.

The season was turning, and a new batch of titles would soon be announced.

Kayako trotted close behind the slim figure of the director, who was striding with both hands jammed into the pockets of his jacket.

Acknowledgments

This book was written with the kind assistance of the following people and organizations. I thank them all, from the bottom of my heart, for graciously guiding a writer who ventured into the unfamiliar field of anime production not knowing left from right, as an almost complete novice.

Animation Director	Kunihiko Ikuhara
Animation Director	Rie Matsumoto
Animator	Hitomi Hasegawa
Toei Animation	Hiromi Seki
	Hiroaki Shibata
Production I.G	Katsuji Morishita
	Keiko Matsushita

Aniplex	Yuma Takahashi Masae Minami Kenta Suzuki
Toho Co., Ltd.	Genki Kawamura
Mainichi Broadcasting System, Inc.	Toshihiro Maeda
ADK	Tomoko Takahashi
Shonan Fujisawa Film Commission	Yojiro Fukushima
Chichibu Anime Tourism Executive Committee	Manabu Nakashima
Good Smile Company	
Kadokawa Shoten	*Newtype* Editorial Department

(in no particular order)

This is a work of fiction, created by mixing the data and anecdotal material generously provided by these experts with a great deal of authorial imagination. The characters and organizations in the story have no connection whatsoever to any existing people or groups.

If this book contains any errors regarding the realities of anime production, those are entirely due to the author's lack of study and discretion, and she bears sole responsibility for any flaws or omissions. Since the anime industry is constantly evolving, this novel may inadvertently contain some insufficient or outdated information. Please accept my sincerest apologies for any shortcomings.

About the Author

Mizuki Tsujimura made her debut by winning
the Mephisto Prize in 2004, with a massive
novel that she started writing in high school
and kept at throughout college. Best known as
an author of dark mysteries, s he won the Na-
oki in 2012. A Japan Booksellers' Award nom-
inee, *Anime Supremacy!* is her first work to be
published in English.

ATTACK ON TITAN

ATTACK ON TITAN: BEFORE THE FALL

The first of the franchise's light novels, this prequel of prequels details the origins of the devices that humanity developed to take on the mysterious Titans.

ATTACK ON TITAN: KUKLO UNBOUND

Swallowed and regurgitated as an infant by a Titan, an orphan seeks to find and prove himself in this official prequel novel to the smash hit comics series.

ATTACK ON TITAN: LOST GIRLS

LOST GIRLS tells of the times and spaces in between the plot points, through the eyes and ears of the saga's toughest—but more taciturn—heroines.

LEARN MORE AT

IN NOVEL FORM!

ATTACK ON TITAN: THE HARSH MISTRESS OF THE CITY Part 1

A stand-alone side story, *Harsh Mistress* tells of the increasingly harrowing travails of Rita Iglehaut, a Garrison soldier trapped outside the wall, and her well-to-do childhood friend Mathias Kramer. **Available in audio too!**

ATTACK ON TITAN: THE HARSH MISTRESS OF THE CITY Part 2

In this concluding half, Rita Iglehaut struggles to turn her isolated hometown into something of a city of its own. Her draconian methods, however, shock the residents, not least Mathias Kramer, her childhood friend. **Available in audio too!**

ATTACK ON TITAN: END OF THE WORLD

In this novelization of the theatrical adaptation, the series' familiar setting, plot, and themes are reconfigured into a compact whole that is fully accessible to the uninitiated and strangely clarifying for fans.

NOW!

AUTHOR NISIOISIN

BAKEMONOGATARI
MONSTER TALE

01 | 240 PAGES | $13.95 | 9781942993889
02 | 328 PAGES | $14.95 | 9781942993896
03 | 224 PAGES | $13.95 | 9781942993902

BEHIND THE HIT ANIME!

DECAPITATION
KUBIKIRI CYCLE
The Blue Savant and the Nonsense User

A dropout from an elite Houston-based program for teens is on a visit to a private island. Its mistress, virtually marooned there, surrounds herself with geniuses, especially of the young and female kind—one of whom ends up headless one fine morning.
   The top-selling novelist year by year in his native Japan, NISIOISIN made his debut when he was only twenty with this Mephisto Award winner, a whodunit and locked-room mystery at once old-school and eye-opening.

NOW ON SALE!

THE SEVEN DEADLY SINS

Seven Scars They Left Behind

Princess Margaret and young Gilthunder know the terrible truth about the betrayal but dare not speak of it, not even to each other.

The aftermath of the event that shook Liones comes to life in seven prose side stories illustrated by Suzuki himself.

Stories by Shuka Matsuda
Created by Nakaba Suzuki

AVAILABLE NOW FROM VERTICAL, INC.